RAVEN MINDER

Lindsay Cummings is the No. 1 *New York Times* bestselling author of nine novels for HarperCollins. She lives in an RV in Texas where she writes full time, accompanied by her husband, two wild-hearted, home-schooled children, and one very vicious cat.

To keep up to date with Lindsay, follow her online at:
www.lindsaycummingsbooks.com
X @authorlindsayc
@authorlindsaycummings
Lindsay Cummings
@lindsaycummingsauthor

Also by Lindsay Cummings:

Blood Metal Bone

THE BALANCE KEEPERS SERIES
The Fires of Calderon
The Pillars of Ponderay
The Traitor of Belltroll

THE MURDER COMPLEX SERIES
The Murder Complex
The Death Code
The Fear Trials

THE ANDROMA SAGA
(with Sasha Alsberg)
Zenith
Nexus

Raven Minder

LINDSAY CUMMINGS

ONE PLACE. MANY STORIES

HQ
An imprint of HarperCollins*Publishers* Ltd
1 London Bridge Street
London SE1 9GF

www.harpercollins.co.uk

HarperCollins*Publishers*
Macken House, 39/40 Mayor Street Upper
Dublin 1, D01 C9W8, Ireland
This edition 2025

1
First published in Great Britain by HQ,
an imprint of HarperCollins*Publishers* Ltd 2025

Copyright © Lindsay Cummings 2025

Lindsay Cummings asserts the moral right to be identified as the author of this work.
A catalogue record for this book is available from the British Library.

ISBN: 9780008297534

Set in Sabon LT Std by HarperCollins*Publishers* India

This novel is entirely a work of fiction. The names, characters and incidents portrayed in it are the work of the author's imagination. Any resemblance to actual persons, living or dead, events or localities is entirely coincidental.

All rights reserved. No part of this publication may be reproduced, stored in a retrieval system, or transmitted, in any form or by any means, electronic, mechanical, photocopying, recording or otherwise, without the prior written permission of the publishers.

Without limiting the author's and publisher's exclusive rights, any unauthorised use of this publication to train generative artificial intelligence (AI) technologies is expressly prohibited. HarperCollins also exercise their rights under Article 4(3) of the Digital Single Market Directive 2019/790 and expressly reserve this publication from the text and data mining exception.

Printed and bound in the UK using 100% Renewable
Electricity at CPI Group (UK) Ltd

For more information visit: www.harpercollins.co.uk/green

*For anyone that's ever wanted to quit on themselves . . .
Stay in the fight <3
(And as always, to my dad, Don Cummings.
Because writing is our thing.)*

PART ONE

THE RAVENMINDER

CHAPTER 1

The raven arrived as it always did.

Just before sunset, to the prison at the edge of the world.

It stayed high above the black rock fortress, silent as it soared past marching guards. They were always in pairs, for one could never be too careful around the prisoners of Rendegard.

Past the turrets and domes, the raven flew, until it reached the southernmost side.

There, the world opened wide.

The prison's rear wall nearly dropped off into the Sundered Sea.

A black rope bridge jutted out over the water. It was so ancient, the entire thing swayed in the breeze, and if one stepped on a board too worn from time and salt air, they might fall to the razor-sharp cluster of rocks far below or tumble into the sea.

A mercy if they drowned before they were eaten alive by the sea wyverns.

The raven cawed, skirting a bit higher as two colossal black fins surfaced above the whitecaps before slipping beneath the churning waves once more.

The bridge ended on a looming black rock isle.

It was Rendegard's most secure block of cells, upon which stood a single tower.

The raven cawed with joy as it came into view, for it had flown long and hard against the night winds and was eager for a chance to rest its wings. It circled, beads of condensation rolling off its dark feathers like morning dew as it landed. It shook the wetness from its feathers, then hopped from the windowsill into the warmth of the highest room in the tower.

The one that belonged to the birds.

The Aviary was a stinking, stained turret, and one of many others just like it across Lordach. A place for the birds to fly to and from, delivering messages about the only thing that mattered these days.

The war.

'You're here late,' said the young woman who sat waiting.

She was small in frame, a dark-haired wisp of a thing who bore the title of Rendegard's Ravenminder.

She was the keeper of the messenger birds, at the furthest point south one could go before Lordach ended and the expanse of the Sundered Sea began.

The Ravenminder sat slumped at a table in the center of the tower, amidst piles of worn parchment and handmade quills, and overturned inkwells that had spilled their contents upon the wood like blood.

Her dark hair was a tangled mess of knots and stray bird feathers, and her gray eyes were as dull as river stones. She was, in every sense of the word, forgettable . . . save for the trio of raised black scars upon her right cheek.

Strange, then, that the Ravenminder bore a name as lovely as *Ezer*.

It had once belonged to a brave and beautiful demigoddess. The very one that hung the moon in the night skies above her tower.

Ezer yawned and plucked a bit of worn parchment off her scarred cheek, stuck there thanks to the drool.

She looked down at the letter and sighed.

Uncle Ervos, it began. *I'm writing to inform you that another month has passed, and yet your sorry, good-for-nothing a—*

Ezer crumbled the parchment and tossed it aside.

A pathetic start to a letter, for her insults had never boasted class. Not that she'd actually intended to send it. Her uncle had only ever written back to her *once* in the two years since he'd left for the war.

She'd sent word to the front in Augaurde countless times, asking for his status. Inquiring whether he was dead or alive for so much time had passed since she'd heard from him. Of course, she sensed in her gut that he was alive, certain she would *feel* it if Ervos had passed.

Their fates were tied.

And Ezer had always been a victim of the cruelty of fate.

She sighed deeply, blowing a bit of hair from her tired eyes. Ervos had never even told her *where* he'd been stationed.

She'd written to the garrison in Tomar, and then Stervist. Then Regalia, and Peddler's Gate, and the troupe at Highgarden. Each camp, spread evenly across the north, holding the line against the dark.

The list went on and on, and not a single godsdamned garrison had word of Ervos.

She supposed silence was better than a confirmed death, for it was Ezer's job, as it was for all the Ravenminders like her, to receive the lists of the fallen. To send those names out of her tower, onward to the doorsteps of those who would discover their loved ones dead and gone.

Two years of receiving those lists, names hastily scribbled upon parchment, and Ervos had never been on one.

He hadn't defected, for she knew he'd die before he ever turned to the enemy's side.

So *why* hadn't he written more? And why couldn't she find him?

With another sigh, Ezer wiped the drool from her face, and did her best to smooth her wild curls.

Ervos wasn't her *true* uncle, not by blood. Anyone could take one look at the giant and see that. He'd discovered Ezer as a babe, the sole survivor of her village after a shadow wolf attack. There was no one left to claim her. Nor was there anyone to give her a name, so he had done it himself.

Ezer, he'd chosen. Because she was found beneath the light of the full moon.

Ervos was once the Ravenminder here, just like his father before him. A talented one at that, for he was a gentle giant that loved the ravens. But he had a betting problem. He drank too much, and practiced his card-play too little, to the point that even Ezer could beat him by the time she turned ten.

Ervos had gotten in way too deep with borrowing coin from the prison master. He hadn't paid any of it back before he'd been whisked away to the warfront, drafted like so many others.

She'd never forget the day the summons came.

All able-bodied men and women were to go and serve, fighting against the Acolyte's dark army in the north. And because Ezer was only seventeen when he left . . .

She was abandoned.

Like so many other underaged children. Left to face the world without a guide.

'I don't suppose *you* brought word from my uncle?' Ezer asked the raven. 'A giant of a man, crop of bright red hair?'

The raven only cocked its dark head left and right, as if wondering why she still hadn't removed the tiny scroll from its leg.

'No,' she said. 'I don't suppose you would have.'

She wiped her hands on her leather apron and stood from her worn stool. Chains clinked between her ankles as she walked, kicking up shavings and the smell of dust.

The shackles had long ago rubbed her ankles raw and covered them in scars, despite the pieces of worn fabric she'd managed to wrap beneath them in hopes of saving her skin. She'd requested salve – *for the poor birds' feet*, an easy lie – and managed to use it on herself enough times to heal the skin.

But the scars beneath would remain.

The ones that went soul-deep, covering the pain of Ervos's abandonment. And now someone had to pay off all his debts.

Of course it fell to his ward to do it.

Ezer would have been boarded upon a wagon heading to one of the gods' temples in Tovar. It was there that she'd be crammed into a room overflowing with other young girls to be watched over by elderly maidens with rapping canes and constant orders to bow her head and pray for mercy to the five gods above, and to the countless demigods beneath them, while they sewed uniforms and gathered baskets of food to be sent to the warfront.

Ezer was no good with a sewing needle.

She wasn't much for prayers.

And she was even worse with following rules.

She supposed having to take Ervos's place wasn't all bad – the only gift fate had ever given her – because Ezer *loved* the midnight birds.

Nobody wanted to be near a raven these days. They were seen as bad omens, too similar to the monsters the Acolyte's army rode to war.

But Ezer saw them for what they were.

Cunning, clever little beasts. *Survivors*, in a world so ridden by death.

'Prison master came knocking *three times* for word of you,' Ezer said now to the raven, as she ran her ink-stained fingertips across his silken feathers.

He was wet from the fog, and smelled something fierce, but she didn't balk at him.

Nor did he balk at her.

Ezer was not beautiful.

She'd always known it, and perhaps that was why she loved the birds. They didn't fear her, not even for the enormous trio of scars that marred the entire right side of her face and had speckled her right eye with flecks of darkness.

They were awful, the scars. Three slash marks of gnarled skin that had healed wrong, so each was raised upon her face. And so dark they looked like stripes of black paint.

The scars had been there for as long as she could remember, stretching diagonally from her temple to her chin.

People often thought her cursed because of them.

And perhaps she was.

She didn't even know who her mother and father were.

She didn't know their names, nor their faces. Ervos, to his credit, had searched for years, but in the end, he came up empty.

Such was the way of war.

She had little memory of the beasts that marred her . . . but sometimes, if she closed her eyes, she saw a dark and shadowed snout. Sometimes, she saw the flash of teeth beneath the moonlight and remembered the sound of her mother's scream.

A sound that had cut off like a snuffed candle.

A slammed door.

A bird screeching before it flew away into the night.

'Is that what brought you here past sunset? It's dangerous to be out after dark, you know,' Ezer said, as the raven closed its eyes and leaned in to her touch. 'They say the moon makes the wolves hunger for blood.'

Its inky black beak clinked against the old ring she wore upon her thumb. It was all that remained of her mother, a tarnished silver hammered with five tiny symbols to signify the gods – one god for each element. She often stared at the ring and wondered which of the Five her mother prayed to most. 'Not that the gods paid any mind to her when the wolves came,' Ezer mused aloud. The raven ruffled its feathers. 'Well. At least you made it here safely.'

All sorts of breeds had gathered to Ezer since she was a child. Anything winged seemed to trust her, to see her as one of their own. But ravens were her favorite, as clever as they were beautiful, and she'd never dared believe the lie that they were *omens*.

For how could an omen give a person so much joy when they were near? They were still the main choice of bird for passing messages across the kingdom, far wiser than pigeons. And all the doves had been placed in pretty cages; they represented the animal shape of Avane, god of the wind, and people truly believed owning a cooing dove might give them some glimmer of the god's protection should the front lines break, and the war fall to the south.

Thank the gods that the Acolyte's army could only come out at night.

They turned to ash in the sunlight.

'Come on, then,' Ezer said to the raven. 'Let's see what you've brought me.'

Another yawn, and she began her work of untying the small scroll attached to the raven's leg.

The wind howled, furious as ever, but inside the Aviary, it was calm.

Ordinary.

Across the tower, another raven cawed and dipped its beak into the small copper dish of seeds and nuts she'd laid out hours ago. An owl hooted and turned its head around as if to avoid the raven altogether. The two had never gotten along. A small starling chirped and a pair of tiny little white finches – only here because they liked Ezer's presence, and not because they were useful at all for delivering messages – fluttered to one side of the tower and back again, playing a game of chase.

'There,' she said, as the string finally came loose and the scroll fell free of its tiny casing. 'That's better.'

She unrolled it and lay it before her on the table. The small nub of a candle had long since burnt out, and had hardly offered a shred of light to begin with, for how much it wavered in the wind that slid through the open window.

But Ezer had always seen better, clearer, in the dark.

It was one of her abnormalities.

Her *strangeties,* as Ervos had called them. Things to keep secret, lest she become a prisoner in one of the cells just beneath her feet. Most of the poor souls had been turned over to the Redguard without a single shred of evidence from their accusers.

It was fear that had them locked away.

Fear that anyone who was different had aligned with the dark.

Ezer's strangeties had begun to arrive at the age of thirteen. It was the age most Sacred – the powerful mages in the north – came into their own magic.

It was rare, though not entirely unheard of, for a Sacred Knight to break their strict laws of purity and leave the Sacred Citadel behind. If they were truly rebellious, they'd fall in love with a *nomage*: a mortal without magic.

Sometimes, Ezer liked to imagine her past lingered in the pages of a romance novel. Perhaps her mother was a Sacred warrioress. Her father, a stable hand or a knight's squire, and the two fell in love, breaking the laws of the Citadel, and the result was Ezer.

Ezer . . .

Who got only shreds of their forbidden, muddied magic.

'*They're the things that make you special, Little Bird,*' Ervos had told her when the birds began to follow her, and even gather to peck at her window until she opened it and let them in. When she began to find things in the dark without ever needing to light a candle. When she woke from nightmares of dark, dangerous things. Things that had yet to come to pass . . . until days, sometimes *weeks* later, when those nightmares suddenly came true.

Sometimes, she thought she saw a shadow of fear in Ervos's eyes when he looked at her. But still, he took her hands and held them close, and whispered, '*Never show your strangeties to anyone. Never forget to hide them and keep them close.*'

She pushed the memory away and focused instead on reading the raven's scroll.

30 dead.
Attack by shadow wolves.

There were bloodstains dried upon the parchment – fingerprints that had been smeared as the other Ravenminder had written it and tied it up and sent the raven south to her tower. It was not unusual these past many months to find a message covered in blood. Ravenminder towers were supposed to be protected by runed wards and kept safe by at least one Sacred squadron. It was the only means of swift communication. Wings were faster than hooves any day.

But the Acolyte was getting stronger. The casualties, more and more each week.

When darkness fell, the wolves always arrived.

And sometimes, the runes on Ravenminder towers wore away before the Sacred Scribes could return and carve their power anew. These days, more often than not . . . they never returned at all.

Ezer read the rest of the scroll, trying to decipher the shaky handwriting as best she could:

Send help to Carvist.

Ezer frowned. She had another three scrolls just like it tucked inside the small basket beyond her locked door, along with several that had scribbled the names of missing men, women and children.

People who'd either been eaten by shadow wolves . . . or disappeared, in the dead of the night.

Tomas Servain. Missing
Zerah Morvani. Missing.
Giuli Avantre. Missing.

All of them had come from messages earlier today, just like the others that came on the days before. The months before. So many had gone missing. Home one day, and gone the next after nightfall, and though their loved ones didn't want to admit where they'd gone, most knew by now.

They were either dead . . .

Or they had journeyed north to join the Acolyte.

He arrived almost twenty years ago, when shadow wolves began to appear in the north, destroying farmlands and crops, devouring innocents in the outlying villages each night when the sun fell.

The symbol began to appear in shadowed places across villages and towns.

Two dark wings.

No one knew their origin.

But it soon became clear it was a call.

And those who understood its meaning laid down their love for the gods, and marched north to join the Acolyte.

His stronghold was hidden in the Sawteeth Mountains, as far north as one could go in Lordach. Protected, at all times, by a storm of pure shadow.

He had *thousands* of shadow wolves. And all those who had disappeared were found with him . . . *changed*. They called themselves Darksouls, with their black eyes, and strange, twisted magic. The strongest ones rode winged hybrid monsters, raphons, into battle. A battle that King Draybor, the ruler of Lordach, had led against the Acolyte for nearly twenty years now.

Sometimes, the warfront felt like a faraway, distant dream.

Like a nightmare concealed by frozen mist and shadow, where few knew the whole truth of what went on. There were hardly any survivors that returned south. And the stories that reached her tower had always felt too wild to be true.

They claimed the Acolyte had created some sort of dark

religion, a following that turned their lifelong adoration of the gods into something twisted.

Something hungry for blood.

Still . . . some part of Ezer had always wondered what it would be like to go north.

She was born there, after all, had nearly died there too.

She longed to see a bird as large as a sea wyvern. To see if her connection to the common ravens would carry across to a beast as fearsome as a war mount.

She doubted so, for Lordach's war eagles *and* the Acolyte's raphons were only commanded by people with true magic.

She had vapors, if anything at all.

'Well now,' Ezer said to the very normal raven who perched before her. 'I suppose the only birds I'll ever connect with will be like you, little corvid.' It blinked up at her with dark, trusting eyes. 'Not that I'm complaining. We're perfectly safe here in the south, far from those awful *mutts* that attacked my village.'

Ezer shuffled across the tower and dropped the bloody scroll through the small slot on the door. It tumbled into the basket beside the others, where the prison master would come for it sooner or later.

'Stay the night,' Ezer said as she turned once more to the raven. It looked exhausted, its wings drooping and its eyes already shining a bit less than moments before. 'Get warm and dry and fed, and we'll worry about what to do with you come morning. I won't be sending you back to Carvist any time soon. We'll choose another route instead. Perhaps one that leads to the gold mines out west?'

The raven cawed joyfully.

As if it heard her words and understood.

They'd always had a love for shiny, shimmering things.

Perhaps that was why Ezer so adored the moon.

Sometimes, she stared out the window for hours, wondering what it would be like to be out *there*. Seeing the places her ravens had been, the places written about in books. Doing more than only taste the wind, or stare into the distant darkness, wondering what it was like beyond these rounded tower walls.

There had to be more than this.

More to *her* than ravens and scrolls.

She squeezed her fist over her mother's ring, a comfort as she crossed to the small cot she'd set up in the corner of the room. With a grunt, she pulled her chains upon it, then lifted her scrap of a worn blanket to her chin and listened to the wind as it whistled past the window. She wouldn't dare close its shutters, for fear of locking out a weary bird that had given its all to reach her with a message tied to its leg.

But she certainly wanted to.

For every so often, Ezer swore the wind *changed*.

Every so often, it went from a whistle to a whisper.

And she swore she heard it calling her name.

She supposed it should have frightened her, that the wind had a voice. But it had never done anything to bring her harm, and each time, the sound faded as soon as she thought she heard it.

But it always caused her to turn her eyes north. To stare out the window of her tower and wonder if there was *more* for her outside Rendegard.

A story still waiting beyond the shimmering black sea.

She felt safe with the birds perched all around her. They would warn her, should anything strange arrive.

Her eyes began to droop, heavy from the day's work.

But on the other side, the nightmares came.

She saw herself hunted by shadow wolves.

She saw herself die, her throat ripped out by a war eagle with eyes like molten fire.

In these dreams, she often found herself adorned in a black cloak, riding on the wrong side of the war. Bowing to the Acolyte instead of the five gods.

Sometimes, perhaps the most peculiar nightmare of all, she

stood at the warfront in the Expanse, a land of snow and ice . . . and it was there that she found herself accompanied by a faceless man, his hood full of shadows.

'*Ezer*,' he breathed as he ran his calloused fingertips across the scars on her face. '*Come back to me.*'

She'd just drifted off to sleep when a caw shook her awake.

As if the raven had heard, seconds before her, the sound of footsteps that now approached from beyond the Aviary door.

The prison master, here to collect the messages, Ezer thought . . . but the gait was much heavier than his.

Her heartbeat hastened.

No one ever visited her tower beyond the servants who delivered plates of stale meals, and certainly not at this hour.

The raven lifted its wings and soared to a high perch, its absence leaving Ezer cold.

'Traitor,' she hissed.

She stood from her cot, chains clinking between her ankles as a pair of skeleton keys rattled outside. The lock twisted, and the heavy black hinges screamed as the door swung open.

A warrior from the north stood on the other side.

A Sacred Knight, with hair as pale as snow.

CHAPTER 2

'I think you have the wrong door,' Ezer said now, heart pounding. She curled her sweaty hands into fists.

A Sacred Knight.

Standing *here* in the south, when he should have been at the front lines of war, fighting back against the Acolyte's darkness with his gods-given magic.

The man who stood in her doorway was most certainly a warrior.

He was her opposite, in every way.

He stood strong and towering when she was small and frail.

His pure snow-white hair was woven into an intricate warrior's braid, while the sides of his head were clean shaven.

She looked at the sigil upon his chest and found her eyes widening. A pair of white eagle wings backed by a crest of deep orange.

A Firemage.

One whose power came from the god Vivorr.

She'd read about the different Sacred magics, seeking every story she could after her strangeties began to kick in.

Each Sacred Knight was born with perfectly controllable magic, from one of five Pillars in the Sacred Text: *Wind, Water, Fire, Realm,* and *the Ehver*.

Each one, represented by its own unique god and their particular power.

Avane for wind, *Odaeis* for water, *Vivorr* for fire, *Aristra* for realm, and lastly, *Dhysis*, god of all mortal bodies. The symbols for each one surrounded her mother's ring.

And though the gods could no longer come down and walk amongst mortal kind, they could still bless them with rare gifts.

Magic had been one of them.

It was the first Godblessing ever recorded, given to the purest of hearts, a group of god-fearing warriors that became the first five Sacred Knights, long ago. They had sworn to protect the *nomages* of the kingdom. And thankfully so. All of Lordach would be dead if it weren't for the Sacred.

But Ezer knew, from the messages her birds delivered, that the tide of war was turning. And it wasn't in Lordach's favor.

She studied the Sacred Knight before her now.

'Ravenminder,' he said. His voice was accented. Northern. She supposed she'd have shared the same accent if the wolves hadn't changed her fate. 'You're . . . younger than I expected.'

She frowned at that.

He looked down at her like he expected her to shrink in the glory of his presence. A massive, jagged scar ran down the entirety of his face, stretching to the neckline of his cloak.

She lifted her own chin as if to better show hers.

Three for his one.

But he was a warrior who had seen more than his fair share of battle. She was just an orphan plucked from the wreckage of a shadow wolf attack. A young woman who had a fragment of useless magic.

Nothing more.

She crossed her arms and stared up at him, fully aware of the feathers stuck in her hair, the ink stains upon her fingertips. 'Who are you?'

He looked young, perhaps twenty, so not much older than she.

But the Sacred aged at a different rate to *nomages*. The more magic they used, the more power required of their mortal bodies . . . the faster a Sacred died.

He eyed her cell with not a hint of emotion on his face.

The open window, the near-shredded blanket upon her stained cot. The piles of books she'd read cover to cover to fill her days alone; the parchment and the bird waste that she'd yet to scrub from the rounded stone walls and perches. All the birds studied him closely, as if they, too, felt the power that emanated from such a godsblessed being.

His eyes lingered a bit longer on her awful scars.

'Well?' she asked and tapped her toe impatiently. Anxiety had always sharpened her edges, made her feel like a weapon poised to attack.

'You *are* the Ravenminder of Rendegard. Are you not?'

The question surprised her, for the answer should have been obvious.

'Who's asking?' Ezer said.

'Lordach,' the knight grunted. He inspected her from head to toe and sighed. As if he were disappointed by what he saw.

But now her heart was racing. Because she knew what it was like when a summons came.

And there was only one person she knew that would bring a summons to her door. One person that had packed his bags and traveled north on a recruiting wagon, two years ago.

'Read it,' the knight said.

And pushed a worn scroll into her hands.

King Draybor Laroux's sigil – a set of eagle wings topped by an arch of five small crowns – sealed the back.

Her legs felt weak. Her stomach was going to turn itself inside out, right here on the tower floor.

She opened the scroll and began to read:

Ezer of Rendegard, Ravenminder, has—

She glanced up, eyes widening.

The Sacred Knight only stared past her, studying the birds.

So, she went back to the scroll and read it hungrily.

> *Ezer of Rendegard, Ravenminder, has been legally drafted into the service of the Lordachian Army on this 12th Godsday of Avane's Month.*

'What . . .' Ezer breathed out.

'You've been drafted.'

'But . . . I'm already in service here.' She doubted he knew about the mountain of debt. 'I can't just *leave*.'

'You can, and you will.'

She crossed her arms. '*Says who*? I'm contracted to work for the prison master until . . .'

She wasn't certain exactly when *until* was.

The Sacred shrugged. 'Your contract is paid off. Your mission is elsewhere now. It's time to go.'

Her heart began to beat faster as she realized what that all meant.

'The prison master *sold me*?' she asked, breathless. 'That *bastard*.'

Heat rushed through her. For two years he'd kept her here, pocketing all the money for her work, only to accept payment for shipping her off to the warfront. To the place where everyone met death.

'Your last Ravenminder,' Ezer asked. 'What was their name?'

'It is not my duty to answer your questions,' said the Sacred. But as he stared at her, he sighed and said, 'He said his name was Ervos.'

She could have sworn the floor fell out from beneath her feet.

'Tall man, red hair, booming voice?' Ezer asked.

'If memory recalls.'

Gods.

She *knew* he was alive. She *knew* she wasn't still alone in this world. For the first time in ages, a bit of hope ignited in her chest.

He'd become the Ravenminder of the warfront. And now he must have been transferred again to another tower.

. . . So why hadn't he written to her?

Why hadn't he come *home*?

Because of the debts, something whispered within her soul.

No, she thought. *He wouldn't do that to me.*

Something suddenly felt off.

'Take me to him,' Ezer said, and stepped forward as if to move from the tower.

'I'm taking you north, to serve as all citizens must serve.' The Sacred Knight's large frame blocked her way. He sighed, as if this entire conversation was already a waste of his time. 'But not to him. He's . . . gone.'

'Gone *where*?' Ezer asked. 'To another garrison, another town? You can deliver me safely to wherever he is and I'll serve—'

It was then that she noticed it. The way his pale eyes had shifted, how his frown had deepened ever more. And it made sense, why Ervos hadn't returned.

'My uncle . . . he's dead. Isn't he?' she breathed out.

His jaw hardened, lips pressed in a thin line. 'War is not kind. People often pay the price.'

Ervos was the only one who'd ever cared about her in this godsforsaken realm.

She'd never imagined a world without him.

And now he was gone.

She could feel the absence of him, suddenly. Like her chest was going to split in two.

Like she was floating, untethered, in a deep black abyss. And there was no one left to reel her back in. To bring her home.

There was not a hint of kindness in the Sacred's words as he said, 'Are you ready to leave now?'

Ezer's head snapped up. 'That's all you can say?'

'I'm here to escort reinforcements north.' He frowned. 'I've already given you more than your fair share of time, if we're to remain on schedule.'

A spike of heat slammed into her. The ravens ruffled their feathers as if they too sensed it, and suddenly . . . she imagined how satisfying it would be to feel his nose crunch beneath her fist. She imagined the pleasure she would feel at making him bleed.

She hated him.

She hated him more than she'd hated Ervos for the past two years for leaving her here without him.

For only writing her a single godsdamned letter.

For never saying goodbye.

'You have two minutes to pack your bags,' the Sacred said. 'Take only what you can carry. The Minder's tower has all the necessary supplies to accomplish your work: quill and ink and parchment, a uniform to be worn. We leave with the next recruiting wagon.'

He turned, slamming the door shut behind him.

The moment he left, her knees buckled. The dust settled around her, but she felt like she was still falling. She curled her hand into a fist around her mother's ring, waiting for the calmness to wash over her. For some sense of peace to settle across her shoulders like it always had.

But there was only silence.

Emptiness.

The birds shifted on their perches, uneasy, as Ezer knelt there in the shavings of her tower, the letter in her hands as she reread it.

Ervos was gone.

And she realized, as all hope died within her, that she was to replace him again.

*

The wind danced with the scent of salt and storms. The stars were so bright, the moon a delicate silver plate balanced in the sky.

Beautiful.

So, so beautiful, the time when death was closest.

She closed her eyes, tipped her head to the sky, and breathed it in.

Freedom, she thought. *A pity, to feel it for a moment . . . only to have it ripped away again so soon.*

The birds followed from above, wings drenched in fog as the Sacred led Ezer away.

After a harrowing, humiliating walk across the creaking rope bridge – a pity, for a Ravenminder's biggest fear to be heights – they reached the front of Rendegard.

There, the prison's steps unraveled down the cliffside like a dark spool of thread.

They ended at the towering prison gates. Beyond them, a thick span of woods separated the prison from the city. Distant smokestacks trailed into the night sky, stretching from spires and tiled rooftops, while candles flickered in second-story windows. Their color was changed depending on the godsday. Tonight, it was green for Aristra, god of realm.

Others had probably donned small carvings of bears on their windowsills to represent Aristra's animal form.

It had been two years since Ezer had stood beside her uncle and lit a candle. Two years since she'd prayed to the Five, some part of her always doubting the words that tumbled from her own lips.

'Hurry up,' the Sacred grunted, drawing her attention back to him.

She turned to see a wagon awaiting her. And not simply any normal covered wagon, but an enormous *prison* wagon, with reinforced iron sides meant for liars and thieves and murderers, all manner of people who'd broken countless of Lordach's laws.

The worst thing Ezer had ever done was curse, and one time she'd kicked a cat in defense of her birds.

Gods, she hated cats.

They entered a room thinking everyone *blessed* because of their presence.

Ezer glowered up at him. Gods, he was massive. 'But you can't mean to make me ride in there, with . . .'

Her voice trailed off as she glanced at the line of prisoners.

'I can,' the Sacred said. 'And I will. It's safer than what we'll face traveling north. The open road is no place for a lady, especially at night.'

'And neither is a prison wagon,' Ezer snapped at him.

A muscle in his perfect jaw twitched. 'You would be wise to watch your tongue, Minder, before you arrive in the north.'

Her eyes met his. 'My tongue, Mage, is of no concern to you.'

She could have sworn his face reddened as he turned away. At least the rumors about the Sacred were true, then. They never laid with another until they were matched.

She watched him walk away as she waited in the rain, shivering like a sewer rat as the prisoners clambered aboard. When she climbed inside, she found herself shoved in the back corner, in the depths of darkness, amid the stink of sweat and piss and prisoners that had at best been petty thieves. At worst, cold-blooded killers.

And perhaps some were like her, with small, spoiled magic, useless to the kingdom but still capable of being feared for their differences, mistaken for someone loyal to the Acolyte.

There was no telling which of them she sat between.

'Escorted here by him?' the woman beside Ezer asked. 'You must be of some worth after all, tiny.'

'And why's that?' Ezer asked as the rain picked up and the wagon doors began to close with a groan.

The woman lifted a filthy brow. 'How long have you been in your cell?'

'Not a *cell*,' Ezer protested, but the woman cut her off with a bark of laughter. 'And why would that matter?'

It was dark as pitch, but with her small magic, Ezer watched the woman's filthy brows rise, clear as day. 'Because anyone with half a brain would recognize that handsome face. He's Arawn Laroux, the Crown Prince of Lordach.'

A whip cracked.

A horse whinnied from outside the wagon as it jolted, and the wheels began to move.

The crown prince of Lordach, Ezer thought.

Strange that he'd come to pick up a wagon full of prisoners, when he should have been using that famed magic for the war.

And *gods*, what an ass Arawn Laroux was.

CHAPTER 3

The hooded man stood before her again. In a glint of light, she saw a dagger of bone on his hip.
He leaned down towards her.
Her heart began to race, a mix of panic and longing coursing through her.
Their lips met.
They were familiar, soft and lovely, and—
White hot pain coursed through her, not an ounce of pleasure, as he broke the kiss first.
Ezer looked down in horror.
And found his dagger, buried handle-deep in her chest.

She woke with a gasp, her first instinct to reach for the dagger in her chest. There was nothing there.

The nightmare was familiar, an obnoxious side effect of sleep . . . but it still rattled her all the same.

Her dreams had often come true, like knowing when a storm was well on its way. Or knowing that Ervos would return home from the tavern with a fresh bruise upon his face.

But when it came to *this* dream . . .

It had never come to pass.

Ezer opened her eyes and blinked wearily, groaning as she remembered where she was. The prison wagon had come to a grinding halt. And it was *cold*, so cold it felt like the very air froze inside her lungs.

Gods, how long had she been out?

Winter's kiss was heavy on her skin.

'What's going on?' someone groaned.

The last time she'd been awake, they were barreling past another ruined village, smoke thick in the air. She'd first pressed her eye to the window, desperate to drink it in as they rolled slowly north. Because though she was not free, it was the most she'd ever seen beyond Rendegard. The closest she'd ever been to the stories Ervos had always shared with her when she longed to hear more about where she'd come from.

But this was not the world Ervos remembered.

There were no emerald hills or valleys, nor lively villages with laughter and music spilling from beneath worn tavern doors.

Instead, the world was quiet. As if it were only inhabited by ghosts.

'We're not moving,' another prisoner said.

Muffled voices came from outside, and then the back door of the transport wagon was thrown open. Light filtered in as it hit the ground with a booming *thunk*, sending up a swell of snow.

When it settled, the Sacred Prince Arawn of Lordach stood in its place.

'Blockage in the road,' Arawn said by way of a greeting. His brows furrowed as if he were already annoyed they hadn't moved. 'Daylight is fading. *Get out.*'

They had yet to trust the prisoners, even if they were soldiers now.

The Redguard had chained them all up, knowing they might take the chance to run before they made it to the warfront and received their stations.

Each was fastened at the waist by chains, and set in two lines, so closely packed together they could shuffle only mere steps at a time as they shakily made their way into the falling snow.

As if they were one body.

Ezer, to her relief, was not chained among them.

Perhaps because she was recruited from a tower instead of a cell.

Trees surrounded the group, mostly thick evergreens as tall as the sky with white weighing heavy upon their lower branches and piled up in drifts at the forest floor. She couldn't see their tops, for how tall they towered. White aspens were mixed in, with ghostly bark and black knots that looked all too much like watching eyes.

She felt dizzy as she followed their ascent. They were far larger than the trees had ever been beyond Rendegard. Like they could stretch to the clouds.

Out in the open, the sheer force of the wind hit her.

This was true winter.

A feeling like knives nipping at Ezer's skin, like she was made of glass and might shatter.

She still wore her shredded remnants of a cloak from Rendegard. It was clothing meant for a life by the sea, lightweight so she could move about taking care of her birds.

Dragging the chains that she did not miss. Her ankles still ached from the ghost of her shackles.

But the sight of the prisoners wearing them . . .

She had to look away.

She peered around the wagon and onto the narrow road, her breath a cloud before her. It was no wonder the wagon wouldn't be able to make it through.

Several enormous trees had been upturned at their roots, their branches already covered up by fresh snow. As if the sheer weight of winter had felled them, though some part of Ezer whispered a warning.

Monsters.

She'd read too many raven scrolls, seen too many names hurriedly scribbled in ink.

'Well?' Ezer asked. 'What happens next?'

Arawn didn't so much as mutter a grumpy hello as he approached.

His enormous shoulders were now covered in a white cloak lined with fur that was thick enough to keep him warm. There were runes stitched into the lining, like he'd somehow magicked the cloak to ward away the cold.

Now that she knew who he really was, it made sense.

He truly *was* handsome. Even through his cloak she could see his muscles were so large, she couldn't help but admire them. Couldn't help but wonder what he would look like in the heat of battle, his body a deliciously honed weapon.

He's a prick, she reminded herself, and that only made his appearance all the more frustrating.

Why was it *always* the heartless ones who looked so damned good on the outside?

She felt like she had daggers in her eyes as she took him in.

His sword was of an extremely fine make, and his thickly knotted braid was so elegant it could only have been done by a skilled servant. It helped to reveal the sharp lines of his perfect face, his full lips . . . and the enormous red scar that spanned down his cheek. Not nearly as hideous as hers, because *of course* it served to his rugged warrior's appearance.

It was fresher than she'd initially thought. The skin was still angry at its edges, perhaps only a few months old.

Strange, that an Ehvermage at the Citadel hadn't healed him.

She thought the Sacred were not fond of scars, especially royals, for it marred them, made them look far less *pure* to their pillared god.

Arawn's eyes snapped to hers as he caught her studying him. 'We'll have to walk. It's a mile uphill.' He glanced down to her ankles as if he could still see the shadow of her old chains. 'Can you walk, or will you require assistance?'

No, she thought. *I'm weaker than I've ever been. I survived on stale bread and salt-tinged water for two years, and now I'm thin as bones, freezing to death in this cold. I most certainly cannot walk a mile uphill, you pompous royal.*

'I'm perfectly capable,' she said instead. 'Not that you cared to offer me the courtesy of asking before. If this is how you treat your new Minder, I'm not certain I'd like to serve in your north.'

His brows furrowed. 'You do not strike me, Minder, as someone who wants courtesy.'

'And you do not strike me, Firemage, as someone who understands anything about what a woman wants.'

His jaw twitched. 'You speak out of line.'

'Because you're a prince?'

She supposed he could have her hung for speaking to him in such a way.

But her anger had replaced her ability to give a damn.

'You certainly didn't act like one when you so callously told me my uncle was dead,' Ezer hissed. 'Your gods would be ashamed of you.'

His hands balled into fists. 'Punishment, Minder, is fierce for those who speak ill of the gods.'

'Go ahead,' she said, and risked a step closer to him, enough that she had to crane her neck back to look him in the eyes. 'Punish me.'

'I wouldn't dare give you the satisfaction,' he said.

'Who said anything about satisfaction?' She smiled sweetly up at him. And because she knew the ways of the Sacred, how they held themselves back for their perfectly pure, arranged marriages, she added, 'I don't need a man for that.'

He squirmed, indeed.

He practically stumbled away.

'You act like a heathen. A disbeliever.'

She laughed, though every muscle in her body was taut. 'Oh, I believe, Sacred. I believe that a *nomage* like me, like my uncle, like all these prisoners who are traveling north to die . . . we are just pawns for you to use in your losing war.'

'You know nothing of war,' he said. His hands curled at his sides. 'And I can assure you, it's one we have no intention of losing.'

She blew out a breath as the prince turned away, the tension finally releasing without his eyes upon her.

With a barked order, he sent three Redguard ahead on horseback, urging them to call for reinforcements at the gates.

Why would they need reinforcements just to march the final mile through the woods to the garrison, where thousands of other soldiers were waiting?

There was no danger here, not *yet*.

Darkness was when the Acolyte attacked, and the battles of the night began.

But the daylight was indeed waning. And the road ahead was thick with untouched snow, deep enough that it would certainly slow their journey.

'First lesson!' Arawn called out, finally addressing them all. 'You're not in the south anymore. You're close enough to smell the blood upon the wind. To hear the cry of the brave men and women who fall in war, fighting for the light.'

Ezer's stomach twinged as she thought of Ervos.

He hadn't fought in this war.

He'd only minded the ravens.

But it had still claimed him in the end. She didn't even know how.

'This is shadow wolf territory, for the Acolyte's beasts like to circle the ward's outskirts like moths drawn to a flame. So, unless you wish to find your intestines strung across the snow . . . you will walk. And you will not utter a single *word*.'

He held out his sword in signal.

The prisoners began to walk.

Ezer turned to follow, frozen to the bone.

But the sword stopped at her middle.

'Not you, Minder,' Arawn said. A spike of fear stabbed her in the gut as those blue eyes narrowed upon her. 'You're staying with me.'

*

The path ahead was far narrower once they passed through the rune-marked trees. It was only a mere six feet across from treeline to treeline. Aspens and pines towered over them, casting everything in deep shadows.

Each glance upwards, Ezer swore the sky was darkening.

Each step, she swore she saw the shadows gathering between the trees. The scar on her face seemed to squirm in the cold, like it sensed the danger that was oncoming if they didn't make it to the warfront before dark.

To the safety of camp.

But what *was* safety, she wondered, on the front lines? They battled in the sky, the mages and their eagles taking the brunt of the attacks from the raphons. They battled on the snow, too, people just like her who were untrained for war, ripped from their homes so they could defend Lordach against a monster.

A monster who made monsters.

At least, that was what she'd always heard of the Acolyte. And suddenly she was terrified, for though she'd held pieces of parchment written this far north, though she'd been in constant communication with garrison after garrison across Lordach . . .

She realized she knew *nothing* of war.

She squeezed the ring on her thumb, a reminder that she had once been loved.

But now her chest ached, and it was not from the cold or the breathlessness in her tired lungs.

In this world, she was now well and truly alone.

The sound of the chains, of boots shuffling across snow, thrummed in time with Ezer's heart.

Her legs began to tremble until she feared she might not be able to take another step. Her ankles screamed, weak from years of little use beneath her shackles.

Gods, the air was thin here.

Her head had begun to spin.

A mile, Arawn said.

It felt like ten.

She glanced at the trees.

The birds would normally be there, hopping along the branches the moment they sensed Ezer's presence. They were always curious, often following her for a while before they got brave enough to soar down and introduce themselves with a clever little chirp.

But there were no birds here.

The forest had gone still.

And utterly silent.

So silent, the back of her neck prickled.

'*Ezer.*'

The wind suddenly sighed her name.

Not now, she thought.

Because the wind only whispered when danger was near.

She glanced over her shoulder to see a prisoner stumble and fall from the exhaustion and cold.

'*Argh!*' One of the others grunted from his spot in line, as they tried to haul the fallen back to his feet. 'Cut him loose. At this rate, we'll never—'

'*Silence*,' Arawn hissed as he spun.

His eyes were wide.

And Ezer knew why when she saw the fresh trail of blood a few paces ahead.

It dripped down the hillside like red ribbons.

'*Ezer.*'

The wind whistled past her ears as she followed its sound and vaguely catalogued the carnage of the Redguard Arawn had sent ahead to the Citadel, mere minutes ago.

They were all dead.

'Avane save us,' a prisoner breathed.

'Come quickly, Odaeis,' said another.

'I said *silence*,' Arawn hissed.

He was the only Sacred. The only one with magic here, and . . .

A stick cracked.

Arawn winced.

And Ezer realized, with a fresh wave of terror, that the prince was *afraid*.

'*Ezerrrr.*'

The wind tickled her ears, sighed her name like a subtle breath.

It had come from her left.

She spun and looked at the trees, where the shadows had too swiftly gathered.

How long until the sun fell?

Minutes, maybe. The pink sky had turned as red as blood.

'*Ezer.*'

Now the whisper came from her right.

She spun, eyes wide, for it had never been so hard to follow. As if it were coming from every direction all at once.

Another crack.

'Move,' Arawn mouthed. He looked back at the group, narrowing his eyes. '*Now.*'

He'd only made it two steps ahead of her when the wind whispered, '*Down! Get down!*'

She didn't hesitate.

She dove, narrowly avoiding the monster that suddenly swept from the treetops, its claws aimed to kill.

A shadow wolf.

She slammed against Arawn, wrapping her arms around his middle. Her weight alone wasn't enough to topple him, but his body seemed to drop on instinct.

She felt the whoosh of cold air over her head as the shadow wolf just barely missed them.

Felt the *snag* as its awful black claws swiped through her hood instead of Arawn's neck.

The prince hit the snow and rolled, his strong arms wrapped around her until they settled.

'Stay down!' he growled.

He practically slung her from him as he came back up to his feet, his sword already out. His muscles had hardened like honed steel, the warrior she'd imagined him to be.

And the wolf . . .

Ezer watched in horror as it slid and whirled around in the snow, then threw back its snout and howled.

The sound gave wings to her panic. She could barely breathe as a howl answered from behind her, and through the trees . . .

Oh gods, oh gods.

Another shadow wolf.

It was canine in shape, with membranous, bat-like wings sprouting from its muscular shoulders. Its limbs were elongated, as if they had stretched to twice the size of a normal wolf. Its dark fur practically rippled, as if it were truly made of shadows. She could just barely see the forest through its body . . . and yet it was a solid creature before her, its enormous jagged claws digging into the snow.

She couldn't even gasp in terror as she stared at the very creature that had killed her mother and father and left its calling card on Ezer's face.

The world swam in and out of focus.

'*Minder!*'

Her mind snapped back into existence as Arawn tossed something at her feet.

A small silver dagger.

'Word of advice?' Arawn said over his shoulder. 'Go for the throat.'

He whispered something – an invocation – and the runes upon his own blade suddenly flared to life.

Fire.

That was orange fire on his sword, blazing like it was dipped in oil.

The scar on his face glowed in its light, stark against his skin.

His other hand lifted, and the wolves backed a step away, as if bracing for the inferno of the Firemages, a legend in its own right. Sure enough, a whirlpool of blue began to stir in his palm, glittering orange at its edges.

Magic.

True magic, the likes of which she had never seen.

She leaned forward, hope filling her lungs.

But just before he struck . . . the light went out.

'Now would be the time to *run*,' Arawn said over his shoulder. He grimaced, as if in pain. '*Go!*'

Ezer scooped up the dagger and whirled towards the procession behind them, hoping to find safety in the crowd of prisoners and Redguard.

Just in time to see three other shadow wolves soar down from the trees and attack.

This was how she would die.

Not by old age, imprisoned in the tallest tower in Rendegard, but by the claws of a winged monster in the north.

She stood frozen, a single dagger in her hand as the world collapsed around her. Blood stained the snow in splatters that looked like wet paint.

You're in shock, a voice told her. It sounded like Ervos. *You must run, Little Bird.*

Run or die.

Arawn's runed blade collided with the first monster's neck. It screeched as black blood sprayed, and that blood turned to shadows – *living shadows* – that went slithering back to the wolf, filling the hole in its neck.

Impossible.

She screamed as it leapt for him.

But when the prince lifted his hand, ready to send a blast of fire towards it . . .

Nothing happened.

The fire in his palm had fizzled out, only a tendril of smoke in its place.

Kill it! she wanted to scream at him. *Use your magic! Why are you stopping now?*

The wolf snarled, and they went down in a tangle of shadows and limbs.

To her right, a monster leapt upon the Redguard at the back of the pack. A male, whose shout was cut off instantly as the beast gutted him with two clean swipes of its front claws.

The wolf shook its head as it began to feast upon his innards, growling and slinging blood.

'Get out of here!' Arawn yelled to Ezer as he stood. Blood dripped down his arm, but he was still alive.

The second wolf growled and lunged, but he batted it back with his sword.

Hope glimmered within as he murmured another invocation and tried to call that magic to his palm.

It was like an ember fighting for life against the wind.

It began . . . and again it fizzled away.

Like the gods had heard his invocation . . . and said *no*.

The prince took to the sword instead, swinging his masterfully glowing blade. A wolf leapt and he spun, using his momentum to behead it in one enormous swipe.

This time, the shadows did not regather.

But another wolf appeared to take its place.

Ezer scurried backwards, her back up against an aspen tree. The solid bark was the only thing keeping her rooted to the spot. With trembling hands, she held Arawn's dagger before her, knowing how useless it would be against the wolves.

She'd seen six Redguard die in a matter of seconds.

Now their bodies were spread across the snow like a garland.

The other beasts down the path killed and killed, as if driven by some carnal need to end every living thing they faced.

Ezer whimpered.

'Please,' she begged whatever gods were listening, if they dared turn an ear to a woman like her at all.

She had no power to help.

She could do nothing but watch the others die.

Something touched her shoulder.

She screamed, and held out Arawn's dagger, expecting another shadow wolf.

But it was only a raven. She could have wept at the sight of it as it landed on her shoulder, a balm to her soul, for now at least she would not die alone.

An omen would be with her.

The raven cawed once before it suddenly nipped at her ear. The pain was enough to shake her for a moment.

'Stop it,' she hissed, but she realized now that her shock was gone.

Her eyesight was clear again as she looked up. Arawn had run down the hill, where the wolves now circled the living as if they would pick them all off, one by one. Somehow, three more had arrived. Shadows seemed to drip from their bodies as they snarled, their maws steaming with hot mortal blood.

They'd kill them all.

And then they'd come for her next.

You will stand now, Ezer told herself. *You will find your own strength and run before you end up like your mother and father.*

But I'm afraid, Ezer thought back.

Now it wasn't her voice that answered, but her uncle's deep timbre.

Who cares, Little Bird?

Do it afraid.

The raven leapt from her shoulder.

'Wait,' Ezer whimpered.

She stood on trembling legs, reaching for it as it soared off into the snowy forest, a little black blur. She took one last glance at Arawn, could see him swinging his sword amidst the howls and snarls.

He'd dragged her all the way to the north, where he led her right to death's doorstep.

I saved you, Prince, she thought. *Consider my debts to you repaid.*

Numbly, she turned and followed the corvid into the woods.

The trees blurred around her. There could be a monster behind any one of them, a shadow wolf hungry to devour her, and yet she kept walking.

She had to get away, to hide and find safety somewhere until she could come up with a clear plan.

Flakes danced in Ezer's vision. Fog clouded the air before her as her lungs heaved. She paused to catch her breath, the sounds of the chaos fading.

For a moment, it was silent. Almost peaceful.

Perhaps the others were all dead.

Overhead, the raven blasted a warning call.

'*Ezer*,' said the wind again. '*Run.*'

Dread filled her bones, for she knew what was to come.

A stick cracked behind her, and she spun, holding Arawn's dagger as two shadow wolves leapt from between the trees.

CHAPTER 4

Death had found her.

The shadow wolves stood twenty paces apart. They'd decided to flank her, so she couldn't pick a direction to run.

And now they moved forward, closing in on her as one.

Each step of their enormous paws left marks of crimson in the snow. The blood of the others from her group still steaming as white tumbled down around them, filling the spaces in between.

Shadows seemed to undulate across their fur, dripping and regathering with each breath as if they were specters given life.

Twin clouds of vapor snaked from their nostrils, which flared as she realized they were scenting her.

Smelling the terror in her blood.

She took a half-step back, nearly dropping the dagger in her fear.

She wanted to scream, but she had no voice. It abandoned her as a low, terrible growl rumbled from each of the wolves' throats.

Her eyes went right to their claws. Each one was jagged and cracked and as long as the dagger in her hand.

Those were the claws that had marred her, that had forever changed the curve of her jaw and her face. Those were the claws that had murdered her parents and countless others in her village.

These shadow wolves – these monsters – had stolen *everything* from her.

Please, she thought to the wind, to the five gods who had never listened. *Please, send something to save me.*

She held the pathetic blade before her as they closed in.

If there was ever a time I needed you to hear me . . . don't let me die like this.

The wind howled in a sudden gale force.

And then the sky erupted in sound.

Ezer glanced up and gasped. Because the forest was utterly *filled* with ravens. Hundreds soared above her at once, appearing from all directions as if the night itself had grown wings.

They circled overhead, a tornado of darkness as they screeched in unison. It grew so loud that it canceled out the snarl of the wolves, the howling of the wind, the roaring of her blood in her ears.

Tears slid down her face.

At least she would die to their dirge.

She would die to the requiem of her ravens.

Ezer thought of a crisp autumn evening in Rendegard, a few days before Ervos was summoned to the war. They stood together in the Aviary, a raven on Ezer's shoulder.

'*They listen to you,*' he said. '*Someday, you'll make a fine Ravenminder in my place.*'

'*And what if I don't wish to become what you are?*' Ezer said. '*I've got dreams of my own, you know.*'

He'd chuckled then, his booming laughter causing the birds around them to stir. '*And what is it that you dream of, Little Bird?*'

'*Elsewhere,*' Ezer said. The raven nuzzled her cheek. '*A place where the wind is wild and free. Where I can find answers about who I am. Where I can write the better half of my story.*'

She would find out who she was, and make it mean something.

Maybe she'd make a friend, fall in love, start a family of her own.

She didn't care, so long as she chose her *own* fate.

Ervos had smiled sadly and placed a heavy hand on her shoulder. '*For now, your place is here, with me. Making a real difference in this war where you are safe and sound.*'

'*And when the war is over?*' Ezer asked.

'*I'll take you elsewhere myself,*' Ervos promised. '*Wherever that may be.*'

Elsewhere never came. But Ezer imagined she'd see it soon enough, in death. The ravens continued to screech as the wolves reached her.

She felt the wind from their current on her face. It dried her tears as their song rumbled in her bones. She lifted Arawn's small blade.

Go for the throat, he'd said.

She would not go down without a fight.

She screamed as she swung. But she never made contact.

A whoosh sounded – a flutter of furious wings so strong it ripped her dark curls free of their braid, and suddenly the darkness filled her vision. She was an anchor in a sea of silken wings that parted around her.

And the wolves were suddenly *engulfed* in ravens.

'*Ezer,*' the wind whispered. '*Look.*'

They were like soldiers, glorious winged warriors as they pecked and clawed and fought for Ezer's life with no care for their own. They went for the wolves' eyes. They shredded those terrible batlike wings, cutting through the membranous skin like it was made of fine paper instead of flesh.

Shadows stretched outwards and away as the ravens tore them apart, pecking at the wolves so fast the shadows didn't have time to regather and heal.

She watched in amazement as the wolves fell.

As the shadows melted into the snow like oil . . . and then faded in a puff of black smoke.

They were gone.

Gone.

Ezer stood frozen as the ravens soared away . . . and then there was only silence.

She'd asked the gods for help out of desperation, not truly believing they'd listen.

But the birds – her beautiful, black-as-night ravens – had saved her.

The cacophony stopped just as suddenly as it started.

Two sets of enormous paw prints were the only sign that the wolves had ever been there at all. Hundreds of black feathers softly settled upon the snow.

Magic, she thought.

It was the only explanation she could come up with.

Flakes tumbled lazily down from the sky, landing on Ezer's nose. The ground was already filling with it, covering the imprints of shadow wolf paws that had been left on either side of her.

A deep inhale to remind herself that she was still alive, and Ezer found her heart settling.

Her vision came back to normal as the panic left her bit by bit. And a strange blanket of peace – a feeling she had not felt in ages – washed over her.

'Minder!'

The sound of a human voice would have been so sweet, were it not *his*.

He was still far enough away that she couldn't see him, but the prince called out again – 'Minder!'

She whirled to find Arawn sprinting through the trees. He hadn't noticed her yet. His eyes were wide and wild as he rushed through the woods, following the path of her footsteps.

'*Ezer*!'

It was the first time she'd ever heard him say her name. The first time she'd heard *anyone* say her name in ages.

Something deep within her winked open, and she realized what a miracle it was that she was here . . . *alive*.

And it was all because of the birds.

Arawn practically skidded to a stop as he noticed her standing there. His chest rose and fell as he looked her up and down from twenty paces away, as if searching for injuries.

He looked nothing like the polished prince from earlier.

Now he looked like the bringer of death.

Black blood splattered his cloak and painted the strands of his hair that had come loose from his long white braid. One side of his cloak and tunic was ripped through, revealing the hardened muscles of his torso beneath, the V that crept towards his waist, and – *gods*.

This was more like it.

No sooner had she thought it than she shook herself, disgusted with the wave of desire.

She couldn't possibly be admiring *him* in this moment.

'Would you stop screaming?' she said. Her voice came out in a raw hiss. 'You'll call the wolves back.'

The sound of her voice seemed to shake him, and he looked down at the pile of feathers surrounding her.

'What happened?' he said.

Not quite a question. A command.

And something about her recoiled at that. It was *her* story, *her* birds, *her* strangety that had saved her. And perhaps that truth was the only thing she'd ever had to call her own.

'Birds got in the way.' Ezer breathed out.

A half-truth to cover a whole lie.

'Birds,' he said, and lifted a brow like he didn't believe her for a second.

Gods be damned.

'The wolves . . . must have run when they heard you coming.'

'They don't run.' His eyes narrowed. 'They certainly don't leave their victims behind *alive*.'

'Then perhaps I'm not a victim.'

She wasn't even sure what she'd meant by the words, but they'd poured out of her like a second breath.

'I told you to run,' he growled, his eyes falling to the dagger still clutched in her fist. They narrowed, like he didn't trust her. 'I'll take that back now.'

'I didn't ask for it in the first place,' she scoffed, and tossed it at his feet. 'And I *did* run.'

'Into the woods, alone, instead of to the others!'

'The others?' She held out her arms, because they both knew what the fate of the *others* had been. 'Death, Firemage, was not something I intended to meet today.'

She told him nothing of the ravens, nothing of the strange lingering sense that she had somehow controlled them, that with a desperate thought thrown into the void . . . they listened.

Perhaps her magic was not so petty after all.

And with the way he was staring at her, *into* her . . .

'Why didn't you use your fire against the wolves?' she asked.

'I did.'

She raised a knowing brow. 'You struggled to call upon it.'

He was the prince of Lordach. The warrior with flames in his hands, already famed for his efforts in battle at such a young age.

He was . . .

Absolutely offended, by the sour look on his face.

'I didn't struggle,' Arawn snapped.

She placed a hand on her hip. 'You most certainly did. And then you ran.'

'To help the others,' he growled in frustration. 'To carry out my command as a Knight to—' His brow furrowed as he seemed to realize what direction she'd been heading in. 'Are you *deserting*?'

'I . . .'

The sun was almost entirely gone, the forest so thick with shadows that even the snow seemed to darken as it fell between them.

It blurred everything like they were inside a snow globe, freshly shaken.

'Well?' Arawn asked.

Ezer sighed. 'I won't be another name on a scroll.'

She'd go as far from the war as possible. She'd discover the truth about herself and her past.

And then she'd finally write her future.

'Minders don't fight in the war,' Arawn said. 'They certainly don't die on the front lines.'

'And yet my uncle, who you said I am to take the place of, would argue against that statistic. I have no one left because of a war he didn't *fight* in.' She fixed her stare upon the prince. And she felt the brokenness in her own words when she whispered, '*No one.*'

He opened and closed his mouth again.

'I . . . understand.'

Rage unfurled within her.

'You understand *nothing*,' Ezer hissed.

But the anger had taken an edge now. It writhed inside her veins, and she didn't have the strength to stop it.

'You live in your perfect white castle upon the hill, gifted with magic to keep you safe while the rest of us suffer. While we wait for news that the war has come for us. A war we didn't start. But a war we're expected to die in, nonetheless.'

His hand tightened over his sword, but he didn't draw it. 'Says the woman who senses when danger is near. I don't think you can count yourself as *nomage*, Minder. You argue for a people you aren't even part of.'

Her blood went cold. 'I don't know what you're talking about.'

A smug smile crossed his lips. 'Tell that to the shadow wolf who nearly removed my head. No one can detect when they're near. And yet . . .' he raised a pale, scarred brow, 'here I stand. How did you do it?'

'I heard them coming.'

'Impossible,' he growled. 'They make no sound.'

Her heart was a war drum now.

He knew about her strange magic. Of course he knew, and she'd been a fool to save him, to give her secret away.

But what was he going to do? Throw her in prison like the others?

He'd have to drag her all the way back to Rendegard to do that, and suddenly she was furious all over again.

'You don't know what it's like to lose, *Prince*,' Ezer spat. 'You don't know what it's like to be left in the darkness, waiting for—'

'I don't know what it's like to lose?' he asked.

She paused, looking up at him. Because his voice had changed.

She'd thought him angry before.

Now?

Now, she backed up a step.

'N . . . no,' she said.

He lifted a pale brow and stalked towards her. 'And how would a Ravenminder, hidden away in her tower, safe and sound from the tide of war, know what a Sacred Knight has or has not lost?'

'You . . .'

She swallowed her words, because now she sounded like a fool, throwing stones when she had no clue of where they should land.

'The Sacred are not given *choices*. We live. We serve. And we die early when the power required takes its toll on our bodies. That is the chief end of those who have magic.'

He said it like a warning.

She met his eyes, and where she expected fury to be on his face . . .

There was only an emptiness that matched her own.

'I understand that to mourn, Minder, is to feel half dead yourself. I understand that there are people we love, people we think we will never lose. We plan things with them, we envision them in our future, and then one day, before we can even *think* of uttering a goodbye . . . they're already gone.'

His chest rose and fell swiftly, like he was short of breath.

Perhaps there was more to the story behind his scar.

'I could have been kinder to you,' Arawn said. 'When I delivered the news about your uncle and your assignment. For that . . . I am sorry.'

She couldn't remember the last time anyone had told her they were *sorry*, let alone a prince. She'd nearly forgotten the word, and it seemed he had, too, for he looked horribly uncomfortable saying it. The word came out with a wince.

And then, to add to her surprise . . . he held out a calloused hand. One that pointed towards the distant woods, instead of the road below.

Her eyes widened.

'You want to run? Then go ahead,' Arawn said. His voice was not gentle, but it lacked the usual gruffness it carried. 'I suppose I owe you a life debt now, anyhow. You saved me from a beheading on the road, and there's not an invocation in existence that can bring a person back from that.'

'Keep your debt,' Ezer said, surprising even herself.

She turned around and stared at the woods.

She would go south, far enough away from the cold that the wolves would not be a bother. She would pick up another job as a Ravenminder there, make enough of a living to scrape by for a time, until the war ended.

She'd start a new life. Earn enough coin to find answers about her family, perhaps pay a visit to the census archives in Touvre. After that . . . she had no plans. It was open-ended, and in some ways that felt like more freedom than she'd ever had.

Ezer took a step towards the woods, opposite from the path where the wolves had melted away. She'd only made it ten paces when she paused.

South, she thought, staring ahead. *Yes, that must be south, just between two bare aspens*. Back towards the nearest settlement, which had to be less than a day's journey . . . if anyone was still left there.

But . . .

No.

That wasn't quite right.

Ezer turned in a circle, unable to get her bearings in the snowy wood, for suddenly it all looked the same.

Perhaps *that* was south, where the evergreens were thicker.

Where are you now, Whisper? she thought.

The wind said nothing to guide her path.

'Confusion,' Arawn said.

She turned back to him, where he stood like a chiseled sculpture, his tattered cape waving in the breeze. He ticked off his next words on his gloved fingertips. 'Shivering. A feeling of exhaustion so strong, you just want to lie down and close your eyes, if only for a moment. All symptoms of slowly dying from the cold. Freezing from the outside in.'

He smirked and looked to the sky as snow continued to pour down over them.

'Storms are worse by night. The cold settles in quickly, regardless of your size. Starvation, too, for you won't know how to find a good enough meal in winter if you're not from these woods. The northern villages are decimated, the Acolyte's wolves have picked off nearly every animal that used to thrive here. And we're not even at Realmbreak yet. *True* winter hits then, in just two months . . . and since you don't have a horse or carriage, you'll be taking at least half that amount to escape the snows given how lost you'd get out here.'

She realized she *was* shivering.

So badly her teeth were chattering, and she couldn't feel her hands anymore, nor any of her toes.

She hadn't even noticed. Her body had gone numb hours ago.

'The shadow wolves always come back to where blood was last spilled. And then there's the occasional darksoul troupe that breaks past our aerial forces. I don't even need to mention the strange ways their magic can make a mortal die. And with the raphons . . . once that sun truly sets . . . the real danger begins.'

He'd crossed his large arms and was now casually leaning against an aspen tree with his broad shoulders, his perfect muscles practically glistening in the fresh moonlight.

He raised a pale, blood-flecked brow, as if he were silently mocking her.

Challenging her.

Bastard.

She huffed out a breath.

'I . . .'

Gods.

He was right.

And she was a coward.

'. . . I will stay. For *now*,' Ezer said, lifting her chin high as she picked up the fringes of her tattered cloak and stepped through the heavy snow back towards him. 'Though I should remind you, I'll ask for that life debt to be repaid in another way soon enough.'

She'd be a fool to give away the promise of a prince.

She began to march downhill towards the road.

'Minder.'

She turned and found him grinning at her like a hungry lion. 'The road is *that way*.'

CHAPTER 5

Ezer had never seen war, but she imagined the aftermath would have been something like this. Bodies were strung across the snow. The wolves had shredded half the wagon's worth. The prisoners who had chosen to become soldiers hadn't even made it to Augaurde, and they'd already been ripped apart piece by piece.

So much blood, so much death.

And . . .

More Sacred had arrived.

Arawn greeted them as if he knew them well.

There were three others checking the survivors who would soon become soldiers.

A Sacred woman, with dark skin and pale white braids, a strip of light leather across her brow. She bore a white and blue crest behind the mark of wings on her chest – the mark for a Watermage. But there was yet another crest beside that.

It was in the shape of a war eagle's talons, poised for the kill.

Ezer's eyes widened.

She was a *Rider*.

And so was the other one beside her. He was enormous, even larger than Arawn, if that was possible. He bore red behind his traditional winged crest, which marked him as an Ehvermage. They often specialized as healers but could make fine trackers as well.

Ezer looked around, searching for a sign of their eagles.

Gods, it would be like a balm to her soul. A way to wash away the horrors of today, if she could just lay eyes on *one* sacred bird, every feather woven by the gods.

The last arrival was kneeling beside a prisoner, his bare hands pressed to the man's throat as he checked for a pulse. His back was to Ezer.

His cloak was white like the others, but he had an interesting gold thread woven on the fringes, and gold silk on the inside of his hood.

Her heart skipped a beat.

An Eagleminder.

The Lordachian army had several different wings, all of them trained in specific areas since they were children.

There were Knights, like Arawn, and Scribes, who trained in the true art of war by inscribing runes upon objects – beautiful, curling script in the Godstongue. It was so vast a language, the runic dictionary took up an entire floor of the Citadel's library. If it weren't for the Scribes, the Minder towers across Lordach would have been leveled long ago.

Like the Knights and Scribes, Eagleminders were born in the Citadel, but there was little known about them. As a child, Ezer often pretended she was one. That her ravens were just tiny fledglings, readying themselves to go into war someday.

But seeing an Eagleminder in real life . . .

'Kinlear!' Arawn called to the kneeling Eagleminder, and he stood, swept the snow from his cloak and trousers, and turned to face them.

It was an effort not to let her jaw drop.

It was like staring at a different version of Arawn.

His hair was dark, where Arawn's strands were white. Tall and lean, where Arawn was all bulk of brutish muscle.

But the face.

The face was the same.

Kinlear Laroux. Arawn's twin brother.

The other prince.

He had a walking cane in one gloved hand, an eagle's head as the handle, which he used to push himself up to full standing. He was undeniably handsome, a softer version of Arawn, with a smattering of freckles across his nose and cheeks. He had dark, messy curls that looked as if he'd just rolled out of bed. Even the white tunic under his cloak was rumpled, the top three buttons undone to reveal pale skin beneath, as if he were dressed for spring instead of an Augaurdian winter.

Not as massive as his brother, but still chiseled enough to prove he'd had his fair share of combat training, as any prince would.

He was a curious, wild sort of being.

The kind that people probably whispered about in the Citadel's halls, for where Arawn was exactly as he seemed . . . Kinlear Laroux felt like a walking mystery.

The kind she'd love to unravel.

She could only imagine what he knew of the War Eagles. What he'd done, and what he'd seen. His cane only served to the mystery surrounding him, as did the small, corked vial he wore on a necklace around his throat.

'You shouldn't be here, Kinlear,' Arawn said. 'It's cold.'

Kinlear shrugged. 'This is Augaurde, brother. Everywhere is cold. And besides, I'm as warm as a furnace, with the runes on my cloak.'

He stopped before them, digging the tip of his cane into the snow. It was a lovely thing, finely carved to look like the long feathers of the eagle's tail swirled all the way down to the ground. 'You were due back yesterday. What happened?'

Ezer found herself glancing back and forth between Kinlear and Arawn.

They were polar opposites.

One, rigid and untouchable, the other, as wild as the wind.

'The journey was slow,' Arawn said. 'Plenty of stops along the way, to visit with the garrisons across the south. They're not faring well.'

She must have slept through each one of them.

'If they're faring at all.' Kinlear sighed and blew a curl from his face. 'Well. It's been terribly boring without you here. No one to tell me to keep my cloak pressed, or to polish my boots.' He inclined his head towards the other two Sacred. 'No one to stop me from paying penance for going a *bit* too overboard on Absolution.' The one night a month that the Sacred were permitted a single release from their rigid, law-abiding life, allowed to imbibe upon winterwine – a northern delicacy – until sunrise. Kinlear chuckled. 'A few Riders were more than happy to allow me a chance to join the thrill of saving you. It's a wonderful thing, being the hero. Not that you'd know.'

'I had it under control,' Arawn growled.

'The body count begs otherwise,' Kinlear said and lifted his chin. 'At least I got to see one of my fledglings, all grown and in action.'

The War Eagles.

Ezer looked past him, searching the woods for a sign of the glorious beasts.

But it was too dark, the snow coming down thicker now.

They needed to leave, to find safety and warmth, and yet all these Sacred seemed perfectly at ease amidst the blood and gore and death.

Kinlear's gray eyes slid to Ezer and brightened, curious as a bird's. 'And who do we have here?'

'Our newest Ravenminder,' Arawn said, and for some reason he took a step closer to her. Enough that the edge of his cloak brushed up against Ezer's arm. 'Brought in from Rendegard.'

'Ah, a *Ravenminder*. How very . . .' Kinlear looked her up and down, as if cataloguing her every detail, '. . . charming.'

A spike of heat went through her.

Being an asshole must run in the family.

'Spent a bit of time with the omens, have you?' Kinlear asked.

'If by omens, you mean ravens, then yes,' Ezer said. 'In some ways, the messenger birds are just as important as the War Eagles.'

Kinlear raised a dark brow. 'A clever sentiment, albeit a false one.'

'It's true, I can assure you,' she said.

His chiseled jaw twitched, as if he weren't used to being challenged. 'Is that so?'

She shook her head. 'It's called communication, Prince. I'm no soldier, but I'm well aware that this war would already be lost without the ability to communicate. You have the ravens to thank for that.' She lifted her chin. '*And* their Minders.'

Beside her, Arawn made a choking sound, as if he couldn't believe the words she'd just spoken.

'And quite a communicator you are,' Kinlear said, crossing his long arms.

They stared at each other, one Minder sizing up another.

She waited for his gaze to slide to her scars, for him to curl his lip in disgust as so many did. As if they saw her scars instead of the person behind them. As if she were merely an afterthought to the wounds on her face.

But this prince never broke her gaze.

Instead, he smiled, a devilish thing, and he conceded by bowing his chin. 'Welcome to the north, then. A size up from Rendegard, for certain.' There was a hint of mischief as he added, 'And of course, I've been so rude. Allow me to introduce myself to you as Kinlear Laroux, Sacred Eagleminder and most loyal servant of Lordach. Though most call me the Handsome Twin.'

Arawn grunted beside her.

'Nothing against you, brother. I'm just relaying what the good people of Lordach say.' A slight cough left Kinlear's lips as he turned to his twin. Seeing them together . . . two *princes*, surrounded by carnage and crimson snow . . .

It was enough to make her dizzy, with how much had shifted since leaving her tower behind.

'I'm due back in the Aviary,' Kinlear said. 'I'll speak to you soon. *Alone*, Arawn.'

Then he looked to Ezer and winked. 'Ravenminder.'

'Eagleminder,' she said back.

Arawn's fists uncurled as his brother turned away.

'We'll escort you safely back, sir,' the Sacred woman said to Arawn. 'Eyes in the sky.'

Kinlear spun and walked off into the woods, the sound of his cane crunching against the snow. The other two Knights bid Arawn goodbye and fell into place behind Kinlear.

'An interesting character, your brother,' Ezer said, for Arawn was still at her side, watching Kinlear walk away.

'Yes,' Arawn said curtly. 'As talented an Eagleminder as I've ever met, despite his . . . edges. But I suppose that's the best way one can stand out, when you're never to rule.'

Ezer glanced up at him. 'Why wouldn't he rule?'

Arawn sheathed his blade. 'Because. He was born seconds after me. By Sacred law, he's not permitted to wear the crown.'

She sucked in a breath.

'*Ezer.*'

Her ears pricked up at the sound of the whisper as the wind skirted past her.

But there was no wolf that appeared, no danger in sight.

There was only Kinlear's cloak as he walked away, softly glowing with gold runes as the wind tugged it from his hip. Enough to reveal the weapon sheathed there.

Ezer gasped.

Suddenly, she wasn't *here* anymore, standing in the frigid north.

In her mind, she was back in her tower in Rendegard, curled in her cot and her chains as a sliver of moonlight kissed her scars.

Because *Kinlear*, Eagleminder and second-born Prince of Lordach . . .

He must be the faceless man she had seen, every night in her sleep for the past two years.

And it was his weapon that she recognized.

His dagger, with its carved bone hilt, that killed her in those dreams.

Arawn led her and the few remaining survivors up the steep, snowy path north.

Walk, she told herself, *the way Ervos once did.*

She imagined his enormous body summiting this very path.

She was so close to resting. To warmth and a place to lay her head, for she didn't give a damn anymore if it was in a soldier's barracks or a seaside cell. She just wanted to sleep and slide back into her dreams.

To see the face of Kinlear Laroux and try to discover when – and why – he would kill her.

You'll warn me, she thought to the wind. *Won't you?*

It had never failed her before.

She almost wept at the sight of the two enormous black towers up ahead.

They were colossal twin onyx formations that sprouted right out of the forest floor. Runes glowed a soft gold upon every stacked stone: giant, curling script that was so otherworldly Ezer had to pause to take it all in.

It wasn't just the stones. That rich, golden sheen emanated from the top of each tower and spanned outwards into the sky . . . a dome of golden light that covered *all* of Augaurde.

The wards.

'The Forest Gates,' Arawn said, noting her stare. 'There are six Gates surrounding the north, each one gifted by the gods on a Realmbreak long ago. This pair marks the southern entrance to Augaurde . . . the *only* space in the north that is safe by nightfall.'

He held out a hand – which, Ezer noted, was still darkened from dried shadow wolf blood. How could they even bleed, when they were spun from shadows? The Acolyte's magic was terrifying, impossible to understand. 'The wards are Godsmade. They will know where your loyalty lies.'

One by one, the survivors stepped through the golden sheen of light. It parted around each person like a curtain, molding back into place the moment they'd stepped through.

What happens if we don't pass its test? Ezer thought.

Because she'd dreamt of too many things coming true. And in her dreams, after Kinlear stabbed her . . .

She saw her own blood, running black.

She clenched a fist over her mother's ring and watched the others step into Augaurde. Everyone passed with ease.

Until she noticed the man before her had fists as clenched as her own.

The second his nose touched the wards, there was a horrible *crackle*. Before Ezer could even yelp, he had been blasted backwards.

His body was already steaming as it hit the snow.

'What . . . what happened?' Ezer whispered.

Arawn knelt at the man's side, his blue eyes narrowed.

'A dark heart,' he said, and used the tip of his sword to pierce the man's skin. A droplet of blood welled out. It was utterly black. Dark as oil. 'He'd already defected in his soul. No telling how long ago.' He whispered a prayer and stood, his gaze sliding back to her. 'Go ahead.'

Her mouth fell open.

'But what about *him*?'

A defector had been among them the entire time. And no one had known. How many others were out there in the realm, walking among them like hidden shadows?

Arawn shrugged his enormous shoulders. 'The wolves will do as they please with him. A fate he deserves, for denying the Five.'

An earsplitting cry suddenly divided the night.

Ezer gasped as the trees tremored above her. And despite the painful tug on her scars . . . when she looked up, she smiled.

A war eagle.

A real, true war eagle suddenly soared over her head.

Its wings were enormous, their color a buttery gold, and so much larger than she'd ever imagined. It banked as it circled overhead, and in the wardlight, it looked like each feather on its wings was spun from the cloth of the gods.

It was large enough that it carried two riders upon its back with ease – the female.

And Kinlear.

A second eagle followed, and Ezer stopped walking, feeling like the world had slid out from underneath her. Like she had instead fallen into the pages of the worn storybooks Ervos had purchased for her when she was just a child.

A child desperate for *more,* anything she could get about the mighty war mounts of the north. Her entire life, her greatest friends had been the birds. And the war eagles . . .

They were magnificent.

Even if the first beast did carry the prince – both lover *and* killer – from her dreams.

'Minder.'

She watched the mounts soar away, until the hilltop and the Forest Gates blocked them from her sight.

'Night waits for no one,' Arawn said. The golden wards shimmered behind him, outlining him like a halo. When she didn't move, he sighed and ground out, '*Please*.'

Ezer lifted a dark brow. 'It has manners now?'

Arawn's gaze hardened. '*It* has a name.'

'And so do I besides *Minder.* Or does everyone always refer to you as your title, Oh Mighty Crown Prince?'

'Oh migh—' He paused to take a deep, calming breath. 'You

enter with me now, or you get left behind.' He leveled his icy gaze upon her. 'The choice is yours.'

She knew he meant it.

But she still stared at him, unmoving.

Waiting for him to meet her demand.

'Ezer.' He finally said her name, exasperated. 'Will that do?'

'Well enough,' she said back. 'Your . . . Majesty?'

'Arawn,' he said, and he looked like he'd been defeated. For some reason, that made her smile. 'Just . . . call me Arawn.'

She stepped up to the wards.

There was truly nowhere else for her to go. At least here . . . she would have a Ravenminder's tower, a space to call her own, a purpose. A job she was certain she could do well.

At least, soon enough, she would be back with the birds, who never made her feel small or insignificant or unsafe.

Please, she thought, as she stepped into the golden wardlight. *Please, let me through*.

Her chest lightened as the wards parted.

But she did not smile as she entered.

Because she knew, like Ervos, she might not ever make it back out alive.

CHAPTER 6

Augaurde sat beneath her like a setting in a dream: a sweeping valley of white that stretched from left to right as far as she could see, before it spanned upwards again to a smattering of sharp, pointed cliffs covered in snow.

The valley itself was scattered with hulking white war tents, mixed through with smoldering campfires that spat smoke into the sky. Countless soldiers – *not enough, as she'd expected* – marched about. Draft horses dragged heavy logs on rolling carts. Mixed among them were the enormous white war bears she'd heard stories of, born and bred to love the cold. She could hear their roars from here. Some were saddled with riders atop them, while others used their brute strength to haul giant boulders across the snow.

Some soldiers practiced sparring or swordplay. They were adorned in red cloaks, the color of the *nomage* uniforms, born without Sacred blood.

The majority of Lordach.

Where the soldiers' barracks fell away, the valley gradually sloped back upwards, and a sweeping stone bridge led to the center of the cliffs, high in the sky. There stood an enormous castle in the clouds.

The Sacred Citadel.

It was ancient and crafted entirely of white stone. It stood so close to the edge of the cliffs that it looked like a strong gust of wind would have sent it tumbling into the Expanse on the other side.

The Citadel boasted five towers, for the five gods, each one spiraling into the snowy sky. Smaller white bridges connected the towers, rounded like the backs of sleeping dragons. The only vibrant colors came from the banners that hung from each tower, near frozen to the stones by a fresh sheen of ice. Five banners, in five colors, for each pillar of Sacred magic and the god they represented.

The Sacred Circle was nowhere to be seen. A place of legend, where twelve enormous standing stones stood in the snow, covered in runes that told the story of Lordach's creation. Ezer wondered if she'd be able to see it from her tower.

If she'd be able to leave it, or if she'd be expected to stay locked away again.

'This way,' Arawn said, and his voice was like a blade as he addressed the exhausted group. It cut into the moment, broke the spell of seeing this place for the very first time. 'To the barracks, where you'll receive your orders.'

She never thought she would walk in the footsteps of a soldier.

Never thought she would lay eyes upon the men and women that would someday, most of them, enter the Expanse.

And die.

She couldn't see it from here. But she could certainly *feel* it: the death and danger that lay in waiting to devour her on the true front lines.

The howling wind lessened with the natural shield of the Citadel's cliffs, but the sounds of the war camp emerged in its place as Arawn led them into the maze of tents.

It was like another world entirely.

She'd been receiving messages from this place and others just like it for years. But somehow seeing a war camp with her own eyes, hearing the shouts of soldiers and the roar of bears, the ring of steel clashing against steel . . .

It felt truly real for the very first time.

She stepped through a cloud of smoke from a nearby campfire and followed the blur of Arawn's white braid and cape through the chaos.

It was the only constant she could hold on to now.

Countless troops marched in all directions. Many seemed dressed for battle, swords sheathed on their hips and shields hefted over shoulders, while others looked to be resting inside the wards for the night. They sharpened their weapons, wrote letters home, scarfed down dried rations that reminded her just how long it had been since she'd eaten any real food.

But she suddenly had no appetite.

'Out of the way, recruit!' a voice grumbled. It was followed by a roar, and Ezer stumbled sideways, narrowly avoiding a giant war bear as it padded past her, its mighty paws leaving deep tracks in the snow. It was harnessed, and dragging a sled loaded with a pile of weapons. The hilts and blades rattled like bare bones.

They went past a tent full of Ehvermage healers: Sacred Knights that had the magic of Dhysis in their veins. The canvas flaps were held open for just a moment to reveal the rows of stained wooden tables, bodies already lying on each of them. The smell came with the familiar reek of cleaning alcohol. *Death*.

She stumbled past a pair of sheep bleating in a pen, and a young girl dressed in Sacred whites, who looked to be in training from the fact that she bore no crest yet. Her lips moved in a constant whisper as she voiced elegant invocations over their water troughs. Blue light emanated from her palms, a dance between her and her god as she manipulated the ice back into water.

Arawn had paused not far away at the entrance to another white tent.

Inside, the prisoners had already begun receiving their uniforms.

A tattered red *nomage* cloak with a hood lined in gray fur. A cap and gloves, a red tunic and thick red trousers, wool socks and a pair of worn leather boots. The toes were stained in dark splotches. As if whoever had worn these uniforms first . . . whoever had stood here at this very tent – *Gods, Ervos had stood here* – they didn't need these clothes anymore.

Which meant she was to wear the clothing of the dead.

Ezer turned, suddenly feeling her stomach twist.

And before she could stop herself, she was vomiting into the snow. Soldiers skirted to the side as they walked past, shaking their heads.

She wiped her mouth clean with the back of her sleeve and turned back to the tent.

'Next!' the soldier barked.

Ezer stepped forward.

And then promptly felt a hand clap over her shoulder.

'Not for you, Minder.'

She turned to look up into Arawn's cold blue eyes and found him frowning down at her. The second their eyes met, he dropped his hand like he'd been burned.

'The Ravenminder's tower is past the Citadel,' he said. He lifted his chin over her shoulder . . . towards the hulking fortress that glowed at the top of the cliffs like a beacon in the night.

'*Past* the Citadel?'

She thought her tower in Rendegard was tall.

But his gaze had gone all the way to the highest cliff in Augaurde, to the right of the Citadel.

Where a single pathway led up to a summit covered in clouds.

She could just barely see the flicker of lights up top; the tower was so tall it nearly pierced the golden wards.

She swallowed the taste of bile and asked, 'I don't suppose you have a tower down here?'

Up close, the Sacred Citadel did not whisper of magic, like the wind or the old stories Ezer used to read in her borrowed books.

It *sang* with it.

Arawn guided her up the sprawling staircase on the cliffside, and finally to the Citadel's innermost gates.

Even the icy wind dropped to only a breath of a breeze when they stepped through. And though she could still hear the rumble of war . . . it felt instantly calmer here.

Quiet.

Like a spell had been cast over the space.

Snowflakes danced lazily above them, landing on a lone tree in the courtyard's center. It was encased entirely in shimmering ice. It looked ancient, its gnarled branches as white as bone, and bare of any leaves.

Swords had been plunged into the snow around it.

Not hundreds but *thousands*. Some were gold and some were silver, some were plain while others had fat rubies or gemstones inside their hilts, but every single one had the sigil of the Sacred hammered into their blades, the winged crest of the war eagles.

She glanced at Arawn. 'What are they for?'

'The fallen Sacred,' he said softly. 'The ones loved and lost. Not just of this war, but of others long forgotten to time.'

He stared at one sword in particular, half his face cast in shadow from the Citadel above. His pale hair had ice formed in the strands, so he almost looked like a form of a god himself.

'How many?' Ezer asked.

Arawn blinked, whatever spell he'd been under, broken. 'How many what?'

'Lives,' Ezer said. 'How many don't come back each night?'

His eyes darkened. 'Too many, these days. Sacred magic is a fickle thing. The more we invocate, the more our bodies dwindle over time. But it's worth the sacrifice.'

Words she wasn't certain she'd be able to say, when speaking of herself.

She did not wish to die young.

She wanted to *live*. To try everything wild and wonderful in life, until she grew old and wrinkled and as wise as the ravens that had saved her.

'This was a godsblessing,' Arawn explained. 'All of it, every stone in its place, granted to an ancient king and queen on only the second Realmbreak, eons ago. A fortress that could never fall. A place to praise the gods on high.'

'So, it's real, then,' Ezer said. 'The godsblessing. *Nomages* celebrate the holiday, but we think of the blessing as only a story.'

Arawn huffed out a laugh. 'There are no stories when it comes to the gods. Only truths.'

He led her to the right, to another infernal staircase, and the uppermost cliff where her tower was. Up, they walked, passing statues of the gods' forms that were littered along the ancient stone railing.

'In the old lore, the Five could come and go wearing whatever body they pleased,' Arawn said, 'whether it be an elderly farmer one day, a beautiful young maiden the next, or sometimes, even a helpless child. Scholars believe it was a way for them to *play* with creating. To show they have no limits, indeed.'

She didn't need the lore explained to her. She'd studied the gods too many times to count, for there hadn't been much more to do in her tower but read. But there was something different about a true Sacred speaking the words. Wardlight sparkled down over the statues as they ascended.

'Aristra, god of Realm,' Arawn said.

The statue they passed had three faces. Male on one side, female on the other, and a roaring bear's maw in the middle.

They passed Avane next, god of wind, with two faces and a third shaped as a delicate dove.

Ezer paused to study Avane's female face. She was carved as a beautiful warrioress, her crown resembling whorls of wind.

Is it your voice that guides me? Ezer thought. *Is it you that watches after me each day?*

'They could end the whole godsdamned war,' Ezer said suddenly. 'If they wished it.'

Arawn sucked in a breath. 'To use their name in vain is unwise. They are always watching, always listening. Especially here.'

Not to me, Ezer thought.

Until she remembered the tornado of ravens, and she thought better of her words.

The higher they walked, the more the rumble of war returned.

And soon she could see the battlefield.

The Expanse.

She paused on the stairwell, breathless as the wind whipped past her ears. There was no whisper. There needn't be, because she knew the sight of death.

For miles, it stretched, a land of snow and ice and howling wind. The battle raged in flashes of light, bursts of colorful Sacred magic.

And far beyond it stood the jagged Sawteeth Mountains.

They were so much larger than she'd ever imagined. It was like another world entirely, a place that could never be fully explored.

But it was the shadowstorm above them that stole the breath from her lungs.

'That,' Ezer breathed. 'That's the Acolyte's power?'

The sky rumbled, and lightning flashed, illuminating the storm of pure shadow that spiraled over the Sawteeth's highest peak.

Unnatural.

Dangerous.

Alive.

Thousands of living shadows seemed to swim up and down the Sawteeth, from the storm to the snow . . . a dark barrier that none could pass.

Not without darksoul blood.

'Shadows,' Arawn said. 'As if he wields the darkness of hell on his fingertips. No one can cross beyond that curtain of dark magic. We've exhausted every option. They all end in death.'

The stories hadn't done it justice.

The Acolyte was the king of nightmares, indeed.

'Does it ever stop?' she asked, as the wind pushed at her back. She closed her eyes and pushed the fear away. She wouldn't fall. Some part of her knew Arawn wouldn't let her.

'No,' he said. 'The shadowstorm guards the Sawteeth day and night, and has never ceased, not in the twenty years of war. His power is immense. His wolves . . . growing in number by the day. His darksoul soldiers, too.'

'Does he ever come out to fight?' Ezer asked. 'Does he ever walk the battlefield?'

Arawn shook his head. 'We believe he sources the storm from within the Sawteeth. A great power that protects the entire dark army. He is too vital to walk the battlefield, to risk death.'

'So why don't you ask the gods to stop him?' Ezer asked. 'Stop the whole war in a flash.'

A *boom* echoed from far away, but she felt it deep in her bones.

Arawn frowned. 'The gods cannot interfere with the affairs of mortals. Lore tells us they aren't the only ones, the Five. There are more. Countless rule over their own realms, represented by our Sacred Circle. Together they form a godhead of many and have laws of their own to abide by. To step down to our realm, to interfere like that . . . it is forbidden.'

'They're gods,' Ezer said. 'Nothing is forbidden.'

'Every power must have a limit, Minder,' Arawn said.

She supposed that was why the Sacred died so young.

Because with every pull of their magic, every invocation the gods granted . . . it took something from them.

Until they had nothing left to give.

They were nearly at the top of the staircase now.

Ezer refused to look down, to allow herself to feel that spike of hideous fear.

'The gods cannot interfere every day. But they *can*, once a century,' Arawn said. 'Much like Absolution each month, as a show of their love and grace, they give us Realmbreak. At the end of it, the gods grant our leader a single blessing. If the heart of the Sacred King or Queen that asks is pure, of course. The intent of the blessing must be gods-honoring.'

'Pure,' Ezer said, and raised her brows. 'I don't think there's any mortal truly pure of heart. Nor are there truly pure intentions. We all harbor selfishness within.'

'You think too little of people,' Arawn said. 'Too much time, perhaps, locked away in your tower.'

'No,' Ezer said. 'I just know living creatures. And in the end, we are all the same, fighting for what is best for *us*, no matter what it takes. Even the ravens are selfish with the choices they make.'

Even kind Ervos had darkness that roiled within him.

Even the gentlest of doves could still peck a person hard enough to draw blood.

Arawn's brow furrowed. 'Think what you will of mortal-kind,' he said. 'But I know the truth. The gods breathed life into us, countless Sacred, countless *nomages* . . . and while we may not share magic, we share the outcome of this war. A war that must end in victory for the light. And if we hope to keep it alive, we must keep fighting for the Five. Until Realmbreak arrives, and with it, fresh hope.'

Ezer should consider herself *lucky*; Ervos had always said that she would get to experience a Realmbreak in her lifetime. Some called it *The Long Day*, which felt more fitting. Because once a century, for three straight days, the sun never set. It was a time when the Five shed all their light on the realm, watching their creation so closely that they could see all the way through to their souls beneath.

If the Sacred had done their job of living in line with their laws . . . the gods would grant them a single, mighty blessing to hold them until the next Realmbreak.

'In a few months,' Arawn said, 'we'll be granted something that could turn the tide of this war.'

Ezer glanced up at him, then immediately looked away when their eyes met. He was far too handsome for his own good. And certainly for *hers*. 'And what will the perfect, pure-hearted Sacred beg of the gods for this time?'

'That,' Arawn said, 'is not information you are privy to. But I'll tell you this. What my father will ask for . . . and what *I* would ask for if I were already King . . .' He blew out another breath that looked like smoke and turned his back on the war. 'They would not be remotely close to the same.'

CHAPTER 7

An ancient black stone temple sat atop the highest cliff.

It was lovely in its old age, the stones worn and uneven as if it had withstood the test of time. And so mighty, it could have housed hundreds of soldiers with room to spare. Her eyes followed it skyward, where she caught the tallest tower. It was covered in shimmering golden runes, with arched windows perfect for birds to soar to and from.

Home, sweet home, Ezer thought, and sighed aloud.

'Am I to go up there and begin my work at once?'

'It's not a prison, Ezer,' Arawn said, and she did not miss the way he said her name with far more ease than he had last time. 'It's a station, like for all soldiers in the north. You're free to come and go as you please.' He looked down at her ankles, her worn boots. 'And no chains.'

A bit of relief flooded her at that.

The doors had lovely sigils emblazoned on them.

Eagles' wings, the crest of Lordach, with five stars arched above them.

She was first hit with the smell inside – not cold and crisp, like the Citadel's courtyard, but the earthy scent that reminded her, undeniably, of *home*.

It was one of shavings and grains, of flickering torches and millet, crushed corn and seeds that she herself had grown so used to scattering across a cold tower floor to feed her own ravens.

The space still held the air of an ancient temple, with beautiful vaulted ceilings and stained-glass windows. But there were no pews. Instead, the stone floors were full of supplies: saddle racks and barrels, wheelbarrows and mucking forks and bags of pine shavings. Torches flickered on the walls, casting everything in a soft, warm glow.

There were countless people in white, gray and brown cloaks milling about, Sacred Knights and Scribes and servants readying for a night of battle.

Ezer paused, watching a Scribe in gray seated on a work bench, a book laid out before her and a dagger in one hand, which she used to prick the tip of her finger.

A drop of blood welled out, and she used it to paint runes upon the enormous broadsword laid before her. The blood sank into the metal like magic, and glowing gold runes took its place. The Scribe smiled and held it out to a Knight who marched over, gave her an approving nod, and sheathed the blade before heading away, fully dressed for battle.

'Come on,' Arawn grunted, and led her on past rows of iron racks upon the walls. And on those racks rested enormous *saddles*. Not for horses or bears, for they were far too large in the girth. Beside them, golden bridles hung on hooks, the chain-link reins so long they were coiled up like ropes so as not to touch the dusty floor.

Ezer's heart skipped a beat.

'This is . . .'

'The Aviary,' Arawn said. 'Home of the War Eagles.'

Suddenly she didn't give a damn if it ached her scars, or if she didn't even want to be here, in the north.

She grinned.

And then she drank it all in like water to a worn and weary soul.

Some of the saddles were new and shining, freshly oiled. Others were stamped with curling runes that had faded, no longer glowing but still a part of the leather, nonetheless. Like fossils, their magic always to be remembered. They were all created by careful hands, each one unique enough that she knew the Scribes had taken great care to customize the runes to their Knight's liking.

If one was to ride in a saddle, *die* in a saddle . . . it might as well be a well-equipped one.

The smell of leather filled her senses, and it reminded her of her Minder's apron, the one that used to belong to Ervos as a young boy, left hanging alone on a hook inside her tower in the south. She'd have a new one here.

And suddenly, she didn't hate the idea of it.

At least here, there were things to see, stories to uncover.

At least here, she would not be so alone.

'You won't see the mounts here,' Arawn said as he walked. 'They live through those runed doors.'

He pointed to the end of the rounded space, where a set of two golden double doors led into the war eagle's area. Softly glowing runes marked them, no doubt to keep intruders out. It had been blocked from her view when they'd stood on the cliffside before.

Gods, she wanted to see the war eagles up close.

Catching a glance of them in the forest wasn't near enough.

She glanced up at Arawn. 'Can I—'

'*Off limits*,' he said, 'to all who have not been chosen.'

Ezer blew out a breath and followed him along.

'Kitchen, bathing chambers, gear room.' Arawn ticked off doors as they walked. She noticed he did not mention the purpose of the black rounded door with bars for a window – not unlike the prison cells in Rendegard.

A pair of young Scribes scurried past them, hauling enormous worn bags over their shoulders, positively full to the brim with leatherbound books.

They paused, glancing up at Ezer for a moment – the scars

on her face, the blackened part of her right eye – before Arawn barked, 'You'll respect your new Ravenminder, or you'll find yourself working for *her* instead of your Knight.'

They squeaked and rushed away.

'I don't know if that's supposed to make the woman feel better or worse, being used as a scare tactic for poor Scribes in training,' a voice across from them said.

Arawn grunted. 'Hello to you too, Indriya.'

Ezer recognized the Sacred woman from the woods outside the Gates, for she was unforgettable with her pale white braids that accented her beautiful black skin, and a smile that reached her eyes. She sat on top of what looked like an old worn treasure chest – there was one beneath each saddle rack, with initials carved into them – eating a stick of dried meat.

She looked as calm as a cat lazing in the afternoon sun.

'Welcome back.' She winked at him. An atypical response for a prince, until she added, 'First Rider, Sir.'

It hit Ezer, then, what she'd meant.

Her head snapped up to Arawn, then back toward the saddles, as if she would find evidence of what she suddenly knew was true.

Arawn wasn't just a Sacred Knight, nor the Crown Prince of Lordach.

He was a *rider*.

And not just any rider.

He was a First Rider, in command of a war eagle aerie.

All this time they'd traveled together, and he hadn't once mentioned a thing about being a rider. Not that they'd spoken much, but . . . it wasn't the sort of thing she thought she'd be able to overlook. War eagle riders were supposed to be the best of the best.

The chosen ones, even out of the Sacred. Even for royalty, a war eagle wasn't guaranteed. It was a fated thing, the kind of position you were either born to handle or not.

But Arawn . . .

Well, so far, he had shit magic, from what she could tell.

She stared up at him as if she could see it on him. As if she could see the mark of the famed bond he'd made with a mighty war eagle.

She suddenly felt like she was meeting him for the very first time.

Several other riders had taken notice of Arawn now. They all marched over, eyes bright, speaking to him like he was . . .

Like he was loved here. Cherished, just as any prince would be. But it was more a true comradery than forced respect.

They adored him.

'So, you'll pick back up where we left off, then?' a male rider asked Arawn. 'A few flight drills should do to shake the dust off, for a record-breaking rider such as yourself. I think that's what Soraya would have—'

'*No*,' Arawn said suddenly.

Several others gasped as the rider's smile fell.

He took a tentative step back, like he'd stepped on a snake about to strike.

'I . . . oh gods, Sir, I wasn't thinking. I didn't mean to . . .' he muttered and ran a hand across his shorn hair. 'I was just trying to—'

'It's all right, Riven,' Arawn said. 'It's already forgiven.'

The excitement, the warmth, the comradery they'd shared just moments before had faded in an instant when that name was uttered.

Soraya.

A death that they all knew, then.

And for Arawn . . .

Definitely closest to him, Ezer thought. *Perhaps his matched lover.*

She couldn't imagine anyone choosing him.

But then again, she certainly couldn't imagine anyone choosing *her*.

Ezer busied herself with watching the flow of people moving about the Aviary as Arawn spoke with the riders.

A large spiral staircase stood at the end of the hall, to the left. The way to the Ravenminder's tower. She imagined Ervos walking up those steps, his enormous footfalls echoing down the tunnel. Her heart ached.

Suddenly she didn't want to go up there. To feel the same emptiness she'd often felt, alone in her tower in Rendegard. Because everywhere she looked, she could feel his absence. It was a living, breathing thing, always just there at her side.

The golden doors caught her glance again, the runes shining as if they'd been freshly inscribed.

War eagles.

She'd longed to see them her entire life.

Ezer's feet itched to move towards those doors, to press her eye to the keyhole and take a single peek inside. To see the mighty birds up close, just once. A dream, if she'd ever had any to claim as her own.

'*Ezer.*'

She flinched.

The voice of the wind was so loud, she swore it was right beside her. It had never been so close in her waking moments.

She looked at Arawn and the others, but no one had seemed to take any notice.

So she glanced to the left, where the whisper had come from. Sure enough, there was a small arched window in the stones, an old thing with cracked and ancient stained-glass flowers: blue ice lilies that could only survive in the north. She could feel the draft coming through the cracks at the edges.

For a moment, she thought it was only her exhaustion. She hadn't slept in ages.

'*Ezer.*'

The wind was louder this time.

She glanced around.

Arawn and the others were deep in conversation. He'd forgotten she was there at all, a circumstance she'd grown used to.

She was always a small, forgettable thing.

So perhaps she could use that to her advantage. No one took any notice when she walked deeper into the Aviary, her footsteps light as she followed the whispering wind down the hall.

'*Ezer. Go inside.*'

It had never been quite so clear.

She stopped, releasing a breath.

It was coming from *beneath* the golden doors.

Off limits, certainly.

But like her birds, she'd always been curious.

Perhaps just one look inside, she told herself.

She deserved something good. She'd gone through hell and back, and it wasn't even her choice to make the journey.

So, with a breath, Ezer steeled herself, rolled back her shoulders, and waited until a few brown-robed servants reached the doors, which opened for them with ease. They each hauled a wheelbarrow . . . and there were a few extras parked nearby, left unattended.

Before she could stop herself, she slipped away, grabbed an empty wheelbarrow, and ignored the feeling in her chest to turn back.

Just before the doors slammed shut, Ezer swallowed her nerves and disappeared inside.

CHAPTER 8

She stood at the entrance to an enchanted forest.

The moment she entered, she felt the buzz of magic.

A free and wild sort of thing, like the whispering of the wind.

It felt as if the trees were alive with secrets, from the lush, emerald pines to the aspens that had not been stripped bare of their leaves, like the ones in the forest beyond Augaurde. Rather, the aspen leaves danced in a delicate rogue wind, a soft, lovely green that made them look like they were made of silk.

The forest floor was covered with a blanket of rolling moss and worn boulders, with fresh fallen needles and pinecones. Flowers bloomed amongst the moss, some nestled atop the boulders, while others ran in delicate vines along the trees.

The smell was like springtime, cool and fresh with a bit of earthy wetness, and undertones of flora and pine. She could hear birdsong, and the chittering of chipmunks as they scurried across the rocks and climbed up into the trees.

It couldn't be real.

It was said nothing could survive in the endless cold of Augaurde, and certainly not up this high on the cliffside, with the howling wind and the storms that constantly raged.

Ezer looked skyward.

Perhaps it wasn't magic at all, then.

The Aviary was *domed*. Like a giant greenhouse made of tempered glass.

Far over her head, a glistening rounded ceiling protected them from the elements, creating a world of its own inside this space.

She walked deeper inside the trees, following a worn path until it spat her out into a large clearing.

And before her stood a large fortress.

Where the rest of the Citadel had been hewn of white marble, this looked like it had sprouted right out of the magic of the forest. Tall cedar logs formed walls, but the gates at its entrance were unguarded, left open as if this space was always welcome for those who'd been granted the gift of being in the war eagles' presence.

Flags with wing emblems hung from each gate, waving slightly as the Scribes passed between them.

No one seemed to pay her any mind as she entered, her head down and her wheelbarrow like a safety net.

She kept going, deeper into the sanctuary, and discovered the center of it all was an enormous, lofted wooden barn. The doors were open at each end, letting the wind dance through the rows of stalls.

'*Ezer*,' it whispered, beckoning her.

She'd made it this far already.

So she ducked inside, passing a row of hooks on the wooden wall that held extra servants' robes. She quickly swapped her tattered prison cloak, the better to blend in, for she could already see several servants cleaning out stalls.

She resumed pushing her wheelbarrow as she headed deeper inside. And instead of horses whinnying, crunching on hay or swishing their tails to ward away the flies . . .

She heard the sound of *birds*.

Her heart did a little twirl.

She came upon the first stall, where a war eagle stood right inside, behind the iron bars. Its breast was relaxed, its feathers a deep gold, with small streaks of white around the base of its neck. A servant skirted past Ezer, head bent and eyes lowered as he carried a dented metal bucket. It sloshed as he set it down and removed a hunk of bleeding, stinking meat from its depths.

A squeak of the hinges, and the servant opened the stall's front window, and held the meat out on a metal gaffing hook. Much like the fishermen at the wharfs outside of Rendegard used to haul in the heavy fish.

'Gentle, Suri,' he warned.

An enormous golden beak appeared at the bars and made quick work of snatching the meat off the hook. It was lovely, sharp and menacing, the tip of the beak dipped with gold that had been placed on like a permanent fixture. Sharp enough to shred through darksoul skin, and it was covered in freshly glowing runes.

The eagle's entire head was larger than the full length of Ezer's body. Its beak, longer than her whole arm from shoulder to fingertips, and each of its golden eyes was as large as her hand.

They were so bright they looked like liquid sunlight.

She stood silently as she watched the eagle eat. His eyes flicked up, then narrowed upon her. Its head cocked to the side in question.

Like it sensed her, the very same as all the other birds. She smiled, wishing she could get a little closer.

'What is it, Suri?' The servant turned, noticing the eagle's stare.

And so Ezer made quick work of disappearing again, deeper into the barn.

More servants in drab brown cloaks tended to them, scraping their stalls clean with mucking forks and wheelbarrows. Some stood *inside* the stalls, grooming the mighty eagles with thick bristle brushes meant to get down to the root of their feathers, while others dabbed dark green salve onto fresh injuries.

Plaques marked the stall fronts – the eagle's name, then its aerie color beneath it – and Ezer read each one, a familiar ease sidling up against her senses. This place had the sounds and the smells that she knew and loved from her tower, the only part of Rendegard that had ever felt like home. It filled her up, the click of beaks, the ruffle of feathers, the snap of wings as an eagle stretched and then settled itself down against fresh pine shavings. Some scratched at the shavings with their talons, as if they were overgrown chickens searching for bugs, while others chittered to the eagles in neighboring stalls, deep in their own unique conversations.

They were, in every sense of the word, the perfect birds.

She'd pay anything, any amount of coin, to be inside one of those stalls.

She finally came to the other end of the enormous barn. A gate led back to the outside.

And there, in the middle of a massive round pen, was a war eagle in training.

A magnificent sight, to see the beast out in the open. A female Eagleminder stood before it, holding her hands out as she ran them across the beast's golden feathers. A group of five others stood around the pen, their hoods colored to show their pillar of magic, one for each god.

They had golden bands on their arms.

And by the way they watched the Eagleminder inside the pen . . .

It seemed like a test.

Curiosity tugged at Ezer as she edged closer.

So easily, the war eagle could have lifted its wings and leapt right over the top railing of the pen, flown off to nest in one of the trees.

But it was utterly still, and silent.

And watching the Minder with an intense and present gaze, its head lowered in a show of respect.

It was a youngling, by the look of its still-white neck feathers, a bit of downy fluff clinging to its breast and sides. Beautiful, though its wings were still a bit too large for its body.

She smiled as she watched the Eagleminder run her hands

across the beast's neck. The woman was near Ezer's age, tall and lovely, with a golden braid that ran halfway down her back.

She stood face to face with the eagle and lifted her left hand.

The eagle lifted its wing to match.

'Good, Tyrn,' said the Minder.

She had a lovely accent, thick and rich like everyone else born in the north. A lift of her right hand, and the beast lifted its other wing.

She tossed it something dark and bleeding – fresh meat – from a pouch that hung on her hip.

The eagle snatched it mid-air and ruffled its feathers as it swallowed the meat in one bite.

It wore a bridle, much like that of a horse. The Minder attached a chain-link lead and began to direct it around the ring. The fledgling followed with graceful steps, its wings tucked, its tailfeathers held in perfect position above the sandy floor.

The five important Sacred inclined their heads or clapped gently in admiration.

The woman led the eagle to the center of the ring next.

She had it bow for the crowd.

Then she directed it in a delicate circle, before it lowered itself to one side, dipping its wing as if to allow a rider to climb easily aboard. A lift of her hands, and it raised both wings.

The Minder removed the halter next and did the same motions. This time, fully free, not a tether upon the beast. It watched her intently the entire time, gold eyes blazing.

'Incredible,' Ezer breathed.

She knew she should go, but she couldn't help the feeling that she was seeing true magic for the very first time. The kind of thing *no one* got to lay eyes on.

A gift.

When it seemed the display was done, and both Minder and war eagle had bowed in the center of the ring, Ezer realized they were heading her way, for she stood at the gate that allowed the eagle entrance back into the barn.

She backed away, trying to fade into the shadows. But the back of her heel landed on a mucking fork that was leaning against a stall door.

'Gods be damned,' Ezer hissed.

She tried to grab it, but her fingers missed by an inch, and before she could stop it, the rake slammed against a pile of empty metal pails in the stall aisles.

The racket was enough to wake the dead, so sudden she felt her own heart rocket into her throat. The Eagleminder's head spun towards the noise.

They locked eyes for a breath of a second, before the war eagle reared up.

With a screech, it lifted its wings, opened its beak . . .

. . . and lunged towards the Eagleminder, like it was ready to kill.

The Minder dove out of the way.

The eagle lunged, beak snapping, and missed her by an inch.

She stood and scrambled for the end of the chain lead, trying to regain control, but it had already been lost.

The others jumped into the pen, a scramble of flurrying cloaks, and surrounded the beast.

In the end, it took magic to settle it.

With a surge of white light from one of their hands, the beast backed down.

The Eagleminder finally managed to halter it again and drag it, flapping and screeching, to the other end of the pen, where she tied it up.

And left it standing there, sides heaving, wings lowered to its sides.

The trainer turned, eyes narrowed, as if searching for Ezer.

But she'd already scurried into the shadows of a nearby storage space full of barrels and bags of shavings and enormous bins overflowing with grains.

Ezer slid behind a rack of blankets and saddles, crouching down to catch her breath. Her heart roared in her ears as the Eagleminder marched past, her cloak soaring behind her like wings.

'I want to know who in the *Ehverloving hell* just ruined my display,' she growled.

Ezer waited, motionless, from her spot in the shadows. A spider scurried across her knee, but she didn't dare move to sweep it away.

She blew out a breath, still stuck in her crouch as the Eagleminder's voice faded.

She didn't realize there was someone behind her until he chuckled softly.

'A dangerous thing, to mess up Zey's demonstration. And before the Masters, no less.'

Ezer yelped and spun to find a white-cloaked figure sprawled out across a bale of hay, a book in his lap. He looked at her with a lazy smile as he corked a small vial back in place.

A vial that hung from his neck on a gold chain.

'Y-your Highness,' Ezer sputtered.

It was Kinlear Laroux.

And they were completely alone.

CHAPTER 9

Oh, gods.

Her eyes went right to the dagger on his hip.

It was sheathed, but there was no mistaking the bone carving that made up the hilt. A fine blade that she knew all too well from her dreams.

'You're not supposed to be here,' Kinlear said. 'This is *my* hideaway when I need a bit of peace and quiet.' He quirked a dark brow. 'You've come a long way from the woods, Ravenminder.'

There was something dark on his lips. He quickly licked it away, then set his book aside and reached for the white cane on the bale beside him, wincing as he stood.

'I . . . I got lost,' Ezer stammered.

He raised a dark brow.

'A difficult thing, to miss the enormous staircase in the center of the Aviary. One could say nearly impossible for anyone with a decent pair of eyes in their head.'

Fool, Ezer chided herself.

He adjusted his grip on his cane and stepped forward.

She took a step away . . . until she heard the footsteps behind her again and wondered if the Eagleminder was coming back.

'I've spent my life learning how to read the body language of war eagles,' the prince said. 'Communication comes in more ways than just words,' he added with a wink, a nod to their first conversation. 'They're quite similar to humans, actually. And I'd be remiss if I didn't point out, Ravenminder . . . you're afraid.'

She was going to throw up again.

Because his hand was moving towards the dagger, and she swore – oh gods, was he going to kill her *now*?

'Strange, that the doors to the Aviary even opened for you,' Kinlear said. He moved towards her with a rap of his cane.

She backed away another step.

And then she heard Zey's voice again, coming around the corner.

'You needn't fear *me*,' Kinlear said, as he watched Ezer with a narrow gaze. 'But Zey?' He tsked and shook his head. 'A dangerous thing, to get in the way of her demonstration. That fledgling was minutes away from being cleared for moving onto saddle work. After that, it would have been cleared to make the Descent, ready to make a difference in this war.'

'I'm sorry,' Ezer whispered. 'I only came to see the war eagles; I didn't mean to—'

'I'm glad you did,' he said.

And then she realized he hadn't been going for the dagger on his hip. Rather, he was reaching for a flask in his inner cloak pocket. He lifted it, then took a long pull before he wiped his mouth on his sleeve.

She didn't realize the Sacred were permitted to drink outside of Absolution. Especially not the prince.

'A tonic for the pain,' he explained, noticing her shocked stare. 'I'm sure you've heard the stories, about the war eagle that bested me a few years ago.'

She hadn't, and she was surprised the Ehvermages hadn't taken care of that for him, just like Arawn's scar.

Perhaps, like her wounds from the shadow wolves, a wound from a war eagle couldn't be healed by magic.

But she nodded as if she did know of his accident, because she sensed he wasn't the sort of person that liked to be overlooked or ignored.

'Zey is a fine Minder, but Tyrn . . . the beast is unhinged. A terrible mount from the moment of his hatching, made worse by Zey's rushed training of him. But of course, it's because she knows that *one more* fledgling broken before this upcoming Descent, and she'd break the record for most eagles taken skyborne. Her ego would only soar higher. We can't have that now, can we?'

Ezer shook her head. 'No. Your Highness.'

'Now, tell me the truth about what you're doing here,' Kinlear said as he screwed the cap back on his flask and returned it to his cloak, 'and perhaps I won't turn you in to my father.'

The King of Lordach.

The strongest Sacred to ever exist, who lived here in the Citadel . . . and had all the power in the world to behead her, should he discover her strangeties, unpillared as they were.

She could try lying again, but what purpose would that serve? The truth was better, in most circumstances. Especially when one was faced with a prince staring her down like she may or may not be an enemy.

'I . . .' Ezer sighed, her shoulders releasing all tension. 'I wanted to see the war eagles. As someone who's spent her entire life in the company of birds, you can imagine how fascinating I find them to be.'

He watched her for a moment, considering.

'Do you swear it?'

'I do,' she said.

His hand gripped the lion handle of his cane tighter. 'On the Five?'

His silver eyes were so cold, so searching. He'd probably discovered a thousand secrets in his life, for though he was her age, the prince felt older. Wiser.

Like he was a walking secret himself.

Her eyes went back to the strange vial on his neck.

'Yes,' she said. 'I swear it on the Five.'

At that, he smiled. 'Dangerous, to swear upon the gods, Ravenminder. One risks getting rebuked from the Ehver above.'

Her mouth was dry. It felt like she was swallowing rocks.

'I am not afraid of the gods,' she said. 'They've been perfectly happy to ignore me all my life.'

He huffed out a laugh.

'A sentiment I can agree with, for reasons of my own. And one that many others feel, but are afraid to speak aloud.' He released a breath. 'If you wanted to see the war eagles, Ravenminder . . . you needed only to ask.'

That was certainly a surprise. 'I asked Arawn.'

Kinlear chuckled. 'Ask the *right* person, is what I should have said. You chose wrong, if you wanted someone who's willing to bend a few rules now and then. There are ways around them if you're clever enough, but my brother is perhaps the most pious Sacred I've ever met. Even more than our father, and that's—'

He paused, mid-sentence, and began to cough. It was a terrible cough, wet and rasping, and for a moment, she wondered if it was ever going to stop.

'Are you . . . all right?' Ezer asked.

'I'm the prince of Lordach. I'm always all right,' Kinlear said as he settled his breathing. 'The dust inside these stalls. It gets to me.' And then his eyebrows raised, and his gaze slid past her to the aisles beyond. 'I'm afraid our conversation here must come to an end. I've somewhere else to be. *Anywhere* else.'

'Why?' she asked.

But then she heard Arawn's voice out in the aisles.

Her blood went cold.

'Gods be with you, when faced with my brother's wrath.' Kinlear quickly bowed his head in dismissal. 'I'll be seeing you, Ravenminder. I do hope you enjoyed your little private tour of the Eagle's Nest. In the future . . . be careful where you step. And where you hide, for you never know who might be watching.'

With that, he winked at her again.

Then he spun on his heel and slipped past her, smelling strangely of black licorice, sickly sweet.

She had one second to breathe before she stepped out of the storage space.

And came face to face with Arawn.

'*Ezer.*'

Oh, gods above.

He looked *furious*, like he had when she'd called him out on his fizzling magic.

'I just wanted to see them,' Ezer tried. 'Just one look, before going to my tower. I swear, that's all I did.'

'You disobeyed a direct order,' Arawn said.

And for some reason, that sparked a fire in her belly.

'I'm sorry,' she said sweetly. 'Are you supposed to be my superior?'

'You have *much* to learn about rank,' he growled. 'I am your *Crown Prince.*'

'Prince,' she said, because there was her reckless fury again. She would *not* be made to feel small. 'Not quite King.'

He looked like he'd been slapped.

And before she could stop him, he reached out to grab her hand.

She gasped at how sudden his touch was, how steady his grip. It was not painful by any means, but she certainly couldn't shake him off. He was the size of a war bear compared to her, all muscle and no give, and before she knew it, he'd whirled her around and was practically dragging her down the aisle of stalls.

Past eagle after eagle, all of which seemed to perk their heads up at the sight of the commotion. One of them released a throaty *squawk*, as if to protest.

Another rammed at the stall door with an enormous beak, but not even the eagles could help her now.

'I told you,' Arawn snarled, his voice low and menacing as he pulled her from the barn, 'that this space is only for the chosen. The ones who have worked to earn their place among the gods' mounts. You had no right.'

'Technically, you didn't apply that to *me*,' Ezer said.

There was no direct command.

'You don't listen,' he said. He was walking so fast she could barely keep her own legs under her. 'You are not from here, and yet you question the gods, question our laws, and break the rules laid out before you. We need to leave this space before anyone else finds out. They'll blame me, as they rightfully should, and I've no room for error on the day of my return. My father will have my *head*.'

'And what will he do to his Crown Prince?' Ezer ground out. 'Punish him?'

She barked out a laugh, but suddenly he whirled to face her.

'*No one* is immune to punishment, Ravenminder. Not the Knights, not the servants. Not even me.'

And that wasn't just fury in his ice-blue eyes.

She saw it now.

It was . . . *fear*.

But before she could ask him anything else, he was dragging her along again. 'Walk faster.'

'I *can't* walk any faster,' Ezer said, and dug in her heels. 'Your legs are three times the size of mine.'

'Then walk thrice the speed,' Arawn said.

'Must you always speak like some pompous, heady *bastard* from the pages of an ancient romance book?' she yelped.

Gods, he made her furious.

They were inside the trees again, on the path back towards the golden doors.

'Let me go,' she said. 'There's no reason to be so rash!'

'You act like a child who doesn't listen. I can't keep tracking you down to save you.'

'I didn't need saving,' she said. 'And if I recall correctly, the one who needed help first was *you*.'

He barked out a laugh. 'Anyone would, in the presence of shadow wolves. You should know.'

'Oh, isn't that noble of you, pointing out a woman's painful past,' she said. 'I suppose I should pick on you for yours now. What gave you that gash on your cheek?'

He said nothing.

'Don't ignore me, Firemage. I asked you a question.'

Still, he hauled her across the path.

'I don't think the problem is me.' She took a gasping breath as she tried to keep up. 'I think it's *you*, a Crown Prince who was sent all the way to Rendegard to pick up prisoners like some grunt soldier. I think you're in trouble already, and I don't yet know why. But it's related to your weak magic, or perhaps the very palpable tension between you and your twin brother. Or maybe it has something to do with someone named *Soraya*.'

He turned around, so fast she yelped.

Because then he was in her face, towering over her, and the fury in his eyes . . .

She'd never seen anything like it on a man.

When he spoke, his voice was a raw whisper. So quiet, she wondered if it was only the sound of the wind ruffling the leaves on the trees.

'Her name,' he said, 'is not yours to speak.'

She held his gaze. They were so close, their chests nearly touched, a steady rise and fall.

'And my hand,' Ezer said back, 'is not yours to hold.'

The spell between them broke.

He seemed to notice, suddenly, how thorough his grip on her was. How small her hand was inside his, a delicate little dove trapped inside a cage.

He released her.

'I . . .'

His mouth opened and closed, like he wasn't certain what to say next. She could practically hear him thinking, going through all the list of rules he must have broken in the past many moments.

'I apologize,' he finally said, 'for my lapse in control. Your words wounded me, and I wasn't certain how to react.'

'Some prince you are,' Ezer muttered, holding her hand to her chest. When she looked back up at him, his eyes were downcast.

He looked wounded. Utterly *broken*.

'The doors are just down the path,' he said, and a muscle in his jaw twitched. 'You're free to go. Anyone can direct you to your tower. A servant will come for you in the morning.'

He made to turn, but this time she grabbed *his* arm and whirled him around. 'So that's it?' she asked. 'We're done here?'

'We're done.'

He nodded, glancing past her. His blue eyes looked faraway, distant, like he was lost inside his memories instead. 'I wish you luck in your time here, Ravenminder. Gods be with you. From here below until the Ehver above.'

For some reason it felt so *final* just walking alone, away from him, after all they'd been through in the woods. He was the only person she'd come to know in the slightest, after so many years in silence inside her tower.

But she was just another face. Another recruit to bring north.

And he had a family of Knights and Scribes waiting for him.

He had a Citadel full of servants, a future and a crown.

And she . . .

She would probably be dead soon, like Ervos.

She turned and took a few steps into the woods.

'Minder.'

She glanced back over her shoulder, with the scarred side of her face. 'Yes, Firemage?'

'Be careful,' he said, 'around my brother.'

His eyes held a darkness behind them. A warning she couldn't quite place.

She nodded, and was about to ask him to elaborate, good-byes be damned, when a *boom* suddenly shook the sky. It was a distant sound, coming from their right. And it sounded like a boulder colliding against metal.

It was followed by a few echoing voices.

Voices that suddenly turned into shouts.

She heard the scream of a war eagle and wondered if perhaps one had broken loose from its stall.

Arawn glanced to the right, a question in his eyes.

'What was that?' she asked.

His brow furrowed. 'I don't know.'

'A war eagle?'

'No, Minder,' he said. His eyes met hers. 'Not a—'

But before he could finish, another *boom* sounded out.

This time, it felt like it shook the very dome over their heads.

'You should go,' he said. 'I'm going to help.'

'Help with *what*?' she yelped.

She could hear other shouts now, across the woods, back where they'd just come from.

'Go,' Arawn said. 'To your tower, before you bring more trouble to either of us than it's worth.'

'*Ezer.*'

She went rigid at the voice of the wind.

No, she thought. *Not now.*

It was coming from behind her. Back towards Arawn.

And suddenly those faraway shouts were louder – the sound of the chittering eagles had grown – and the whisper was now an insistent hiss.

'*EZER!*'

'What?' she screamed out loud as she turned.

She nearly toppled sideways at what she saw.

Because there, just over Arawn's shoulders . . . a shadow had appeared in the tops of the trees.

It can't be, Ezer thought, as she felt her own eyes widen. And she began to tremble in fear.

She watched as a monster – a beast that was half raven and half black panther – climbed down from the treetops, heading straight for them.

CHAPTER 10

She screamed.

And this time it was Arawn who lunged for her.

His strong arms wrapped around her torso, and then they were falling. Soaring backwards, the force of his hit so strong she felt her nose crack against his collarbone as they slammed against the forest floor.

The pain was white-hot beneath her skin.

They hit the ground and rolled, the weight of his body pulling her with him as they landed on the moss.

'Don't move,' he gasped as he straddled her, holding her in place.

She could barely breathe beneath his weight, and her own blood dripping down her face.

But she saw, from over his shoulder, the beast that had appeared from inside the trees.

Gods.

The stories were true.

All of them, *true*, for though few survivors returned from the warfront, their tales had still spread across Lordach like wildfire in the wind. Every scroll that came to her tower, every soldier's name and cause of death . . .

She'd read all she could about the raphons, *the raven-cats of nightmares.*

And in the fleeting glimpse she caught of the beast . . . she felt like her own heart might stop.

Horrifying, *beautiful,* a nightmare incarnate as it leapt with boundless grace from the branches of one tree to another.

'Raphon,' Ezer breathed, and pain flared in her face from her broken nose, but Arawn shushed her, and held her still and silent. His breathing mixed with hers, their bodies flush, the first time a man had *ever* been so close to her.

But there was no desire.

There was only panic.

It couldn't see them, she realized.

Because they were hidden in a small nook between two boulders, the thick moss and vines concealing them from above.

Arawn rolled away from her slowly, silently, a finger pressed to his lips.

For a moment, she thought, *perhaps he knows it's here, perhaps it's meant to be here.*

But then she saw the shock on his face. And she saw how taut his muscles were, even down to the veins on the back of his hands as he reached for the sword on his hip.

And paused.

Ezer's eyes widened.

The sword wasn't there.

He'd taken the entire damned weapons belt off before they'd entered the Aviary, for why in the hell would an aerie rider, a first-in-command – a *prince* – need to protect himself inside a space that was practically his own home?

And what was a raphon – the Acolyte's beast – doing *here*, inside such a protected place?

Together, they watched the beast as it slunk across the tops of the trees, as if on the hunt for something.

It was smaller than she'd expected, up close, at least half the size of the war eagles.

No larger than a pony. A young one, perhaps.

Its body was lithe, and perfectly honed to be a predator.

The fur was so dark it could have been a shadow, could have

been spun from the night. It had a sleek black cat's tail. But where the panther part of the raphon ended, the raven part began: a seamless transition from furred shoulder blades to feathered black wings. And a beak so sharp and dark – a beak that was so perfectly curved and feathered as to belong to a *raven* – she couldn't help but be amazed.

The raphon scurried up a tree trunk and disappeared into the canopy, leaving claw marks in the bark.

Ezer could hear her own breathing, her blood thrumming in her ears. She could barely *think* past the throbbing pain on her face.

'Where is it?' she mouthed to Arawn.

He crouched beside her, so utterly still he could have been a statue.

He placed a finger to his lips again.

She nodded.

Then he held up a hand.

'*Stay*,' he mouthed.

At that, her eyes widened. She shook her head. *No*.

There was no way in hell she'd be staying here, alone inside the woods. With a *raphon* on the loose.

The hybrid beasts hungered only for humans, and she was covered in her own fresh blood.

More shouts came from deep in the woods.

Like they were hunting the beast.

How did it get inside?

Arawn raised himself to standing, so silently she couldn't even hear the whisper of his cloak on the leaves.

She reached for his hand.

No.

He gently pried her fingers away – and held a hand down, like he was commanding a dog.

Stay.

'No,' she whispered, as quietly as she could, though it sent a spike of pain rushing through her from her nose. '*I am not going to sit here like bait, while you—*'

His eyes widened, and he lunged forward and pressed a hand to her lips, silencing her.

She froze beneath his touch.

She could taste the sweat of his palm on her lips, the dirt from the forest floor. He leaned in, his lips skimming her ear.

'Please,' he breathed against her. 'Please, Ezer. *Stay* until it's safe.'

She nodded.

Not to please him, but because she didn't want to die, and for whatever reason, she trusted him.

He turned and snuck away through the trees, following the path of the young raphon.

And there she stood, alone. Her back pressed against a tree trunk, her heart racing. Overhead, she saw nothing but the domed ceiling, and beyond it, the subtle flashes of light that meant the Sacred were still out there fighting with the gods' magic, far beyond the wards.

She looked to her right. They were almost at the edge of the woods, back to the golden doors and the warm halls of the Aviary.

She could make it, warn any other Sacred that didn't yet know of the threat.

A raphon is loose inside the Aviary! she imagined herself screaming.

The mere thought was wilder than even her worst dreams.

A gentle breeze slid past her temples, and with it came that trusting whisper.

'*Ezer.*'

It was leading her back to those golden doors.

'*Go.*'

She didn't need convincing. She pushed away from the tree and inched her way across the ground.

Be soft with your steps, she told herself, for despite his size, Arawn had crept away like he was at one with the woods.

But she . . .

Two steps, and a twig broke beneath her heel.

Panic surged through her, but she heard nothing in the trees.

And the wind . . .

She trusted it now to warn her, so she kept going.

She dared look up.

The treetops had settled. There was nothing there at all.

Another step.

She was close enough now to see the golden doors, perhaps thirty paces away.

She would yell for help when she was close enough to throw her body against them, to open them wide to the Aviary halls.

She risked two more steps, and nothing followed.

She was going to do this.

She would make it out of here, alive.

'*Go!*' urged the whisper.

She was walking faster now, as fast as her tired legs could carry her. In her mind, she dared pray to the gods, if they were even listening. She didn't know if it was them who had sent the ravens in the woods.

Or maybe it was Ervos, out there in the Ehver. Maybe they were sent by her mother and father, looking down on her from above, even though she never knew them.

Help me, she begged. *Please.*

Each step, more blood dripped from her nose, leaving a trail of crimson on the leaves.

Step.

Drip.

Something rustled in the trees behind her.

A whimper left her lips.

Step.

Drip.

Something cracked, not twenty yards back.
Step.
Drip.
She was running now, for she swore she could feel the eyes of the beast on her back.

She could sense that it had turned around, that it had followed the scent of her blood . . . that she was being *hunted*.

She was nearly at the doors.

She opened her mouth to shout for help, too afraid to think clearly anymore, when the wind suddenly whispered a word it never had before.

'*Stop.*'

A shadow passed over her head.

She heard the scratching of claws, the rustle of leaves as something large leapt from one tree to another.

And before she could take another step, before she could throw her body against the golden doors . . . the raphon landed before her on the forest floor.

She nearly lost all control of her body as she stood face to face with the beast.

It wasn't as large as she'd expected it to be, its beak level with her face.

But there was no mistaking the threat.

A low growl emanated from its throat; the catlike sound carried out through its curved black beak.

Its body rippled with muscle and silken fur. Beautiful, feathered black wings protruded from its shoulder blades, the feathers as long as swords. Its tail twitched back and forth as the raphon lowered itself into a crouch.

Oh, gods.

She knew that motion.

She'd seen it countless times, for it was the gesture every cat made before it pounced.

She *hated* cats.

And now she was to die by the devil's version of one.

Slowly, it stalked towards her.

Strands of her hair pulled away from her face as it breathed in through the slits on its enormous beak. There was a massive, jagged white scar that ran across it, like lightning in a black night. She could hear the rumble deep in its chest, a low growl as it breathed her scent back out.

It smelled like blood.

It smelled like death.

I'm afraid, Ervos, Ezer thought.

A line, cast out to the only person that had ever loved her.

The thought of him was an anchor, the only thing she could cling to when she was lost in a raging storm. The ghost of Ervos's voice whispered into her mind: along with a memory, the last time she'd spoken to him.

He'd stood on the front steps of Rendegard, one large boot already planted on the recruiting wagon that would carry him away from her. He had a worn leather bag in his hands and a desolate smile on his face.

'*Of course you're afraid, Little Bird,*' he'd said, as he placed a warm, calloused hand on her scarred cheek. '*Fear is a part of life.*'

He'd said it like he felt it too.

But he had embraced the feeling when Ezer had not.

'*We cannot erase fear. We certainly cannot kill it, for it will follow us all the days of our lives, stalking us like a panther stalks its prey.*'

'*Then what am I to do?*' Ezer had asked. She wanted to hold on to him, to grab onto his leg like she did when she was a child, doing her best to keep him from walking out the front door.

'*Do it in spite of the fear,*' he said to her. '*Do it afraid. All of it. Every moment in life. That's how you beat the fear. You do it all afraid, and suddenly, it isn't so scary anymore.*'

She didn't know what he meant then, as he climbed aboard the wagon and left her behind.

But some part of her understood now, as she lifted her hands before her. They formed a pathetic shield between her and the raphon, but it was all she had.

Blood glistened on her palms, still wet from wiping her broken nose. She didn't know what her bare hands could do, but she knew she'd at least be remembered as someone who did not kneel in the face of death.

'Go ahead,' she whispered, as she locked eyes with the monster, darkness incarnate. And curled her lips in a snarl. 'Make it count.'

The beast leaned forward.

And pressed its scarred beak against her bloodied hand.

She had only a moment to gasp at how smooth it was, how utterly warm despite the cold in her bones. She had only a moment to feel the *zing* that went through her, like she'd just been shocked by a bolt of lightning.

Every part of her body went taut, and the fringes of her eyesight darkened as a strange vision pulled her under.

A midnight feather, floating alone in an endless dark sea.

And that was sorrow she felt. A sorrow so deep it washed over and through her like a rogue wave, filling every part of her body until she felt she would drown in it.

Tears poured down her cheeks as the vision broke.

As the raphon screeched in pain. She felt it like a stab to her own body, a hot flare that began in her neck.

She gasped, thinking she'd been struck by an arrow or a sword.

But there was nothing.

The raphon stumbled away from her, then dropped to its knees in the moss. It toppled sideways, releasing a strangled cry as it fell. Its wings were splayed out behind it. Its catlike tail twitched once before it went still.

A strange, glowing arrow had struck the beast on its side.

An arrow marked in gold runes.

And on the other side of the raphon's body, standing there with a crossbow in his hands . . .

Was Kinlear Laroux.

Her knees went out from under her, but he was already moving towards her, his cane abandoned as he reached out. He caught her just before her head hit the ground.

'Are you all right?' he asked.

Arawn arrived just after him. '*Ezer.*'

Their twin faces hovered above her, morphing together like darkness and light, until she wasn't certain which prince was holding her in his arms.

She could still feel the warmth of the raphon's breath dancing across her skin as she was lifted up.

She tried to hold on, but darkness embraced her.

The last thing Ezer saw before her eyes closed was the dark shape of the raphon's body, splayed on the forest floor.

With her bloody handprint on its scarred beak.

CHAPTER 11

For the first time in years, Ezer dreamt of something new.

She was standing in a dark and icy labyrinth, a depthless place with frost-covered walls of black stone. Tunnels lined the walls all around her, gaping mouths of shadow that looked the same, no matter which direction she turned.

Ezer shivered, her breath forming in thick white clouds.

'Hello?' she whispered.

Only the echo of her own voice answered back.

She looked down, and realized she held a flaming torch in one hand.

And in the other, a black sword.

It was a short blade, with wings for a guard. And though Ezer knew nothing of swordplay . . . it was comfortable in her grasp. It was covered in strange, angular markings. Symbols she'd never seen before, for they were not quite runes. She felt that they were something other. *She ran her bare fingertips across one, surprised when a shiver ran through her body.*

It was not from the cold, but from the feeling that she was skimming her hands across the gravestone of a loved one she had not seen for centuries.

Familiar.

But not enough to spark any sort of memory.

The air was bitter cold, tearing through her cape despite the lovely flame-shaped runes that had been stitched into the fabric.

'This isn't real,' *Ezer told herself.* 'I can wake up from my dreams any time I like.'

And yet, try as she might . . .

She couldn't.

'Nightmare, then,' *she muttered.*

She angled her torch, searching for a way out. Strange, that she could not see without the firelight. That the darkness here was so deep, it stole even the small magic she had in her scarred eye.

The same damned tunnels were all around her, carved out of black rock and the ice itself.

She could not keep track of them, so identical that—

'Ezer. This way.'

The voice of the wind had come from just behind her again.

She spun.

And found herself on the threshold of another tunnel.

The darkness inside was full of doors.

Endlessly, they stretched on, lining the frozen, rounded walls. There was a groove to her right, filled with sticky black oil. Instinctively, she dipped her torch into it.

The groove blazed to life, snaking far into the tunnel until it illuminated the whole place with a soft orange glow that bounded off the frosty walls.

The doors were all ancient, dark as pitch, though a slight golden shimmer sparkled in each one. Like the darkness was webbed through with glittering veins.

They had no handles, no windows, no sign of what lay in waiting beyond.

But there were worn plaques on the stone walls beside each door, and the inscriptions had been carved in that same strange, angular writing as on her sword.

At the end of the tunnel, the path forked two ways.

Ezer took a right and found herself at the threshold of another tunnel, identical to the last. Twist after twist, turn after turn, each passage was the same.

The deeper she went into the labyrinth, the worse the cold became, until she could scarcely move her fingertips for the ice now coating her veins. Even her torch protested, but she continued to dip it into oil-filled groove after groove, grateful for the path the fire made through the maze.

She came to another fork.

The tunnel on the left was undisturbed – and so thick with a curtain of ice-crusted cobwebs she would have had to sweep them aside to pass through.

She turned to the right instead, and found the frost had formed so thickly on the floor that it looked like snow.

And . . . it had been disturbed.

It was not footprints that marked it, but rather a thick, sweeping line, like the fringes of a long cape.

Ezer's hand dropped to her sword.

Some part of her sensed that in this dream, in this labyrinth . . .

She knew how to wield it.

She knew how to kill with it in a thousand ways.

She had just knelt to run her fingertips across the marking, when the air behind her shifted.

The hair on the back of her neck prickled, and suddenly she could feel the weight of eyes upon her back.

As if she were not alone in here, after all.

There was nowhere to go, nothing to do but force herself to turn and face whatever was watching her from the darkness.

Her hand on her blade, Ezer stood.

She could have sworn she saw a shadow slip around the corner.

'Who . . . who's there?' she whispered. 'Show yourself!'

Perhaps it was only her mind playing tricks on her. Only the fear coming to life.

But then the ground kicked up, and with a whoosh, *a sudden gust of wind soared down the tunnel.*

And her torch went out.

*

Ezer woke with a jolt to the smell of burning wood, her body warm and . . .

Was that *snoring*?

The dream faded like candle smoke. She yawned, opened her eyes in full . . .

And promptly sat upright so fast her head spun.

She was in the middle of a large room, the walls and ceilings made of white stones with ornately carved wooden beams. A wall of windows to her right – the source of the soft light spilling into the room – was covered by sheer white curtains from floor to ceiling. Lovely, with delicate golden-stitched runes that swirled across the fabric.

The Citadel, Ezer thought.

She was surrounded by rows of ornately carved wooden beds covered in plush white blankets – and sprawled bodies. All women, some as young as thirteen or fourteen. Others could have been twenty, like her. None were much older. Sacred didn't last that long in times of war.

They were all asleep from the sound of snores and steady breathing.

Some wore gray, the color of Scribes.

Some wore white, with color-backed patches to depict their pillared god, while others had golden hoods. Eagleminders, like Kinlear.

They were all *Sacred*.

Ezer reached up to rub sleep from her eyes, then hissed through her teeth at the hellish pain that suddenly blossomed across her face.

Gods be damned.

She'd broken her nose, and with another terrible throb came a wave of memories as she pieced everything back into place.

The Aviary.

The raphon.

It was night when she'd survived the run-in with the beast, but now gentle morning light winked in through the long white curtains. Had she slept here one night or more?

A quick check revealed the ring on her thumb was still in place. Someone had placed a heavy blanket over her, the fabric edged with plush velvet and embroidered ice lilies. She pushed the blanket off, trying to keep quiet. She winced as the young woman next to her snorted and rolled over, turning to face Ezer.

Ice filled her veins.

It was *Zey*.

The blonde Eagleminder from earlier, whose demonstration with the fledgling Ezer had utterly destroyed.

What in the name of the gods am I doing here?

She needed to find someone to explain to her why she was *here*, with the Sacred . . . instead of inside the Ravenminder's tower alone with her birds.

She swung her legs over the side of her bed and noticed she had a trunk.

She nudged the lid open to find it had an outfit folded carefully inside. A quick inspection revealed it was a pair of black leather trousers and a long-sleeved tunic, a heavy black velvet cloak – the clasp at the throat was a pair of dark wings – and a pair of black leather boots that looked to be just her size.

The fabric was lovely, the stitching of every piece of finer make than anything she'd ever held.

A doorway to her right creaked open, and a young woman in a brown servant's cloak entered. Ezer caught a glimpse of the hall behind her – arched ceilings, a wide white stone hallway – before the door snapped shut.

'Oh! You're awake.'

Her voice was delicate, a gentle squeak of a thing that reminded Ezer of a little tavern mouse. Her eyes widened – bright blue, like Arawn's – and she waved Ezer over. 'Well, come on! Get dressed and join me by the fire before the rest of them wake. They're not entirely pleased about this.'

She kicked off her boots, leaving them beside the door before she walked as silent as a doe to the enormous hearth with flames flickering merrily on the farthest side of the room. A large worn leather couch sat across from it, with an old wooden table and chairs, and several bookshelves loaded with yellowed tomes.

Like a common area in a dormitory.

Slowly, Ezer stood. She had on her old tunic and trousers, but the brown servant's cloak she'd borrowed inside the Eagles' Nest was nowhere to be found. Which meant at some point, someone – gods only knew who – had carried her from the Aviary. Removed her cloak. And tucked her into a foreign bed.

Her stomach churned, for the last face she had seen was that of the prince.

Princes, she corrected herself, because it had been both Kinlear *and* Arawn, melding together into one.

With a sigh, she quickly changed into the new clothing, all too aware of how each piece, even the boots, was a perfect fit. She secured the dark cloak over her shoulders with the winged clasp, feeling for all the world like a specter in shadow-black.

A color that stood out, painfully, in a world of pristine snow-white.

Silently, she tiptoed across the cold white marble floors, making her way past the others still sound asleep in their ornate beds.

'Um. Good morning.' Ezer kept her voice low as she approached the young woman, who sat with her head back and her eyes closed, as if she were finally gathering a moment of peace. She had soft brown hair braided in a band across her head and was not much larger in stature than Ezer.

She winked open an eye, as if she sensed the shadow of Ezer standing over her. 'You're blocking the fire.'

So Ezer sat down beside her.

The young woman lolled her head to the left, as if she couldn't be bothered to sit up all the way. 'The clothing fits as nicely as I'd hoped. But *you*, my friend. . . well, gods know I can't lie. You look awful.'

'I broke my nose,' Ezer said.

A log split in half, sending a wave of sparks upwards into the hearth.

She didn't mention the raphon.

'I can see that.'

Without a word, the young woman reached into her deep cloak pocket, produced a small tin of green salve, and passed it to Ezer.

The very same kind she'd seen smeared on the war eagles' injuries earlier.

'It smells something dreadful, but it takes the pain away entirely. Ehvermage-crafted. Helps the servants, when we spend too long scrubbing floors. I'm only nineteen, and I swear I've worse knees and knuckles than my nan. She died at forty-three. It's quite old for a Sacred, these days.'

Ezer realized, suddenly, that if she was a servant . . . it meant this woman wasn't a Knight or a Scribe.

She was a Null.

Sacred-born, with no magic at all. Born to do nothing but serve.

Without a word, Ezer unscrewed the lid on the salve – and nearly choked on the smell of it. It was like rotten milk left too long beneath the sun. But she dipped a finger into the greenish substance anyway and spread it across the bridge of her nose.

It felt warm at first, like she'd traced a line of hot water down her face.

But then it cooled – so rapidly, it felt like ice.

The relief was instantaneous. She hadn't realized how bad it hurt until the pain was gone.

'Thank you,' Ezer said, handing her back the tin.

'Keep it,' the servant said. 'I've a feeling you'll need it more than me in the coming days.'

Something about that made her stomach twinge.

Still, it was the first time anyone had done something truly *kind* for her in a long time.

Longer than she liked to admit.

'I can get more,' the young woman said, and smiled. 'No shortage of mages here. No shortage of penance marks, either.'

She wasn't certain what *penance marks* were, but if it required the salve, it couldn't be good.

'Izill Brezevayne.' The young woman held out her small hand for Ezer to take. 'And . . . your name?'

'Ezer,' she said. 'Just Ezer.'

Izill smiled. She had a natural sort of beauty, disarming with her mouse-brown hair and freckles scattered across her cheeks and the bridge of her nose.

'*Lovely* name, Just Ezer. Now I need to thank *you*. You've earned me sixteen silver coins. They'll get me plenty of fun on Absolution.'

Ezer blinked. 'And why would that be?'

'Because,' Izill said, as she pulled her knees to her chest and began to chew on her thumbnail, 'the other servants wagered it would only last for two. But I had the winning bet. You've been asleep for three days.'

'*Three days?*' Ezer yelped.

Izill shushed her, glancing nervously over her shoulder. 'Runic stasis,' she said, and pointed to Ezer's wrist, where a mark she hadn't noticed before now sat like a fresh scar on her skin. It was white, like a rune whose power had already faded. 'It was ordered by the King himself.'

Ezer felt sick at the sight of it, at the mention of the King.

Someone had *marked* her . . . to knock her unconscious?

'But why—'

Izill shushed her again. 'You're loud enough to wake the

gods. I'm not supposed to be here long, but sometimes . . . well, it's nice to take a moment. Now, keep it down,' she whispered, 'unless you've the skill to fight a cranky war bear, and that's the best way I can describe Zey when she wakes even one *minute* too soon. But of course, it looks as if you've fought something greater and survived. Beyond the raphon, I mean.'

So, she knew.

Did the others?

Izill nodded at Ezer's trio of raised black scars. 'Do tell.'

'Shadow wolves,' Ezer explained. 'They attacked my village when I was a child. I was the only survivor.'

Izill whistled and spat a chewed fingernail into the fire. 'Not many of you out there,' she said. 'Survivors, I mean. You're godsblessed.'

Ezer doubted that, so she changed the subject to more important matters.

'How did you know about the raphon?'

Izill grinned. '*Everyone* knows about the raphon. Zey saw it. And so everyone knows because Zey knows.'

'Zey,' Ezer repeated, glancing over the back of the couch to the rows of beds and the blonde Eagleminder still sound asleep.

Perhaps she'd get lucky, and the woman would never wake up at all.

'Eagleminders,' Izill said with a sigh. 'You know how they are.'

Ezer just stared at her.

Izill's eyes widened. 'Ehver above. So, it's true, then. You really are an Unconsecrated.'

'A what?'

The word sounded foul on Izill's lips, like a curse.

She'd never heard it before.

But she'd also never heard of a *raphon* being inside the Citadel. Clearly the countless articles she'd studied about the Citadel and its Sacred hadn't come from very reliable sources.

When Ezer didn't answer, Izill added, 'An *Unconsecrated*. A Sacred, born and raised *outside* the Citadel. Likely because one, or even *both* of your parents decided to lay down their oaths and leave.' A pause as she tapped a fingertip on her lips, considering. 'What's your magic, then? Realmist? No. The dark hair, the scars, the mysterious glint in your eyes . . . you look a bit like an Ehvermage to me. No offense.'

Ezer pursed her lips. 'Not a mage,' she said.

'A Scribe, then?'

'I've no magic at all,' Ezer said, because she didn't know this woman, didn't dare breathe a word about her connection to the birds. Her ability to see so well in darkness. The voice on the wind.

And certainly not her strange dreams of the prince.

She held out her empty hands. 'I'm just . . . me.'

Izill stared at her for a moment, and Ezer wondered, not for the first time, just how convincing she could be at telling a lie.

Kinlear wasn't fooled.

Arawn wasn't either.

But Izill shrugged, as if she were instantly convinced. 'Welcome to the club, then. Unfortunate, in this space, for there aren't too many of us. They do try hard to weed out the weak when they match Sacred.' She lifted her chin. 'I'm nothing to be ashamed of, though. At least, not in my mind. I've always said a Sacred is a Sacred, even if they've just one *drop* of our blood in their family tree. Even if they break their oath and leave the Citadel behind.'

She was kind. An easy companion, Ezer could tell.

'So, who was it?' Izill asked. 'Your mother or your father that broke their oath?'

'Neither,' Ezer said. 'At least . . . not to my knowledge. They died in the attack. I don't even remember their faces.'

'A surname, then?' Izill said. 'You'd be surprised how many names you come across when you're delivering laundry to every door in the Citadel.'

Ezer shook her head. 'I've never known.'

'Gods, they weren't lying.' Izill smiled sadly at her. 'You're quite a mystery, indeed.'

She wasn't used to being spoken about, used to being looked at or considered by anyone at all. Something about it made her skin crawl to know she'd been the topic of conversation inside the Citadel. While she'd been utterly gone to this world . . . for *three damned days*, unable to tell her side of the story.

'Whatever the case, you've Sacred blood,' Izill said. 'No one, and I mean *no one,* can enter the Citadel without it. You don't see any *nomages* walking the halls, now, do you?'

'No?' Ezer said.

She hadn't had the chance to consider that.

But now that she thought about it . . .

It was only the Sacred. The Scribes, the Knights, the Eagle-minders. Even the Null servants, for though they were the only ones not to have magic . . .

They still had Sacred blood.

Another little mystery unfolded before her, and it was one she'd never discovered in the pages of her books.

Ezer supposed she should have been shocked.

But she wasn't. She knew the stories of those who'd defected, not to join the Acolyte, but to leave the ways of the Sacred entirely. It was either for love or fear or a need to live out one's life without the pressing weight of the Sacred laws.

She couldn't imagine the sheer weight of living so *perfectly* all the time, beyond the one damned day of Absolution to blow off a month's worth of steam. Perhaps it was why she'd seen such fear in Arawn's eyes, when faced with the reality of failing.

That wasn't living. It was *marching,* always to the beat of someone else's orders.

'Can you tell me where I am?' Ezer asked, changing the subject, because it was too heavy to bear in the moment. Too much to process, in so little time.

'Tower of Dhysis,' Izill said matter-of-factly. 'Shared dormitories line every floor of this tower. If you want your *own* quarters, you'd have to be of advanced Sacred status. Most of them are in their thirties by now. The Masters grant them more privacy than us. Makes the rapid decline . . . less intrusive, I suppose.'

A terrible thing, the toll magic took on a Sacred after time.

'And how, exactly, did I get here?'

'You're a guest of the princes,' said a voice from just behind them.

They both whirled to find Zey, the Eagleminder.

'And *you*,' she said pointedly to Izill, 'are not supposed to be here, Izill.'

'My orders are to clean your dorm. It says nothing specifically about how long it takes me, nor what I'm permitted to do in the in-between. But if you must know, I've been reassigned.'

'To what?' Zey growled.

Izill shrugged. 'To her.'

'What?' Ezer spun to face her again when she realized Izill was speaking about *her*.

A servant. For a Ravenminder?

'The prince wants you to have an attendant,' Izill explained with a smile. 'Someone to help escort you throughout the Citadel, and help you learn the ways.'

Zey barked out a laugh. 'That's preposterous. She doesn't belong here.'

'She belongs as well as you,' Izill said, as Zey practically snarled like a hungry lion.

Ezer had no clue how long the Eagleminder had been standing there, but she had her arms crossed over her full chest, a pale brow raised in disapproval. Lovely, buttery yellow waves tumbled over her shoulders now that her braid had been let loose, and despite the chill, she wore a sleeveless tunic to reveal the fine muscles on her toned arms.

Ezer swallowed.

Because the woman wore a look of pure, seething hatred on her face.

'Zey,' Izill introduced them. 'This is—'

'The one who interrupted my Demonstration earlier this week. I never got the chance to thank you properly for it.'

It was said with a snarl. A shiver tiptoed up and down Ezer's spine.

It nearly made her sick, how someone could be so beautiful on the outside when they were clearly *curdled* within. Because she knew in an instant, Zey was rotten to her core.

'Ezer,' she said, introducing herself. Refusing to bend to the piercing glare Zey leveled at her. 'We've met.'

Zey bared her teeth like a lioness. 'Well, Ezer. Next time you find yourself in a space not permitted for *your* kind,' she looked pointedly at Izill, as if to rope them into the same category, 'I'd suggest you swiftly find yourself back *out*. There's only so many times a Sacred can resist the urge to defend what is theirs. A delicate balance we must hold.' She looked at her fingernails, feigning boredom. 'I'd hate to see that balance shift on Absolution. We wouldn't want to get another mark on your face. Though I'm not sure there's room for more.'

Ezer had dealt with plenty of lashing tongues in her life. The comments hurt when she was younger. Sometimes, she refused to leave the house until Ervos bribed her with books and sweets. But these days they rolled off her like morning dew on the feathers of a bird.

Nothing could hurt her the way the past had.

Not anymore.

'I apologize for what happened with your demonstration,' Ezer said. 'An accident, if there ever was one, and believe me, I'd take it back if I could. Though, I'm not entirely certain it was my fault.'

'No?' Zey asked.

Ezer shrugged. 'No. In my expertise, a bird's behavior is a

direct reflection of its master. Your eagle is unhinged. A danger to itself and others, practically feral. And given that a spilled bucket set it off in such a way . . . well.' She clicked her tongue. 'I'd hate to see what a wave of shadows would do in the middle of an all-out war.'

Zey looked like she might leap across the couch and strangle her. But she only flipped her lustrous hair over a shoulder and tipped up her nose. 'And what sort of expertise would an Unconsecrated have?'

'Enough to know a feral beast when I see one,' Ezer said. 'But that depends, of course, on whether you trust the opinion of a scarred little vermin like me.'

Others began to wake behind them, the movement enough for Zey to pause, glance over her shoulder, and settle her breathing.

'I suggest you leave,' Zey said softly. 'Go back to whatever shit-stained tower you came from and— *Your Highness.*'

Her face paled as she suddenly glanced past Ezer's shoulder, where another woman had quietly opened the door to a knock.

And standing in the doorway, an amused expression on his face, was Arawn.

CHAPTER 12

The Crown Prince was dressed in his white Knight's cloak, but the clothing beneath was different.

For the first time, he looked like her future king.

He wore elegant black trousers and a fine white silk tunic with golden runed stitching around the neck. A deep V at the top revealed not only his absurdly large pectorals, and the gold chain with Vivorr's flame sigil upon it – but also the furious scar that stretched even deeper than she'd initially thought.

Like it had nearly reached his heart.

His pale hair was braided back in elegant knots, the sides freshly shaved to reveal the devastating lines of his face.

His blue eyes narrowed as he glanced from her to Zey and Izill, then back again.

As if he knew exactly what had transpired.

'Your Highness!' Zey's voice had changed from storm clouds to a bright, airy breeze, and she bowed her head in respect. 'You're back.'

Everyone else bowed and came up wide-eyed, as if they, too, were surprised by his presence. Ezer could have sworn one of the younger girls actually *sighed* in admiration.

'*Bow*,' Izill whispered to Ezer, as if she were throwing her a lifeline. She felt Izill's small hand on her shoulder and gave an awkward curtsy.

The corner of Arawn's lip quirked. She saw his eyes move across her, the salve and the swelling on her face.

'At least the uniform fits,' he said with raised brows as he beheld her, all in black. 'We're going to be late. Izill, I'll take it from here. Thank you.' He nodded his thanks to the servant, then gave Ezer a pointed glance. 'Come on, Minder.'

She hadn't the faintest idea where they were going, but for the first time, she didn't need convincing to follow him. She practically fled the room like it was on fire.

'Good luck!' Izill hissed as she reached the threshold.

Arawn closed the door behind them. They stood in a narrow hallway, ancient white stones all around them, and towering arched ceilings with wooden beams covered in runes.

He cleared his throat.

She felt suddenly *small* in his gaze.

Someday, he'd have a golden crown on his head. Someday, he would be her *king*.

'Making enemies with Zey is unwise,' Arawn said.

His tone unraveled all semblance of royalty and any admiration she might have felt.

Instead, there was only annoyance.

'I can handle Zey,' Ezer said, and crossed her arms. She was plenty used to bullying, plenty used to being underestimated. 'But *you* lied.'

His eyes widened. He looked like she'd accused him of murder. 'I'm a Sacred. I do not *lie*.'

'The Citadel doesn't allow anyone without Sacred blood to enter,' she whispered, as a servant in brown walked by, quickly bowing at the sight of their prince. 'You knew, the entire time, that I'm—' She waved a hand at herself, as if it would make it all make sense, because she'd heard the way even soft and kind Izill had said the word. As if Ezer was somehow even *less*. 'I'm an outsider. An *Unconsecrated*.'

Somehow the word felt spoiled. Like a curse she shouldn't utter inside these walls.

But Arawn didn't look at all surprised by it, like he truly had known the whole time.

'You didn't ask,' he whispered back. 'I assumed you knew, with your magic.'

'I don't have magic,' she lied.

'You do. And for whatever reason, you're hiding exactly what it is. Why?'

Her fists curled in frustration.

'You're afraid,' he said. 'Because you cannot control it. Is that it?'

She barked out a laugh. 'No.'

'Then what is it?' he asked. 'You are here now, where all Sacred belong, whether they were raised beyond these walls or not. This is your true home. So, tell me why you seem to have everything against it.'

She released a breath.

How could she tell him?

The list was far too long.

Because I've watched people thrown in prison for accusations of spoiled magic just like mine, she wanted to say.

Because for two years, I've fallen asleep to their cries echoing through the floor of my tower in Rendegard.

Because I've read about all the pillars, tried to find space for myself within one, and I cannot. I do not fit.

Because people fear the omens, and I find sanctuary in them.

And if she was really being honest with herself . . .

It was because she did not love the gods with her whole heart, like Ervos did. She'd tried. For years, she had lit the right colored candles and said perfectly recited prayers, and she sang all the songs on Allgodsday beneath the light of the full moon. She'd memorized the stanzas in their Book, and she'd even blessed the bread each time she and Ervos sat down for a meal.

And still, the Five had abandoned her.

Still, they had allowed terrible things to happen to her, and she did not have it in her heart to forgive them. To give her entire heart and mind and soul to serving them.

Not yet.

Not until they answered her.

Not until they showed her they were *real*.

And she had not been forgotten.

'I am not my father,' Arawn said, keeping his voice low. 'You'd be wise to trust me with your gifts.'

A spike of fear jabbed her in the gut when he spoke of King Draybor Laroux.

He was double-pillared, capable of sending invocations to not one but *two* gods. Very few Sacred had ever been capable of surviving the power that this required.

For twenty years now, King Draybor had torn himself down, bit by bit, to defend them from the Acolyte in battle. He could wield both fire and wind at once, a deadly combination. And with each granted invocation that surged power through his body . . .

She'd heard the rumors that he was aging fast these days.

That he was on the battlefield less and less, needing to recover between bouts of using his magic.

And if the rumors were true, then soon enough, Draybor Laroux would be well on his way to a classic Sacred end.

A death, too young.

Another sword plunged in the snow.

And then *this* man before her, this cold prince of the north . . .

He would become his father.

And she would be another anomaly that the kingdom feared, just like her ravens. *Different*.

Dangerous.

She wouldn't dare give Arawn an inkling of her strangeties.

It wasn't safe.

Arawn seemed to sense the battle writhing within her, because his voice softened. 'If you allowed me to help you with that hidden magic of yours . . . it's worth honing. It's worth discovering which pillar you lean into, because it saved me. And it can save you, too, with what's coming next.'

'What's that supposed to mean?'

Fear washed over her anew.

Arawn's jaw twitched. 'You have been reassigned.'

'To *what*?'

'To Kinlear,' he said.

She raised a brow.

'To do what you do best,' Arawn said. 'Minding.'

Without another word, he turned and marched down the hall, his pressed white cape sweeping out behind him as if caught in a rogue wind.

She sighed and followed as he led her down the Citadel halls. They were endlessly twisting, the stones painted with runes that glowed like stars as he guided the way. Stained-glass windows showed depictions of the gods in their triad forms.

Each person they passed bowed when Arawn came into view.

Their future king walked amongst them.

But she could feel their eyes on *her* back instead, as he guided her away.

Something like nausea roiled in her gut.

They finally paused before a towering set of ancient wood doors. Two guards bowed and opened them for Arawn to pass.

She followed him inside, expecting a throne room, or perhaps a torture room of some sort . . .

But to her relief – and surprising delight – it was only books. They'd entered into an enormous room, with rows of massive wooden shelves that could only be held aloft by runed magic. They were the largest Ezer had ever seen.

Her eyes widened.

'A library,' she breathed.

A true library, not like the dusty, shadow-filled pawn shops

Ervos had taken her to, where very few books on magic remained.

After the war began, King Draybor had most of the books on Sacred magic, war eagles, raphons, runes – anything, beyond the literature on the Five – rounded up and sent to the Citadel for safekeeping.

His guards had taken all they could find and handed out the Sacred Text instead.

It held the laws that all mortals must keep in order to become as close to the Five as they could. To fail was to deny the gods. And with each failure, a dark mark was placed upon one's soul, dimming the light that the gods needed to find their soul when death came.

Too many laws broken and that light would go out.

There would be no Ehver.

No eternity in peace with the Five.

Instead, the soul would be tossed into a lake of darkness, a cold and endless abyss with not a shore to be found. Of course, that fate was too harrowing a task for every mortal.

So, the gods had children . . . and so were born the very first Sacred.

The Sacred were given magic – and invocations to call upon it – as a way for the gods to keep their power in check. With it, they were sworn to protect the innocent and strive for perfection on the *nomages*' behalf, apart from one Absolution Day a month to keep them appeased.

The Sacred had always been the sacrificial lamb.

Without them, Ezer guessed they'd all be souls, heading for that lake of darkness.

The Sacred Text was the first book she'd ever read, cover to cover, and it was lucky she *could* read at all.

Most of the children in the temples were taught only wartime things.

Like how to cook or grow crops or sew uniforms for the

soldiers. Most were taught simply how to survive, in a world where the chances of being drafted into the war were much higher than the chances of finding a good storybook.

But Ervos had valued books, and he knew Ezer would, too.

A child needed something to escape to, a place to feel safe and separate from the horrors of the war.

So he did all he could to purchase the ones left over for her.

He brought her books with stories of brave knights.

Stories of princes and princesses and dragons, where she'd learned that not every character needed saving.

And not every villain needed to be slayed.

In books, she learned about love. She learned about heartbreak, too – and vengeance – things she knew all too well.

Each story watered the seed that had been sown in Ezer's soul long ago: the desire to live out her own choices.

It gave her hope that there was *more* for her outside of her tower. That the world was full of color, instead of scrolls scribbled in black and white.

So when the doors of the library shut behind her now, and Ezer was wrapped up in its warm embrace . . . she felt like she could hardly breathe from the sheer beauty of it.

She had *never* seen so many books at once.

They took up an entire turret of the Citadel. The walls were rounded behind rows upon rows of shelves.

An ornate curving staircase of gold stood along the library's far wall, stretching upwards like a mighty dragon. Arched windows in the stone revealed the entirety of the soldiers' barracks and the Thornwell Forest beyond, their edges lined with hoarfrost.

Each step was made of white marble and carved with depictions of the gods in their many forms.

Exquisite, in every sense of the word.

There were carts of books amongst the rows of shelves. And tables stacked to the brim with books. And books holding up other books – enough that she couldn't count them if she spent a full week here.

And the *smell*.

Gods, it was lovely.

Ezer closed her eyes and breathed deeply.

It was of leather, worn paper, and crackling wood from an enormous stone fireplace that stood like a beacon in the center of it all. It was round, to allow Sacred to sit on the hearth from all sides, and it stretched all the way up to the library's domed glass top.

Wardlight bathed a soft, golden glow on everything below.

Several Scribes sat at the scattered tables, amongst pen and ink and haphazardly stacked piles, busy practicing inscribing their runes. It felt like a school.

The kind of thing she'd never experienced, growing up in the south.

She'd never even spent much time around anyone her age.

It was only Ervos.

Only the birds.

'The Scribes,' Arawn explained, keeping his voice low as he led Ezer into the space, 'consider the library a second home. They come here each day to prepare their Knights for battle. They test out new runic combinations, for there are millions. Truly *millions*, enough that it would take multiple lifetimes to scratch the surface of what the godstongue can do.'

They passed by a Scribe using his dagger to prick the tip of his finger, drawing a bead of blood that he used to paint a delicate rune upon a bit of stone. Strange, that it did not look painful.

Rather it looked like an artist at work, peaceful and practiced.

The stone began to tremble.

And then it disappeared, gone in a flash, as if had never been there at all.

'They spend their entire lives studying and perfecting, through trial and error,' Arawn explained. 'Learning how to inscribe them perfectly, because any error in the formation, and the rune won't wake. When we take to battle, we are heightened by their countless hours spent preparing. Their knowledge of the gods-tongue far surpasses a Knight's. Without the Scribes, we would die from the first hit we take in battle. The first scrape of a darksoul claw.' He looked sidelong at her. 'Our war eagles, too.'

'I've no knowledge of the eagles,' Ezer said, as her ears perked up at the mention of them. 'The prince is a fool if he thinks I'm to be of any worth to him in Minding them.'

Though a part of her could imagine it.

A part of her *wanted* it.

Arawn led her to the gold staircase, up to the next level of books. She avoided looking left, where the wall of frost-covered windows revealed just how far a person could fall, should the glass give way. 'And *you* are a fool if you utter another negative word about my brother inside this space.'

The next level was the same in shape and size as the ground floor, but the books on the shelves looked far more worn and well loved. They were all leather, with ornate curling script stamped on their spines.

If there was anywhere she could learn about herself, whatever strange ability she carried within, how far back in her family line a Sacred was – who they were and why they left the Citadel – it would be here that she'd find it.

Arawn led her to yet the next level up. She didn't dare look down as she followed him up the steps. Didn't dare risk letting go of the gold railing, either.

And finally, they came upon Kinlear.

Each time she'd been around him, he had walked with a swagger, a confidence that she supposed only a prince could have, and somehow his cane only added to it. Like he couldn't be bothered by anything.

But today, he didn't look princely or overly proud of himself. He just looked like a scholar, at peace amongst piles of books.

Not at all like the man who killed her over and over again in her dreams.

Certainly not like a famed Eagleminder, nor a prince.

He had his white cloak on, laced with the gold silk hood, reflecting the firelight as he sat at a massive old oak desk before the rounded hearth. His cane was left on the table before him, abandoned. His dark curls were mussed, and he leaned his chiseled jaw on a fist, while his fingertips skimmed down the pages of an open book. His lips moved as if he were busy searching, speaking to himself as he went page by page. That unusual vial still hung on a gold chain around his throat.

In a story of mysteries and murder, Kinlear Laroux would be the main character.

She just wasn't certain, yet, if he was the villain or the hero.

'This is as far as I go,' Arawn said.

'And why is that?' Ezer asked.

His eyes darkened as he looked at his twin. 'Because my brother is about to perform one of his dramatic speeches, and I'm not certain I have the willpower to survive it today.'

And before she could ask him anything else, he turned and left, his white cloak snapping after him for how fast he seemed to want to leave.

Whatever was between the twins, it certainly wasn't good.

She supposed that was how it worked with siblings, especially when one was destined to wear a crown. And the other . . .

She didn't know what Kinlear's future held. He'd be involved in the running of things and would live a life of luxury until he was ever called upon, should something happen to Arawn.

He's a backup king, she'd once heard spoken of him.

And she couldn't imagine the stigma that came with it. To be a runner-up for all your days.

She approached his table slowly, unsure whether he wanted to be disturbed. He didn't look up, but he must have heard her approach. 'Sit,' he said, and turned another page.

She went to the chair across from him and sank into the worn leather without a sound.

Better to face him, to keep her eyes on his hands, should he reach for the bone blade he carried at his waist. But she doubted he'd kill her here, in the middle of the library.

One would have to be a monster to risk getting blood on books.

He finally looked up from his page. 'It's interesting, the literature from our past. This book is centuries old. Do you know what it's about?'

So, he would play it this way, then. Like a calm, casual conversation.

Like he hadn't just had his brother deliver her here, with no explanation for why she'd been in a runic sleep for three days.

'No,' she said.

He locked eyes with her. '*Raphons.*'

For a second, she held his stormy gaze, remembering the last time she saw him. The blood on her hand, the raphon crumpled at her feet. Herself, caught in his long arms and his face melding with Arawn's as if the two were one.

'Many claim that raphons are poisonous,' Kinlear said. 'That to touch one is to die a terribly slow death. What do you make of that claim, Ravenminder?'

She looked down at her hand.

The one that had left a bloody imprint on the raphon's beak.

'I think I wouldn't be here right now, if that were true,' she said.

He looked like he was holding back a smile. 'An excellent observation. I have something for you. A reassignment, signed and sealed by my father.'

He reached into his cloak pocket.

She tensed.

But he just tossed her a letter signed with the King's five-starred stamp. She skimmed it, and indeed, she was no longer a Ravenminder.

She was, instead, a title she'd never seen before.
Raphonminder.
The blood drained from her face, and she dropped the letter as if it were on fire.
'What is this?' she breathed.
'We'll get to that.' Kinlear leaned back in his chair, ignoring the shock on her face. He tapped the pages of his book with ringed fingers. 'Many believe that to even lay eyes upon a raphon is to greet death. It is why no one settled in the Sawteeth before the Acolyte. Because too many explorers had become dinner for the feral flocks.' He smiled and met her eyes. 'I'm not surprised by your survival. Because we at the Citadel know that theory – that raphons are untamable – to be untrue.'
He said nothing, waiting for her to respond.
Like he was playing a game with her, and if she wanted answers, she'd have to oblige him with the right questions.
'And why is that?' Ezer asked.
Kinlear shrugged and swept dust from the book in front of him. 'Because we have been capturing them for years now.'
At that, she raised her brows, truly surprised.
'How?' she asked. And then she added, '*Why?*'
He smiled. 'Runes, my fellow Minder, can do a lot more than people think. People love to overlook the Scribes, to think of them as less than the Knights. But I find they are bolder, braver than anyone who wields magic or a sword, for there is little limitation when you have knowledge. Did you know, before I was chosen as an Eagleminder, I trained as a Scribe?' He held out a hand. 'I've never been able to wield like my brother. *This* is my battleground, the library. My weapons cache, the books, and with them . . . myself, and countless others, have discovered a way to capture raphons, hold them in stasis, so we can study their behaviors. See what makes them tick. To know one's enemy . . . it is the true art of war.'

She had a feeling this information was not common knowledge, beyond the confines of the Citadel.

'A few months ago, we discovered one of the raphons we'd captured – a female, wounded in battle after her darksoul rider was rightfully slayed – was pregnant with a litter of pups. None of the books cover a raphon's birth. We found they don't lay eggs, not like the raven half of them. They birth them warm and wailing, like panthers. The mother perished. But we managed to save a litter of six. Small, screaming things, thirsty not for milk but for blood.' His jaw quirked. 'A traitor – a *monster* – disagreed with our plans, broke into the catacombs, and slaughtered five of the pups before we managed to stop him. There was only *one* to survive.'

It felt wrong.

It felt dark, to know that all this time, raphons had been held prisoner here.

A servant arrived to add another few logs to the fire.

Kinlear kept silent, watching Ezer as they waited. He looked so much like Arawn in the face . . . and yet so different. Even their postures were unique, the way he carried himself so calmly, when it seemed like every part of Arawn was always tense.

He coughed again, and quickly uncapped the vial at his throat, taking a small sip of the liquid.

It smelled overly sweet.

As he wiped his lips and recorked the vial, he said, 'The raphon that broke out of its cage in the catacombs three nights ago, that managed to break through an iron portcullis *and* a sealed back door into the Eagle's Nest . . . it was the final pup from that litter. The last survivor, and only a fledgling, six months old.' She remembered the scar on its beak, a jagged white streak to break apart the darkness. 'It was due to be put down days ago, for my father's belief is that the research on them, the risk, outweighs the minimal chance of reward.' He released another small cough, then smiled as he recovered. 'And yet . . . there *is* a chance for reward. I've fought for years to maintain control over the Black Wing Battalion: a code word for our studies, for we don't need the kingdom catching wind of it.'

The realm would be in uproar.

They'd done a fine job of keeping the secret thus far.

'Despite the pup's size now . . . it will grow quickly. Enough time to be fully grown, by the time Realmbreak comes around. And by then, we hope to have it tamed.'

'You can't be serious,' Ezer said.

It was well known that the raphons were wild beasts, as fearsome as dragons in her children's stories. They were cold-blooded killers who hungered for human flesh. Some even believed that like the ravens they called omens, the raphons had been a rejected creation of the gods, long ago.

Which was why the Acolyte probably found them the perfect mounts for his darksoul warriors. Raphons feared nothing. Not even the war eagles that were double their size.

'This is a feat previously thought impossible,' Kinlear said. 'Myself and several other Eagleminders have all applied our best efforts. Our strongest Scribes have applied their greatest runic combinations to try and tame the pup.' He sighed. 'Alas, the raphon's trust has been quite hard to gain. Everyone that's tried has failed, and I am no fool. I'm willing to admit when I've met my match, to bow out when it will most certainly end in defeat. And I *was* defeated.' His gray eyes met hers. 'Until I met *you*.'

She wanted to shake her head. *No.*

Instead, she just sat there frozen, staring at him as he stared at her, his lithe body outlined by a halo of flames from the nearby fire.

'What happened the other day wasn't part of the plan. I apologize for the trauma you have been put through in the north thus far. It isn't how we want to treat our recruits.'

She wasn't sure he was being sincere, but she listened as he continued.

'I believe the gods knew otherwise and disagreed with my father's hope to shut down the Black Wing Battalion. They are the only beasts that can fly to and from the Sawteeth, untouched by the shadowstorm. They hold an immunity to it, and by proxy, so do the riders upon their backs. I believe, along with a majority of the War Table . . . that the raphon pup is our answer.'

'The answer to what?' Ezer asked.

Kinlear was deadly still. 'To assassinating the Acolyte.'

'You're mad,' Ezer said, shaking her head. 'You can't ride a raphon! Certainly not *that* raphon.'

'Why not?'

She blinked at him. 'Because . . .' Gods, she couldn't believe she was arguing with the prince of Lordach, and about a raphon, no less. 'Because it's not even *trained*, for starters. Has it ever even seen the sky?'

'No,' said the prince. 'But that isn't my problem. It's yours.'

A spike of cold went through her. 'I'm not sure what you're getting at, Your Highness.'

'Raphons don't hesitate,' he said. 'But in the woods, when it was faced with you, the perfect victim, small and scarred and alone . . . it hesitated.'

She could still remember the feel of that moment. The racing of her heart, the wind telling her not to run, but to *stay*. The feeling of the raphon's warm beak on her hand, its breath hot as it swam across her skin.

And a vision that brought sadness.

A single black feather, floating alone in an endless, dark sea.

'Now, I'll be quite clear,' Kinlear continued. 'Some furious deliberation has gone on in the days you've been at rest. A runed rest, I might add, for it was necessary to keep you subdued in case it was decided that you are to be treated as a threat. The jury is still out on that one, as there is no birth record in Touvre for an *Ezer* that matches anyone near your age.'

Of course they'd looked into her.

Of *course* they would see her as dangerous, because she was different.

She certainly hadn't chosen that fate.

And by no means was she a *threat* to Lordach.

'It's probably because my parents never had a chance to report my birth or take me to the census themselves,' Ezer said. 'When I was old enough, I showed up every year for it. I dropped my name in the box, the same as all the others, so you could call upon us. The weak and magicless ones, when you needed more to use as cannon fodder in your war.'

He took the insult with ease, the same way she would have.

'And why would your parents have skipped out on such a joyous occasion?' the prince asked. 'They would have been compensated finely for ensuring the kingdom knew your year of birth and your name.'

Every citizen that reported their newborn children was given rations. A sack of coins for each child, if only because when they reported them, their names all went down in the kingdom's register and when they turned eighteen . . . they could be called upon for the war.

'They didn't report me,' she said, curling a fist around her mother's ring, 'because shadow wolves razed our town a few days after I was born. I was the only one left. My uncle found me, raised me as his own. And when your father called him away, when he *ripped* him from my grasp, the prison master of Rendegard forced me to fill his position as Ravenminder. Without pay.'

He paused, and for the first time, his eyes slid to her scars.

'I am truly sorry for your loss,' he said. And it sounded like he meant it. 'Your part in this war is vital, Ezer, and if you lean into it . . . it may well give you the chance for vengeance.'

'I . . . didn't say anything about vengeance,' Ezer said.

It was a word she hadn't heard in the mouth of a Sacred before.

He only smiled knowingly. 'You didn't have to. I can see it in your eyes. It's the same look every survivor has. *You* were a victim. *You* were the weak one. And now you have a chance not to be seen as such anymore.'

His eyes went to his cane and narrowed.

She had the feeling he wasn't just speaking about her.

He cleared his throat. 'The War Table took a vote. And it was voted that we give you a chance to mind the raphon pup. To train it, teach it how to behave as any good mount should. Teach it to trust you. So that, in two months' time . . . we can assign it a rider. And take the beast to the skies. That rider will journey across to the Sawteeth on Realmbreak, using the sunlight of the Long Day to go behind the shadowstorm unbothered by darksouls . . . and assassinate the Acolyte. Before it's too late.'

She couldn't hide the fury on her face.

'I train *ravens*!' she yelped. 'Ravens to fly from one tower to another. Not *raphons*! Pick an Eagleminder! Pick . . .' A furious blonde woman appeared like a haze in her mind. 'Pick Zey. She clearly wants to prove her worth. She might be the perfect fit for the pup's wrath.'

But Kinlear only shook his head. 'They have all tried. The Citadel's best, the Citadel's brightest, every Eagleminder and Bearminder we have in our ranks. And all have failed to get close to the beast. But you . . .' His eyes were practically glowing. '*You* are different.'

She just stared at him, frozen in horror.

'I'll die,' she said.

'Death is coming for us all eventually, and sooner rather than later in times of war. You're the only one who's made it close enough to touch the pup. To live to tell the tale. It may learn to trust you yet.'

Slowly, he grabbed his ivory cane and pushed back his chair. When he stood, for a moment she swore she saw him wince. His fingertips shook as they gripped the eagle handle.

'You will feed it. Clean up after it. *Mind* it, as if it were your own. And each day you survive, you will be compensated handsomely. Upon completion of the job, you'll be granted a full pardon from your service, free to carry on about your life as you please. No more summons. No more war.'

'And if I die?' she asked as he turned to go.

He shrugged. 'I suggest you work on your relationship with the Five. Would be a shame, Raphonminder, if you missed out on the Ehver. You begin tonight. I'll send for you.'

And with that, he turned and left her behind, alone in the library with her stomach in knots.

No one could save her now. Not the wind, not the ravens...

Perhaps *this* was how she would truly die.

PART TWO

THE RAPHONMINDER

CHAPTER 13

The day crawled by much to her anxiety's delight.

Every minute that passed, Ezer felt more tension building in her shoulders and chest, like she was a coiled wire about to snap.

She wondered if this was how prisoners felt before their march to the gallows.

If this was how Ervos had felt when he climbed aboard the recruiting wagon and faded into the mist.

She read for a while, discovering the book Kinlear had left on the table was an old Realmist's account of training war bears. There was more on war eagles, from basic ground motions to the most intricate commands in the saddle.

All things she'd never learned, for she hadn't even ridden a godsdamned *horse*.

How was she to get close enough to touch the raphon, let alone get a halter over its beak – then a *saddle*? Did they even have saddles and bridles, strong enough tack, to fit the raphon?

Of course there was nothing on training them.

Probably because such training had never existed, and if anyone had ever tried, they hadn't lived to tell the tale, let alone write a book about it.

'Death,' Ezer said aloud, and blew out a long, slow breath. 'The only end to this is death.'

At some point, Izill came by to check on her, the only truly friendly face she'd met in the Citadel thus far.

'*There* you are,' Izill said when she arrived, pushing an empty kitchen cart. Apparently, she worked most of her time in the Citadel's kitchens. 'Oh, Dhysis bless you. You look faint.'

So Ezer shut the book and told her of her fate, in part because speaking it aloud helped the reality of it settle in a bit more. And also because if she was to go back to her bed, settled right beside Zey's, she wanted at least one person she could turn to.

It felt like walking into a den of hungry wolves.

'I'm going to die,' Ezer said.

Izill simply waved a hand and said, 'How do you feel about tea?'

The Citadel, it seemed, had the best food Ezer had ever tasted, for Izill then scurried away, returning half an hour later with so much food it could have fed an army.

It consisted of a delicious creamed lentil soup, a croissant piled high with roasted meats and melted cheeses, and when they were done with that, Izill introduced Ezer to the sweet cinnamon rolls that she claimed were the King's favorite, so there was a fresh batch every day.

And after that, a mug of steaming mint tea.

They talked and ate, and talked some more, and when Izill left to see to her own duties, Ezer buried her nose in a book again, hoping her mind would settle.

It never did.

'What are you reading?'

Ezer glanced up from her book at the sound of Arawn's voice. The moment she saw him emerging up the stairs, the spell of the library seemed to break.

'A study on death,' she said. 'And how, exactly, the raphon chooses to kill its prey. It stalks them, in case you're wondering. And then it tears them apart, limb by limb, and eats its fill. It leaves the rest of the body behind, but the biggest, most marrow-filled bones, it carries back to its nest. Like a dragon hoarding treasure.'

He looked at her like she'd just sprouted three heads.

'Thanks for the warning,' she grumbled at him.

He paused by the hearth.

'It isn't my job, Minder, to warn you of what's to come,' he said. 'My loyalty is to my family first. Kinlear is my blood. And with his work, he has tamed many war eagles. My own mount he trained so well that she's saved me countless times in battle.'

It was the first time he'd spoken of his war eagle.

She wondered which one it was, if she'd passed it in the rows of stalls.

'Then why do you seem to hate him so much?' Ezer asked.

Arawn's face flushed with red. 'Because family is complicated. And sometimes, the ones closest to us can hurt us the most.' He sighed. 'I warned you about asking questions. Let's go.'

'Manners wouldn't hurt, for a woman standing at death's door,' Ezer said.

So he sighed, held out a hand as if to help her up, and added, 'Please.'

She didn't take it.

And as she followed Arawn out of the library, she couldn't help but stop on the threshold and glance back at the books, feeling like she was seeing them all for the very last time.

The walk upwards to the Aviary was just as harrowing as before and, it turned out, far worse with a full stomach. By the time Ezer clambered to the top, frozen to the bone and nauseated from how high they were, she threw up on Arawn's boots.

'You're weak,' he said, when she stood up and wiped her mouth with the back of her dark sleeve.

'And?' Ezer asked.

He looked more annoyed than disgusted as he kicked fresh snow over the mess.

'And you should equip yourself with something to combat that weakness. A training routine, for starters. So you can move swiftly on your feet when you're minding the raphon.'

'And if it grows hungry and decides to make a meal of me?' Ezer asked.

He balked at her.

'A joke,' she said, 'which I am beginning to learn is wasted on you. Or do you only save your fun side for Absolution?'

He turned away, not looking back as he said, 'I was under the impression that jokes had to be funny.'

The Aviary was already in full swing with the preparations for battle. This time, the others who had ignored her now stared as she and Arawn entered.

She wanted to shy away from their gazes. Instead, she kept her chin high as she followed Arawn, even when she passed by Zey, who sharpened her blade as she locked eyes with Ezer.

'Careful, Wolf Bait,' Zey whispered, as if she knew all Ezer's fears. 'The pup likes to dine on the scrawny ones the most.'

She winked as Ezer turned the corner, following Arawn through a black door with heavy bars on its rounded window, like an entrance to a castle's dungeons.

'The catacombs?' she asked.

They walked down a single rounded tunnel lined with blue torches. The ground slowly sloped downwards, until it was so cold, she could see her breath forming before her in clouds. Frost glistened on the walls, reminding her for a moment of the labyrinth inside her dreams.

'Couldn't afford to heat the place, I guess,' Ezer grumbled.

'Raphons nest in the Sawteeth. They like it cold,' Arawn said. 'Did you read anything of use in the hours you had to prepare for tonight? Anything to set you up for survival, Minder?'

'I ate,' she said. 'My last meal.'

He stopped walking. 'Would it be so bad to consider yourself capable? To consider that you just might survive in there? The fact that you're still here, alive and well, is proof that you must have some gift the others do not.'

She was surprised by how stern his tone was.

'Positivity, Minder, goes a long way towards survival. Every soldier knows that.'

'Says the king of scowls and snarls,' Ezer said to his back. 'And scars upon his face.'

'Indications that I have, indeed, survived. And I intend for you to as well.'

The corridor opened up to reveal the exit. A runed portcullis gate was raised over their heads.

They nodded to the Sacred standing guard – Ezer noted the runed crossbow leaning against the stones – and entered into what looked like some kind of enormous cave lined with iron cages, built right into the rocky walls and also lit by blue magefire torches.

They were empty of any beasts, though all of them were full of objects: barrels and old buckets, bags of grain and extra saddles that looked too worn to be of much use.

It was a glorified storage bay . . . save for the last cage.

The one with Kinlear Laroux standing before it.

It was the largest of them all, big enough to hold several war eagles inside, and she could see a dark shape in the corner of the cage behind him.

The raphon pup.

'Ah!' Kinlear turned as they arrived and limped across the dark stone floors to greet them, the rap of his cane echoing with each step. He coughed once before he stopped in front of her, grinning from ear to ear. 'Our brave Raphonminder is here!'

Bastard, Ezer thought as she glared at him.

It felt wrong, being here. Like she was a prisoner walking to her death. And in this dark wing of the Aviary, there was not a single source of natural light.

She felt trapped.

Like a bird inside a cage.

'Shall we begin?' Kinlear asked.

Ezer wasn't sure why, but she glanced back at Arawn. He nodded curtly.

'Good,' Kinlear said. 'Come along then. And Brother? You're free to go. Work with the younglings until you prove yourself again.'

Arawn stiffened beside her.

If she wasn't terrified, she'd have been more curious.

Her heart rate hastened as Kinlear reached for the cell gate. Her feet felt leaden as she approached.

The hinges screeched as he unlocked it and swung it open.

She expected the raphon to leap from the cage.

To tear out her throat.

But the raphon didn't even move a muscle. She could barely see it, could barely decipher its legs from its head and wings, with how curled up it was in the corner of its cell.

But she'd always known the youngest creatures to be the most unpredictable.

Please help me, she thought to the wind. *I don't want to die like this*.

Kinlear stared at her expectantly as she stood at the threshold. Like he was just waiting for her to dive in. She glanced back to find Arawn had stayed. He was still there, a steady presence in the background, and suddenly she felt no ire for him.

The sight of his calm face was a relief.

'We'll use the Long Day to our advantage, send the raphon across while the darksouls are incapable of coming out beneath the sunlight. Seeing as this is less than two months away, and we're pressed for time . . .' Kinlear shrugged as he looked inside the cage. 'It's best to just jump right in.'

She felt his hand on the small of her back.

And before she could stop him, he shoved her inside the cage.

She was frozen.

Utterly frozen in shock, in rage, for here she was, her back pressed against the cold bars, while the twin princes stood safe and sound on the other side.

'You *bastard*,' she hissed, as she whirled to face Kinlear.

She pushed on the gate, but he'd latched it shut.

She was too weak, too small . . .

And she was trapped.

'Let me out.'

'Best to keep calm,' he said. 'And never turn your back on a predator. Just a little tip.'

At that, she spun.

Her entire body was trembling, head to toe.

For even though the raphon had not moved, even though the dark lump of fur and feathers was still facing the wall opposite her . . . she knew it was fully aware of her presence. And fast enough to attack, the second it wished.

'Let me out,' Ezer begged Kinlear, without turning around. '*Please.*'

'No,' he said to her back. 'Because I believe in the gods. I believe in fate. A little trust in the process, Ezer, and I think you'll believe, too.'

She hated him.

She hated him so much she wanted to take the blade from his hip, the blade that was to end her . . . and thrust it into his chest.

Let *him* be the one who died, again and again and again.

That would turn her nightmare into a dream.

'Please,' she said one more time.

'*Kinlear*,' Arawn tried. She didn't turn to face him, but she could hear the rage in his voice. Careful, controlled. 'This is madness! Let her out. Try another way.'

She was going to die.

And both men were going to stand back and watch it happen.

'Trust me,' Kinlear said.

Arawn practically snarled. 'The way I trusted you with Soraya?'

That name again.

She risked a glance back as he actually moved to try and open the gate, but Kinlear lifted his cane and placed it on Arawn's chest.

'Leave her,' he said, his voice a low, menacing purr, 'or defy a direct order from Father. Defy the gods *again*, Arawn, and see what becomes of you.'

Ezer locked eyes with Arawn, all her desperation hopefully passed to him.

But his face was pained and broken. His gaze fell from hers as he backed down. As he left her there to die.

No.

This was cruel, this was wrong, this was . . .

Behind her, the raphon shifted.

She wouldn't have heard it, were it not for the sound of clinking chains. A sound she knew all too well.

And she saw, then, how the beast's ankles were covered in shackles.

Thick black bands above its paws, almost blending in with its fur.

The chains were tied to anchor points upon the back wall, embedded deep in the stone. They were runed, glowing a gentle gold she hadn't been able to see until the beast moved. And the chains were short.

Certainly, not long enough to allow the raphon to reach her if it lunged.

'I'm not going to get my last hope killed, Arawn,' Kinlear said. 'If you had any trust in me at all, you'd never have doubted for a second.'

Chains or not . . .

She was far from safe.

With her back up against the bars, Ezer watched the beast. It had turned, just enough that it could watch her with one lazy eye.

Its enormous curved raven's beak was large enough to bite her head off in one snip. The white scar on it was awful. Like the blade used to kill the raphon's siblings had just *barely* missed.

Strange how seamlessly its birdlike head turned into a panther's body.

Its giant wings were pressed flat to its back, its body curled up the way a cat would laze in the sun, the tail twitching with each second that passed.

She didn't know whether to speak or move or scream, whether to hold out her hand and try to reach for it. *No*, she thought. There was no way she'd try that.

But then she saw the stain on its scarred beak. Her own handprint, still there, as if she'd left it on the raphon like a brand. For three days, it had breathed in her scent, carried a part of her with it.

She prayed – gods, she hoped – that today would not be her last.

She still had too much of her story to write, too many questions to answer. She would not die unsure of who she was.

What do I do?

She'd never been so desperate for a lifeline. For the whisper of the wind.

She could scarcely stand for how hard her legs shook. Slowly, she sat, lowering her body to the shavings.

But she did not dare take her eyes off the raphon.

What she had told Arawn had been wrong. She had read *plenty* about them in the hours she'd spent leading up to this, and one thing was a common theme in the texts she'd found.

They were bloodthirsty predators. They killed swiftly. They preferred to attack at night, under cover of darkness, when they could blend in with the sky and the black mountains from which they came. And, like ravens, they were far too clever for their own good.

But they could also go for a full week without feasting.

And Kinlear himself had said the pup ate last three days ago. What that meal entailed, she shuddered to think, because they only wanted blood.

But if luck was on her side, it wasn't hungry . . . yet.

She didn't know how long she sat staring at the raphon. It stared back at her, breathing steadily, only moving to stretch its wings or scratch at its head with those enormous black paws.

In many ways, it acted like a cat.

Each paw was easily the size of her face and could certainly shred the skin from her with a single swipe.

So why hadn't it even tried?

At some point, Arawn left.

And returned with a plate of steaming food and a jug of water, which he promptly passed through the bars.

She'd never felt more like a prisoner, like the people who'd slept and died beneath her tower in Rendegard all those years she spent locked away in Ervos's place.

'Thank you,' she said to Arawn. Their gazes met, and something silent passed between them.

He would not leave her again.

He sat down beside Kinlear, and the two muttered quiet conversation with one another.

Curt, short phrases, stiffness in their voices.

How is Father doing?

Fine.

How is Mother?

An angry huff from Kinlear.

Hell if I know, you're the one she fawns over like a newborn babe.

And then it fell silent. Like they couldn't be trusted to speak another word without fighting, the tension between them so palpable.

Whatever history was between them had scarred deep.

Ezer didn't know what time it was, but eventually her legs grew numb, so she stood slowly again, expecting the beast to attack.

It watched her with unblinking, dark eyes, in the way that only birds could. As if she were merely a strange little mouse visiting its cage.

At some point, she began to pace, watching the way the raphon's eyes trailed her. But it never lifted its beak from the shavings, never moved to spring itself upon her.

When she grew hungry enough, she sat back down and ate from her dish of food.

The raphon's nostrils flared at the smell, but when she tossed a piece of meat before it, it did not even flinch.

Not hungry, she told herself.

'What do you feed it?' Ezer asked as she cut into the meat. Arawn had brought her a fancy cut of steak, delicious and fragrant. A scent a predator should have adored.

But still the raphon did not move.

'Grains and meat, like the war eagles,' Kinlear said.

'And does he eat it all?' Ezer asked.

'*She*,' Kinlear said.

So, the raphon was a female.

For some reason, that surprised her.

'And no,' Kinlear said. 'She does not.'

'Does she have a name?'

He chuckled at that. 'Call her Six,' he said.

'A number is not a name,' Ezer said.

He shrugged. 'And a raphon is not a pet.'

'It is, if you're to make me tame her.' Ezer sighed and took another bite of meat, her head leaning against the bars.

'Two minutes,' Kinlear said. 'That's how long the last person to enter her cell survived.' And then he smiled. 'You've been in there for five hours.'

Interesting, indeed.

And the longer she sat, the more she looked at the raphon, and the raphon at her . . . the less she was afraid. She could see the physical signs that the beast was a pup. Her neck was still a bit downy, like she hadn't yet lost those first hatchling feathers. Her cat paws were far too large for her frame.

And Ezer hadn't seen her fly.

For in the Aviary . . . the raphon was crawling in the trees. Stalking her, like a cat.

Like she didn't even know she was meant for the sky.

Ezer was nearly done with her food now. 'Does she just lie here all day?'

'No,' Kinlear said. 'The past many months, she has spent her time wearing holes in the floor with her pacing. We had to replace the bars from how much she'd slammed her body against them, before we finally resorted to the chains to keep her from hurting herself.'

'As would you, when placed in a cage,' Ezer said.

The prince yawned and lifted a dark brow. He looked tired, but his eyes still lit up when he spoke to her. 'Do you always speak to royalty in such a way?'

'*Yes*,' Arawn said beneath his breath.

Ezer lifted her chin. 'Do you always lock women inside cages?'

'Fair enough.' Kinlear chuckled. 'Six didn't stop moving until she met you. She's been this way, a lump of feathers and fur, ever since.'

'Perhaps because she tasted freedom for the first time since her birth. I'd be depressed as well,' Ezer said, and shook her head. She sliced back into her meat with the kitchen blade. 'And now, after her first glimpse of the outside beyond these cursed walls . . . you've tossed her right back into – *damn it*.'

She winced and looked down as a sudden stab of pain went through her finger. She'd sliced her thumb, deep enough to draw an instant swelling of blood. Deep enough to need stitches, for certain.

'I don't suppose you'd let me out of my prison for this?' Ezer asked and lifted her bleeding thumb.

The prince never answered.

Because suddenly the chains clinked from the corner of the cell.

And she turned to find that the raphon had sat up.

'Kinlear.' She could sense the tension in Arawn's voice. 'Let her out.'

'Not yet,' Kinlear answered.

The raphon's wings were flat against its back, and even as it stood, as it crouched and lowered before her across the cell . . . the slits on its beak flared.

In the same way they had before in the Eagle's Nest.

Slowly, *so* slowly, it moved towards her. The chains clinked with the first step.

Ezer's heart roared in her ears.

Gods, she prayed. *If you can hear me, if you're there at all . . . don't let it harm me.*

The raphon took another step. She lifted the small knife in front of her with trembling hands.

She hated how her legs shook again, how she felt like she was going to soil herself in the monster's gaze.

It took another step. Then another.

Perhaps it was the fact that she trusted the memory of their first meeting, and how she couldn't look away from the dried, bloody handprint still marking the raphon's beak. How its scar marked it as a survivor . . . just like her.

But on instinct, she lowered the blade and stuck out her hand instead. Just as she had before. She took a step closer, bridging the gap.

'Come on.'

She held her breath as the raphon leaned, breathing in the scent of her blood.

It dripped on that glimmering black beak and ran down the white scar like a delicate rain.

She swore the beast began to purr.

Like her blood was a balm to a worn and weary soul.

'Hello,' Ezer whispered, her voice a trembling thing as the raphon leaned ever closer.

And pressed her beak to her bleeding hand.

The shift was instantaneous. Ezer's vision went dark at its edges, like a black cloud of oil had overcome her. And there it was again: the image of a single dark feather, floating alone. Lost in an endless sea. She gasped, for she could still feel the raphon's beak, still feel its hot breath on her skin, and when the vision broke, she realized she was crying.

The raphon pulled away.

The chains clinked as she went back to her corner, circled a few times, and slumped back down on the worn shavings.

This time, it closed its eyes, and she was certain the beast fell asleep.

The gate behind her opened. So loud it made Ezer jump, for she was still standing there, frozen, with tear tracks on her cheeks and her bleeding hand dripping into the shavings.

'Well done,' Kinlear said. 'Raphonminder.'

Arawn was staring at her like he had in the woods. Like he was slowly unpeeling the layers of her, breaking down her walls . . . and some part of that made her feel bare.

She wiped her tears with the back of her hand.

She was cold and tired and feeling like her insides had twisted up in a knot . . .

But beyond that.

She felt, for the first time in ages . . . *alive*.

She settled her gaze on Kinlear.

'If you *ever* lock me in a cage again,' she said, 'I don't care that you're a prince. I will skin you alive. And I will feed your bleeding corpse to my raphon.'

She was surprised at how much she meant it.

And even more surprised at how his only response was to smile.

CHAPTER 14

Arawn found her in the warmth of the Aviary, minutes later, seated on a bench just beside the doors.

'Minder.'

She looked up to find the prince walking towards her, ever the picture of Sacred glory . . . beyond the redness in his face that revealed he might have just left a screaming match with his twin brother.

Thank the gods Kinlear was nowhere in sight.

'What do you want?' Ezer asked.

The bravery she'd felt moments ago was gone. In its place, fresh waves of pain from her wounds. Her hand oozed blood, and her nose . . . the salve had certainly worn off.

'Izill is waiting for you in the courtyard,' Arawn said, and frowned down at her like he expected her to leap to her feet.

'I'm having a *moment*,' she said. 'Allow me the courtesy of a second to breathe before I fall prey to yet another order today.'

A sigh as he removed his cloak and sat down beside her.

'I only meant—'

She heard the sound of something tearing and looked over to find he'd ripped part of his beautiful white cloak into a strip. He held it out to her. 'Here,' he said a bit gruffly. When she didn't take it, he softened his tone. 'So you don't bleed out before you make it to the infirmary.'

'Oh,' Ezer said. 'Thanks.'

She tried to wrap the cloth around her wound, but her damned hands wouldn't stop shaking.

'Let me,' Arawn said. The bench shifted from his sheer size as he turned to face her, their knees almost touching.

And with careful fingers, he wound the fabric around the cut on her hand. Red bloomed across the velvet as he continued to layer it. He had scars on his skin, his fingertips and the backs of his hands . . . the marks of a warrior who had killed and nearly been killed.

Strange, that he could be so gentle.

'You did well in there,' he said.

She hissed as he tied the cloth tight.

'For a Ravenminder?' she said darkly.

'No,' Arawn said. He glanced up to meet her gaze, forgetting to remove his hands from hers.

His were warm.

Calloused, and strong.

'You did well for *anyone*,' he said, and to her surprise he smiled before he realized he was still touching her, and quickly pulled away. 'Seasoned warriors have run from Six screaming, but *you* . . .' He looked at her like he was trying to put all the pieces together. 'You are . . . an anomaly.'

She quirked a brow.

'Well, Firemage. Coming from you . . . I suppose that's as good a compliment as any.' She stood, nodded her thanks, and turned to open the enormous wooden doors to the outside.

'Tomorrow,' he blurted.

She spun back around. 'Tomorrow . . . what?'

He was still sitting there on the bench, his hands held before him like he wasn't certain what to do with them after touching her.

'Perhaps we could speak more then. About your magic.'

Snow danced around her, the cold already piercing her back as she stood in the doorway. 'I don't have any magic,' Ezer said, and pulled her dark hood over her head, bathing herself in shadow. 'And I haven't the time to think about tomorrow when I'm still in the middle of trying to survive *today*.'

Without another word, she headed out into the cold.

After a long, harrowing walk down the upper cliff steps, Ezer finally found herself back in the Citadel's embrace.

Izill waited in the courtyard, wearing a path in the snow.

'Gods above, Ezer!' She gasped when she saw the wrap on Ezer's wound. 'Tell me *everything*.'

She grabbed Ezer by her good hand. And where normally Ezer would have flinched, unused to being touched by anyone, she found herself strangely disarmed by Izill's warmth.

The servant began hauling her towards the Healer's quarters, asking questions the whole way.

It was towards the lowest floors of the fortress: a calm, quiet space with a courtyard entrance, easily accessible to any Sacred wounded in battle.

Ezer had never spent much time in hospital rooms, but she'd certainly helped Ervos stumble his way to a local healer a time or two.

She remembered how sterile it smelled. How it was a place meant for healing, and yet so many entered and never came back out.

I wish you could see me now, Uncle, she thought. *I wish I could share all of this with you.*

The infirmary was strangely warm and comforting, with magefire torches dotting the walls, large stained-glass windows overlooking the distant Thornwell Forest, and a Sacred Ehvermage who was as lovely in appearance as she was kind.

She looked old enough to be Ezer's grandmother, but her smile was still youthful, full of life, with enough wrinkles at the corners of her eyes to prove she was well-versed in smiling.

'Alaris,' Izill greeted the woman with a kiss upon the cheek. 'The princes' new guest, Ezer. Would you see to it that she's healed?'

'Ah. And how is the Black Wing Battalion faring these days?' The healer winked. 'Don't look so surprised. Someone had to inscribe that stasis rune upon your wrist. Now, come on.' She *tsked*. 'Izill, gone with you already. I won't have you clucking about like a mother hen. I'll take good care of her. Grab these rags here and see to it that they're cleaned.'

Alaris waved her away with a towel she plucked from a nearby table – one complete with all classic healer's supplies. She probably saved her magic for the worst wounds. Sacred had to be cautious about wielding too much, lest they steal more years from their own life. And they needed all the Ehvermage healers they could get in this war.

Izill paused at the door. 'Zey goes to bed around eleven. If I were you . . . I'd find a reason to stay out late.' She left before Alaris could shoo her off again.

It fell silent and calm.

'Now, let's see, child,' Alaris said. She sat down on a stool and motioned for Ezer to seat herself on the edge of an open bed. She was surprised by the smell that hit her the moment she touched the sheets. It was earthy, like a warm summer's day in the south, tinged with salt and a fresh bit of parchment.

'Strange,' Ezer mused. 'It smells just like home.'

Alaris nodded. 'The sheets are stitched with runes to make them smell soothing. A way to disarm the senses, for no one enters a Healer's tent at ease. Smells like lavender and lemon drops to me.'

'Clever trick,' Ezer said.

'Runes can do a great deal,' Alaris said. 'I imagine they must be quite foreign for someone not raised in the Citadel.'

Ezer glanced up. 'Is it that obvious?'

The woman smiled. 'I know an Unconsecrated when I see one, dear. Like you've one foot in the world, and one foot here with us and the gods. Your mother and father. Who were they?'

Ezer shrugged. 'They hailed from Torvir. I'm afraid I never

even learned their names. I was just a babe when the shadow wolves attacked.'

The woman considered. 'Poor thing. There are plenty of others like you, orphaned by the Acolyte.' For a moment, her eyes lost their light. Like she was remembering all the swords in the snow outside her door. 'Well, I suppose like some of the others, and mind you, Unconsecrated are a rare few these days, you've someone far back in your lineage that broke the vows of the Sacred. Any idea who your grandmother or grandfather were, dear?'

Ezer shook her head. 'No. I've only ever known my uncle, Ervos. He was Ravenminder here, and . . . well, he wasn't even my blood.' She looked down at her bleeding hand as Alaris removed the wrap. The wound *was* deep, enough to have hit bone. 'He's gone now.'

Something shifted in the Healer's eyes. 'Like so many others, thanks to that spineless demon across the Expanse. And don't worry about the wounds you're certain to gain at your new post. As much as you like, you can come to me. Working with Prince Kinlear . . .' She chuckled beneath her breath. 'He's quite the reputation in these walls. A wayward wind, I always say, and Prince Arawn is the wall he crashes against.' She shook her head. 'Now, let's see about this hand . . . too deep for needle and thread, if you're to be back at your post tomorrow. Only magic will do.'

The woman began to whisper, so softly Ezer almost couldn't hear it.

Invocating sounded like poetry, like words that could shift seamlessly into song.

In a few seconds, the woman's hands began to glow with a delicate white light. She pressed them to Ezer's wound. Her skin was cool to the touch, and soon came a feeling a bit like bubbles popping gently over Ezer's skin. She moved to Ezer's nose next, shaking her head like a disapproving mother as she looked at how swollen it had become.

Another invocation, another strange feeling upon her skin, and the pain was gone.

For good this time.

'There,' Alaris said. 'All done and fixed up, child.'

Ezer lifted her hand and grinned.

Without magic, the gash would have taken weeks to truly heal, and then it would have scarred, but here in the Citadel . . .

She flexed her hand, marveling at how perfectly stitched together her skin was. And so fast, it had taken only a breath.

She was brand new once more.

'Thank you,' Ezer said. 'I know what it takes to invocate. To use your magic.'

It was a cherished gift, the realization that a Sacred would use her precious energy, give of herself to channel the gods' power . . . for *her*. A stranger.

Alaris waved a hand. 'Healing requires far less magic than wielding in battle. I've plenty of years left. It's why you're not likely to see a Sacred quite as elegantly aged as an Ehvermage Healer.' She ran a hand across her graying braid. '*Nomages* don't often appreciate the beauty of aging. The joy that it gives to know you're still living, while others haven't been quite so blessed. I'll take the wrinkles any day.'

Her smile fell away as she studied the trio of dark and jagged lines across Ezer's face.

'I can't do anything about the scars, I'm afraid. The Acolyte's magic is utterly unfazed by the power of the Five,' Alaris said. 'It's why this Realmbreak is so important. Why we all must be in prayer for the gods to grant us a blessing.'

'Could it end the war?' Ezer asked.

Alaris pursed her lips. 'That, I do not know,' she admitted. 'But it could give us a fighting chance.'

Ezer nodded, and noticed Alaris' eyes were still on her scars. 'I'm not certain I'd know what to do with my own reflection, anyhow, without the scars. I guess it's fitting for a

Raphonminder. I'm more suited for a dirty cloak than Sacred whites.'

'Ah,' the woman said, smiling. 'Well, for what it's worth . . . I think the most beautiful attribute in a woman is strength.' She placed a warm hand over Ezer's. 'Seems you've more than enough of that.'

When she slipped out into the halls now, they were nearly empty. It was just the crackling torches and the sound of the wind howling against the stained-glass windowpanes. They were lovely, marked with swirling gold runes, depictions of the gods' many forms, and some with war eagles poised for flight.

She took her time exploring, until she found herself back on the path towards the library. Like her mind simply knew it longed to be among books.

She passed a few servants, who inclined their heads and kept pace. In darkness, the Knights were out fighting, and the Scribes were busy sleeping off the hard work of preparing for war during the day. The Eagleminders were probably busy inside the Aviary – still off limits to her, not because of Kinlear, but because she knew if she entered, she'd run into Zey.

She wondered, come morning, how many Knights would return from the Expanse.

And for a surprising moment . . . she was grateful Arawn would not be among the fighters.

He would be with the younglings, if what Kinlear said was true. It seemed a demotion for a crown prince. A punishment.

But for what?

She tucked the thought away as she reached the library.

It was calm inside, save for the crackling hearths and every so often, that telltale rumble of the war beyond the Citadel's stones and windows.

She began where she started, with the stacks of books she'd

left. There was a cozy spot on the third floor, where a chair sat before the fire, so large it could have held two people with ease.

Ezer sighed as she sprawled out across the cushions, the tension leaving her shoulders. There was no company as lovely as a comfortable chair and a good book. Though, she supposed, she could do with more entertaining literature, for the book in her lap was an old, dusty tome, and had nothing to do with ravens or raphons. She'd decided to learn about the panthers instead: the enormous ones that ran wild in the Dornan Hills out west.

Birds, Ezer knew plenty about. Cats? Now that was a different story entirely. And perhaps that was what she'd need to brush up on instead, if she was to truly tame the beast waiting for her. It was half cat, after all.

She spent some time flipping through the pages, past sketches revealing the way a panther hunted, how they truly had the behavior of large house cats, sometimes. But other times – they were cold-blooded killers, eager to stalk and hunt and shred their prey with their sharp claws and canines.

She learned that sunlight was a cat's best friend.

She doubted Six had ever seen much of it, had ever truly felt it warm her fur or her wings. She took note of that for later, and shut the book, yawning.

By now, Zey had to be asleep.

She stood, slowly stretching her arms, and had just begun her way down to the first floor, when she heard the library doors swing open.

Several figures entered.

The first two wore white robes, with golden bands on their arms.

The War Table.

The highest-ranking Sacred Masters, in charge of each pillar of magic inside the Citadel.

And behind them . . .

Alaris, the Healer. She spoke in hushed whispers to a broad figure in long white robes who seemed intent to leave her behind.

He had a crown upon his dark curls.

Ezer's eyes widened.

The King.

She hadn't seen him in years, not since she was a child and he rode through town in the Allgodsday procession. He was a large man, a warrior built for battle instead of the luxury of a throne. She knew he reigned from here, in the Citadel, while Queen Dhyana stayed in Touvre to watch over the southern half of the kingdom.

For some reason, Ezer feared him.

She'd heard he was not a kind ruler. Rather, a bold one, furious as he set his sights on destroying the Acolyte.

She quickly ducked behind one of the shelves and watched from the shadows as the group walked by.

'It's the third time this season,' Alaris said softly. 'How many times can one pay penance?'

Penance.

A word Izill had mentioned . . . She backed further into the shadows, with her scarred eye still seeing clear as day.

'As many times as it takes,' said the King. His voice was deeply accented, eerily similar to Arawn's. But he had Kinlear's dark curls, peppered through with bits of gray. He'd paused to lean against one of the shelves and catch his breath. Strange, for a warrior so famed to struggle walking across the flat, even ground as if he were climbing up a hill.

Alaris reached out a hand. 'Do you need—'

'*No*,' the King growled. He stood back up to his full height, though she could see it pained him. 'Save your strength. It is needed for the mark.'

'But . . . she's one of our best,' Alaris pleaded. 'And sometimes, I fear she might—'

The King spun round, his gaze fierce.

His *face*.

It was gaunt. Dark shadows pooled beneath his eyes, as if he hadn't slept in days. He did not look like a man in his forties, fresh-faced and dark-haired like he had been in the processions only a decade ago.

But it looked like *many* decades had passed for him, given how gray his curls were, how pale his skin.

The rumors were true.

Channeling the gods' power was truly taking its toll.

'We do as the gods say,' the King growled. 'Or we risk facing their wrath.'

'Of course,' Alaris said, taking a step back. 'Forgive me.'

'Ask the gods for forgiveness,' the King said. 'Not me.'

Their voices faded as they continued deeper into the library.

Ezer risked a glance out of the shadows. She wanted to follow them – her curiosity would be what killed her someday, Ervos had always warned – but she also wasn't a fool. She wouldn't spark the rage of the King, and risk getting caught.

Penance.

The word made her insides turn.

A yawn left her lips, unwelcome and unavoidable.

It had to be past eleven by now.

She'd wasted enough time that the coast was clear, at least . . . so she crept back out into the main corridor. She'd made it halfway across the common area, past the crackling hearth, when she heard another door creak open.

And then footsteps were heading her way.

Ezer glanced left and right, but there was nowhere to go this far out in the open in the center of the library.

She turned on instinct, glancing over her shoulder.

And froze.

Zey.

'By the gods,' Ezer whispered to no one. She braced herself for a slew of hurtful comments as she locked eyes with the Eagleminder.

'Here to spy, Wolf Bait?' asked Zey, as she came into the firelight.

Her eyes were red, like she'd been crying. It took her harsh edges away. Made her look, for a moment, a bit more human.

'You're . . . what is that?' Ezer said and pointed at Zey's hand.

It was a fresh rune of some sort, but furious red, almost charred at its edges. More like a burn than carved with magic. It was in the shape of a small five-pointed star, the sigil of each Pillar at its points. A small flame, a water droplet, a curl of wind, a mountain for the realm, and a tailed star for the Ehver.

Zey pressed her hand to her side, failing to hide her wince. 'It's none of your concern. Now get out of my way. I'm ten minutes past my bedtime, and I don't like to break my schedule. I need my beauty sleep if I'm to keep looking this good.'

She tried to shoulder past, but Ezer reached out a hand. 'Did . . . did they do that to you? The War Table?'

'Get your hand off me unless you wish to lose it,' Zey growled. 'I did this to myself, brought it upon myself when I failed in the demonstration earlier this week.'

'But . . .' Ezer stared at the wound.

That was *her* fault. In a way.

Was this what Alaris and the others were here for?

Penance.

She couldn't fathom the healer having done this to anyone. The King, perhaps . . .

But they wouldn't lay a hand on their own Sacred.

Would they?

Zey stared at her, considering. And then she surprised Ezer when she said, 'You're new here, Wolf Bait. So let me give you a piece of advice. If they ask you to take their vows, to become reinstated as one of us . . .' She glanced over Ezer's shoulder, into the shadows. '*Don't.*'

Then she turned and left before Ezer could reply.

Ezer was about to follow her, when the doors opened again.

And Kinlear Laroux strolled in.

Don't notice me, Ezer thought as she ducked her head and tried to avoid his gaze.

'Raphonminder!'

Damn the gods.

She paused, sighing deeply before she turned to face him. She just wanted to go to sleep, to bury herself beneath her blankets. She'd had more than her fair share of speaking to *people* today.

'Your Highness.' She forced a smile. 'Shouldn't you be Minding an eagle, or flying in battle, or . . .'

Or locking people in cages with bloodthirsty raphons, she thought.

'If you must know, I was banned from battle years ago, thanks to my injury,' Kinlear said. His hand tensed over his cane, and she realized, in horror, that she might have just offended him. If he was injured . . . he wouldn't be able to fly in the war, like all the princes before him. And after him.

Penance.

The memory of Zey's hand flashed before her eyes.

She should be more careful when speaking to the son of King Draybor Laroux. Somehow, Kinlear felt different from Arawn in that way. Like a wayward wind instead of a steady gale.

'I'm sorry,' she said carefully. 'I didn't mean to offend you.'

'Offending me, Raphonminder, is not an easy thing to do.' He waved a hand. 'And partaking in the battle is not a thing to desire, despite how glamorous many of the Knights may make it seem. *Ending* it, however . . . that is my dream. My heart's desire. And we've only until Realmbreak to do it.'

She nodded. 'Because of the Long Day?'

'There's more to it than that.' He limped closer to her, looking stiffer tonight than he had in the daytime. Some wounds worked that way. 'Can you keep a secret, Raphonminder?'

She backed a step away. 'I don't suppose there's anyone here I would tell one to.'

Izill, perhaps.

But she'd always found that, like Ravenminders, servants seemed to know more than they let on. They were the eyes and the ears, the hidden soul of a place. It was just as likely Izill already knew the Citadel's secrets.

'My father will ask the gods for a blessing, as happens only once every century.'

Ezer nodded. Arawn had confirmed that earlier.

'And what will that blessing be?' Ezer dared ask.

'Think of it as . . . a hypothetical shield, instead of a sword,' Kinlear said. 'Something to bring about peace, instead of heighten the brutality of war.'

It wasn't a true answer, but it was more than Arawn or Alaris had given. Bigger wards, perhaps? Extended sunlight hours, to keep the darksouls hidden away?

'Walk with me,' Kinlear said.

She didn't think she had any choice but to follow. One did not say *no* to a prince. But she certainly kept her distance as he led her towards the stairwell and began the ascent.

It was slow going as they moved up, floor after floor, until they were both breathless.

They were higher than she'd dared go before, so close to the top floors she swore she felt the warmth of the wardlight as it shone down over them from the other side of the domed ceiling.

'I've spent my life inside this Citadel,' Kinlear said, as he paused halfway up another flight. He pointed at the windows covered in frost, where she could just barely hear the howling winter wind trying to batter its way through. 'This was always one of my favorite spots to pray to the Five. Do you see why?'

She dared risk a glance out the windows, the harrowing drop on the other side of the glass, and—

She gasped.

'The Sacred Circle.'

It was small from here, enough that she could have covered it up with her hand.

But she knew up close, the Sacred Circle was enormous.

It stood all the way past the *nomage* barracks, up a cliff and beyond another set of black obelisk gates that protruded from the forest – another exit from the golden wards.

But there, even taller than the gates, stood a ring of twelve enormous white standing stones. She wouldn't have seen them, had it not been dark outside.

Even from this far away, she could see the golden runes glowing on every standing stone.

The stones were said to have the earliest recorded history of the realm upon them. They were a scholar's dream, the oldest artifact Lordach had.

'There are twelve,' Kinlear said as he came up beside her. She tensed . . . but did not hear a warning upon the wind. 'Each one represents an individual realm.'

She nodded. 'I'm well aware.'

Every child was told the story of the Sacred Circle.

He shrugged. 'They are white as the snow, representing, of course, that the gods created them with purest intent. But did you know . . . there used to be thirteen?'

At that, Ezer glanced to him.

'But that can't be.'

The prince sighed, as if he were bored. 'Of course, anyone raised beyond the Citadel wouldn't know that ancient truth. But, alas, it remains. Come along.'

He turned and continued further up the stairs until they came to another floor of the library. He walked through it with ease, navigating the stuffed shelves until he came to a stop before one. 'Here we are.' There he knelt, leaning his cane against the spines. A flourish of his gloved hands, and he removed a book with yellowing pages.

A History of Arivahda: Lordach, Volume 1.

'This book is as old as these walls,' Kinlear said. 'I trust its pages more than I trust any half-witted knowledge, passed from one town to another until it reached the south.'

An insult, but she didn't mind.

She was used to them. There were *far* worse things said to her over the years.

He flipped through the pages, nodding to himself until he came to an image of the Sacred Circle. 'See for yourself.'

There it was, just like she'd seen beyond the windows, a perfect sketch of standing stones in a circle . . .

Ezer's eyes widened.

There were indeed *thirteen*.

'But . . . that can't be.'

'Why can't it?' Kinlear asked. 'We live in a world of magic, Raphonminder, and oftentimes, strange things happen that we cannot explain.'

She glanced past the book to find him smiling like he knew a secret, leaning against a shelf with his dark curls hanging in his eyes. With his soft lips and hard jaw, his fine clothing and the sea of books all around him . . .

He could have sprouted right from the romance novels she so dearly loved.

A younger Ezer would have swooned.

But a flash of her dreams came to her.

His lips against hers, his blade buried in her chest.

She found herself taking a small, casual step away.

'There were once thirteen stones,' Kinlear explained. 'Until one of them turned black, about a century ago. I suppose right around the last Realmbreak. That stone crumbled to ashes and dust and is now all but forgotten in our history.'

'What happened to it?' Ezer asked.

Because despite her healthy fear of him, she was too damned curious.

Because she loved a good mystery, and here one was, unraveling before her.

'Something terrible, I assume,' Kinlear said with a shrug. 'No one knows, though the War Table has certainly speculated. When the stone crumbled, so did the runes marking its story. Its history. Each one represents a realm, you see. Ours is but one in a string of others. And . . . well, it's quite unfortunate that it was the stone directly next to *ours*, that crumbled and fell away.'

Their realm, Arivahda.

And their kingdom, Lordach, was the largest one in it.

'When my grandfather was a boy, Arivahda's stone got its first fracture. A hairline – so small it wouldn't have been noticed, were it not the deepest tendril of black. If you've ever seen the stones up close, you know just how pure a white they are. Brighter, even, than the snow.'

She felt her eyes widen.

He smiled, like he was enjoying spilling the secret, bit by bit.

'The fracture grew after that, and each year the war goes unending, it grows wider still. And the stone darkens, bit by bit. It's estimated that by the time Realmbreak arrives . . . the stone will crack in half.'

'And . . . when that happens?' Ezer breathed.

He'd stepped closer to her.

She could smell the strange sweetness on him, the scent that came from his vial.

He shrugged. 'No one knows. But I can assure you . . . it won't be good. It's why we need the godsblessing. Why we need *something*, anything the Five can give, to help us survive. Our numbers are far too slim as it is.'

Incredible, how the news of the stones hadn't reached the south. How people had been so distracted by the war, the deaths and the disappearances and the shadow wolves, that they hadn't passed stories of the Sacred Circle along.

Probably because there was no one left alive here in the north beyond the soldiers.

And none of them had made it home to tell the tale.

'The Acolyte,' Ezer said, her heart racing. 'It's him, isn't it?'

'We believe so,' Kinlear said. He coughed and motioned for her to follow him out of the shelves. Their footsteps and the clacking of his cane echoed through the space as they emerged back onto the stairwell and descended together.

'It's why he must be stopped *before* Realmbreak. It was the day the last stone fell, if our calculations are correct.'

'What makes you think it's that easy to stop him?' Ezer asked. 'If he's done it before. If it's his dark magic that made the neighboring realm fall . . . and *they* didn't stop him . . .'

'We aren't without hope.' Kinlear cleared his throat, fighting away another cough. 'I believe the stones are there from the gods as a gift. A warning bell that's been ringing for years now, trying to ensure we do not make the mistakes of the realms beside us. And while we don't know for certain what went on, for it's impossible for one realm to speak to another . . . we have *some* leads. Raphons aren't the only thing we capture.'

She couldn't hide the shock on her face.

'The darksouls are tricky to seize alive, but we've managed a few. It's messy to question them, difficult to fully trust, but thanks to our Ehvermages, we've managed . . .' His eyes skirted away and his jaw worked back and forth for a minute. It struck her how identical his facial features were to Arawn in that moment. But the feeling she had around Kinlear was not nearly the same. 'They speak of one similar truth. A black door in the mountains, that his beasts enter and leave through. A hidden domain, where he rules from a throne of darkness. He goes there each night, before darkness falls. It's the only time he's guaranteed to show . . . just waiting for a runed blade to sink beneath his cursed skin.'

It was suddenly too cold, too quiet in the rows of shelves.

'What happens if I fail?' she whispered. 'If I can't get Six gentled for an assassin to make it across?'

And beyond that, what happened if the assassin failed?

The Long Day was the best chance they'd have – seventy-two hours without a drop of darkness in the sky. But even then, it might not be enough time to make it there, find this mysterious black door, and manage to navigate inside to kill the Acolyte before darkness fell again . . . and his army re-emerged.

Kinlear's eyes met hers. 'I can't say for certain. But I suggest you try your hardest to tame the beast, if you don't wish to find out.'

He fell into another coughing fit, and with that, he dismissed her, taking another sip from the vial at his throat.

She descended the steps quickly, eager for silence and space.

She'd nearly made it down to the next flight when Kinlear called her name.

'Ezer.'

She paused, her skin burning with the need to *run* as she looked back up at him. From here, he was backlit by the wardlight, his face cast in shadows. Just as he always was in her dreams. 'Yes?'

'What was Zey speaking to you about?'

Something in Ezer's gut twisted.

'*Lie*,' said the wind. It came from nowhere, whispering past her ears.

'The war eagles,' Ezer said, her fingers curling around the golden railing. 'I was simply picking her brain about them. I figured . . . maybe it would help me with Six.'

He seemed to study her face, searching for the lie.

Her eyes went to the dagger on his hip. 'Is that all?'

He nodded. 'I expect you in the Aviary at dawn. You're dismissed.'

She turned, and exited the library as fast as she could, and by the time she made it to her dorm, she was shivering. Zey was already snoring, cradling her wounded hand.

Ezer stared at her for a moment, remembering her warning.
If they ask you to take their vows . . .
Don't.
She fell asleep clutching her mother's ring, hoping the wind would protect her, watch over her, until morning.

CHAPTER 15

The moment she fell asleep, the strange, new labyrinth was waiting.

'Not again,' Ezer said, her breath forming before her in a thick cloud.

She'd never dreamt of this space before arriving in the north.

She found herself standing in the same entry spot, the sword in one hand, a torch in the other, the circular mouths of tunnels, all around.

The shadowed figure was here somewhere in the winding darkness.

The wind whistled. Here it was like it lived and thrived, and she swore it whispered her name.

'Ezer.'

This time, it came from the tunnel to her left.

'If you're to say my name so constantly,' Ezer whispered, 'at least give me an indication as to why. And what you're leading me towards.'

It was icy cold as it whistled past her tangled hair again, pushing her towards the tunnel to the left. A beckoning, if there ever was one.

She dipped her torch into the oil-lined ridge on the wall, expecting a living shadow, a monster, to be waiting for her at the farthest end.

But there were only doors.

Countless doors, just like the last tunnel. They each held the same ancient plaques beside them. The same strange symbols.

She paused to touch one, reaching out her hand.

But the wind suddenly whistled again, kicking up the folds of her cloak as if it were insistent that she keep on walking.

'Fine,' Ezer said.

She continued past frozen cobwebs that hung from the rafters. She used the sword to carve them aside. They tinkled as they fell to the icy tunnel floor, a sad little melody.

This place – her dreams – felt alive.

Every detail, important.

She followed the wind until the tunnel ended.

She'd come face to face with an enormous black door.

It was old, an ancient thing made of iron, but it had no markings. No plaque.

Ezer set her torch on the empty sconce beside it and tried the handle.

She didn't expect it to be unlocked. But when she put her weight on it . . .

It clicked open.

There stood a different world entirely on the other side.

A house.

No, a tiny little cottage, and she stood right at its threshold.

Moonlight glimmered through a small cracked window across from her, sending a spear of silver light inside. Dust motes danced through the air as she took in every detail.

The walls were stone, the wood floors were worn and covered in a thick layer of grime. Whoever had lived here hadn't been inside in quite some time.

There was a small bed at one end of the room, the quilt handstitched. Northern ice lilies for the pattern, she noted, like some of the ones she'd seen inside the Eagle's Nest.

Beside the bed was a small table made of knotted wood, a candlestand with the candle long since melted away. On the other side was a small kitchen, a basin and a few cracked dishes, shaped from clay.

She tried to peer out of the window, but it was too filthy, and despite using her sleeve to try and clean it . . . the glass remained opaque, only allowing the moonlight to slip through.

She crossed to the hearth and breathed in the scent of woodsmoke that still lingered.

'What is this place?' Ezer asked softly.

The wind slid past her, tugging at the ends of her cloak until she came to a trunk at the foot of the bed. It was not unlike the one she had in her dormitory. An old wooden one of lovely make, with golden detailing across its edges.

The latch was broken, hanging by one rusted screw.

She glanced back over her shoulder, feeling as if she were being watched. She'd left the cottage door ajar, afraid she'd somehow wind up locked inside.

But there was just the tunnel, still glowing a cool blue, no monster waiting to trap her.

So Ezer knelt and opened the chest. She found a small bundle of cloth inside.

The fabric was stained, thick beneath her fingertips as she slowly unwrapped it.

Inside was a large black key.

A skeleton key, the brass detailing worn from time. It sat there, nestled in the bottom of the trunk like a treasure indeed. A tarnished chain hung around its top, the clasp open as if it were begging to be put on.

'And what do you open?' Ezer whispered to the key.

She thought of the darkness beyond this strange, forgotten room.

The doors she could never open, because they needed a key.

With trembling hands, she lifted the chain, holding the clasp as if to secure it around her neck.

But just before she did . . .

She thought she heard something shift in the hallway behind her.
The wind suddenly whistled past her ears, angry and cold.
And the door behind her slammed shut.

She woke to the sound of her own gasp, drenched in sweat.

'Gods,' Ezer hissed and sat up inside her bed in the Tower of Dhysis.

Her dreams were getting stranger, wilder, since arriving here.

Strange that Zey wasn't sound asleep beside her. The Eagleminder was usually the first thing she saw when she sat up.

But her bed was empty.

'Breakfast?'

Izill had arrived, her voice barely a whisper.

Ezer yawned as she dressed in a fresh set of black clothing she found carefully folded inside her trunk.

'If we're to do this every day,' Izill said with a smile as she joined her by the hearth, 'we might as well get to know one another. I'll go first.'

Izill was nineteen: a year younger than Ezer – a fast talker, but gentle as a turtle dove. And despite her lack of magic, she knew anything and everything there was to know about the Citadel.

'I spend most of my days in the library when I'm not in the kitchens,' Izill said. 'Or on duty for Head Servant, tending to odds and ends. But it's not so bad. I've a goal to make it to every floor of the library – to read every tome – before I'm called to the Ehver above.'

'But that's impossible,' Ezer said. 'There's far too many.'

Izill shrugged. 'Not if I'm only reading the spines.'

Ezer laughed at that. Then she leaned closer and asked, 'The laws the Sacred are to keep. How many are there?'

Izill's smile fell. 'A thousand. We make a vow when we come of age and show our magic – or lack thereof, in my case – that we will keep the laws until our death.'

'What happens if you don't?' Ezer asked.

Izill frowned. 'Penance.'

'You mean the brands,' Ezer said.

Izill nodded. 'I suppose that's one way to put it. They say the brands are kindest. A moment of pain to absolve a lifetime of punishment. Centuries ago, it was far more barbaric. The removal of fingers or toes, or tongues, even . . . depending on the severity of the law broken.'

'Zey had one last night,' Ezer said. 'A brand.'

Izill pursed her lips. 'She is one of the strong-willed ones. A good trait in a Sacred. But sometimes . . . well, that trait must be softened. Honed, at the very least.' Izill shrugged. 'Zey wants to be the best. Sometimes her methods lead to breaking a few laws here and there. The War Table is quick to catch her falling short. They cannot have the younger ones looking up to a Sacred who follows her own ways, instead of the Five. Too many mistakes . . . and one might think she's lost her allegiance.'

Ezer took a sip of steaming coffee. 'And what if *penance* isn't enough to keep a Sacred in line?'

Izill's eyes softened. 'That's why we have Absolution. Although I should warn you . . . steer *clear* of Zey when the festivities begin. You think she's bad now? Imagine her when she's two goblets of winterwine deep.'

Not a comforting thought. And yet a small tremor of excitement went through her. She supposed the next Absolution was coming, sooner or later. Bit by bit, she was getting a chance to see *beyond* the veil of the Sacred. To uncover the mysteries so many in Lordach would never know the answers to.

'But what about beyond all that?' Ezer asked. 'What if a Sacred refuses to obey?'

Izill frowned. 'Well . . . there's a tale they tell us all when we are younglings, to help us understand the value of keeping the gods' laws. The story of Wrenwyn the Wrong.'

Ezer's ears perked up and she paused, mid-bite of her brown-sugared oatmeal. Izill had forced her to pile on three heaping spoonfuls, clucking over her weight like a mother hen. 'I've heard of Wrenwyn. It's a favorite of mine.'

Izill raised her brows. 'Where?'

Ezer nodded and said with a full mouth, 'My uncle Ervos told it to me when I was a child.'

Izill frowned, either at the way she ate, or her knowledge of Wrenwyn.

Ervos had told her the tale as a birthday present, when they hadn't the funds to buy something tangible. But Ezer knew better than most children just how valuable stories could be.

How they lasted longer than flowers or sweets or lovely little trinkets.

How they so often took on a life of their own.

'Strange,' Izill said. 'It's a tale they tell us all as younglings. One as old as the walls themselves. But . . . well, I suppose some parts of an old Sacred story may have made it into the Outside, after all these years.'

Ezer wiped her mouth with her sleeve.

'Here.' Izill pursed her lips and passed her a napkin. 'Wrenwyn's story is a strange and dark tale, my friend.'

Ervos had said the same thing. It was more of a story to scare young children into remembering to say their prayers and stay in the Five's favor.

But the story hadn't scared her at all.

It had fascinated her.

Ezer nodded and said over a mouthful of scrambled eggs, 'A terrible fate she met in the end.'

Izill's eyes lit up. 'You *do* know it. Did you know her final resting place was somewhere near the Sawteeth?'

At that, Ezer laughed. 'It's only a story, Izill. Wrenwyn wasn't *real*.'

Izill smiled. 'Perhaps to an Unconsecrated, raised beyond

these walls. Here, we believe it's ancient truth. At least, the parts that matter.'

'I guess we'll never know,' Ezer said. She considered the breakfast spread before them and decided on a piece of buttered toast next. 'Tell me your version?'

'Of course,' Izill said. She leaned forward, eyes wide, like she'd been waiting for years to find a new set of ears to tell this specific tale.

And as Ezer listened to her new friend speak, suddenly she was transported back to her Ravenminder's tower, the stones around her eaten away by salt from the sea, a raven perched upon her narrow shoulder.

And an uncle that was still alive, telling her this tale for the very first time.

'*Wrenwyn was one of the first Sacred younglings. She was a beautiful princess. Like you, Little Bird.*'

'*I'm not beautiful,*' Ezer had protested, reaching up to touch her thick and angry scars. '*And I'm certainly not a princess.*'

'*And who are you,*' Ervos asked with a patient smile, '*to decide what is beautiful – what is noble – to me?*' He'd picked up a crown of dried white flowers, one he'd made himself to celebrate her turning nine, and placed it upon her dark curls. '*The story of Wrenwyn is as old as the mountains are tall. Someday, it may teach you something that I cannot.*'

Ezer closed her eyes and listened to Izill tell the rest of the story.

'Wrenwyn was the youngest of three,' Izill began. 'Her magic was lovely, for Wrenwyn had the ability to make the realm dance. She could grow vines with her fingertips, call a field of delicate flowers to sprout between cracked stones. She could make the ground shift, could reshape a river with a swirl of her hands. She was gentle and kind and pious, keeping the gods' laws like every good Sacred should.'

Ezer had always thought the idea of Wrenwyn was an inspiring one.

Not because of all the times she obeyed.

But because of the one time she didn't.

'When Wrenwyn came of age, she was set to be Matched with another Sacred. It was her duty, the Masters said, to marry her chosen. To mate with him and carry on the bloodline . . . to keep her Realmist pillar pure. So Wrenwyn arrived at her Matching Ceremony as one should, dressed in a gown of spun gold. All of Lordach was in attendance, eager to see the beautiful young princess be Matched. Her chosen was handsome and powerful, well connected to the gods, for he had never broken a single one of their laws.'

'*A fine match,*' Wrenwyn's brothers told her. '*A beautiful union.*'

Izill smiled. 'The people of Lordach adored him, just as they adored Wrenwyn. He uttered his vows aloud, and promised to stand by Wrenwyn's side, to give of his own flesh to create another with such pure magic. It was a dream, that day, the sun high in the sky, the butterflies dancing and the flowers blooming.'

Her voice softened. 'But when the Masters turned to Wrenwyn, and asked her to recite her vows . . . she told them *no.*'

The Masters warned her of what would come should she disobey. It was a command. It was her duty, passed down from the Five who breathed life into her veins.

'*I do not fear the gods!*' Wrenwyn shouted. '*If they are real, then they will prove to me their wrath.*'

Izill's eyes widened as she continued. 'And in that moment, in the bright light of a perfect day, the sky turned black. Wrenwyn was struck by lightning. And she died on her wedding day. Only her bones were left by the time she was done burning. They buried them in a small, meager grave, a reminder to all of us, to this day. No one defies the gods and gets away unscathed.'

Izill sat back, the tale done.

'Izill.'

They both whirled to find Zey standing there behind the

couch, her eyes tired, her hand covered in a fresh bandage. She looked like she hadn't slept all night. 'Don't you have somewhere else to be? Toilets to scrub. Dishes to clean?'

Izill's jaw hardened. 'Good luck today,' she said to Ezer as she stood and quickly pressed a hand to her arm. Then she glared at Zey and left.

'Servants,' Zey said, and to Ezer's surprise, she slumped into the seat across from her and took what remained of Izill's meal. Her blonde hair was wild and tangled, no longer in its exquisite braid. 'Wrenwyn didn't die that day, you know.'

Ezer lifted a brow. 'I've certainly not heard that version before.'

'You wouldn't have, being that you're Unconsecrated.' She folded a piece of bacon in half, and ate it in one bite, groaning at the taste. 'There's another version, passed around in silent whispers. One that's far more exciting.'

'What's your version, then?' Ezer asked, crossing her arms.

Zey picked up a cinnamon roll, and began unfurling it, inch by inch. 'No lightning strike. But her brothers did subdue her then cut out her tongue, and locked her away in their castle for the rest of her days. She was supposed to die there, for her defiance.' She took a bite and licked the icing off her fingertip. And Ezer realized, suddenly, the familiar smell upon the woman. The strange glaze in her eyes.

She was drunk.

And today was *not* Absolution Day.

'In that version of the story, she could no longer wield, of course, because she had no way to invocate. But she *did* find a way to break out. She had help, some say, and she disappeared across the Expanse, never to be seen or heard from again.' Her lips broke into a cold, cruel smile. 'Some believe that was just before the thirteenth stone turned black.'

Ezer's blood went cold for a moment.

'Of course, it's only a story,' Zey said, and shrugged. 'She's got a grave out there, somewhere in the woods. Someone broke into it, years ago. And when they did, do you know what they found?'

'What?' Ezer asked.

Zey smiled. '*Nothing*,' she said, and slurred the word. 'Not even a finger bone. Think about that, Raphonminder, and tell me which version of the story you believe.'

A knock sounded on the dormitory door, and Ezer jumped.

'Run along to your little prince,' Zey said. 'But you should know. The women he spends his time with . . .' A devilish smirk. 'Well, if they aren't his betrothed . . . they have a mysterious reputation for dying.'

She didn't believe her for a second.

Especially when she opened the door and found Arawn standing there, a small black box in his hands.

'What's this?' Ezer asked as Arawn held the package out to her.

He was dressed in more casual clothing today, still with his white cloak, his classic warrior's braid. But instead of silk, he wore a linen tunic and trousers. The fabric showed all too well the lines of his body. He frowned as he held out the box. 'It's a gift.'

'I can see that,' Ezer said, and glanced back over her shoulder at the dormitory door. 'Do you need me to deliver it to someone inside?'

Surely he had a Matched, or at least someone he hoped would be.

'No.' He cleared his throat. 'It's . . . for you, Minder. Consider it a lifeline.'

Her eyes widened.

She hadn't been given a gift since she was a child, before Ervos lost himself to the betting and drinking.

The box was wrapped with a silk bow, no larger than the palm of her hand.

She lifted the lid, and felt her brows rise on instinct.

'It's . . . a rock.'

He'd given her a *rock*. One that could have fit easily in the palm of her hand. Gods, the ways of the Sacred were strange.

'Not *just* a rock.' Arawn's blue eyes were eager, like he was letting her in on a secret. 'It's a *speaking stone*.'

She turned the stone over, and sure enough, it had a freshly glowing rune that looked like twin tailed stars encircling one another, never quite touching.

'Right . . .' Ezer said slowly.

He sighed. 'It's so we can speak to each other, Minder.' His brows furrowed, like he'd practiced this speech and it wasn't coming out right. He reached into his own pocket and revealed a matching stone. 'Kinlear and I used to use them as children. It stretches across the entirety of Augaurde. So that, no matter where you are . . .' He swallowed. 'You can call on me. Should you need me.'

'Oh,' she breathed.

Gods, was it hot in this hallway?

She had the sudden urge to roll up her sleeves.

'May I?' he asked.

She wasn't sure what to say, what to even do, so she scooped up the stone in her box and held it out to him.

But instead of taking it from her, he curled her fingers around it.

'What are you—'

'You'll see,' Arawn said. Their eyes locked. 'Patience, Minder.'

The stone began to grow warm in her grasp, or maybe that was from *his* skin, too hot over hers.

And then she could have sworn . . .

'*See? A speaking stone.*'

His voice filled her mind.

She yelped and dropped the stone back in the box like it was on fire.

He chuckled.

'They're runed to share internal thoughts like conversation,'

Arawn explained. 'All you need to do is squeeze it. And . . . I'll be able to talk to you. Any time at all.' He cleared his throat again. 'To help, I mean. To answer questions, or . . . be an ally.'

It was a thoughtful gift. A very *personal*, close gift. And she didn't know what to make of it.

Yes, it truly *was* too warm in this hallway.

'I . . .' Gods, where had all her words gone? She nodded and placed the stone in her inner cloak pocket. 'Why?'

'I just thought, with the danger of your mission . . . you need someone you can trust. Someone . . . to perhaps help you feel not so alone.'

A twinge of something new unfolded within her.

She felt . . . strangely light.

A bit panicked, too.

She felt like running far away from here, if only to give herself a second to breathe and clear her mind.

'Thank you,' Ezer said instead, because he was looking at her far too intently. 'It's a lovely rock.'

'Speaking stone,' he corrected her.

'Right. A lovely speaking stone.' She nodded up at him.

He shifted uncomfortably.

It was so silent, she swore she heard him swallow.

'Well. I'm off to attend to my duties,' Arawn said.

'All right,' she said.

Gods, her mouth was dry.

He nodded. 'All right.'

And with that, the Crown Prince of Lordach turned on his heel and left.

She stood there alone, the weight of his gift in her pocket as she watched him slip through a side door, ever the brute soldier.

And yet . . .

She'd just unpeeled another hidden layer of him.

And it frightened her how much she enjoyed what she'd found.

CHAPTER 16

'Good morning, Prince,' Ezer said, breathless as she finally made her way through the outer doors of the Aviary.

She wiped sweat from her brow and kicked snow from her boots, feeling for all the world like a wet cat. That insufferable walk up to the Aviary cliff had nearly killed her, both from how difficult it was to breathe to the fear of falling that sent her anxiety into a spiral, time and again.

But she'd done it, and she was proud of herself at least for not turning back.

Kinlear stood past the saddle racks beside the black door, waiting for her as promised with a chained stopwatch in his hand.

'You're thirty-five minutes late,' he said, and tucked the watch into his pocket.

Ezer shrugged. 'My schedule should be of no concern to you.'

Kinlear raised a dark brow in challenge. 'It is my mission. Therefore, it is my schedule. And I do not like to be kept waiting.'

'Well, it is my *life*,' Ezer said back. 'For which you seem to have little concern.'

At that, he chuckled. 'You challenge my patience. It's a wonder you bond so well with Six.'

He looked handsome today, effortlessly disheveled to the naked eye, but Ezer wondered if perhaps it was only a part of his mask. A sort of shield he wore, so that no one really got to know the true prince beneath.

He had on his normal Eagleminder's cloak, white with gold silk inside the hood, but today the front folds were open to reveal the tunic he had on was a cool, springtime blue. It was unbuttoned nearly halfway down his chest. He wasn't muscular, like Arawn. He was tall and lithe and toned.

And he was pale, like he'd never left the confines of the Aviary. Like he'd never seen the summer sun.

She supposed not many in the north had. It was another thing she missed about the south, those few and far between days when the sea glittered so bright, it ached to look upon it.

The birds had always loved those days.

'Well?' Kinlear asked. 'What's your excuse?'

Her eyes slid to the small corked vial nestled against his chest, the glass too dark to see what was inside. He'd added a few more rings to his fingers, which clacked as he held open the Aviary door for her.

Her fingers grazed the speaking stone in her pocket.

'I got lost,' Ezer lied. 'You spend enough time locked in a tower, and you're likely to lose your bearings, too, in a place as large as this.'

'It's interesting, the tells people have,' he said as he looked at her. 'You squint when you lie.'

She could have sworn his eyes narrowed as they slid towards her pocket. But he couldn't know. Surely not.

'You can be honest with me. You are *safe* with me, despite what my brother may say.' She didn't realize she'd backed up against the door to the catacombs. He reached around her, his hand barely skimming her waist as he grasped the handle. 'I am not your enemy, Raphonminder.' He swung open the door into darkness. 'Not unless you want me to be.'

*

Six was in the same spot as before, so far in the shadows of her cage that it was hard to decipher her tail from her beak.

It reeked inside, far worse than a Ravenminder's tower ever did.

'Is she always there?' Ezer asked, curling her fingers around the icy cold bars. Her heart did a little tremor at the sight of the raphon. It struck Ezer how *beautiful* Six was, in a darkly dangerous way.

Just like her ravens.

Kinlear stopped at her shoulder. 'She's a creature of habit, for certain,' he said. He reached down to the vial on his neck and uncorked it, allowing the smell of black licorice to pour out. 'But so am I, I suppose.'

And he took a small sip, plugging the vial up at once.

'What is it?' Ezer asked.

'This?' He shrugged. 'A clever little tincture from Alaris. After the injury . . .' He looked down at his leg and lifted his cane as if that explained it. 'I wasn't able to move around as much. I fell deathly ill, and it had its way with my lungs. This eases my symptoms.'

'But what about magic?' Ezer asked, looking at the vial.

He chuckled softly, as if he'd explained this a thousand times before. 'It isn't the magic that makes the final call, Raphonminder. It is the gods, and what invocations they are willing to grant.'

The look on his face told her not to question him further.

But now, she wondered . . . what had he done, what sins had he committed against them, that they'd refused to heal him? A prince.

A flash of her dreams crept up again, the image of his dagger in her chest after he broke a heated kiss.

She turned to Six to distract herself.

'Is she always this tired?' Ezer asked. 'This . . . lazy?'

The raphon's tail twitched, and Ezer could have sworn the beast huffed in annoyance. Happenstance, of course.

Kinlear shrugged. 'Most birds are up and singing before the start of dawn. I suppose that's the cat part of her.'

'Unless they're busy hunting for birds,' Ezer said beneath her breath.

'Not a fan of cats?' He lifted a brow nearly hidden beneath his dark curls. 'That may pose a problem, considering Six is half of one.'

'I don't need reminding,' she said darkly.

'You die . . . we all die,' Kinlear said. 'Her chains remain. And for what it's worth . . . I'll be here the whole time.'

He was different today.

More relaxed, less showy.

'Such a relief,' Ezer said beneath her breath. And motioned for him to open the gate before she could think better of it. 'My warning from yesterday remains, Prince.'

'I've thought of nothing else since,' Kinlear said with a wink, as he gently shut the gate behind her. 'No locks. You have my word.'

Ezer's feet rustled the shavings as she edged inside the cage, eyes on the beast.

Six didn't move.

But her breathing was certainly not deep enough to be true sleep.

'Faker,' Ezer said, as her eyes adjusted to the darkness inside the cage.

She'd be a fool, as good as dead meat to think one shared touch last night meant the raphon had truly accepted her. But there was certainly less terror in her gut entering the cage a second time.

It felt a bit more like . . . anticipation.

A tremor in her heart, as she sat down against the bars and said, 'Hello, Six.'

The beast didn't move other than to twitch her long, catlike tail.

It clinked against the heavy chains that were anchored into the stones: four chains, one for each shackle still attached to Six's ankles.

The sound sent a ripple running through Ezer; a mental flinch that reminded her of chains upon her own ankles, a heaviness she bore for two long, lonely years.

She glanced away, focusing on Six's wings instead.

They were relaxed, spread out across the pup's body. The tips of her long black feathers were coated in shavings. A messy sleeper, she supposed, but so was Ezer, always waking up tangled in her own sheets.

'Are you going to greet me this morning, or shall I bleed for you again?' Ezer asked.

Six lifted her head and blinked warily at the sound of Ezer's voice.

The slits on her scarred beak flared, as if she were pulling in Ezer's scent.

But when her large, dark eyes fell on Kinlear . . . they narrowed.

She twitched her tail twice and quickly tucked her head beneath her dark wing.

'It's *you*,' Ezer said. 'I think she's afraid of you.'

Kinlear scoffed. 'I hardly believe that, considering I am the only one in this Citadel that has overseen her survival since her birth. If it weren't for me, my father would have had his way, and the pup would be a pile of ashes on the wind. Here.'

He stood, reaching for something in one of the other empty cells.

A heavy clink of chains sounded, and something landed at her feet.

'What is—'

'If we're to have her starting groundwork by the end of the week, she must be haltered *today*.'

Ezer looked down at the pile of black chains. It was like a halter for a horse, though much larger, and certainly stronger.

She hoped.

She'd never haltered anything before, but she'd seen it done. She didn't think it could be all that difficult: just lacing it through

Six's beak, while avoiding her swiping paws and razor-sharp claws, and . . .

'How in the hell,' Ezer asked, as she lifted the chain-link halter, grunting beneath its heavy weight, 'am I supposed to do this?'

The prince only shrugged and sat down on his stool like he was ready to witness a show. 'That sounds like a "you problem" to me.'

It very much *was* a problem. But it wasn't Ezer's.

It was Six's.

The moment Ezer laced the halter over a shoulder and inched her way towards the raphon, something seemed to shift in the air.

'Just ease it over,' Kinlear said from outside.

'I've got it,' Ezer said as she adjusted her grip on the heavy chain-link.

Six turned and watched her with wary eyes. But she did not move to harm Ezer.

She didn't even blink.

'All right.' Ezer kept her voice low. 'Here we are, Six. Nice and easy.'

She held out the halter, the chains clinking at the motion.

'*Ezer*,' said the wind, a whisper that reminded her of a disappointed sigh. '*No*.'

And that was all it took.

Six screeched, her eyes going wild.

Ezer tried to move out of the way, but the beast leapt to her feet, her wings snapping out so fast that Ezer couldn't avoid the hit.

And then she was in the air, thrown backwards from the impact.

Ezer landed with a bone-splitting crash against the water trough at the other end of the cell. Which promptly spilled on top of her, soaking her to the bone. She came up sputtering, gasping – so cold, that for a moment, she thought Six had broken her ribs. She thought she couldn't breathe.

'Ezer!'

A blink, and she came back to her senses.

'Are you all right?'

Kinlear's voice called out to her from the other side of the bars.

'I'm . . . I'm fine,' she gasped, as she sat up to find the raphon back in her curled-up position again. 'Coward!' she yelled. 'You're three times the size of me. How *dare* you—'

But then she realized what she'd held in her hands, what she'd carried towards the beast.

And it seemed to *pop* into her senses, like a rubber band snapping into place.

Her stomach dropped to her toes, regret filling her.

Because . . . Six's ankles were already bound in chains. She stared at them, the deep black shackles that were so like her own, the heavy bolts in the stones that the raphon was connected to, and it broke her.

She'd carried the burden of them for two long years, alone and forgotten.

A prisoner to a life she had not chosen.

No, someone else made that decision for her, and it was hers alone to drown in. Hers alone to suffer through in silence, and she would have lost herself entirely, if it weren't for the birds.

'Cut them loose,' Ezer said.

Six was huddled in the corner. A predator, acting as prey.

And Ezer – the halter at her feet – had been the catalyst.

She threw it out of the cell. The sound was deafening, the slam of chain upon ancient stones. She flinched at the same time Six did.

'What are you doing?' Kinlear asked.

She heard his cane as he came as close as he could towards the bars.

'What I should have done first,' Ezer said.

She didn't know if it was the sound of her voice, the stillness of her body, but when she turned to look at the second Prince of Lordach . . .

He was staring at her, his eyes haunted.

'Please,' she said, swallowing the lump in her throat. 'Cut her loose.'

She expected him to laugh at her, to ask whether or not she was concussed. But instead, he swallowed and said, 'Okay.'

He reached inside his cloak and produced a ring of keys, which he passed through to her.

They were warm in her hands.

Her heartbeat roared in her ears as she cautiously approached the raphon. She lowered her gaze, not wanting to challenge the pup.

Tonight, they were one and the same.

After all, they shared a cage.

She felt Six's hot breath on her neck as she knelt and reached out, ever so slowly, towards the first shackle.

'I'm setting you free,' she whispered. 'Don't eat me.'

She nearly broke again when she saw how utterly raw the skin was beneath each ankle. How the lovely dark fur was matted and wet from blood. Her hands shook as she reached out, not making a sound.

She didn't even dare breathe.

The key fit into the lock, and the shackle came loose.

Six hissed.

Ezer flinched but held fast. The pup waited patiently, a statue, as Ezer moved to the other front paw and removed the shackle.

And when the final two were off, when the raphon was truly *free*, enough that it could kill her, devour her, feast upon her bones if it wanted . . .

She felt something nudge up against her shoulder.

She flinched again, but it was warm, and it was gentle, and when she risked a glance down, she found the beast's head pressed against her.

Six's eyes were closed.

Her purr filled the cage, the sound rumbling off the walls.

Ezer reached out and placed her hand on her beak. So large, it spanned her entire torso, and Six wasn't even fully grown. The scar was deeply indented, like a blade truly *had* swiped across her, barely missing her throat. She probably carried the memory of that blade, the feel of it . . .

Like Ezer carried the whisper of shadow wolf claws against her skin.

'No more chains,' she promised the pup. 'I swear it.'

The moment she said it, the beast leaned forward, pressing harder against her palm.

She was gone in an instant.

Her body, here in the cell. But her mind . . .

It carried her away, back to that same vision as before.

She saw that dark, endless sea, the waves rocking slowly from side to side. There was no shore in sight, nothing to mark where it was, beyond the single feather.

It floated alone. No matter which way the waves carried it, it never sank. And there was that awful feeling again. A deep, unending sadness, like Ezer was lost. Like no one would ever find her, and this dark, endless sea was all she would ever know.

Ezer gasped as she pulled her own hand away.

The vision cleared at once, and there was Six, standing there before her, dark eyes intent.

'You're lonely,' Ezer whispered. 'Aren't you?'

The raphon's tail twitched once.

And she swore Six inclined her head.

So Ezer lifted her other hand and placed it on the raphon's neck.

The feathers were soft, delicate and silken.

She'd never felt anything so lovely before.

'It's all right,' Ezer said. 'I'm here now.'

And she meant it.

Before she left, she removed her outer cloak and dropped it on the floor of the cell.

It was something Ervos always did, when a new raven arrived at his tower. A way to get the birds to trust him, to know him, not just when he was there in the present, but when he wasn't there at all.

He wanted them to think of him like a fond memory. A space to be safe and sound.

'She's done for the day,' Ezer said, as she turned away from Six.

She met Kinlear's eyes, nearly forgetting he'd been there the whole time.

'I expect a new halter for her, one *without* chain link of any kind.'

'I'll see to it,' Kinlear said.

He was looking at her like she was a puzzle, like a set of stars in the sky that he couldn't quite remember how to name.

He stood slowly and opened the door for her without a word. His eyes were limned with silver.

He coughed, and turned away, leaning heavily on his cane.

'Are you all right?' she asked.

'Never better,' Kinlear said, and offered her a small smile. 'Thank you.'

'For what?' Ezer asked.

She couldn't help but notice how hollow his breathing was, how he sniffled and ran a hand across his eyes again. How his cane rapped heavier than it normally did as they walked away.

'For hope,' he said. 'Someday, they'll sing songs about you. The Raphonminder who changed the fate of Lordach.'

And then he was silent.

She turned back only once to find that the raphon had scooted a bit closer to her cloak. And buried her scarred beak in the fabric, as if to breathe Ezer in.

CHAPTER 17

Ezer spent the rest of the day alone, curled up in the corner of the library beside a flickering fire. Her body was bruised something fierce, but a bit of Izill's salve took the pain away.

She had lunch on the third floor while she scribbled notes down in an old worn journal, the sound of the nib scratching on parchment like a balm to her soul.

Her pocket warmed suddenly.

She nearly yelped from the heat, like an ember had sparked to life on the speaking stone. She grasped it, hoping that would settle the surge of runic power.

Arawn's voice caressed her mind from far away.

Alive and well after today's session?

She'd never get used to that feeling of a human voice in her mind. It wasn't like the wind's whisper, a delicate thing that commanded her very *soul* to listen.

This was like he was well and truly here with her. She swore she could even smell his earthen scent.

I'm alive. But am I well? She thought back, then winced as a bit of ghostly pain echoed across her ribs. *That remains to be seen. I could do with a bit of sugar to take the edge off.*

He was quiet for a moment, and she wondered if he'd gone.

But then the stone warmed again, and his voice filled her mind.

I may die if this meeting with my father and the southern

emissaries reaches its fourth hour. Should I survive . . . I'll see what I can do.

The stone went cold, like he'd dropped his own hand from his.

She spoke to no one else over the next hour beyond the librarian, who was an older Sacred Scribe, bent at the back as he wheeled past, pushing carts of books. A small orange cat followed him, tail twitching in a very Six-like way.

'Excuse me,' Ezer said. 'Excuse me?'

She'd never been very good at approaching people, always unsure of what their reaction would be when they saw her scars.

But the librarian did not balk at her.

In fact, he squinted at her, as if he could scarcely see. 'If you're looking for more literature on raphons, I'm afraid you'll have to search a bit higher than I've time for these days,' he said, glancing up. 'Upper levels.'

'Ah,' Ezer said. 'That's . . . unfortunate.'

He didn't ask why.

He just shrugged as the cat began to circle around his ankles, purring loudly.

'May I?' Ezer asked, holding a hand towards the cat as it yowled up at him.

The librarian shrugged. 'The choice is his,' he said. 'Not mine. Gods help anyone who ever dared tell a *cat* what to do.'

So Ezer knelt, reaching out to scratch it behind the ears. But the second she did, the cat hissed and darted off towards the shadows between bookshelves like a little orange demon.

'I suppose I'm not the best with cats,' Ezer said with a sigh. 'Birds mostly.'

The librarian only chuckled. 'I wouldn't take it personally. Well, now . . .' He clucked his tongue and put his glasses back on, as if he'd just noticed something important. The lenses were so thick his eyes looked thrice the size as he leaned in. 'That's an odd, ugly little thing. But worth far more than it looks.'

'What?' Ezer asked, recoiling.

'The ring, child.'

She looked down at her mother's ring, the symbols of the gods surrounding it. 'It was my mother's,' she said.

'May I?'

She shrugged and held out her hand for him to examine it. 'Curious. It's been quite some time since I've seen one of these.'

'What is it?' Ezer asked.

He stared at her thumb a moment longer, twisting his mouth sideways. 'A Ring of Finding,' he said. 'Given from one Sacred to another. A symbol of love, really, meant to be worn even in the grave. So that even in death, the bearers of the rings can find one another. This is . . . quite sad, really.'

'Why?' Ezer asked. 'Seems more romantic than sad to me.'

'It would be romantic,' the librarian said, frowning, 'if the ring was still on the bearer's finger. Your mother's, you say?' His brows raised higher than the lenses of his glasses. 'Won't help with finding her now.'

He turned, *tsking*, like he didn't know he'd just dropped a hammer across her soul.

She looked down at the ring and frowned.

If the librarian was correct . . . that meant her mother's ring, the ring meant to connect her to whoever had given it to her . . .

It hadn't gone with her to the grave.

A lump formed in Ezer's throat as she squeezed her thumb around it.

Ervos had taken it off her mother's body, hoping to bring something back to Ezer. He'd meant it to be a gesture of kindness, a way for Ezer to keep some part of her mother. He couldn't have known what removing that ring might do.

If it's even real, Ezer thought, for there were plenty of made-up things in this realm. Many stories. And she was learning plenty of different versions in the Citadel, compared to what was believed on the Outside.

A mystery for another day, and so she busied her mind again with books.

She quickly settled into a book on the characteristics of cats. How they lived, what they ate, what they enjoyed doing.

Perhaps Six had been captive for so long, she didn't even know she could be anything *other* than a house cat. That she could spread her wings, feel the strength of them as they carried her through the sky.

She'd start there, as soon as she found a way to halter the beast. But one thing was for certain.

There would be *no* chains.

Soon, with the feel of the pages between her fingertips and the heat of the fire at her feet, she dozed off.

She did not dream of her labyrinth.

She dreamt, instead, of Kinlear.

It was the same as it always was, the dream where he killed her.

But this time, instead of a dark, shadowed hood . . . she saw his face.

She saw how his dark hair curled long enough to just get into his soft silver eyes. How he had a vial of dark liquid on a gold chain around his neck. How his cane clacked as he approached her, the sound echoing through her.

This time, they weren't standing in the abyss.

They were standing in a dark space, with a strange soft purple light casting a glow upon them.

She had her back against the wall as he leaned over her and kissed her fiercely.

His tongue tasted like red wine.

She gasped as he breathed her in, and she ran her hands up the sides of his neck, her fingertips skimming past the gold chain. She curled them into his dark hair, pulled him closer as he pressed against her. His hands skimmed the hem of her tunic, setting her skin on fire.

It was not she, but he that pulled away.

And when the kiss broke . . .
It was no longer Kinlear pressed up against her.
It was Arawn.
His blue eyes were not hungry like Kinlear's. They were soft as he stood above her, looking down. His hands cradled her face like she was fragile, made of glass and might break.
And his fingertips were on her scars, undisturbed and unbothered by the marks that had worn themselves deep into her skin, that had labeled her as different.
'Ezer,' he whispered. 'Come back to me.'
And when he leaned in to kiss her, she wanted it.
She wanted it because he was looking at her like she was the moon on a dark night. Like she was—
'Ezer?'
She bolted up right to find—
'Arawn,' Ezer gasped.
Oh, gods.
She blinked up at him, mortified.

Because she was breathless, and flustered, and did he know how *passionately* he'd just kissed her in her dream?

Did he know what they were just doing . . . together . . . behind her closed eyes?

He looked down at her with a half-smile on his face. Like he knew he'd caught her with her back up against the wall, but . . . no, he couldn't. So she tried her best to look cool and nonchalant, to think of the swirling snow and cold, icy wind beyond the Citadel's windows.

She'd never longed for anyone before. Never had such vivid dreams of what a man could do, how he could make her burn when he got too close.

You fool, she told herself. *Get yourself in check!*
You care nothing for either one of them.
You will never, not until the grave calls you under, fall for a Sacred Prince.

Because Kinlear was unhinged.

And Arawn . . . well, he was *Arawn*.

And he was holding a plate of cinnamon rolls in his large hands.

'Is that . . .'

'You requested them, didn't you?'

'I didn't think you'd actually deliver them,' Ezer said.

She paused to yawn, unable to hold it back.

Arawn chuckled. 'Tired, Minder?'

'As you would be, if you'd spent time with Six,' she said, and tucked her hair behind her ear. Gods, she still reeked like a raphon.

She'd taken a shower in the dormitory, of course. But she supposed she'd have to scrub her skin with a whetstone to get the raphon grit off.

'Calling her by name now?' Arawn asked and raised a pale white brow. 'I believe that sounds like progress.'

'Shouldn't you be at war?' Ezer asked. 'With all the other Knights?'

She stood and swiped her hands across her cloak to settle the wrinkles.

'No,' Arawn said, his eyes downcast as they walked. 'I am on . . .' A twitch of his jaw. 'Temporary reassignment from the skies.'

'Liar,' Ezer said.

He looked shocked. 'I do not lie, Minder. It is one of the first laws of the Five.'

Penance, Ezer thought. To break it would be to earn penance.

'If I'd a war eagle at my disposal, I don't think I'd be willing to leave their side. So why aren't you with yours?'

He did not answer as they came to the next level, and he led her towards another set of exit doors. 'If you won't talk about that, at least tell me where we're going?'

'We are going to train,' Arawn said. 'Because *you* are weak, and a growing raphon is not.'

Her heart sank. Physical training sounded like a death sentence. 'Kinlear put you up to this, didn't he?'

They came out into the torchlit hallway. 'So many questions, Minder.'

They passed several Sacred in full armor, marching out for another night of war. Many were young, between their twenties and thirties, but some of the Sacred had telltale whispers of ageing too soon. They passed one who had paused, taking a knee to catch his breath, his sword like a cane to support him. He had dark circles beneath his eyes, deep wrinkles that looked out of place on his young body. His red hair was flecked with white and gray, though he couldn't have been more than twenty-five.

'Gods be with you, Brogen,' Arawn said, and helped the Knight stand. 'To the end of your days.'

'And to the Ehver after,' the Knight said. He took a breath and rejoined the current headed for war.

'Why aren't you going with them?' Ezer asked as he led her along.

'More questions,' Arawn called over a shoulder.

'And so few answers,' she said. 'It's called conversing. In person, face to face, instead of with a stone.'

He still said nothing.

So she reached into her pocket and gripped the stone until it warmed.

Is this better?

He sucked in a breath beside her, like he was surprised at her voice sidling up against his mind.

The stone is supposed to be for emergency purposes only, Minder.

They forked left down another set of stairs.

And what was earlier? Ezer thought back.

A test of the runic magic, Arawn answered.

You missed me, she said. *Admit it. I'm not so terrible as you once thought, now, am I?*

At that, he chuckled aloud. Then his voice filled her mind as the staircase wound down, down. *I never thought you terrible, Minder. Though I think* you *thought that about me.*

He wasn't wrong.

She risked pushing him further. *Why are you on leave?*

His silence was answer enough.

She tried to keep her next thoughts gentle. *If I'm to trust you, to be your ally, as you said . . . then I need something to go off. Let me get to know you, Firemage. Please?*

He paused before they reached the bottom of the stairwell. And when he turned to her, they were nearly at eye level, even though she was two steps above.

She felt her eyes drop to his chest, where even through the pale linen tunic, she could see the outline of his angry scar.

A bit of truth about you, she whispered into his mind as she clutched the stone. *That's what I require if we are to be friends.*

He swallowed and opened his mouth like he was going to speak.

But then the words came into her mind instead, and she could hear the carefully veiled sadness in his voice. A wound . . . that hadn't quite yet healed.

I am not in battle, he thought, as his chest rose and fell so close to hers, *because my magic has been denied by the gods. And it's all my fault.*

The stone cooled in her grasp, signifying that he'd dropped his. That the conversation was over. But he'd given her a truth, just as she'd asked.

And she didn't like it one bit.

They entered a torchlit, rounded hallway. And there stood a small figure in brown robes.

'You came!' Izill's hood fell from her head as she rushed to grab Ezer by the hand. 'And just barely in time.'

A pointed look at Arawn, who held out his hands in apology. 'She walks slowly, Izill.'

'Or perhaps *you* arrived too late to collect her,' Izill chided him. She sighed, exasperated. 'Door, please?'

Ezer smiled at the way such a small, mouse-like servant could boss around a Sacred Prince the size of a war bear.

'Of course.' Arawn inclined his head respectfully and swung open the door for them.

The room on the other side was enormous. It was lovely, with ornate white stones with golden veins striking through the floors and the walls. It was domed, like a massive ballroom, but beyond the tall white marble pillars, one enormous circular window stood on the other side.

It took up nearly the entire wall and overlooked the Expanse.

The war.

There were several others standing before it.

They were all younglings, children no older than ten, at best.

The sky was almost dark. She could see the jagged Sawteeth in the background, the peaks so sharp they could have been refined by a whetstone.

The shadowstorm felt closer than ever. Like a living, breathing black crown atop the Sawteeth. Some parts of it were darker than others, tendrils of deepest black that she imagined she could feel from here, for it made the hairs on the back of her neck stand on end.

She'd never seen a storm so alive, so angry.

So ready to cover its enemies in darkness.

He's mad, Ezer thought of Kinlear, *to think anyone can fly beneath that cloud. To make it inside the Acolyte's domain.*

Snow poured from the sky in buckets, concealing the view as the alpine wind gusted past. It rattled the windows, shook the floor, had her shivering even though the dark cloak she wore was well made.

'Come on,' Izill said, taking her by the elbow. 'The sun is about to set.'

Ezer glanced back at Arawn. He just nodded his head towards the window, his eyes on the sky.

'What are we waiting for?' Ezer whispered to Izill.

Izill grinned. 'You'll see.'

She nodded her small chin towards the view ahead of them, where the sun was slowly dipping behind the Sawteeth. And where, if Ezer dared look down . . . she could already see the line of ground forces snaking out into the snow.

They were only two stories up, but on their cliffside they stood high enough that the soldiers looked like ants. Horses and war bears rode among them, the ground soldiers in Sacred whites, while the *nomages* were in bright, bold red. Like smears of blood in the snow. They marched towards the black obelisks that were the Snow Gates.

The exit, where the wards would no longer protect them . . . and death surely awaited the moment darkness struck.

'Almost there,' Izill breathed.

All around her, the children were practically giddy, hands pressed to the icy window.

Arawn appeared beside Ezer, his body warm and his shoulder nearly touching hers. She glanced sideways to find him watching, too.

'Sunset,' he said, so softly she almost didn't hear it. 'The Descent.'

The bleeding sun dipped beyond the Sawteeth.

And then something suddenly *fell* past them, on the other side of the glass.

A blur, a rush of golden color.

A war eagle, aimed like an arrow as it leapt straight down the cliff's face.

Ezer gasped and pressed her own palms to the glass, daring to look down as four others followed in a perfect V formation, the eagles' curled talons so close to the window she swore it rattled in their wake.

Her heart roared in her ears.

She took a step back, because she couldn't watch.

They were going to fall. They were going to splatter upon the snow.

She clutched her speaking stone on instinct, the warmth her only anchor.

Look, Minder, Arawn's voice whispered into her mind.

She opened her eyes and gasped.

At the last second, the War Eagles pulled up, snapping out their golden wings.

The children cheered all around her.

The aerie riders were pressed close to their eagles' backs, expertly staying in their saddles as they climbed into the sky. So fast, they'd fallen past the window, and so fast, they soared back up, sending a wave of snow against the glass.

It was like watching the stars fall. Beautiful, lovely, and deadly in their golden grace.

The cheers settled.

And then all around her, whispers sounded.

Prayers, Arawn said into her mind. *For safety, for strength, for swords to strike true and invocations to be granted.*

She didn't even know they could be denied, throttled, until she met him. And he was about as Sacred as one could get.

What did he do, she wondered, *to earn their wrath?*

Beside her, she heard a child pray for an aerie by name, each rider within it, as the eagles fell past the window, then snapped out their wings and rose to the sky.

They headed straight towards the distant Sawteeth, where she could just barely see the flickering blue torchlights beneath the layer of frozen fog. Ground soldiers, heading to clash against the darksouls.

There. Arawn's voice sighed into her mind. *It's what I wanted you to see.*

She looked all the way to the black mountains, where the

shadows had already begun to strike, rattling the glass, rumbling the very floor beneath her feet. And a cloud of winged darkness rose from between the peaks.

Dark wings.

Lithe, catlike bodies.

Raphons.

Raphons, and their darksoul riders.

They're slower than the war eagles, in a straight flight, Arawn thought to her. *But watch when close combat occurs. There, on the right flank.*

Where the first eagle aerie had clashed with a pack of raphons.

She saw a blaze of fire erupting from a Sacred firemage's hands. It was coupled by a beam of blue ice from a watermage, sent spiraling into the raphon pack. Power that great . . . it was no wonder it sucked the life from the Sacred after too many years of battle.

Ezer held her breath.

They would not miss.

But at the last second, the raphons split, and dipped, smaller and shiftier than the war eagles.

And before she knew it, they were rising from beneath the war eagles, attacking from below, where the giant birds' bellies were soft and unprotected. The eagles banked and split up, and the raphons gave chase.

The war in the sky is a dance, Arawn explained softly as she clutched the speaking stone. *A rider must always be ready to pay attention to which partner, which step, will come next. From all angles.*

They grew closer, enough that she could make out the sheer size of the raphon in front.

Its wings were enormous, easily three times the size of Six's. Bits of shadow, like black smoke, trailed from behind the rider's dark robes.

A Sentinel, Arawn explained, his voice thrumming against her mind. It felt strangely comforting, like she wanted to lean deeper against it. *The strongest warriors lead the packs and wield some of the Acolyte's magic. Their numbers are far less than ours, but we must invocate to wield. Their darkness flows freely. Endless, in battle.*

As he said it . . . a tendril of shadow soared from the Sentinel's outstretched hand.

It spiraled towards the eagles, and as the one in the back of the aerie dipped . . . the tendril of shadow dipped, too.

It trailed the eagle like it was *alive*.

'No,' Ezer gasped out loud.

She didn't want to watch anyone die.

But when that shadow suddenly exploded against rider and eagle – it bounded right off, dissipating in the sky.

The runes, Ezer thought.

Arawn nodded, still watching the sky.

We're protected for several hits, thanks to our Scribes, and hopefully the aerie will be able to make one count.

What is their weakness? Ezer asked.

Daylight, Arawn answered. *If it weren't for the sunrise, this war would have been lost long ago. Sacred magic slows them, but it won't always kill them. It must be the removal of their heads or wings . . . a hit they cannot heal with their shadows.*

Just like the wolf in the woods.

She imagined Six out there in the battle.

Imagined a Sacred's blade driving deep into the pup's belly, and she shuddered.

She felt sick.

How do the Riders decide, Ezer asked, *that they want to be in the sky?*

His voice was gentle, faraway, as he thought back to her. *It's in our blood, Minder. Just like that feeling you said you get. Now . . . the Descent is over. It's time we train.*

Her stomach sank.

And when she turned to him, he looked like a warrior again. Cold as the stone in her pocket.

'Please,' she said out loud. 'I've no desire to train in any sort of physical activity, Arawn, especially against children half my age.'

Not because she feared she'd best them.

But because she knew they would all kick her ass.

But as Arawn shrugged and turned away, she realized they weren't going through stances, or wielding training swords, or getting ready to spar.

'What is this?' Ezer asked, as she sat down beside Izill.

Everyone had sat in their own spaces on the floor, where one of the older servants had begun passing out wooden trays. Each one held a bowl of water, a seed, two candles – one lit and one unlit – and finally, a small dagger.

'The night class,' Izill said. 'For those – mostly the younglings – not yet settled on their pillar, because they've yet to wield at all. If they fail to settle before they turn thirteen, odds are they'll never settle at all. And as of now . . . well, I suppose it's also a class for you. And me.' She sighed. 'A special circumstance, given our advanced ages, but every Sacred's got to start somewhere. We've a rare few that settle in their later years.'

'Settle with *what*?' Ezer asked.

Izill smiled. 'Your *magic*.' She pressed a finger to her lips as everyone turned to face the front of the room . . . where it was Arawn who stood waiting like an impatient professor.

Of course.

This was what Kinlear had meant when he said *to look after the younglings*.

He'd said it like it was embarrassing. A demotion, or a punishment.

She couldn't stop herself from looking at Arawn's hands, remembering when his fire had fizzled out in the woods. All the stories about the crown prince with the gods' glorious magic . . .

It's all my fault, he said.

What had he done . . . what could be so bad that the gods would deny the invocations of a crown prince? The King was dwindling. And with Arawn next in line for the throne, they couldn't afford to lose him. He'd die as fast as the *nomage* troops without magic.

His eyes fell upon hers as he said, 'Let's begin.'

CHAPTER 18

Perhaps physical training would have been better.

For the next hour, they sat and practiced magic.

Ezer, much to her unsurprise, had achieved *nothing*.

Arawn was a fine enough teacher. He walked them through a basic invocation of certain syllables, in the godstongue, in which they would place an object upon their outstretched hand, close their eyes, and focus on imagining what they wanted it to do. And if they were to succeed . . . it would mean that specific god had claimed them.

It would mean they were truly meant to be a Sacred Knight who could wield magic in battle.

But they must be careful when they asked for a bit of granted magic. Too much, too frequently, and it would shorten their days.

Magic *always* required a price.

Arawn ran through each pillar with surprising patience, his voice gentle as he showed the younglings how the invocation should sound. It was the same utterance for each: a blanket phrase in the godstongue that meant, '*Show me whose I am.*'

A prayer meant to request a bit of magic to one's bare hands.

Ezer's tongue tripped over the phrase countless times as she spoke it aloud. She felt like a fool, because children half her age spoke with grace and confidence, and she . . .

She sounded like she was slurring her words.

Like Ervos used to sound on his drunkest nights.

For the water in the bowl, the invocation was meant to raise a single droplet. If she succeeded, it would mean she was a Watermage, a child of Odaeis.

For the unlit candle, it was to draw a flame. Success would make her a Firemage, a child of Vivorr, like Arawn.

For the seed, success would be to get it to sprout. If so, she'd be considered a Realmist, a child of Aristra.

The dagger was meant to be used to draw a single cut across one's palm and heal the skin back together again. That would make her an Ehvermage, a child of Dhysis, like Alaris.

And for the lit candle, it was to conjure just enough of a breeze to blow it out. They would be a Windmage, a child of Avane.

It was the one Ezer leaned towards the most.

The wind was her friend, her guiding voice. And so naturally, she held out a hand to the lit candle, thinking that it would be doused by Windmage magic. She'd simply never had the means to call upon it before.

Show me whose I am, she thought, and whispered the strange new invocation aloud.

She waited, staring at that tiny flame.

And just for a moment, she believed that it would go out.

But nothing happened.

So she tried again.

Please, she thought. *Show me whose I am.*

She was here, after all, given entrance to the Citadel, like Izill had said. So even if she *was* an Unconsecrated, born and raised beyond these walls . . . she had magic in her blood. She just needed to know how to bring that magic, whatever it was, *out*.

But when she thought of the ageing Knight in the halls – the King she'd seen in the library the other night – she wasn't sure she wanted to pay the price.

It didn't matter anyway. No matter how many times she tried, the candle stayed lit.

Arawn paced about the room, speaking over them all. 'Imagine the outcome while you invocate. You must believe in your heart, your soul, that you are a true servant of the gods. That if they grant you a bit of magic to do their bidding, then you will serve them, uphold their laws in the Sacred Text until the end of your days. And even if our days are shortened, even if we do not see old age because of the power required of wielding . . . that is a Knight's true purpose. To be a vessel.'

Ezer glanced away from the flame.

Until the end of her days?

She hadn't even started her own life yet . . . not truly. She'd yet to learn who she was, and now she was busy trying to survive Six – a gift, in its own strange way – but beyond that?

Kinlear had promised coin for every day she survived. Mountains of it, enough to buy herself passage anywhere she wished, to see the places she'd read about in stories. She could do *anything*. Fall in love, if she wanted, or perhaps decide she didn't want a man at all. But it would be *her* choice.

Her steps would be free, untethered, because there would be no laws to stop her.

A thousand of them, Ezer thought.

The weight of that reality hit her like a rock to the chest. Because all she could think of was her old chains. All she could think of was dragging a thousand of them behind her for the rest of her days.

She would rather go back to Rendegard.

She would rather die young and free than grow old beneath the weight of a thousand laws she could never keep. She would rather die powerless than watch her youth crumble in the mirror because of a gift she didn't even want from the gods in the first place.

So why did failing make her so *mad*?

'Gods be damned,' Ezer hissed beneath her breath. 'I can't do it.'

A few eyes glanced at her.

So she focused and tried again. But the candle refused to obey her command.

A growl, and Ezer set the candle down. 'Just go *out*, you son of a—'

Her words died as the stone in her pocket warmed.

She sighed and closed her fist over it.

Yes, Your Highness?

His shadow fell over her, and she glanced up to find his blue eyes narrowed. His scarred face twisted in carefully controlled anger.

Mind your tongue. His voice slid into her mind. She hated how good it felt, how familiar he was already becoming. *There are children here.*

I'm well aware, she thought, holding his gaze. Several had already invocated successfully.

His voice sighed against her, and she gave an involuntary shiver. *You can't invocate through heightened emotions, like sorrow or anger. Humanity blocks your connection to the Five.*

Then show me, Ezer said. *If you're so capable.*

He raised a brow at her challenge, especially after the truth he'd given earlier.

For a moment, she wondered if he *would* fail.

His stone cooled as he released it.

And then he took a breath, and stood ever so still, as if he were placing every part of himself aside.

When he opened his eyes, he practically sighed the invocation aloud. On his tongue, the words were gentle. Natural. The flame flickered . . . and then flared with a *whoosh*. Tall enough that she yelped and shoved the candle into the bowl of water.

It splashed all over the floor, and a few children broke out in laughter.

Ezer could see their eyes on her. On him.

Her face grew hot, even as he seemed surprised at his own success.

She plunged her hand into her pocket and grasped her speaking stone.

Fine, she growled into his mind. *You lit a candle. That does nothing to help me. The gods do not answer my call.*

Because you are angry at them, Arawn's voice snapped back. She swore she could *feel* his frustration, even as he turned and walked away, pacing about the space as if he weren't speaking to her at all. All the while, his voice caressed her mind. *Trust me. I understand more than you know. You feel abandoned by the Five. You feel insignificant. But they are still here, Minder.*

Across the room, she saw him pause and place his hand over his own heart. *Here, where it's quiet.* Then he reached up and tapped the side of his head. *Not here, where things are often a battleground of their own.*

You know nothing of my mind, Ezer thought to him, even as he was currently *in* it.

He smiled at that. *I wasn't talking about you.*

Then he was back before her again, his shadow overpowering as he knelt before her, and plucked her dripping candle out of the water.

He whispered an invocation into her mind, practically purring the request for power.

It had nothing to do with her.

But it left her breathless, wishing she could hear him sigh the invocation all over again.

Before her, the wet wick flickered to life.

His fingertips just barely grazed hers as he handed it back to her, still lit.

Then he leaned even closer, enough that she could smell the scent of woodsmoke upon him, could feel the heat coming off his skin, like he was a raging fire. His breath tickled her ear as he whispered aloud, 'You saved me, in the woods, when my own magic failed. You have power, Minder. The gods chose you to be here. And when you finally come to know it . . .' He paused, and chuckled, his eyes meeting hers as he backed away. 'Gods help anyone who stands in your way.'

And then he was back to pacing the rows of younglings.

She watched him go, all too aware of how close he'd just been.

All too aware of her pounding heart.

Little by little, the room cleared.

And still, Ezer tried.

Truly, she did, but eventually her head began to spin, so she set her candle down, and spent the rest of training staring out of the window instead. Watching the flashes of war, a place that Six would someday soon enter . . . and leave Ezer behind.

The thought pained her more than she cared to admit.

Eventually, Izill bid her goodnight with a gentle squeeze on her shoulder.

'Don't give up,' she whispered. 'It's only day one for you. It's been over a *decade* since I first tried, and I'm still here, hoping and praying.'

Ezer felt selfish, and terrible, as Izill walked away.

And then it was just her and Arawn, alone in the enormous room.

'Tell me about your magic,' he said, watching her closely. 'There's no reason to hide it. And besides. It's *your* turn to tell a truth.'

Even if it was unpillared, stained magic.

But he wasn't going to imprison her again. She trusted that much. So she sighed and tucked a dark curl behind her ear. 'I have always had a connection with the birds. It isn't just a liking, it's more like . . . they see me, and understand me. As if we are one and the same. And sometimes . . . I hear a whisper.'

'A whisper?'

'A warning on the wind,' she explained. 'It's a bit like the power of the speaking stone. But when your voice speaks, it's right there. I can . . .' She frowned. 'I can *feel* you in my mind.'

She didn't know why that made her stomach give a strange little flutter.

'The wind is more like an echo. A whisper that watches over me. It has since I was a child. But I can't call it. I certainly can't control it. I couldn't even blow out the candle.'

She glanced back at him, his pale eyes and scarred face. He was staring at her, so she slid her gaze to the warfront instead.

'Though it's different to most, the connection to the wind comes from Avane,' Arawn said. 'Perhaps . . . yours just manifests in a different way.'

'Without invocating?' Ezer asked.

'There . . . have been rare instances. A very rare few.'

He frowned for a moment, like he was considering something.

Her heart raced a bit faster until he leaned in, his voice full of wonder. 'Just imagine what it would be like if you *could*.'

'That's the problem,' Ezer said. 'The gods don't answer my prayers. They never have.'

He raised a brow. 'Haven't they?'

She blinked at him.

'You survived a shadow wolf attack. You're protected by the wind if what you say is true, and of everyone in Lordach, *you* have been chosen to tame a raphon.' He smiled sadly. 'Take it from me, Minder. Spend too much time doubting the care of the gods, and eventually . . . they might take away their gift.'

He looked down at his hands. She did not forget the way he'd reacted days ago, when someone spoke a name aloud to him. *Soraya*.

'Will it ever come back?' she asked him.

He shrugged. 'If that is their will. Months ago, I couldn't even conjure a flame.' His gaze slid to the wall of windows. 'I suppose some progress is better than none.'

'What happened to cause it?' Ezer dared ask.

What did you do?

He tensed. She'd pressed too hard, and she could sense that his walls were back up. 'It's getting late.'

'You're right,' Ezer said. She was about to bid him goodnight when she realized he was walking *away* from the exit doors . . . to a small rack of wooden training swords in the corner of the room that she hadn't paid any mind to before.

Her heart sank.

'No,' Ezer said. 'Absolutely not.'

He tossed a wooden training sword at her feet.

With a groan, she knelt to scoop up the sword and held it back out to him. 'I am *not* a soldier.'

'Not yet,' Arawn said with a shrug of his enormous shoulders. 'But by the time I'm done with you . . . you will be.'

Morning came, and Ezer woke as stiff as a corpse. Every muscle in her body felt like she'd been run over by a prison wagon.

'I *can't*,' she groaned as Izill paused at her bedside, clucking at her to get up before she was late. 'I can't do today.'

'Dear gods, what did he *do* to you?'

'Physical fitness.' Ezer yelped as she rose on throbbing legs. Even lifting her arms to rub the sleep from her eyes was hell. She hissed between her teeth.

For two hours, Arawn had made her train, barking out commands like a true soldier. She'd hefted the wooden sword, failing at blocking his advances. And then he'd moved on to hand-to-hand combat.

He'd finally finished the entire lesson with pushups and squats.

She was so tired she'd fallen into her bed last night without taking her boots off.

But sleep had been hard to come by, because for some reason, the second she closed her eyes . . .

She saw the way he'd looked with sweat beading on his brow.

She remembered every line of his body, all the hard angles and wiry muscles beneath his skin. And how it had felt when his hands had lingered on her hips, ever so gently showing her how to perfect her stance.

How she'd found it hard to breathe . . . and it had nothing to do with how exhausted she was.

She needed to get herself *away* from the Crown Prince, before it caused her another bout of trouble she didn't want.

She was nothing to him.

And he was nothing to her.

'Why would anyone *choose* to put themselves through that hell?' Ezer asked now.

Izill frowned and helped her towards the fireside. 'To survive. Which Arawn is going to have a hard time doing, prince or not, when I'm done with him.'

Despite the pain in her ribs, Ezer laughed.

The Aviary was almost empty when she arrived, drenched in sweat despite the cold.

It had taken her three times as long as it normally did to make the ascent, every step like a knife to her thighs.

I hope you're true to your word, Izill, Ezer thought darkly as she ripped open the Aviary doors and entered. *I hope you make Arawn pay.*

She groaned when she stepped inside . . . because Zey was already there.

Today, the Eagleminder looked tired as she gathered a saddle from one of the racks on the walls. Her blonde hair was falling out of its braid, the strands greasy as they hung over her face. She reached up to tuck them behind her ears.

And Ezer's stomach sank as she noticed the mark on Zey's hand.

Her *other* hand. Like she'd paid penance yet again.

She had a small youngling with her and was busy piling the heavy things into the child's scrawny arms. Ezer waited until the boy was gone before she approached.

'Zey.'

'Ah, if it isn't Wolf Bait,' said the Eagleminder. 'Still standing? I'm surprised the raphon hasn't killed you yet.'

Even her devilish smirk was off kilter.

She smelled like liquor again as she tried to step past Ezer.

'I could say the same about you,' Ezer said. She looked at Zey's hand. 'You were punished again. Why?'

Zey glared at her. 'Get out of my way.'

'No,' Ezer said. She glanced over her shoulder, but nobody else was around. 'This isn't right.'

'And what would you know about *right*?' Zey asked. 'There are laws. Sometimes we break them.'

'And so they break you in return?' Ezer asked.

The Sacred were supposed to be pious, pure, but if they broke a law . . .

Physical penance was not something she'd ever seen in the writings of the gods, nor whispered about in the south. Nobody knew the truth about this.

It was *wrong*.

Zey's youngling came back around the corner, but a glare from Zey, and he suddenly seemed to remember he had elsewhere to be.

'We don't speak about it,' Zey hissed. 'We do as we are told, and if we mess up, we pay penance. Our blood pays the price for our sins against the Five. It is our way.'

'But it's not *right*,' Ezer said.

Zey's eyes hardened. 'And why should I care about the opinion of an Unconsecrated?'

Ezer crossed her arms. 'Because nobody deserves to be treated like . . .' She looked down at her ankles and remembered the way her chains used to weigh heavy upon her. 'Like a prisoner.'

'I can leave any time I like,' Zey said.

'And risk getting kicked out of the Ehver, spending an eternity in darkness because of it?' Ezer asked. 'That's what the punishment is for laying down your vows. Isn't it?'

She didn't want to think about her mother or father, whoever had been Sacred, ending up with that same fate.

The Eagleminder's jaw went taut, but she glanced past Ezer's shoulder. 'I have a job to do. I cannot be late.'

'What would happen if you were?' Ezer asked.

Zey didn't answer, so Ezer caught back up to her, reaching out.

'Touch me, and I swear it will be the last time you use that hand,' Zey growled.

Ezer dropped her hand. On instinct, she reached for the stone in her pocket . . . but decided against it.

She did not need Arawn to fight her battles for her.

She followed Zey instead, keeping pace with the Eagleminder despite the soreness in every step.

'You hate me,' Ezer said, 'because I took the job you wanted. Is that it?'

Zey flicked her blonde hair over her shoulder. 'The Sacred do not *hate*, Wolf Bait.'

'Then you strongly dislike me to the point that you'd rather me be as miserable as you,' Ezer said. '*Why?*'

For a moment, she thought Zey might actually hit her. Surely there was a law about that. But the Eagleminder surprised her when she paused her walking and said, 'Because you have what I cannot.'

'I don't have anything,' Ezer said back, exasperated.

Not a home, nor a family.

She wasn't even certain she had true magic, despite what Arawn said.

'You have *choices*,' Zey growled. 'Don't ever let anyone take them from you.' She was tall and beautiful and everything Ezer was not. But she looked miserable, like the swiftly ageing Knight she'd seen marching into battle last night. There was no life in her eyes. 'You never should have come here. If I were you . . . I'd leave before it's too late.'

Ezer's breathing hitched. 'Too late for what?'

But Zey had already turned and left.

CHAPTER 19

Kinlear was not waiting for her at the black doors.

Instead, there stood a servant boy in brown robes. He had Kinlear's key around his neck and a letter in his hands.

'Where's the prince?' Ezer asked.

'His royal highness is indisposed,' the boy said. 'He sent me to deliver this.'

He pressed a small scroll into Ezer's hands, the seal unbroken. It was the crest of Lordach, the familiar outspread eagle wings with five stars above, but Kinlear's own initials had been marked into them. Ezer popped it open, and read:

Dearest Raphonminder,

I will be indisposed for the next several days, attending to a private matter. Please continue your efforts with the pup. I expect that you will have it haltered and gentled enough for ground training by the time I return. You have five days.

With eagerness,
Prince Kinlear Laroux

P.S.
I needn't remind you of what will happen to Lordach should you fail to meet the deadline.

The success of the Black Wing Battalion rests upon your shoulders.

Ezer scoffed at the letter.

As if gentling a wild raphon pup was something that could be met by a *deadline*.

She hated deadlines. They were like stamps on a grave, crippling her creativity, her methods. Each time she'd had to rush training a new raven for the messaging route, it had never returned to her tower.

To dare rush a *raphon*?

She may as well ask it to eat her for supper.

'Am I able to send a letter back?' Ezer asked.

The boy brought her a bit of parchment and ink, so Ezer quickly knelt to the stones and scribbled a response.

Dearest Prince,

Please, do take your time with your duties. I will give my utmost efforts to successfully halter and gentle the beast before Realmbreak, but I cannot make any promises, as some creatures tend to be driven wild by force. Even wilder, by timely force.

With patience,

Your Most Loyal Raphonminder

P.S.
I needn't remind you what may happen should the pup decide to kill your last and final hope at completing the mission of the Black Wing Battalion.

She smiled and folded it up, handing it back to the boy.

'I'll be back at noon,' he said as he unlocked the door to the catacombs, 'as per the prince's orders.'

And then Ezer was alone in the tunnel, heading towards Six.

The torches were dimly lit today, but she didn't mind. With her scarred eyed, she could navigate the shadows just fine. Sometimes, she felt more comfortable in the darkness anyhow.

True to his word, Kinlear had left a new halter hanging beside Six's cage. It was leather, marked with softly glowing runes she assumed were meant to strengthen it, and not a single bit of chain.

And he'd kept Six's shackles off, though they were still in the corner of the cell, abandoned like the sloughed skin of a snake. Six was in the opposite corner, as far from them as she could get.

Ezer's cloak was still held beneath her paws like a little treasure.

A classic *raven* thing to do, for they'd always collected trinkets in their nests. A little *pang* reverberated in her chest. She missed her ravens dearly, though being with Six filled a few of the holes.

'We'll remove the chains from your cell,' Ezer promised. She bit back a yelp as she settled her aching body on the soft shavings across from the pup. 'But first, I'm going to need a bit of cooperation from you. How do you feel about haltering?'

Six just watched her in silence.

'Of course, you don't understand. But I've always spoken to my birds, and I'm to do the same with you. Even if you *are* half cat.'

Six blinked slowly, and she swore the raphon opened its curved beak and yawned.

'I'm sorry,' she said, 'am I *boring* you?'

The raphon just lifted its too-large paw and scratched its feathered neck with sharp black claws, the motion positively catlike.

'Well.' Ezer chewed on her fingernail. 'If we're to do this, as the ever so *lovely* prince requests . . . then we'll have to speed things up a bit. Yes? I've a new halter for you, just there on the hook. Black leather, no chains . . .'

She mused aloud, talking as much as she would with her own ravens. Six watched her intently the entire time.

You want the birds to see you as a comfort, never a threat, she remembered Ervos teaching her about the ravens long ago. She could still picture him standing there in the tower, while he held a raven on his enormous wrist, and the bird slept soundly. *You want the bird to look forward to your time together. Like you are an old, trusted friend, so that when it leaves, it will return. So that when you move to tie the scroll to its leg, it will trust you. It will welcome your touch.*

So, for the next two days, Ezer sat and spoke.

Nothing more.

And on the third day, true to Ervos's word . . . Six was sitting up, waiting for her expectantly.

'Hello,' Ezer said, smiling at the pup. Kinlear had still not returned, and she was beginning to enjoy her solo visits.

Especially because *here* there was no Arawn to force her to train. And train, they had.

Her body hated her for it.

But her mind . . .

It was not a safe space to be in, especially when she lay down each night and replayed every second of their session. The earthy smell of him, the feel of his body as he'd pushed her backwards to the mat and whispered into her mind, *You're dead, Minder. Get up and do it again, and this time . . . don't hesitate.*

And then, each night when she finally fell into bed, soaking wet from a cold shower . . . it was *his* voice that whispered against the walls of her, the speaking stone hot in her hand. They spoke for hours, never going too deep with the truths they revealed about themselves, but she found she was hungry for more of his words.

More of his whispers.

Last night, he'd called her by her name.

Goodnight, Ezer.

Goodnight, Arawn.

And she dared face the truth that she *cared* for him. In a way that was not at all safe.

She'd finally placed the stone inside her trunk so she could sleep, unwilling to go further down the road they were both traveling.

Six's head cocked to the side now, as she watched Ezer gingerly settle down on the shavings. The white scar on her beak looked almost orange in the nearby torchlight.

'Training,' Ezer groaned. Every part of her ached, down to her bones. Even her mind.

Because along with the physical training, she'd still attended her magic sessions each night – the same damned routine with Izill beside her, both of them trying and failing to garner any sort of power.

The gods would not answer.

'Good thing here, we can hide and be safe from the mean prince,' Ezer said with a groan. 'Princ*es*, actually,' she corrected herself.

Six's tail twitched once.

In the darkness and silence, Ezer whispered soft words to her, telling Six a slew of tales the way she used to with her ravens. She spoke of Ervos and showed Six her mother's ring. A Ring of Finding, utterly useless now. She spoke of her fear of heights, the whisper upon the wind, and the shadow wolf that had nearly killed her in the woods.

She showed her the speaking stone, at which Six huffed in annoyance.

Like she didn't want to share any part of Ezer, and she supposed that was fair.

'It's best here with you and I, anyway,' Ezer said, and she meant it. 'Girl time is good for the soul.'

She wasn't even sure if Six could understand her, but each time she paused her talking, the pup would twitch its catlike tail and place its dark eyes upon her, as if to say, *another story, please*.

'All right,' Ezer said, 'then I'll continue the tale of—'

It surprised her when Six rose to all fours.

And quietly, carefully, padded over to settle down with her head on Ezer's lap.

The weight of her beak was enough to make Ezer grunt, but she found the warmth of Six instantly soothing. It washed the cold of the cell away.

Ezer relaxed back into the stones.

'Hello there,' she said. 'I dare say we're becoming friends.'

She kept her hands to herself, allowing Six to lay calmly across her.

She spoke for a time more, telling Six all the tales of her childhood, how Ervos had changed before her eyes, how he'd left her . . . and how she'd been alone, a floundering thing, ever since.

'And now, if I don't have you visibly *gentled* within the next two days,' Ezer started, 'I'm not certain what my fate will be. Nor yours.'

She often spoke with her hands, and when she lowered them back down to rest on Six's scarred beak, her vision suddenly shifted.

It grew dark at the edges, and before she knew it, she was sucked into a vision.

No longer was it the single feather, floating alone.

Five others floated alongside it. All identical in shape and size, and Ezer watched as they began to sink. One by one, they faded beneath the dark waves, never to be seen again.

The vision lasted until Ezer pulled her hand away.

She had to push past the sadness she felt in her core. The sense of mourning that she'd had in her own heart since losing Ervos . . . and she knew it came from the raphon.

'It's you, isn't it?' she asked Six. 'The dark feather in your visions? The only one left. The prince told me about what happened to the others in your litter. Your siblings.'

Six's tail twitched, only once.

And then the beast sighed deeply, and Ezer could have sworn Six turned her head just so Ezer could study her scar.

'You're a survivor,' Ezer said, and turned her own cheek. 'Like me.'

Six's breath washed across her face, as if she were studying the shadow wolf marks.

'I'm sorry,' Ezer said, 'that you've been in here this whole time. You can leave, you know. You need only work with me. We've a mutual goal to get out of this awful cage.'

The vision hit again, just as sudden as before.

She felt her body rooted to the spot, but in her mind . . .

It was the same dark feather floating in the sea. But now another joined it, caught up in a current, only this one was white.

Like a delicate dove.

The vision broke, and Ezer was left staring down at the top of the raphon's head again.

It was positively jarring, and yet . . . something sparked in the back of her mind. A story Ervos had told her once, long ago, about a princess and her pet dragon. A magical companionship, as lovely as it was fearsome, for the two had forged a lifelong bond.

When the dragon died, a part of the princess died, too, for they'd forged their souls into one being. It was heartbreak that killed the princess in the end, for she was unable to live without that bond.

Ezer had cried the first time Ervos told her the story. It wasn't real, she knew, for dragons didn't exist in Lordach. Only wyverns.

But perhaps she could take something from the tale.

'You use the visions to speak to me,' she said as she scratched the top of the raphon's head. 'Is that right?'

She barely noticed when Six's tail twitched, just once.

'I don't suppose that would be possible. But . . .'

Another twitch of Six's tail.

Ezer widened her eyes.

'You *are* speaking to me. Aren't you?' Ezer asked. 'Show me again.'

It seemed impossible that the raphon could do such a thing. Because that would require *magic* of some sort. Magic that would allow a single touch to spark a vision into Ezer's mind. Magic that no one seemed to know about, in all the books she'd read on raphons, in all the journal entries she'd looked back on thus far.

Not even Kinlear knew about what the beast could do.

But the vision suddenly came again, as if truly on command, stealing her sight away to that dark and swirling sea.

Two feathers floated side by side, one dark and one light.

Ezer kept her hand on the pup's head, desperate to hold on to the image in her mind. It faded anyway, as if Six was done speaking.

'It's you,' she said. 'And me.'

She felt it, as sure as she felt the stones behind her head, the coldness lingering inside the cell.

And Six's tail twitched again, just once.

'*Yes*,' whispered the wind.

Its arrival was sudden, but not unwelcome. She'd missed its voice lately, but she supposed that meant she'd also been out of any true danger.

Ezer grinned.

'Do you have magic, Six?'

A single twitch.

Yes.

'Incredible,' Ezer breathed. 'Does anyone else know?'

This time, the beast twitched her tail twice.

No.

No open-ended questions would do, but at least they had a way forward now. A mutual understanding of one another's wants and needs.

Ezer's heart began to pound in excitement.

'The others,' she said. 'All the Eagleminders that came before. Did you try and speak to them, too?'

A long pause, and Ezer's heart roared in her ears as she waited for Six to respond.

Then a single twitch of her tail.

Yes.

Which meant that, for whatever reason . . . she was the only one who'd ever heard. The only one who'd ever received the messages from the pup and understood.

The question was . . .

Why her?

When Ezer made it to her dorm that afternoon, she found Zey curled up by the fire, a book in her hands. Her pale hair was down, not smooth as before but tangled like she'd just awoken from a restless sleep.

'Zey?' Ezer approached her slowly, the way she would have a wild raphon. She'd rarely seen the Eagleminder sitting with anyone, even when they took meals. She seemed a floating island . . . all alone. 'I need to talk to you.'

A moment passed, and she wondered if the Eagleminder would ignore her entirely.

But then Zey sighed and aggressively turned a page in her book. 'I'm busy. Why don't you run along and find Izill instead?'

'You're the only Eagleminder I know,' Ezer said. *And Kinlear is still nowhere to be found.* She waited until the silence was painful before she added, 'Please, Zey.'

Another flick of the Eagleminder's pages.

'What's in it for me?'

Ezer crossed her arms. 'We're fighting the same war, aren't we?'

Zey chuckled. '*You* are not fighting, Wolf Bait.'

Without her cloak, in just a tunic and trousers, she looked thinner than Ezer remembered. Her eyes looked tired and shallow. Eagleminders did not wield, so they did not age supernaturally as the Sacred Knights did.

No, this was a different sort of fading away. It seemed to come from her very soul.

Ezer sighed. 'I'm still doing my part. I only need two minutes of your time, Zey. I don't think that sacrifice is too much to ask of you.'

At that, Zey shut her book with a *snap*.

And her pale eyes slid up to meet Ezer's.

'Easy to speak of sacrifice,' she mused, 'when you aren't the sacrificial lamb.' She picked at something on her cloak. 'Go on. Ask your questions. The clock is ticking.'

Ezer swallowed the lump in her throat. 'What happens when you train an Eagle? Tell me about it from the start.'

Zey yawned, like she was already bored. 'The war eagles have lived and bred in captivity for centuries, so their nature is already to obey. But each beast takes time. Trust must be gained before they'll really listen. When a Sacred is young, we're introduced to the war eagle fledglings.'

'And they choose you,' Ezer said almost reverently, remembering the stories she'd always heard. How magical it must be to be chosen by one of the godmounts.

But at that, Zey laughed bitterly. 'You poor, naive little creature. Do you believe every story you've heard from the *nomages*? Eagleminders are *assigned*, not chosen. There's a sort of trial, every few years, with each crop of fledglings. The War Table starves the beasts for three days. Then they set us loose in the Eagle's Nest – weaponless – with buckets full to the brim with bleeding meat. It is only the ones who do not run away screaming that are given the job.'

Ezer leaned forward. 'But that's cruel.'

And not at all what she'd been told.

'And you think they care about that?' Zey said. She produced a silver flask from her pocket. 'You came here with stories. Rumors. Mythical ideas about what it's like to be a Sacred. Some of the *nomages* fear us, but most revere us, dreaming of what it would be like to have our magic. They think we are immune to feelings, to temptation—' She raised her flask, and Ezer realized she'd probably been drinking here all afternoon. 'Well, I'm happy to be the one to darken your stars.' She took another long sip. 'My title may be Sacred. But I am just a woman, taught to ignore my instincts. And the eagles are just eagles, forced to do the same.'

A log broke in the fire.

For some reason, Ezer jumped.

'But . . . it doesn't make any sense,' Ezer whispered. 'The gods wouldn't want it that way.'

'And what way would they have it be?' Zey asked.

Ezer didn't have an answer. But this felt dangerous. Utterly raw, and she suddenly felt the urge to look over her shoulder, because if she was caught speaking this way . . .

She feared finding marks upon the backs of her own hands.

She actually feared what would happen to Zey, who seemed to be sliding down an icy slope, with nothing but darkness at the end of her descent.

'How do you train them?' Ezer asked. 'Surely a bond begins, after all the work.'

'We lead them through the motions of haltering, saddling, mounting, following the pattern of Minders who came before. Eventually, we break through the fledgling's desire to fight back.'

'But what does it *feel* like?' Ezer pressed.

'It's not a feeling,' Zey said, exasperated. 'It's a march. The result of time spent doing the same thing again and again. *Repetition leads to success*.' She frowned. 'Why are you asking me this?'

Ezer sat back, deflated. It couldn't be true. She was eager to understand her own place in this, with Six, because she'd tapped into something.

And she thought maybe it was the way it always was, when a Minder found their match in a winged beast.

But now she only had more questions. About herself, about the raphon. About her magic.

'And how do you get them to trust you when it really counts? To obey even when the war rages, and a Knight's life depends upon their eagle?'

Zey's green eyes met hers.

'The same way a Sacred learns to obey the laws. We break them. We shatter every instinct they have to disobey our commands. Look closely at the war eagles, and you will see they are branded. Just as I am.'

A cold sweat formed on Ezer's forehead, and she suddenly wanted to put out the fire. 'The eagles pay penance? That's—'

'Cruel?' Zey asked, with a dark laugh and another sip from her flask. 'It's the Citadel, in the midst of a twenty-year war with an enemy we cannot see nor understand. An enemy the War Table would do anything to defeat. Even if it means letting our King waste himself away.'

'So, there is no bond,' Ezer said softly. 'No magic that connects a war eagle to its trainer, its rider, soul-deep.'

Nothing that would give reason to how Six and I share a bond.

Or how I can see the things she sees.

How I can feel her pain like it is my own.

'Sometimes stories are just stories,' Zey said, and stood. 'And sometimes the truth is far worse. My best advice? Don't get too close to the raphon. It will be gone soon, given to someone else to finish out its journey, just like all the eagles I have spent my life training. Give it your heart, Wolf Bait . . . and it will fly away with it. And once it reaches the other side of the wards . . . there's a good chance it's never coming back.'

Her eyes were red as she stood and left, her book discarded in her spot.

'Wait,' Ezer said, and scooped up the book. 'You left your—'

She frowned, pausing as the yellowed pages fluttered open, pushed as if by the wind.

'*Look*,' it whispered suddenly. '*See.*'

Ezer stared down at the pages, confused.

Because the book Zey had been reading, so intently . . .

Every page was blank.

CHAPTER 20

The next day, when Ezer woke, she received the news.

It was given in the form of hushed whispers, of worried looks and shock and for some, even poorly veiled smiles.

'What's going on?' Ezer asked as Izill wheeled in the day's breakfast.

'You haven't heard?' Izill wore one lovely, long braid today, and she twisted the end nervously around her fingertips. 'Zey took an eagle early this morning, when she wasn't slated to fly. Nobody noticed until it was already too late.' She locked eyes with Ezer. They were red, like she'd been crying. 'I've served her my entire life. She wasn't always awful. Not all at once. At one point . . . she was a part of us.'

'Where did she go?' Ezer asked, heart racing. Her eyes flicked to the book she'd left on Zey's trunk last night, not wanting to bother the Eagleminder again.

But she already knew, even before Izill said, 'She was last seen going north . . . towards the Sawteeth. To defect.'

'Did anyone go after her?' Ezer asked.

Izill shook her head. 'Her eagle came back without her, and there's no telling if she made it, with how heavy the day's snows have been. Even if there was a body to recover . . .' A sniffle as Izill looked away and whispered, 'She would have been left for the wolves to devour. She made her choice. She's *gone*.'

Ezer placed an awkward hand on her shoulder and sat there silently while Izill cried.

She should have been horrified. Perhaps she even should have been relieved the Eagleminder was gone, for Zey had not had a shred of kindness to share.

But in her mind, in her heart . . .

She hoped that Zey was out there, somewhere. Alive.

Free.

News of Zey's defection had spread across the Citadel like wildfire. People whispered about the marks on her hands, the harshness of her words, the way she'd failed in her demonstration with the eagle, and perhaps *that* was why she'd run . . . because she couldn't handle the embarrassment.

Some said she'd gone with no hopes to defect, but rather to escape her vows to the gods entirely. To die as she pleased.

Her story became a spectacle. A rumor.

But no one beyond Izill seemed to care about the absence of *her* as a person . . . the yawning emptiness that should have been present in their eyes, knowing one of their own was gone.

It put Ezer in a foul mood, made her breakfast tasteless, her conversations short. Zey's face stuck in her mind as she left the dorm behind.

She couldn't quite place why until she came into the courtyard and stood before the ancient frozen tree. Her breath clouded before her as she stared at the swords plunged into the snow, one for each of their fallen comrades.

She reached her hand into her pocket, feeling for the stone she didn't dare leave behind in her dorm. It was like a comfort now.

An anchor that kept her grounded.

The stone warmed almost instantly.

Will there be a sword for her? Ezer asked. She gave no greeting, no hello.

And she was breathing too hard, panicked for some reason she didn't quite understand.

For Zey? No, Minder. His voice sighed gently against her mind, and she closed her eyes, leaning into the safety net the sound of it had become. *When a Sacred leaves their post and their vows behind, no matter the reason . . . they are dead to us. They are forever gone, wiped from the records. As if they never existed at all.*

That would explain why Ezer had yet to find anything on her mother or father.

So nobody mourns her, Ezer thought back.

They mourn. His voice was unusually gentle. *Just . . . not where others can see. To do so would be to show some sort of allegiance to Zey's choice, over our allegiance to the gods.* He was quiet again, and she thought he'd gone until his voice whispered, with an almost palpable wave of sadness, *She made her choice. We must learn to live without her now.*

She didn't think he was speaking entirely about Zey.

The stone went cold.

How many others, Ezer wondered, who had spent their lives here, trying and failing like Zey, were dead without anything to remember them by?

And then Ezer wondered, with a lump in her throat . . .

Would anyone mourn me?

She hoped Izill and Arawn would, and Kinlear was more a mystery now than ever. But beyond them . . .

Her loss would be like the countless other names on scrolls. There would be no sword plunged in the snow. No stories told.

And she hated the thought of it. Of fading away, forgotten to time.

Snow kissed her nose and cheeks as she looked skyward. Past the Citadel, to the normal world she'd been plucked from. Full of *nomages* and Ravenminder towers and so many innocents, who would all die if she did not succeed.

War had stolen too many lives.

It had left too many children like Ezer behind.

They'll sing songs about you, Kinlear had said. *The Raphonminder who changed the fate of Lordach.*

And as the snow fell around her, and she followed the pull of the wind towards Six . . .

She decided, then and there, that she would be remembered.

No matter what it took.

After that, Ezer spent every second she could with Six.

Each day she arrived, she found Kinlear missing, even when his deadline of five days had passed. She supposed it should have been a relief that he hadn't yet returned. Her dreams were a warning that she could not trust him.

But it only left her with a sizzling sort of fury.

He'd been quick to throw her into service with Six . . . but hadn't the decency to return to check up on her progress in person. Like he couldn't be bothered.

He left a letter for her each new day, written in lovely black ink.

And with each one, he now sent gifts.

Piles of books tied in delicate silk ribbon.

Heaped bags of milk chocolates, or fresh strips of polished leather to hold her curls back in a braid, to show he'd learned her likings. Like he had eyes watching her.

It was both a comfort and a subtly veiled threat.

She took the gifts anyway, grateful for something to do with Six to pass the hours. She read the books aloud as she walked, and discovered Six had no patience for romances. No, she liked cold, blood-soaked thrillers instead.

'You may be a raphon, but I'm not certain this content is appropriate for a creature not even a year old,' Ezer told her.

Six had left a pile of waste upon the romance books in response, and so thrillers it was.

Ezer brought in a wheelbarrow and mucking rake, and cleaned Six's cage. It was exhausting work, and her sore arms throbbed as she cleaned the shavings, despite Six's annoyance.

The raphon hated the mucking rake and had even tried to swipe it from Ezer's hands with a paw.

'It's not a weapon,' Ezer said as the pup twitched her tail twice – a very obvious *no*.

Six still sat there, glaring at the rake as if it were a snake.

Ezer supposed she shared the same look when Arawn handed her a training sword each night.

'This place reeks of death, and I'm not certain I'll survive another few hours in here with you. Now move, *please*, so I can clean it all up.'

The raphon scurried away, tail twitching near her face as Ezer continued to clean.

She managed to take Six's measurements for a saddle, another dance that had Six skittering away from her – even knocking her against the wall and earning her a sprained wrist. She'd gone to Alaris to fix it, and the healer had only clucked her tongue like a disapproving grandmother.

'Progress is slow, then?' Alaris asked.

Ezer sighed, and asked, 'Can I borrow that pair of forceps?'

The healer had offered them up, confused, as Ezer smiled and left the room.

She had discovered that she had to offer a shiny bauble to Six as a gift each day:

Alaris's silver forceps. A tiny golden teaspoon from her breakfast.

A copper candlestick from her dormitory.

Even a book with gilded edges, courtesy of Kinlear's daily gift.

They were silly things, but they were all glowing and shimmering and to the raven side of the raphon, each one was utterly irresistible. And Six had been perfectly pliable when given such gifts, enough that Ezer could lift her paws, and touch her tail, and polish her scarred beak.

Enough that Six finally bowed her head and allowed Ezer to get the halter close enough to slide it on.

And when a full week passed . . .

Kinlear still didn't show.

But he had sent another letter back with Izill. Ezer practically growled in frustration as she tore it open.

It was beginning to feel familiar, the *being left behind* sort of thing. The waiting.

Dearest Raphonminder,

My messenger informs me that you are making slow, if any at all, true progress with the pup.
Consider this a gentle reminder, while I am away.

The fate of Lordach rests on your shoulders.

With Fervor,
Prince Kinlear Laroux

'Sorry,' Izill said with a wince, as she handed Ezer another gift.

This time, it was a shiny golden bangle for her wrist.

She gave it right to Six.

Yet another week passed, and Ezer practiced haltering and un-haltering the raphon, until they reached a perfect little dance together.

Six skittered away, tossed her head, slashed her paws.

Ezer cursed at her, earned some sort of wound, and in the end, she had to offer up a shiny item until Six finally relented and allowed her a chance to buckle the halter over her neck and beak.

Each afternoon, Ezer spent curled up in the library, warmed

by the fire and the smell of old books, until her training began. She spent hours researching Sacred magic, hoping to track down someone who could share visions with a beast of any kind. She'd even had the librarian search through the archives of those born in the Citadel. There were hundreds of books, names scribbled in ancient ink. But her eyes had crossed after only a few tomes.

'You're distracted,' Arawn said, on another night inside the training room.

Their routine was now something she'd begun to look forward to.

Not because of the training – gods, she still *hated* that – but because he'd quickly become a true friend. Someone she could be herself with, no matter how bad her attitude, nor how much she smelled like a raphon.

'Because your brother still hasn't shown to check up on my progress with Six.'

She yelped and lifted her wooden sword as he advanced.

'And that's a problem, *why*?' Arawn asked.

Gods, he was strong, even though she knew he was holding back.

'Because he doesn't even care to see me!' Ezer growled, then lunged forward. 'He has no clue about the work I have done with Six.'

He tripped her with his sword, then caught her before her face could slam against the floor.

'As much as I do not wish to defend my brother's honor,' Arawn said with a sigh as he set her back upright, 'he has good reason to be absent. Give him time.'

'And what reason could be as good as ensuring his Raphon-minder isn't *dead*? It's been two weeks.'

She whirled and avoided another hit, proud of herself . . .

Until the tip of his sword hovered just beyond her throat.

She growled in frustration, sweat dripping down her temples.

His hand slipped into his pocket, where he always kept his speaking stone.

Have you considered that maybe he trusts you to do your job? Maybe he's allowing you the space you need to succeed on your own? A smirk, and he added, *You're dead, by the way.*

I can see that, Ezer thought back as she gripped her own speaking stone. *I do not like to be kept waiting. I do not like to be ignored. The gods have done that plenty, when it comes to me.*

He frowned. *He'll return soon enough. And . . . it also sounds like your heart still isn't right.*

My heart? She released her stone to wipe sweat from her eyes, and spoke aloud next, needing him to understand. 'My heart is *fine*. I'm just not a warrior, Arawn. I'm a Minder. Hence, I do things *with my mind*, and not a godsdamned sword. Certainly not with magic, for how many nights I've tried. What's the point of this anyway, if I'm only to ready Six to fly with a rider and not go across myself . . .?'

His face gave nothing away. 'The point is that you're a Sacred. It is your birthright to learn. And the gods, much like my brother, are on their own timetable. Sometimes it is to our benefit to wait.'

She tried to strike him in the chest . . . but he easily batted her sword to the floor.

'Lose your weapon and die,' Arawn said gently. 'Pick it up. Try again but remember to keep your arms strong. Mean it, Minder, when you strike to kill.'

'I wasn't striking to kill,' Ezer said sweetly. 'I was striking to piss you off.'

He lunged for her, faster than she could evade.

'You must have clarity of mind –' he struck, she failed to block – 'and heart –' another blow landed to her chest – 'each time you invocate.'

His body slammed against hers, and she hit the ground with a *whoosh* of breath, and then he was standing over her, with his sword poised just over her heart.

'Dead. *Again*.' He frowned. 'What will you do when a darksoul or a shadow wolf comes for you? If you cannot invocate *now*, how will you do it when your life is in mortal danger?'

She winced, remembering the fit she'd had earlier that evening, when she'd lost *all* clarity of mind and thrown the candle in frustration. The wind would *not* come to her call, despite how well she'd learned to invocate the request to Avane.

Her attempts at wielding were more like . . .

Furious desperation.

'There isn't going to be a darksoul or shadow wolf that comes for me,' Ezer tried.

He struck harder, faster.

'We have no clue what the future holds.'

She sidestepped and ducked to avoid a hit to her temple.

He wasn't holding back tonight.

'We have the wards,' she said, and swung.

But he was ready for her and rapped her on the ribs. Hard enough to make her yelp, but not hard enough to truly break anything. He was helping her learn her own grit. Helping her see that she could take a hit and keep standing on her own two feet.

'And what if you find yourself *beyond* those wards?' he asked. 'What happens then?'

She paused and raised a brow. Because they both knew what happened last time.

She'd nearly been eaten alive . . . until the ravens.

'I don't *know*,' Ezer growled.

'That is exactly why you must train.' His eyes fell to her sword. 'Again.'

'No,' she said. 'I'm tired.'

'You're *quitting*?'

'Yes,' she hissed. 'I'm never going to need to—'

'You *must* learn, Ezer, or someday you will *die*!' he growled. 'You will die out there. And it will be *my fault* for not training you hard enough.'

His voice echoed off the cavernous walls.

'I'm . . . doing my best,' she said, and she couldn't hide the hurt in her voice. 'I'm sorry if that's not good enough for you.'

But he sheathed his sword, and when he met her eyes again, some part of him was gone. 'Sometimes . . . I swear you were sent to punish me, Ezer. Because you act just like *her*. And when it counted . . . when it mattered the most . . . she couldn't save herself. And I couldn't save her either.'

His words hit her like a brick to the chest. Suddenly it was hard to breathe, hard to think straight.

She didn't even know what to say. But it didn't matter anyhow.

Because before she could reply, he'd already turned and gone.

The entire next day, the stone in Ezer's pocket remained cold.

After a session in which Six had panicked over a mouse scurrying through her cage, Ezer limped to Alaris's office, nursing what had to be a broken toe.

She'd navigated the route back to her dormitory plenty of times, but she was so stuck in her head, lost in her thoughts, that this time she took a wrong turn.

And somehow ended up on the threshold of a door she had not seen before.

It was a lovely thing.

As golden as the Aviary doors, and so heavy she didn't think she'd be able to heave it open, were it not already ajar.

She wouldn't have gone inside if she hadn't heard the sound of music.

Gods, it had been so long since she'd heard music.

It was soft and delicate, a trilling instrument that reminded her of the old days with Ervos, when they sat on the outskirts of the city and listened to the faraway concerts that were saved mostly for the wealthy.

She knew the song it was playing.

A mournful tune . . . one she often heard like an echo when she thought of her mother.

She slipped inside, too curious to stop herself.

And paused when her feet found fresh-fallen snow.

Another courtyard, Ezer thought, as she entered.

She had to be in the center of the Citadel, the rounded white walls around her protected by the enormous fortress on all sides. Snow danced down from the sky, kissing the space.

Marble pillars spanned to her left and right, carved runes twinkling beneath the wardlight. Somehow the snow still trickled through it, another mysterious kiss of the gods' magic. Rows of long worn wooden benches stretched all the way to a raised dais. They, too, were rune-marked, the snow hissing before it touched the ancient wood, so they remained clear and dry.

Pillowy white drifts had piled up all around them, so the entire space seemed nestled.

Tucked away for when it was needed most.

Beside the dais – upon which sat five pillars with five bowls of fire, one for each color of pillared magic – sat a harpist.

She wore gray robes, a hood covering her long black tresses from the snow. Her long fingers stroked the strings of the golden instrument, every note as sweet as the snowflakes that danced gently around her.

Ezer sighed and slid onto a bench, reveling in the warmth of the runed wood.

Ervos would have loved to hear this song.

I miss you, she thought. *I wish I could see you one last time. I wish you could help me with Six.*

Because if *she* had a gift with the raphon . . . surely, Ervos would have been better.

For a time, she simply listened, allowing the song to swim

through her veins. She stared at the depictions of the Five carved all around her . . . strangely at peace.

Which was broken by the sound of footsteps, then the groaning of a bench as someone sat down just behind her.

She glanced back, thinking it would be Arawn arriving to explain himself after his outburst. Or perhaps Izill, making sure she kept to her eating schedule for the day.

But when she turned around . . .

Her peace shattered.

And she looked right into the cold blue gaze of King Draybor Laroux.

She knew she should have bowed, should have averted her gaze, but she was frozen.

'Y-your Highness,' Ezer sputtered.

He hardly looked like the man she had seen just weeks ago. His shoulders, once broad and enormous with muscle, seemed to have shrunk even further. His face was so deeply lined with wrinkles he looked like he'd melted, like a wax figure left to sit beneath the sun. His hair was now fully white, thinning beneath his golden crown. Two marks, for his two pillars.

The magic that was clearly killing him, each time he had to invocate in battle.

No one in Lordach truly knew how bad a Sacred's ageing was.

No one really knew what it was like when they spent themselves like this.

When they wasted away for obeying their gods.

'My second-born seems to think you are making progress with the beast,' the King said. 'I expect it to be ready for a Demonstration soon enough.'

No greeting . . . he went straight for the throat.

'Several weeks of training, and you have yet to settle upon a pillar of magic,' the King said.

Ezer's veins went cold.

Of course, he knew. He had to know.
Had it been *Arawn* that told him?
No.
He wouldn't.
But . . . would he?
This man, wasting away before her eyes, was his father. And she was only an outsider in this space. His loyalty would be to his kingdom first.
Not to her.
'Answer me, Unconsecrated,' the King spat. 'Have you made any progress at all?'
'W-with Avane, Sir.' Ezer forced the words out, grateful he wasn't an Ehvermage who could sense her lie. 'I . . . am leaning towards Avane.'
One of his two pillared gods.
His blue eyes narrowed.
Could two Sacred sense one another if they shared a god? She suddenly felt like he'd catch her in the lie, though it wasn't entirely untrue.
'Avane,' the King said. 'A god that has great power. Tell me, can you sense the current upon the wind now?'
She tried to swallow. But it felt like rocks were in her throat.
'Tell me which direction the wind is flowing. Tell me what you sense right now.'
'I . . .' She glanced back at the harpist as a new song began. It suddenly felt too high-pitched. Too fast. 'I'm not entirely—'
'*South*,' the wind whispered to her.
'South,' she echoed it. 'Towards the Sawteeth, Your Highness.'
He nodded his approval and she released a nervous breath.
'It often does, these days. Like it pulls us towards the darkness. Like Avane is insisting we stay in the fight. And fight, we will. Even those who are not trained properly. Even those . . . who may only be talented at minding ravens . . . and brandishing a lucky guess.'

Her stomach roiled again.

She hadn't been convincing enough.

'You were chosen by the gods,' the King said, and she caught a glimpse of his hands as he settled them in his lap. He wore rings like Kinlear, each one worth more than her life. His skin was papery-thin and bruised, swollen with arthritis at the knuckles. They were not at all the hands of a man in his forties. 'And certainly chosen by Kinlear, who believes you to be something *special*. But make no mistake. No one is special. Not even me.' He nodded to himself, as if he appreciated his own line. 'You would *not* be my choice, Raphonminder, as you are clearly from a bloodline incapable of holding their vows to the Five.'

She didn't dare defend herself.

Not to him.

She just took his wrath as he dealt it, knowing she would prove him wrong.

'You are not trained in magic,' he said. 'By the looks of you, frail as you are, you certainly are not capable of doing *anything* to protect my son should the beast turn upon him.'

Darkness writhed inside her.

'She won't harm him,' Ezer said. 'She will do as I teach her to do. She *will* be ready. I have faith in that.'

'Faith means little when it comes from an Unconsecrated.' An uneven breath, as he seemed to grow tired of their one-sided conversation. 'Make no mistake. If you fail to reach the deadline, if you fail to get the beast ready in time . . . it will have no place in our world.'

She sucked in an icy breath.

She didn't want to believe his words, didn't want to imagine that he would dare harm a creature as gentle, as lovely as Six.

But the second she met his eyes . . . she knew he *would*.

He would do anything, even waste himself away, if it meant saving Lordach.

'I voted yes on this final mission in order to appease my son,' he said. She felt small in his gaze. She felt powerless. She *was* powerless, next to him. 'He has always been a loyal servant to the Five, capable of sensing things that others may not. But hear this, Raphonminder, and take it to heart. Should you fail him . . . should you fail *me* . . .' He smiled, and she felt her insides curl. 'We will let the gods decide what your penance will be.'

He stood with a grunt.

But before he walked away, he paused, his shadow darkening the wardlight.

'I suggest you get back to work, Raphonminder. And do not come to this temple again. Until you've proven yourself . . . take the one for the servants.'

She waited until he was gone.

Then she fled from the temple as fast as her sore legs could carry her, not breathing until she was in the safety of the shadowed halls beyond.

Morning came too soon, sleep evading her yet again.

She'd fallen asleep reading, too afraid to slide into her nightmares so soon after the King's haunting words. She couldn't erase the chill of them away.

'Good morning.' Izill swept in, hauling a breakfast cart as usual. 'By the gods, you look exhausted. You need more rest.'

'Hard to rest when the dreams turn into nightmares,' Ezer said. 'But you're right. Coffee would certainly help, too.' She quickly scooped up the book and tucked it into her cloak pocket for safekeeping, grateful Izill's attention had gone to the pot of steaming coffee instead.

The book was Zey's.

For some reason, Ezer had grabbed it a few nights back, unable to bear seeing it sitting there on Zey's trunk . . . forgotten. She went back to it each night, thumbing through the blank pages. Perhaps she'd missed something on them, for Zey had been reading it so intently by the fire that final night.

But there was nothing, so Ezer decided it wasn't a book at all, but rather a journal that Zey hadn't the story to fill its pages with.

In some ways, it was easier to commiserate with Zey now that she was gone. The Eagleminder had been trapped here, all her life . . . like a Ravenminder in a tower.

A short breakfast later, during which Izill announced she'd counted Ezer's yawns – *seven, to be exact* – and Ezer bid her friend goodbye.

She made it to the upper cliff without vomiting, and her legs did not ache as much as they had in the days before. Perhaps her training with Arawn *was* paying off.

Celebrate the small victories, Ervos had always said.

Ezer smiled to herself, wishing he were here to walk the steps with her. She wondered what he would think of Six. What he would think if he saw Ezer dressed in Sacred robes, conversing with two princes, taking orders from one and training with the other each time the sun set.

She was in a story of her own now, writing the pages fresh each day.

The stone in her pocket suddenly warmed.

About time, she thought, for she felt Arawn owed her an explanation of some sort. But before she could grab the stone and speak to him, she paused.

Because a single pair of footsteps marked the snow on the doorsteps of the old temple. When she went inside . . .

It was Kinlear.

CHAPTER 21

'Oh,' Ezer said, as she approached. He was sitting on the bench beside the door to the catacombs, his legs sprawled before him, his white cane balanced on his lap. 'You're back.'

He wore his white and gold Eagleminder's cloak, but today his shirt wasn't unbuttoned as normal. In fact, his cloak was freshly runed, glowing with what looked like little flames. Runes to warm him, perhaps, though the godstongue was still foreign to her. He wore white gloves, and she could still see the gold chain with the vial around his throat.

'Oh?' Kinlear asked, as she came to a stop in front of him. 'That's all you can say after a millennium apart?'

'It was hardly that long. And forgive my disappointment,' Ezer said and placed her hands on her hips, 'after receiving your handwritten threats. And I am *not* easily appeased by gifts.'

'Then I suppose I'll take the books back.'

She gasped. 'You wouldn't *dare*.'

He chuckled at that. She was surprised at how light his laughter was, despite the dark circles beneath his eyes.

'I find the best threats are handwritten ones, Raphonminder. And if I recall . . . you sent me a threat back.'

He raised a dark brow. 'Did you miss me, Ezer?'

'Like a knife to my brain,' she said. 'And in case you're wondering, I've haltered the raphon. *That* task is done, so you can hold off on whatever hellish punishment you had in mind for me. We won't be needing it today.'

'A shame,' he said, feigning disappointment with a deep sigh. 'It would have been . . . quite artistic, the way it would have made you bleed.'

'There was never a punishment to begin with, was there?'

He shrugged. 'I guess we'll never know.'

And for the next several moments, they just stared at each other, as if sizing one another up.

'I hear the magic and combat lessons are going . . . well,' Kinlear said. 'Despite the instructor's shortcomings.'

Ezer glowered at him. 'You're wasting his time and mine, sending me there.'

'I didn't realize magic is a waste, Raphonminder.'

She crossed her arms. 'Magic isn't. Trying to pull it out of *me*, when it requires the blessing of the gods . . . that most certainly is.'

'And why would you think that?' he asked.

'Because the gods have turned a blind eye to me,' Ezer said. 'I told you before, and I'm more than happy to tell you again.'

He glanced over his shoulder, holding back a smile as he looked at the black door. 'You think the gods will answer with words or wielding. Whatever it is, to show their *yes*. But that is not always the case. Sometimes . . . they say *no*.' He sighed, looking at his injured leg. Then he looked pointedly back up at her. 'And sometimes their answer might be a raphon.'

He grunted as he stood, like it truly pained him.

'My mother is traveling to the Citadel as we speak,' Kinlear announced. 'My father's magic requires much of him. Too much, in his later years, at least for a Sacred. While she's here . . .' His eyes met hers, and for a second, she could have sworn there was a shift in them. Not quite fear. But something close. 'She and my father wish to meet you and see a Demonstration. With Six.'

Ezer's stomach dropped to her toes. 'What kind of demonstration?'

Kinlear waved a gloved hand. 'We have several days until her arrival. And if what you've said is true, then you'll have no problem saddling the pup today . . . and getting her ready for a rider by tomorrow.'

'*What?*' she yelped.

'No time to waste, Raphonminder!' he said, and opened the black door for her. 'We've got a King and Queen's blessing to earn, and after that – an Acolyte to kill!'

She glowered at him.

He was mad if he thought Six would be ready for a rider.

But just before she passed him, Kinlear began to cough.

It sounded like it came from deep inside his lungs. He reached for a handkerchief inside his cloak, pressing it to his lips.

When he was done, he waved her forward.

'Apologies. I contracted a bit of a cold in my preparations for my mother's arrival. Lack of sleep. Little water, and far too much winterwine . . . you've no clue how large the Citadel's collection is. Just wait until Absolution. You slept your way through the last one.'

She stared at him for a moment, noticing how pale he was. How truly tired he looked.

She wondered, for the first time, what it would be like to be royalty. Even if he wasn't the Crown Prince, he still had a responsibility to his kingdom. His people.

'Let's go, Raphonminder,' Kinlear said. 'The clock is ticking, and there's a war to be won.'

Just before she entered the darkness, she paused and looked back.

She could have sworn, as Kinlear quickly tucked the handkerchief back into his cloak . . . there was a smear of red upon it.

*

Six was waiting for her when they arrived, pacing the cell as if she was already frustrated that Ezer was late.

It smelled like fresh pine now, instead of raphon waste, and Ezer grinned as Kinlear seemed to take notice.

'A change,' he said, 'in the right direction. Though not big enough.'

Ezer reached for the leather halter she'd left hanging on a hook outside the cage door and paused. 'What the hell is that?!'

There was a leather saddle on a rack outside the cage.

Ezer stared at it like it was a nasty little spider, unwelcome in a space that was supposed to be safe.

'She won't let me put that on her. There is no way. The halter was bad enough.'

He shrugged and pulled up his usual stool. 'Then I suppose we'll discover what that punishment is, after all.' His smile was wicked.

She sighed. 'Fine. But *you* will remain *outside* the cage.'

'And you,' he said, as he approached the door and unlocked it with his key, 'do not give me orders. Are you aware how many war eagles I've minded? How many I've saddled and sent to the skies?'

She shrugged. 'Quite frankly, Your Highness, I don't give a damn.'

She slipped inside the cage, slamming the door shut behind her before he could follow her in.

Six's tail flicked once as she approached.

'Good morning,' Ezer said. 'You're looking positively chipper today. And just in time. We've an audience. And *orders*.' She looked back over her shoulder at the saddle, then turned back to Six, and whispered, '*Please*. Can we make this quick and easy today, Six?'

Six's tail flicked twice.

Ezer wasn't at all surprised, but she approached the raphon slowly anyway, reaching out to place her hand on her neck. No visions, for it seemed Six was content to remain silent.

But the raphon's dark eyes were on Kinlear.

They narrowed. And she flicked her tail twice again.

'I know,' Ezer said as she pulled away. She began securing the halter around Six's long, curved beak, taking care around her scar, then up around the back of her neck. 'But he's here, whether we like it or not.'

'You know I can *hear* you, right?' Kinlear asked from outside the cage.

Ezer ignored him.

'Now, today we're just going to try out the saddle. Just a little weight on your back, nothing you can't handle, with how strong and lovely you are.'

'Complimenting the raphon, I see,' Kinlear said aloud.

Ezer closed her eyes and sighed.

Gods, he was obnoxious. She missed her silence with Six.

'I promise it won't hurt,' Ezer said. 'I won't even buckle it.'

'You most certainly will,' Kinlear said, 'unless you wish to spook her more when it slides from her back and gets tangled in her paws.'

At that, Ezer spun to face him.

'*Enough.*'

He chuckled. 'Brave, Raphonminder. And curiouser, each time I'm near you, you seem to forget your place.'

'Oh, I know my place quite well,' Ezer said as she exited the cell. 'And it is here. *Alone.* Just me and Six.'

The saddle was light, at least, as she hoisted it over a shoulder. Kinlear made no move to help, just sat back and watched like a proper palace cat.

The second she entered the cell, Six skittered backwards, sending a wave of shavings towards her boots.

'That's enough fear out of you,' Ezer told the raphon. 'It's leather and buckles, and it's oiled black to match your feathers and fur. At least they got the color right. Imagine if they dressed you in white, like him.'

Six's tail twitched twice again.

'If you don't put this on,' Ezer said, 'then *he* will stab me. I'm assuming that's what the punishment will be.'

She glanced back over her shoulder at the prince who stood watching and waiting.

'Not even close,' he said, and coughed into his sleeve.

Ezer looked back at Six. The beast had lowered herself down to a sitting position. And once again, she twitched her catlike tail twice.

'Six,' Ezer tried. '*Please*. I'm not up for a battle today.'

She plunked the saddle into the shavings, earning a gasp from Kinlear, who probably liked his tack as nice and neat as his clothing.

Ezer lifted her hand out, no longer afraid. And when she touched the raphon's scarred beak, a vision sucked her under.

A fish caught in a net, washed ashore as it struggled to breathe.

Now the vision shifted; *she saw a tiny bird caught in a cage, flapping its wings to no avail.*

She felt the dread like it was her own, even as she broke the moment and the vision fizzled out. Six's dark eyes held hers, wide and panicked.

'I'm sorry,' Ezer whispered. 'But I will be right here with you.'

Two tail flicks.

'*Six*.'

The raphon turned away from her.

And laid a pile of waste on top of her boots.

'Now, that's just *rude*,' Ezer growled and called her a terrible name.

One that had even Kinlear balking from the other side of the bars. 'Perhaps progress hasn't happened at all,' he said, and lifted his hand to sweep aside his dark curls. Ezer caught a glimpse of the fat rings shining up on his fingers, made clear by the torchlight.

And an idea sparked in her mind.

'Stop laughing,' Ezer growled at him. 'Neither she nor I were prepared for this today.'

'It's clear you've never saddled a beast before. You don't prepare a war mount. You simply *do*. You haven't even tied her down.'

At that, it was Ezer's turn to gasp. 'I will do no such thing.'

She looked back at Six, who continued to flick her tail twice in a constant rhythm, pausing enough time in between for Ezer to get the message.

No.

No.

And another no.

Ezer closed a fist over her mother's ring. 'What will it take, Six? A gift?'

A pause.

Then a single twitch of Six's tail.

Yes.

She blew her hair from her face and marched to the bars where Kinlear stood. 'Your rings,' she said. 'May I borrow one, please?'

Kinlear looked like he'd been stabbed. 'These are precious heirlooms! A true rarity from Lordach's past.'

'And your mission is about to be considered an heirloom, too,' Ezer said, and reached her hand through the bars, 'if you don't give me something to use as an offering.'

She looked back over her shoulder, pointedly, at the pile of treasures in Six's cell.

She could see his eyes narrow, then widen. 'Are those . . .'

'*Hers*,' Ezer said, 'and so is one of your rings. Now choose which one, or we'll make no progress here today. She requires payment for what she's to do for you.'

He blinked at her. 'What in the Ehver happened while I was gone?'

'A mutual understanding,' Ezer said. 'Ring, please.'

His face was pained as he placed a fat emerald with a gold band into her palm.

Even in the torchlight, it shone like a beacon, and Ezer could see at once that Six's dark eyes slid towards it.

'All right, Six,' Ezer said, as she turned to face the pup. 'A saddling for an emerald, and a royal one at that.'

Kinlear sighed. 'I hardly think the beast can understand you.'

Ezer ignored him, reaching up to run her hands across the raphon's feathered neck, until her fingertips touched fur. So soft, so seamless, the transition from raven to panther. Her wings were lovely, the feathers long and perfectly tapered. And so dark, they nearly looked purple in the torchlight.

'Here we go,' she breathed.

She could see the space on Six's back where the saddle was to go. It was smaller, thinner than a horse's saddle so it could fit between her wings, and was meant to buckle more like a harness, in front and behind, so it wouldn't slide.

Carefully, so, so carefully, she touched the leather to Six's back.

'No chains,' Ezer whispered. Six's eyes flared at the touch of the leather on her feathers . . . but she did not move. 'Good girl.'

She eased it over the raphon's neck, allowing it to rest there.

'Wrong,' Kinlear said.

Six flinched and backed away.

Ezer huffed and let the saddle drop to the shavings. 'What exactly, dear prince, is wrong?'

She glanced over her shoulder, to where he stood with his arms crossed and an eyebrow raised. 'Everything about your form. You've positioned yourself so that if she spooks, she'll probably break your nose or your wrist. *Again.*'

Ezer glowered at him. Of course he knew about the visits to Alaris.

But she adjusted her position and tried again. Six stood well, even as Ezer held the saddle just above her back, skimming her smooth black fur. Her arms shook as she let it hover, and slowly, lowered it to rest in between her wings.

'Wrong again,' Kinlear said.

'Out!' Ezer yelped and spun towards him.

Six skittered backwards, and the entire saddle flung off her back, slamming against the bars with a loud clang.

And then Six lay down and curled herself into a ball, wings hiding her face.

Her tail twitched twice in a final *hell no*.

'Out, *please*,' Ezer said to Kinlear, breathing deeply. 'And don't come back until you're called.'

He looked positively shocked, like he'd been slapped. 'It's unwise to speak to a prince as if he is a dog.'

'I don't particularly care what is *wise*,' Ezer said. '*You* placed me in here, *you* put me in charge. When we work, we are silent. And that, Your Highness, is something you cannot seem to be.'

He just stared at her, open-mouthed.

So she curled her fingers around the bars and said, 'I was perfectly fine, making progress the past many days without you. You could have left me for dead, and you wouldn't have known. You wouldn't have cared, until you came back to find your little project pet sitting over my corpse!'

She was mad at him, she realized. *Furious*, because it felt just like Ervos leaving her.

Why was *she* always the one left behind, waiting?

Why was she always left to struggle, to suffer, in the wake of *men*?

He started to speak, but she held up a hand.

'To you, I am just another servant. Just as my uncle was.' She let out a breath so deep it hurt. 'You've no care for the fear I have encountered, the sleep I have lost, and have you thought for one *second* what it is like to be me? To be ripped from a tower – where I spent two years alone behind a locked door just like this one. And furthermore, if you've no respect for me,

Prince, then consider what it is like to be Six. To be born and raised in the confines of a cage.'

He blinked at her, silent.

And with his face growing red.

'No. I didn't think so,' Ezer said. 'Because a prince cannot possibly understand the plight of a pauper like me.' Another deep breath, as the wind suddenly rattled past her ears, and whispered, '*Stop.*'

And where have you been, Ezer thought to it, *the past many days? You, too, left me for dead!*

She glared at Kinlear.

'If you've a problem with what I do, Prince Laroux, then I will gladly step aside and allow you to mind Six yourself. Punish me if you wish. But there is nothing you can do to me. Nothing you can take. Not magic or family or—' She paused to swallow a sudden lump in her throat. 'There is *nothing* left.'

She crossed her arms and turned to face him, even as she felt Six's beak rest heavy upon her shoulder. A deep sigh came from the raphon – she felt it against her back, warm and soothing, like Six wanted to remind her.

She wasn't alone.

The ice over her heart cracked. A little warmth poured in.

'That is,' Ezer added, reaching up to place her hand upon Six's beak, just over the ridges of her scar, '*if* she allows you to keep your brains intact when you come for me.'

Kinlear's eyes went from her to Six and back again.

He grabbed his cane and stood with a wince.

'I apologize if I hurt you. That was never my intention,' Kinlear said. 'But for what it's worth, Raphonminder, you have no clue what sort of confines I live within. What pain I live with. And what sort of fate awaits *me*, if this plan fails.'

CHAPTER 22

For hours, Six fought Ezer's attempts at buckling the saddle.

Each time she tried, the pup panicked. Each time Ezer settled her again, she received various visions of trapped creatures flooding her mind.

And felt the panic within her own soul.

'It's a means to an end,' Ezer said, on the third hour.

She'd long since removed her cloak and was covered in shavings, sweating despite the frigid temperatures inside the dark space.

'The end is *freedom*, Six,' Ezer said. 'You can leave your cage. You can *fly*.'

Six walked slowly towards the saddle, which was left crumpled and abandoned on the edge of the cell, half-buried in the shavings.

'That's it,' Ezer said. 'It's safe.'

Six swiped out with her front paws. And positively shredded the seat of the saddle.

'*Fine*,' Ezer growled. 'You don't like that one, then I'll commission another. And another after that, until you do as you're told.'

Six grabbed the saddle with her curved beak, sharp as a sword itself. And flung it across the cage. It landed in her water trough, drenching Ezer in a wave.

'Gods,' Ezer said.

She slumped down, soaked, breathless and too damned tired.
A familiar burn started behind her eyes.

No, she thought.

It was weak, crying. At least, that's what she'd always thought, for Ervos only cried when he was drunk, too buried beneath the weight of alcohol to think clearly.

She often brought him a mug of steaming coffee, for it seemed to be the only thing to sober him up. She'd take his large hand in hers and help him stand and hobble towards the couch, where he'd slump down, his eyes half-open.

She could feel the tears on her face, hot despite the cold around her. She could feel the pain in her heart, the emptiness that came from not ever getting a chance to say goodbye.

Not to her mother or her father or to Ervos, who took the place of both.

Hot breath suddenly warmed her face, and the tip of a sharp beak nudged her chin.

'Go away,' Ezer said. 'Please.'

But the beast lay down and placed her heavy beak on Ezer's lap. Her body had grown, the weight of her head had grown, in the past many weeks alone. She almost didn't even look like a pup anymore, unless Ezer paid attention to the downy feathers still clinging to her neck.

'What are you doing? What am *I* doing?' Ezer wiped her tears and laughed to herself, a sad and desperate sound.

And then she placed her hands on Six's beak and lowered her forehead against it.

'I'm sorry,' she said.

She wasn't certain if that *sorry* was for Six or for herself, for all she'd endured.

The beast huffed out a warm, stinking breath.

And a vision stole her away.

This time it was a true vision. A memory, perhaps.

She saw the Eagle's Nest.

The trees and the lush springtime forest, and when she looked down, she could just barely see the tip of a curved black beak and two awkward, too-large raphon paws, Six's paws, as the beast climbed across the treetops, leaping and bounding like only a cat could.

From branch to branch, the raphon went.

Ezer recognized the memory as the day Six broke out.

The day they first met.

It felt like ages ago, now.

Six reached the domed edge of the Eagle's Nest, where the runed glass was all that stood between her and that harrowing drop far below.

She could hear the war eagles screeching, could hear the Sacred calling out as they tried to give chase. She had seconds, maybe, before they caught her.

But she couldn't tear her eyes from the sky behind the glass.

A boom rattled the world.

She felt it in her body, through her paws and all the way to the tips of her lovely black wings.

Lightning illuminated the storm that hung over the Sawteeth. Shadows swam through that infernal cloud, like stretching fingertips. They danced down the mountainside, a web of darkness that none could pass. And beyond the shadows, beyond the Sacred Knights and golden eagles . . .

She saw the raphons.

Her own kind.

They soared from the Sawteeth, a flock of dark feathers and fur.

She could hear the wind calling to them as they rose, even from here.

It danced past her hearing, whispering that the path for the raphons was safe, that the shadows spilling down from the clouds would not harm her kind.

Each rider was held expertly between their raphon's wings.

There were no saddles. No bridles. Only a beautiful, unbreakable bond between darksoul and raphon, and when they reached the curtain of darkness, alive and swarming down from the mountaintops . . .
They passed on through.
And dove into the war, ready to kill.
Ready to claim all in the name of the Acolyte.
The vision broke.

Ezer pulled away, lifting her eyes to the raphon. Six's beak was wet from her tears, her jagged white scar shimmering in the torchlight.

'You aren't to be gentled, are you? *Broken.*' She growled the word, like Zey had. With disgust. 'Not in their way.'

A single twitch of the raphon's tail.

'All right then,' Ezer said. 'That settles it.'

She picked up the saddle from the other side of the cell. Shavings tumbled from it as she lifted the soft leather into her arms. 'We'll just destroy this obnoxious thing, so that you never have to—'

Her words trailed off as she turned to find Six kneeling before her, leaning so far down her beak nearly touched the ground. She'd dipped one wing, as if she were making room for Ezer to climb aboard.

'What are you doing?' Ezer asked.

Six huffed, sending shavings outwards in a wave. She twitched her tail once. *Yes.*

'Yes, *what*?' Ezer asked.

And then her blood went cold.

'Oh, no. No way.' She held out her hands. 'I'm certainly not going to ride you.'

Six's tail twitched again. *Yes.*

'Absolutely not,' Ezer growled. 'I won't do it.'

One dark eye slid towards her and narrowed. A growl left her throat. Her hackles raised.

'Six.'

Another growl.

'I can't be your rider!'

A single tail twitch.

Yes.

'No.'

Yes.

Ezer put her hands on her hips. 'I'm not arguing with you about this. I'm the Minder.'

She marched over and reached for the halter, to pull the raphon back up to full standing. But instead, the second her hand touched Six's feathers . . . another vision came.

And this time it wasn't a memory. This time, it was . . .

It was Ezer, seated atop Six's back.

Ezer, soaring out across the cliffside, and Six was glorious, full-grown and wonderful as she tore through the sky, and together they were one. Together, they were fierce and wondrous as they angled towards the Sawteeth and never looked back.

Ezer ripped her hand away, breathless.

'I can't fly you, Six. I'm not a Rider. That's not what this mission is for. You are to be matched –' her voice broke at the sadness she suddenly felt – 'with someone *else*.'

'It doesn't have to be that way.'

Ezer spun at the sound of Kinlear's voice.

She didn't know how long he'd been watching, but it had to have been long enough.

'She speaks to you, doesn't she?' he asked. His head was cocked, his eyes narrowed as he studied them both. 'I wasn't certain before, but now . . . gods, it's impossible to deny, the bond you share. Of course, I was hopeful before, when I first saw the beast standing before you in the Eagle's Nest. But now . . . well, it took long enough for her to do it.'

'To do what?' Ezer asked.

Kinlear grinned. 'To choose.'

Something strange began to move through Ezer, deep in her core. 'What are you talking about?'

'The book you've been searching for in the library. You won't find it, because quite frankly it doesn't exist. But the darksouls know. I told you before about the interrogations. About the things they tell us, when they are tortured.'

He had a new expression on his face.

He looked . . . like he was staring into the flames of a crackling fire, spilling his secrets. Ones he'd held on to for far too long.

'The war eagles are assigned at random. They usually lean towards one or another, but in the end, they are all capable of being controlled by any Rider.' Just as Zey had said. 'Not so with the raphons.'

'You knew this?' Ezer asked. 'The whole time? And you didn't tell me . . .'

He shrugged. 'The process must be organic. It cannot be forced, and I apologize for holding it back, but it wouldn't have mattered. Because in the end . . . the raphon chooses the Rider.'

She couldn't speak.

She couldn't breathe, because she knew what he was saying.

And it terrified her, more than anything ever had in her life.

More than the shadow wolves, more than the summons to war.

'And according to what she's done now, Ezer . . .' Kinlear glanced past her, where Six was still bowing low, as if waiting for her to climb aboard. He smiled, his eyes limned with silver as he said, 'She has chosen *you*.'

The sky is a dangerous place for a girl without wings. Ervos's words echoed in her mind. A warning each time she'd strayed too close to the windows in their tower.

'I won't do it,' Ezer said now, as she stomped after Kinlear.

They'd left the tunnel behind and burst through the door into the main hallway of the Aviary. The smell of leather filled her senses – saddles on the walls – and it made her all the more angry. All the more *terrified*. 'I'm not a Rider.'

She wanted to scream at him. He'd given her hope that she'd be dismissed, that she'd get to walk free with enough coin to sustain her for life, once Six was handed off to her Rider . . . and now?

Now, *she* was to be that Rider.

Which meant she'd have to go across the Expanse.

'Then you'll become one,' Kinlear said, turning left towards the outer doors. 'Several weeks is plenty of time before you make the Descent. It's daunting, but from what I've seen thus far, I trust that you and Six will demonstrate your skills as a duo just in time.'

The Descent.

She felt like her stomach dropped to the floor as she realized he meant the display she'd been watching all these nights with the others in the training room. The war eagles diving down the harrowing cliff face, towards death.

'I'll die!' Ezer yelped.

Kinlear waved a hand. 'You said that before and look where it's landed you.'

'You're mad,' Ezer growled. 'Utterly mad.'

He crossed his arms and raised a brow at her. 'You'll be fine.'

'Fine?' She threw her hands up, searching for the right words. 'If you won't see reason about the flying, then see reason about this. I am not a *murderer*,' Ezer said. 'You want me to soar across the Expanse and waltz into the Acolyte's domain myself, stab him with a blade, and—' Anger writhed in her. 'Why are you *laughing*?'

'Because it perplexes me, Raphonminder, how you can think so highly and yet so utterly lowly of yourself in one moment,' Kinlear said.

He'd paused by the doors, the two of them several paces

apart. The wind howled as one of the doors opened, and a gust of swirling snow spilled inside. A few younglings took notice of them – the snarling Raphonminder, the smiling prince – and promptly rushed past.

'I certainly do not expect you to be capable of killing the Acolyte. That honor is to be bestowed upon someone else. Someone the Citadel can trust. To be quite frank . . . we hardly know you.'

'And yet you have decided my fate,' she said. 'Like Lordach has done for the rest of us.'

His jaw twitched. 'I don't question the decisions of my father and his War Table. I certainly won't question the gods.'

'I suppose you wouldn't, when you've spent your life protected. Knowing you'll never have to go into war, never have to risk your own neck when the rest of us will do it for you,' she spat. 'We die. So that you can live.'

'Careful,' Kinlear warned. 'You don't know what you're speaking of.'

'Don't I, though? Who's the one that spent the past weeks in the cage, while you were . . .' She waved a hand, searching for an answer.

'While I was what?' Kinlear asked, raising a dark brow.

The door opened again and a few Scribes entered. They bowed to him, and he inclined his head, the picture of respect.

Another spike of rage went through her. 'While you were gallivanting about the castle in your silly little outfits, all prim and proper, and—'

'We needn't bring the outfits into this,' Kinlear said, like she'd truly wounded him.

'While you were reading books, lazing about in your plush quarters, drinking winterwine from your precious flask when it's not even Absolution Day. While you were—'

'I'm dying, Ezer.'

The words left his lips so fast she almost didn't catch them. She paused.

'What?'

He inclined his head towards a small window seat in a shadowed alcove, where few would overhear their conversation.

She sighed and followed him to it. He sat gingerly, wincing, and turned to face her.

She did not sit.

'I'm dying,' he said again.

She shook her head. 'I'm not certain what you're getting at.'

'The truth,' he said. He raised a brow, like he knew she wasn't getting it. '*Dying*. You know, the way people do when the gods decide they are no longer worthy of spending time in this world. The kind of dying that ends with a freshly dug grave.'

It was outlandish.

He didn't wield, so there was no reason why he'd be on his deathbed already. He was young, and he was the prince, and they lived in a world of magic.

But then he coughed, and the sound was wet, like he had water in his lungs. He reached for that vial around his throat and uncorked it, his hands shaking as he took a sip.

'I was born sick, barely hanging onto life, while Arawn was born strong,' Kinlear said, as he recorked the vial. He put his head back, letting the sickly-sweet liquid wash over him. And when he opened his eyes again, they were heavy with sadness. All the anger had fizzled out of her body, gone in a rogue wind. 'The Masters, Alaris, all the best Ehvermage Healers we know in Touvre. They saved me at birth. But . . . they cannot fix me now.' He looked at the cane in his lap and sighed. 'There was no accident with the eagles that gave me my limp. Not as many would believe. No illness, that gave me my cough. My body, Ezer, is giving up on me.'

He removed his outer cloak, while she just stood there staring at him.

And when it fell from his shoulders, she nearly gasped at how *thin* he was. How his shoulders and lithe frame seemed to have shrunk.

In a matter of weeks.

'What is it?' Ezer asked. 'The illness.'

He leveled his gaze on her. 'It is my fate. Many things have been eradicated from Lordach, thanks to magic. But some diseases still linger. I've spent my life serving the gods, praying to them, and . . . for whatever reason, magic can't heal me.'

'But there must be some mistake,' Ezer said. 'Surely something can be done. You're the *prince*.'

'Death doesn't see status,' Kinlear said. 'It doesn't care whether you've a crown on your head or hardly a coin to your name. It chose me. It chases after me. And soon—' He sighed and ran a hand through his dark curls, pushing them away from his eyes. 'It is why this mission is pivotal. Not just to the kingdom, to the women and children and men that call Lordach home. But to *me*. I want to see him die. I want to see the war end before I go.'

Before I go.

Three words that seemed too resolute. Like he'd decided upon his fate.

It was utterly horrifying to imagine.

'How much . . .' She couldn't believe she was asking this to someone so young, someone who didn't even wield. To someone that, beyond his strange disappearances and the cough and the limp . . . seemed vibrant. Full of *life*. And someone, she realized now, that she had come to care for in their short span of time together. Even if he annoyed the hell of out her, she'd come to appreciate their banter. She'd come to enjoy the mystery that was Kinlear Laroux. 'How much time do you have left?'

It felt cold to ask. It felt callous. But she had to know. She had lost so many people already, and now she was about to lose another. The one that had given her Six.

'I don't know,' Kinlear said, and placed his heavy cloak back over his shoulders, fastening it beneath his throat. It hid his shrinking frame well. 'It goes through phases. Days when a healer must attend to me and help reignite my strength. Days when I think the end is near, but then the worst of it passes, and I'm back to my old self again. There are ways to combat the exhaustion, the cough, the weakness my muscles experience. Thank the gods for runes, but in the end . . . it continues to eat away at me. Like a poison. And nothing can stop it.'

She had no words.

She sat beside him, suddenly seeing him differently.

The wind rattled against the windowpane, and she trembled.

'Do others know?'

'The ones that matter do,' Kinlear said. 'The others speculate. They whisper.' He shrugged. 'I'm sure you understand what that is like.'

She nodded and stared down at her hands.

'I have to make it to the other side. I have to see it through to the end, Ezer. So that I will know, when death comes calling . . . that I did something of worth. That I wasn't just the bonus prince, the shadow to Arawn. I don't want to be just another portrait hung in the castle in Touvre, for my mother to mourn as she walks past. My father will die soon, and when he does, they'll remember him forever for all he's done to protect Lordach. I want the same thing for me. I want vibrant stories told, and songs written. I want them to marvel about Kinlear the Brave. Kinlear the Bold, the prince who saved us all.'

And suddenly she understood.

Her blood felt cold.

'We're doing this *together*, Ezer,' Kinlear said, his voice almost worshipful. 'You're the Rider. I'm the Assassin. All I need, all you have to do, is get me there. Take me to the other side, so we can ride Six through the shadows. So that I can use this . . .' he lifted his cloak to show the pale dagger on his hip, the one that had driven into her own chest, time and again in her dreams, '. . . and kill him. I can end this, once and for all.'

She had no words left.

She could see the truth in his eyes. He'd been dreaming of this, preparing for this, for quite some time.

And he hadn't told her the truth.

'Take the rest of today off,' Kinlear said and winced as he stood up, leaning on his cane more heavily than before. 'Go to the bathhouse.'

She glanced up. 'What?'

A strange thing to say after such news.

'Take some time there. Sit in the silence with your future. Your calling from the gods. Wrestle with it, war with it, for it is not without consequences. But in the end . . . the best outcome is for you to cede to it, Ezer. Let it win. Do it afraid.'

She was so taken aback by the words, she almost gasped. 'What . . . did you say?'

He shrugged. 'An ancient phrase, taught to us when we are just younglings. Everyone born in the Citadel knows it. It means to accept that you cannot defeat fear. So you take it with you and do the thing you fear anyway.'

'I . . . know what it means,' Ezer said.

She'd never heard anyone but Ervos speak that phrase.

And for some reason, it made her gut twist. Because . . . where had *he* learned it?

'I've accepted my fate,' Kinlear said. 'It's time you accept yours. At least . . . we'll be together.'

He bowed low, and when he came back up to standing, he looked like a prince again.

Healthy.

Happy.

Not at all doomed to die.

He turned and walked away, pausing to speak to some younglings who were busy cleaning saddles. She watched him, wondering why a part of her still feared him, and why a part of her actually liked his company, so long as he wasn't telling her what to do with Six.

Her dreams certainly hadn't warned her that *he* would be the one dying.

And suddenly, his words echoed into her mind.

All you have to do is get me there.

She realized with a pang in her gut . . . he'd told her to take him *to* the Sawteeth. That was the mission. But he'd never once mentioned her bringing him back.

CHAPTER 23

The stone in her pocket warmed as she walked, alone, down the steps towards the Citadel.

She didn't answer, partly because she was in shock.

And partly because she didn't think she could tell Arawn about her fate.

The stone went cold again by the time she reached the courtyard, passing by the swords driven deep into the snow.

She wondered if Kinlear would soon have one to join them.

He truly wished to go north. *All* the way north, to face an enemy he knew little of. To kill him.

And hope that it would be enough to stop the war.

She felt shaky and utterly frozen, so she ducked inside, making her way through the halls until she came to the set of twin golden doors that marked the bathhouse.

A cloud of fragrant steam billowed out when she opened the doors.

'*Gods,*' Ezer said, choking on the sudden heat. But it was *wonderful*. The warmest thing she'd felt since leaving Rendegard's southern sea wind behind. She instantly removed her cloak. The steam smelled like eucalyptus, earthy and vibrant enough to open her senses in a rush.

The walls were rounded dark rock, the ceilings low over her head. Water trickled down them, a delicate, natural sound that had her instantly sighing as she stepped further inside, following the torches that lined the walls.

The room widened when she came to the end of the tunnel.

Her jaw dropped.

It was an enormous rock cavern, utterly *filled* with natural hot spring pools. Delicate gold light emanated from each pool, from runes that marked their bottoms. Steam danced from each of them, clouding the entire space with an otherworldly haze.

A servant in a brown cloak tended to one of the pools. There were eels swimming inside it, every few seconds sending sparks of blue into the water until it bubbled hot and blazing.

Ezer made a point to avoid that pool.

She cleared her throat awkwardly, and the servant glanced up and spent a few moments walking her through the various benefits of each one. It was the Sacred bathing chambers, with healing properties inside each pool.

'Your clothing will be laundered and returned before you conclude your time here,' the servant explained. 'You could use a deep clean, my dear.'

Ezer couldn't disagree.

The servant left to give her privacy, and soon she'd piled her robes upon a rock and was standing stark naked in the middle of the cavern, her arms wrapped around her middle as she crept to one of the steaming pools . . . ensuring first that there were no eels inside.

Only softly glowing golden runes, their shapes morphed by the rippling water.

A sigh left her lips as she dipped her toes in.

And then she decidedly dove in, submerging herself beneath the soothing waters.

She came up feeling immediately refreshed, washed clean and – gods, her muscles felt instantly loose, all the knots and bumps and bruises painless for the first time in weeks.

She leaned with her back against the warmed stones, the water bubbling gently around her.

She'd just closed her eyes, allowed herself to relax into the moment, the water barely covering the curve of her breasts when she heard footsteps.

And she looked up, horrified, to find Arawn.

Standing half naked in the steam, with only a small towel around his bare waist.

'Away!' Ezer yelped and submerged herself up to her neck in the hot waters, praying the steam on the surface hid every bit of her bare skin. He just stood there awkwardly, wide-eyed as a deer faced by a hunter in the woods. '*Look away!*'

'I'm sorry,' he blurted, and turned away so fast his towel slid further down his hips. 'I didn't see anything.'

But *she* certainly could. She could see the small of his back, the rippling muscles, the steam clinging to his scarred skin . . .

'What are you doing here?' she asked.

He was staring at the wall.

He was so damned close to a torch it nearly licked the top of his pale white braid. 'I tried the stone twice today, and you didn't answer.'

'Because I didn't want to!' she yelped.

His voice softened. 'I came to check on you.'

'Congratulations, you've checked on me. You can go now.' She reached for a towel, but it was too far away. *Gods be damned.* 'Don't turn around.'

She would die if he saw her naked. *Had* he seen her naked?

She lunged out of the water awkwardly, hissing as she scraped her bare stomach upon the stones. She gripped the fabric and pulled it to her, covering herself before she'd even fully climbed out of the water.

'Oh, come *on*,' she groaned as she looked down at the towel.

'What?' Arawn asked. 'What is it?'

'Nothing of your concern,' Ezer growled. The towel was too damned small. It hung not even halfway down her upper thighs, revealing *far* too much skin.

She needed to get out of here.

'Are you *decent*?' he asked. 'The torch is going to melt my face if I don't back away, Minder.'

'Decent enough,' she said, damning the servant now for having taken her clothes. She'd take the raphon stink over this . . . this *moment,* both of them half naked and alone in the dark.

Arawn turned, his face almost pained from the heat.

They locked eyes for a second before he cleared his throat and looked away again.

But she saw enough.

Her jaw dropped.

It wasn't because of his muscles, nor how low that tiny towel hung on his hips, revealing the telltale V she'd seen in her dreams. Gods, why did it make her skin warm, why did it make a strange little quiver turn in her stomach?

And it wasn't because of the enormous pectorals and biceps he had, and the way the steam was rolling down his skin like sweat, like—

Stop it, she told herself. *This isn't one of your godsdamned dreams!*

But she couldn't look away from him. There were penance scars upon his chest, which were all older than Zey's – like they'd branded him into submission long, *long* ago.

All of the above would have given her pause.

But her eyes were stuck on the enormous scar he had, still angry and raised, that spanned from his collarbone to his waistline. A scar large enough it practically split him in two.

'I'll go,' he said, still looking off into the steam. His jaw twitched, and his hands curled into fists. If she didn't know any better, she'd think he was uncomfortable. Miserable, actually. Her cheeks warmed, and something that felt like disappointment crossed her mind. 'Take the space. I'll bathe in the dormitories tonight.'

He turned away.

'Wait,' Ezer blurted.

She truly hadn't meant to, but she couldn't stop herself. He turned back, his eyes expectant.

He was staring at her face.

Quite pointedly at her face, like he didn't dare look away, and the expression on his own was almost pained.

'What happened?' she asked. 'Your scar.'

He slowly looked down. This time, at his own body, where it looked like he'd been split open and sewn back together again.

'War,' he said.

She raised a brow and held the towel tighter around herself. 'Arawn.'

He flinched at his name on her lips.

'The truth, in exchange for trust, remember? It's your turn.'

'I . . .' He looked pained when he swallowed, like he had rocks in his throat. And then he met her eyes. 'I made a terrible mistake.'

'Tell me?' She swallowed. 'Please.'

He wiped sweat from his brow.

'Three months ago, one of my aerie riders took an eagle without clearance. She went rogue, trying to cross the Expanse on her own.'

'Why?' Ezer asked.

Zey's face flashed in her mind.

'Because she was searching for answers,' Arawn said. 'Searching for something she thought she might find on the other side. She was speaking of strange things, hiding something from me, and . . .'

'What sort of things?'

He shook his head. 'Places far away. Another world. She

showed me a book, something she wanted me to see, but . . . the book was empty when I opened it.'

'Empty?'

A curious feeling came over her, as she thought of Zey's book.

Arawn nodded. 'I feared for her life. For her mind. When she ran . . . I went after her. She'd settled into her pillar late, wasn't ready to face the darksouls alone. Night fell just before she reached the Sawteeth, and the battle began. A darksoul attacked her and severed her eagle's wing. She crashed. I made it to the ground before the wolves swarmed us. There were too many. And there was nothing I could do.'

His voice broke, and Ezer's heart did a terrible twinge. Today was full of awful revelations.

'I tried to bring her back to Alaris, but it was too late. The wolves were closing in, and I had to fly away. I had to . . .' He took a shuddering breath. 'I had to leave her behind. So that I, the future of Lordach, could survive.'

His eyes were downcast. Terrible, the expression on his face. He looked like he hated himself.

'I went back after the battle ended, to recover her by sunrise. To bury her the way she deserved. But when I got there . . . she was gone. I found the site; I could see the blood in the snow.' His voice broke. 'And now . . . now she fights on the Acolyte's side.'

It was silent for quite some time. She watched the rise and fall of his chest, watched the way he seemed to let the grief wash over him, before he forced it away.

'How?' Ezer asked.

He shrugged. 'The Acolyte's magic is dark. A terrible thing. We're told not to leave the victims behind, because the Acolyte . . . he has the power to bring the wounded back from the edge, with a loyalty so strong, they don't fear death any longer.'

That was news to her.

And it made the Acolyte all the more terrifying.

'What was her name?' Ezer asked.

His eyes met hers, and they looked so utterly sad. 'Soraya. She was betrothed to Kinlear.'

Of course.

That name . . . she'd heard it countless times now, spoken between Kinlear and Arawn like a curse.

An untouchable thing.

It all made sense now, why they seemed to hate each other. Why they stiffened in one another's presence.

'I failed her,' Arawn said. 'I could have trained her harder, could have paid more attention, and—'

'You tried,' Ezer breathed, and suddenly she understood why he'd spoken those hurtful words to her the other night. They weren't about her at all. Not really.

Because when he looked at Ezer . . . he saw the ghost of Soraya.

It hurt her more than she cared to admit. Was that why, all this time, he'd been drawn to her? Why he'd given her the speaking stone, why he'd tried to train her to fight and wield?

Was she a way for him to fix his mistakes?

She wrapped her arms even tighter around herself, wishing she could fade into the steam.

But that would require walking away from him. To leave him standing here, alone and broken . . . and she didn't know if she had the strength to do it.

'I didn't try hard enough,' he said.

She remembered the words he'd uttered to her in the woods, when he'd first empathized with her about losing her uncle. About her own grief. And so she echoed those words back to him now.

'I understand that to mourn . . . is to feel half dead yourself.'

His lips parted, like he remembered, too.

'My magic – my connection to the gods – it has struggled since losing Soraya. She is why I'm not in battle, Ezer. She is why I'm too weak to fight, a liability if I go to war before it returns.

We grew up together. I had hoped . . .' His cheeks reddened. '. . . that maybe she and I would be matched. She made me feel things I didn't know were possible in this life. She made me feel *free*.'

Ezer could see the light leave his eyes when he spoke of freedom. It was something the Sacred did not have . . . and for him, it had died with Soraya.

'I never told her how I felt. And thank the gods, because they chose Kinlear for her instead.'

A terrible turn of fates.

She imagined it would have been worse than heartbreak, to love someone . . . and see them end up in the arms of your twin brother.

'Why did she run?' Ezer asked. 'If she was betrothed to Kinlear, wouldn't she want to stay with him? To be with him, when . . .'

He locked eyes with her, his gaze searching. 'He told you, then?'

She nodded.

'She tried to defect *because* of Kinlear.' He spat his brother's name like a poison. 'When he finally told her about the illness . . . Soraya changed. She'd fallen in love with him by then, and she became desperate to save him. She thought she could find the Acolyte. That she could somehow reason with him, beg him to heal Kinlear with the same power he'd used to bring back the others on the battlefield. She was distracted. She stopped praying on Allgodsday, stopped showing up for training. He didn't see it, for he loved her too much to find fault. But I knew her inside and out.' His hands clenched into fists. 'Soraya had changed. By the time I got to her, I think she'd already chosen to lay down her belief in the gods. I think . . . in her heart of hearts, the Soraya I knew and loved was already gone. She was a talented rider. The best I've ever known. But I think she *wanted* to fall in battle, to get so close to death that the darksouls would come for her and take her to the Acolyte.'

He was breathing harder now, lost in his memories of that night.

'She wouldn't let me save her. I begged her. I thought she wasn't thinking clearly, maybe her head had been hit in the fall, but when I tried to haul her away . . . she did this to me.' He looked down at his enormous scar.

And suddenly it seemed a thousand times worse, knowing the woman he'd loved had done that to him.

She'd broken him.

'The wolves closed in when they smelled my blood. My eagle took the brunt of the attacks for me, but there were far too many of them, so . . . I flew away. Like a *coward*, I left Soraya behind.' He released a shaking breath. 'My eagle passed from her wounds shortly after. And my magic hasn't been the same since.'

Gods.

It was too much for anyone to bear.

'I'm so sorry, Arawn,' Ezer said. 'Truly.'

She reached out as if to place a hand on his arm, because no one should have to look so broken. No one should have to suffer heartbreak alone.

But her towel nearly slipped, and she paused, making sure to squeeze it tight around her, not missing how his eyes slid down, then back up to her face again.

She swallowed, despite the dryness in her throat. 'If you ask me, the gods are *fools* not to grant your invocations. You did the best you could. It isn't your fault, what she decided in her heart. What she chose. That fate is hers alone, Arawn.'

'Sometimes I think they're punishing me. For not seeing it sooner with Soraya. For not stopping her. I don't even know *how* the darkness leached into her soul.' He shook his head. 'I don't know what she came across, who she might have spoken to . . .'

It was a mystery why people disappeared.

Why even a Sacred, created by the gods, would turn to the shadows. But Ezer had seen it with Zey. Subtle signs at first, and even the night before she fled, with how strange she'd been acting . . .

Ezer still would not have guessed the Eagleminder would be gone by sunrise.

'You have to forgive yourself,' she said, meeting Arawn's eyes.

He looked pained. 'I can't.'

'Not today,' Ezer said. 'Not tomorrow. But at some point, you have to *try*.'

She knew she wasn't the first to say it, but maybe she would be a part in his healing. A path to someplace better and brighter.

'For what it's worth, you're a fine man, Arawn Laroux. Soraya was lucky to have your heart for the time that she did.'

He blinked in surprise. And then a hint of relief softened his features as he smiled. 'Was . . . was that—'

'A compliment,' she said. 'And one I won't offer again.' She sighed. 'Ervos was always good at giving them. Me, not so much.'

Something flashed behind his eyes.

'I'm sorry,' he said again. 'That you did not get to reunite with him as you'd hoped.'

'Hope is a fleeting thing,' Ezer said. 'It's my own fault for thinking I could hold onto it as long as I did.' She looked down at the ring on her thumb and added, 'Sometimes, it's easier to think about what I could have done to stop him from leaving. But in the end . . . fate had its way with him. And there is nothing I could have done to change that.'

They fell silent, but for the first time it was not an uncomfortable silence.

And with their backs turned to one another, they agreed to sink into neighboring pools.

The steam rolled between them. She was painfully aware of their discarded towels, the heat in her body that was not entirely from the water temperature. The sound of his sigh as he sank into the pool just behind her.

This is dangerous, Ezer thought to herself, as she leaned back and stared at the steam. *Just like your dreams.*

He was clearly still in love with Soraya.

And *she* was clearly a replacement, a project to fill the void of him missing *her*.

She suddenly felt the urge to fill the silence with something, *anything*.

'Six chose me to be her Rider,' Ezer blurted. 'She chose *me* to be the one to carry Kinlear to the Sawteeth.'

'I know,' he said, and she could sense the change in his voice. The anger boiling beneath the surface. 'Kinlear told me.' A pause, and he added, 'You're afraid.'

She huffed out a laugh. 'Of course I'm afraid. I won't do it. I can't.'

He was the only one who truly understood why. He'd guessed her fear of heights long ago, but beyond that . . . it was more than the heights. It was the promise of dying – terribly – that came with it.

It was entering the Ehver and discovering that no one would be there waiting for her.

That love did not stretch beyond the grave, that her mother and father wouldn't find her in the Ehver, and she would *never* know who she was.

She would die a stranger to herself.

The water trickled behind her as he shifted in his own pool. 'Are you going to run?'

She'd considered it.

But for some reason . . . she couldn't imagine walking away from Six.

'Would you stop me?'

'No,' he said, and that surprised her. Some part of it pained her, deep in her gut. 'I owe you a life debt still, remember?'

She smiled, her chest lightening. 'Right,' she said. 'The life debt.'

'You're capable, Minder. I know you are. And I'm grateful.'

'For what?' Ezer breathed.

The steam was even thicker now. The heat, too strong.

And his voice had softened even more, so that it made her heart feel strange and heavy, and . . .

She turned, and he turned at the same time, and they locked eyes through the steam as he said, 'Thank you for seeing me. For telling me that I am more than my pain. More than my mistakes. And for what it's worth . . . I think you'd make a fine raphon Rider. I think you'd make it to the other side. And I think hell itself couldn't hold you down from making it back.'

She smiled. And then he cleared his throat as the servant arrived again, saw them seated there with locked gazes and quickly turned right back around.

CHAPTER 24

She left the bathing chambers with heaviness in her heart.

She couldn't stop thinking of Arawn. Gods, she was *way* too attracted to him. There was no denying that. But . . . it wasn't simply because of what he looked like. It was how he'd spoken, how he'd shed the armor from himself, and shared his pain with her.

A shame that his heart was set on another.

And beyond that, he was forbidden.

Them being together could *never* be . . . not that he was ever an option to begin with. Especially now that he was soon to be king, when his father passed.

He'd be Matched with someone powerful.

Never her.

She didn't even know she was headed towards the Aviary again until she found herself back out in the snow, marching up the steps as sunset arrived, and the war raged to her left.

She made it to the cliffside, and stared out just in time to see the Eagles rise from the glass dome. One at a time, they tore into the sky. Magnificent, enormous beasts, their bodies like spears as they climbed up, up, up, riders poised in their saddles.

As soon as they reached their peak, they dipped downwards.

And soared straight down the cliffside, making the Descent.

She watched them fall, one by one. Like the tips of arrows, brave and brilliant and so far from what she could ever be.

Her hands trembled.

What if she died?

What if Six was a terrible flier, not at all like Kinlear hoped she would be, and she killed them both?

It didn't matter to Kinlear. His fate was sealed, his death imminent. But Ezer . . . Ezer could live.

She could turn and run, right now.

She spun and looked back behind her at Augaurde. A world of white. The war tents spat smoke into the sky, and far below the garrison was alive with activity. Soldiers who had either signed up or been drafted, never wanting to be here in the first place.

But they were *here*.

They didn't run away from battle.

They marched straight in to protect people just like her.

'You're a coward,' Ezer told herself.

Because when she turned back around, she imagined every single one of those riders had fallen, splattered against the snow, and then she saw herself among them, and Six's body broken.

Gasping for breath that would not come, she closed her eyes and tried to push the vision away.

'*Ezer*,' said the wind. '*Look*.'

She opened her eyes as a war eagle soared past her.

It was glorious, so fast a flight that it sent a gust of wind pushing her backwards.

It screeched, and the sound went through her. It set her soul ablaze.

You could be that way, Ezer told herself. *If you weren't so afraid*.

All her life she'd been nothing, and no one.

Forgotten.

Left behind.

But not by Six.

She turned, and suddenly she was running across the snow,

towards the waiting Aviary doors. She burst through them, ignoring the glances from the younglings.

She ran until she made it behind the black door, surprised to find it unlocked. She sped down the dimly lit tunnel, and stopped in front of Six's cage.

And then she curled her hands around the bars and gasped, 'Why did you choose me? *Why?*'

Tears poured down her face, and she hated them, every single drop.

'Tell me *why*!'

She screamed.

Six didn't even flinch.

So she marched to the cage door . . . and found it unlocked. Like Kinlear had known she would find herself back here in the darkness, her heart too drawn to Six to stay away. And Six's, too drawn to hers to even attempt escape.

'Why not someone else?' Ezer asked.

Six blinked up at her from where she lay by her pile of treasures, guarding them with her front paws.

'I'm not a Rider.'

Six's tail twitched once. As if to say, *I know.*

'And yet you still chose me.'

Another twitch.

'I won't do it.'

Six chirruped her beak once, as if to say, *why not?*

'Because you haven't flown before,' Ezer said, to which Six let out a soft growl. 'It's the truth, and your fussing isn't going to change that. Why did you pick *me*?'

She could have sworn, as Six blinked up at her . . . the raphon shrugged.

'You don't know?'

Two tail twitches.

Ezer sniffled and wiped her tears away. 'That's not comforting.'

Six huffed into the shavings.

'Riders train their entire lives before they make the Descent. And that's what the King and Queen will wish to see, Six, to approve this partnership. Are you willing to do that?'

Six's tail lifted.

Paused, as if considering.

And then twitched once.

Yes.

'Well, I'm not.'

Six just blinked at her innocently, like she hadn't a clue why Ezer was so concerned. So Ezer crossed the soft shavings and slumped down with her back against the raphon. It was warm, and Six began to purr.

'I'm nobody,' Ezer said. 'I never wanted this.'

Six huffed again, as if to say, *neither did I.*

A vision of five sinking feathers floated into her mind. They sank beneath a dark, endless sea, never to be seen again. Six's siblings.

'I'm sorry,' Ezer said. 'I know it wasn't your choice, either.' She sighed and wiped her face dry with her sleeve. 'I have scars, Six.' She felt the raphon's hot breath on her cheek. On her shadow wolf marks. 'Not these. They're the kind you can't see. The sky is a dangerous place for a girl without wings.'

Ervos's words tumbled off her tongue, the first time she'd ever spoken them out loud.

Six paused for a moment, as if she weren't sure how to respond.

And then Ezer felt two dark wings drape over her shoulders, holding her close. It was so simple, the act. But it made Ezer's heart twinge. And as Ezer leaned her head back, cradled in Six's warmth, another vision filled her mind.

She saw Six, soaring alone in the sky.

Shadows swam behind her, making her black fur and feathers even darker.

Six was magnificent. Proud and beautiful, with her enormous black wings outspread as she traversed the sky. Her paws clawed at the air as if she would tear it apart.

But Ezer was not focused on the raphon.

No . . .

The vision pulled away, until Ezer could see the rider on Six's back.

She looked fierce – not beautiful, but haunting, with the wind tugging at her dark black braid . . . and the trio of jagged black scars on her face.

It was Ezer, wild and free, as a rider on Six's back.

And she was not afraid.

'I see,' Ezer said, as the vision broke.

She was breathless, feeling like she'd just been in the sky. Like she and Six were out there, *together*.

'What would you say if that vision didn't come true?' Ezer asked. 'What would you say, Six . . . if I ran from here, tonight? If I never came back?'

The wings tucked tighter around her body, holding her close.

But then . . .

Six huffed.

And slowly, so slowly . . . those wings lifted, setting her free.

Ezer turned to find that the raphon had laid her head down, her beak heavy against her pile of treasures.

'You would let me go?' Ezer said. 'You'd let me leave you here alone?'

The raphon huffed again.

And her tail, ever so slightly, twitched once.

So Ezer imagined it for a moment. Standing from the warmth, walking away from the raphon, closing the door shut. Leaving the Citadel and never seeing Six again. Never seeing Arawn or Kinlear or Izill.

The thought of those three ached her, for she'd never had friends before. And they'd come to be exactly that. She imagined those goodbyes would hurt, but she would heal. She was used to being on her own.

But it was the thought of leaving Six that broke her.

It was like watching Ervos ride away on a transport wagon, knowing she'd never see him again.

It was like holding on to a hand that grew colder as it died.

'I can't leave you, Six,' Ezer said, sighing. 'I won't.'

Because when she was with the raphon . . . she was *home*. For the first time in her life, she knew it was where she was supposed to be.

She leaned her head back against Six's warm side. She felt the raphon's heartbeat, steady and true.

'I will try it. One time,' Ezer said. 'But if you drop me . . .' Her stomach twisted, and she had to work past the fear again, the image of herself broken in the snow. Six's wing tucked tighter, as if she sensed it, too. As if she would keep that fear at bay. 'I swear to the gods, Six, if I am *ever* to fall from your side, you had better catch me.'

Six's tail twitched once.

Yes.

And with the purring and the warmth, the softness of her wing feathers . . .

Ezer fell fast asleep.

'*Ezer.*'

She found herself back in the labyrinth, the ring of identical tunnels all around.

And in her cloak pocket, she now held the ornate black key.

'*We'll have to see what you belong to,*' *Ezer said as she held the key to the torchlight. She looked up, as if the wind might hear her.* '*I don't suppose you'd be of any help tonight?*'

A breath passed, and suddenly the wind sighed past her, pulling the tips of her hair towards the tunnel to her right.

It led her to a door. The wind whispered around its edges, like it was beckoning her to go inside. So, she removed the key from her pocket . . .

And placed it into the lock.

She glanced back over her shoulder but found no shadows shifting in the darkness. No eyes, blinking back at her, nor the owner of the footsteps she'd seen in the frost, nights ago.

She turned back to the door.

And when she turned the key, the lock clicked.

And the door swung open, silent as a grave.

Inside . . .

She gasped.

Home.

She was back in the tiny little apartment she shared with Ervos, long ago. The details were muddled, as if she were looking at it through smoke, but she knew the shape and feel of it all, nonetheless.

There was the squat woodburning stove they used to keep warm on the coldest nights.

There was the couch with the worn cushions, the small creaking table that Ervos had placed his feet on, time and again.

The kitchen sink, copper and stained green from the salt air that clung to every bit of Rendegard's outer town.

Ezer gasped.

There was Ervos, walking through the open doorway of the bedroom. He looked younger, still vibrant with life. Not a hint of the bloodshot eyes she'd grown so used to in his later years.

She nearly cried at the sight of him. His summertime smile, his shock of red hair, his full beard, and his enormous frame in the doorway.

'Ervos!' she breathed.

She rushed across the room, stepping over the worn floorboard that squeaked like a field mouse, reached for him . . .

And went through him.

'Get some rest, Little Bird,' Ervos said.

His voice.

It was the voice that had raised her, comforted her, shaped her into who she was.

'Uncle,' Ezer begged, reaching for him again. But her hands went through his arm, as if . . .

As if she were a ghost.

'But I'm too excited about tomorrow!' said a small voice behind Ezer.

It was young, and innocent . . . and it was hers.

She turned at the same time Ervos did, until she was standing face to face with herself.

'You won't see tomorrow any sooner, Ezer,' said Ervos. 'But it helps to close your eyes. Put an end to today. You'll see the King and Queen soon enough.'

Ezer stared at herself in shock. She was so small, standing there in her nightgown. So tiny, her little arms, her hands and feet. And the scars on her face . . . they were furious. Far worse than she remembered. As if they were only a few years out from her accident.

'Come on,' Ervos relented. 'One more story, Little Bird.'

They walked past her, and the room began to grow dim.

And then she was standing at the closed door again, as if she'd been kicked out of the memory.

Ezer rushed to the next door, and the next after that, using her key to enter.

Each time, they opened and revealed to her a memory.

Some were short. Little snippets of scenes, the core things she remembered about her life, like the first time Ervos allowed her to mind a bird. When the memory ended, it spat her back out.

Perhaps . . . the doors were all in order, all leading towards her older years the further she made it down into the depths of the labyrinth. Perhaps she could go back to the beginning. Perhaps it would show her who she was.

So Ezer went back out into the tunnel and turned left. She jogged at first, and then she was running, the key in her hand, hope in her heart.

She could discover who she was.

Perhaps the answer had been here all along.
She went all the way back, to the very beginning. The first door in the mouth of the tunnel . . .

She woke to the sound of a chuckle, and then Kinlear's voice.

'I was hoping access to the bathing chambers would serve to refresh you. Not lure you right back into the den of the beast, where you could acquire more of her smell.'

Ezer opened her eyes to find him kneeling on the other side of the bars, staring down at her with a smirk on his handsome face.

'What in the name of the gods are you doing here so early?' he asked.

'Sleeping,' Ezer said with a groan. 'And not nearly long enough.'

She was on her side, her back against the raphon's belly, her head on Six's front paws like a pillow. Six's wing was still tucked over her like a blanket.

'I can see that,' Kinlear said.

He looked truly shocked to see her.

'I wasn't certain I would lay eyes on you again.'

'I considered leaving,' Ezer said.

He inclined his head. 'I . . . had a feeling the thought crossed your mind.'

'Which is why you left the cage door unlocked,' Ezer said.

He shrugged. 'I've never been much good at persuasion. Six, however . . . seems to have quite the talent for it, if the bareness of my hands is any indication.'

He had but a single ring left today.

At that, Ezer smiled.

'I have a gift for you,' Kinlear said.

Ezer sat up, blinking blearily as he held something through the bars. A new cloak, with a fur-lined collar, to match the one he wore now.

'What's this for?' She held up the cloak.

She caught a glimpse of the blade on his hip and instantly felt a pang of panic race through her.

He won't hurt you, she told herself. *It's just a dream.*

She wanted it to be, more than anything.

'That, dear chosen one, is my apology.'

She frowned. 'You don't know me very well if you think a bit of clothing will make up for your hiding the truth of my fate.'

He sighed. 'I would have told you if I could. But I am bound to certain parameters, as is every other Sacred in this place. And for all my stretching of those boundaries . . . there are some even I cannot cross. And for that, I *am* sorry.' He looked truly earnest. 'I would beg your forgiveness, if it were easy for me to take a knee.'

And then it looked like he *would* kneel before her.

'No,' she blurted. 'Gods, don't do that.'

To make a dying man beg.

To make a prince bend a knee before her . . .

'If I put on the cloak, will that suffice for forgiveness? Or is it better that I toss it to Six to curl up with?'

She held it out, like she would drop it on the shavings.

Kinlear's head snapped up. 'That's a magicked thread count, Raphonminder. It defies all others in Lordach. Please, don't—'

She smiled wickedly.

Because she'd forgiven him already. His fate was twisted with hers. She had known it from the moment she met him in the woods, and if they were to fly together . . . there was no sense in hating him.

She slid the cloak on, earning a sigh of relief from him. Gods, the fabric truly was stifling, in the very best of ways. It was not missed on her that Kinlear wore his runed cloak even indoors.

'Are you going to tell me what this is for?' she asked.

At that, he grinned. 'We're taking her *outside*. It's time you learned to ride.'

CHAPTER 25

It was not as peaceful as Ezer had guessed.

It was not a beautiful, tear-inducing moment: the day when an orphaned raphon pup, raised in the darkness, finally got to break free and see the sky.

Rather, it was like herding a wet cat.

An *angry* cat, for it turned out Six was terrified of the snow.

They'd gone through a back door in the catacombs, a similar tunnel protected by a portcullis with a door to the outside, guarded by two enormous Sacred.

They'd winced as Ezer walked her out, even though Six was perfectly pliable in her halter and lead.

She was surprised to find the snow had stopped. A rare day in the north, when the clouds didn't unleash a barrage of it upon their heads. And if she didn't know any better, she thought they might see some sunshine. Kinlear had ordered a few Scribes to set up a magical pen of sorts: a circle of small boulders with runes inscribed on their sides.

It was far enough from the domed Eagle's Nest, far enough from the edge over the Expanse, that Six didn't risk going overboard or panicking about the shadowstorm. The others spread out, leaving Ezer and Six alone in the center of the circle. Arawn arrived to watch, his arms crossed and his eyes narrowed as he beheld her with the raphon. She couldn't help but notice he'd brought his sword.

She reached for the stone in her pocket.

Gods help you if you come after Six with that blade.

She could hear his chuckle as her own stone warmed. *I think you have it all under control, Minder. I'm just here to enjoy the show.*

She huffed out a breath. *That makes one of us, at least.*

It wasn't as jarring to be outside in the cool light of morning. And certainly, without the flashes of Sacred magic going on during battle. There was no other beast in the sky.

Only the one before her, twitching her tail twice. *No.*

'Come on,' Ezer said, tugging gently at the lead rope. Everyone was watching, and she felt her cheeks redden. 'It's not going to kill you. This is *your* weather, Six. The weather of your ancestors, all the flocks before you. Snow!'

She picked up a handful, holding it out towards the raphon, who stood with her back arched, her paws on tippy toe, as if she were a housecat about to be struck by a snake.

Her tail twitched twice.

No.

'Don't be a baby,' Ezer said.

Six nudged against Ezer's cheek, filling her mind with a sudden vision.

A raphon pup, so small it was still closed-eyed and yowling as it nearly drowned in swiftly gathering snow.

'Don't be ridiculous,' Ezer said, and broke the vision as she pulled away. 'You're not a baby anymore. It's time to grow up, Six, and it starts with being a real raphon. In the snow.'

She held out the handful.

Six huffed hard enough to send the snow skyward in a cloud of white.

'It's fluffy!' Ezer said.

Two tail twitches.

No.

'It's pretty. When the sun hits it, it *glitters*.'

Two more tail twitches.

No.

'It comes from the sky, Six. Where you belong.'

No.

'We aren't going back inside.'

Six promptly used her tail to send a wave of snow soaring towards Ezer's face. It was cold and wet and utterly humiliating.

'Stop it!' Ezer hissed.

Behind her, the others were laughing. Even Arawn, who never dared smile. Ezer felt the stone in her pocket warm.

Is this really the time? She sighed into Arawn's mind.

Just making an observation, he thought back, a smile on his words. *She reminds me of someone else during her own training...*

Why don't you come over here right now, Ezer thought back, *and let me borrow that very sharp, shiny sword of yours, Prince?*

His answering chuckle was all she got before the stone went cold.

'*Six*,' Ezer hissed, her attention back on the raphon. 'Pull yourself together.'

The beast turned away, ready to go back to the darkness. To the bars of her cell. Fury roiled in Ezer's belly. All the work she'd done, all the time they'd spent bonding so Six could understand what it was like to be *free* . . .

'You aren't meant for a cage,' she growled. 'And neither am I.'

Because if she failed in this mission, she feared Six would *never* taste freedom again. The king wouldn't free her. He would have her killed.

'It's time for me to ride, like *you* requested,' Ezer spat. 'Now lower yourself to that pretty little kneeling position, just like you did yesterday, so I can climb aboard.'

Six only flicked more snow at her.

So Ezer cursed at her, the runed cloak suddenly too hot on her skin. Her blood roared in her ears, and then she did something she never thought she'd do.

She bent over, picked up a handful of snow, packed it tight . . .

'Two can play at this game,' Ezer growled.

And launched a snowball at the raphon.

It hit Six right between her tucked wings. White exploded against her fur, enough that Ezer winced.

Even Kinlear gasped.

Arawn's jaw fell open.

Six snapped out her wings, as if to shake the snow away. But suddenly the wind picked up, furious as it came from beyond the cliff. It was so fast it whistled, a wild gust that had Six's eyes turning wide. Her feathers ruffled as snow danced between her and Ezer, a wall of white.

'*Ezer*,' it whispered, not a warning but a hello as it arrived.

And Ezer swore . . .

Six cocked her head towards it.

As if she heard the whisper on the wind, too.

It tugged at Ezer's cloak and hair, cold and biting and trusting, and Six's eyes widened, two dark orbs. She cocked her head the way all birds so often did, testing the feel of it. She lifted her beak, breathing in the smell of winter and woodsmoke.

'That's it,' Ezer said, hands before her. 'That is the wind, Six. A *friend*.'

The beast closed her eyes, leaning into it. It was like watching her breathe for the first time. Like watching her *live*. She lifted her wings higher, so that it ruffled through her feathers, tugging at the enormous blades of black that someday soon would carry her into the sky. They had grown.

She had grown, taller than she was just weeks ago. All her downy feathers were gone, and her paws seemed more suited to her body. She was the size of a war horse now, instead of a small pony.

'You're meant for this,' Ezer said, stepping closer. 'The sky, the snow, the cold. And there in the distance, Six. That is your *home*. You can go there, if you learn to fly.'

Six's tail twitched back and forth, not in conversation, but on instinct. She stared out across the cliff as the wind danced away.

Towards the Sawteeth, and that roiling shadowstorm.

Towards her true home.

'We'll do it together,' Ezer whispered. 'Every step of the way.'

She realized, suddenly, that Six wasn't just a raphon.

She was a friend.

A confidante.

A safe space for Ezer to rest her weary heart.

She was *hers*.

Ezer picked up the lead rope.

And this time, when she held out her arm as Kinlear had showed her, asking Six to break into a lunge . . .

The raphon obeyed.

'Good,' Kinlear said gently from the edge of the circle. She'd forgotten he was here, and the sound of his voice snapped her back to the present. 'Lead her through several minutes, so she knows the patterns. Then we'll try with you on her back.' He smiled at Ezer. 'You're doing it. Just like I always knew you would.'

She smiled back through her scars.

Six set her paws in full against the snow, lowered her wings against her sleek, catlike body, and began to move. It was beautiful, watching her jog. Ezer stood in the center of the ring, and Six practically pranced past her, keeping in a perfect circle.

The wind whistled past, ruffling Six's neck feathers as she broke into a run.

'Yes,' Ezer said. 'Good girl, Six!'

'She's magnificent!' Kinlear laughed beside her. He placed his hand on Ezer's arm. 'She is *everything* we've been waiting for, Raphonminder!'

Together, they marveled at Six.

Her paws were soundless on the snow, and it was the first time she'd ever looked graceful. The first time she looked truly lithe and – Ezer's heart did a sad little tremor – she looked *full grown*. Her dark body shimmered, feathers and fur like liquid ink as the clouds broke, and a spear of sudden sunlight trickled through them. Ezer gasped and glanced skyward at the same time Six did. Through the wards, the light was pure, blazing gold.

Gods, it had been ages since she'd seen the sun.

And Six . . .

Six had never.

The raphon paused, as if she weren't certain what was happening above her.

'It's all right,' Ezer said. 'It's the sun. Cats like the sun.'

Six huffed out a breath, and padded softly over to stand by Ezer's side, her beak still tipped towards the sky. And then she began to purr.

Ezer laughed, a joyful sound.

'It's lovely, isn't it?'

She'd forgotten what it felt like to have the sun on her face.

Kinlear sighed beside her, his eyes closed as he, too, reveled in the sudden golden warmth.

'It's a beautiful day,' Kinlear said. The sun lit up the freckles scattered across his nose and cheeks. His hair shimmered bronze beneath the light, and for a moment it struck her how handsome he was. The other side of a coin she'd forgotten to flip over until now. Today . . . Kinlear Laroux glimmered with life.

'Just . . . beautiful,' he said.

He wasn't looking at the sky or at Six.

No . . . he was looking right at her.

A tendril of electricity sparked through her as he said, 'If I didn't know any better . . . I'd say you were born for this.'

'For what?' she asked.

He smiled knowingly and nudged his chin towards Six. 'For *her*.' He swallowed, and said, 'For me.'

Her eyes widened.

She flicked her gaze to Arawn . . . but found the space empty where he'd just been. And the stone in her pocket utterly cold.

'For . . . you?' Ezer asked, eyes back on Kinlear.

Her mouth had gone dry.

She wasn't supposed to feel *that* way.

Not for him.

'Oh, Gods, I mean . . .' Kinlear clear his throat and chuckled. 'I mean for me and this mission. I feel as if you have been godsent, Ezer. The answer to the prayers so many of us have sent skyward, hoping the gods would take pity on this realm. I've never met a soul like you. You're . . . unburdened.' He smiled, and she realized he had a dimple on one cheek. She'd never looked at him this closely before, always too afraid of her dreams to dare search his face. It was endearing, the softness in him. 'There is no greater joy than to share this moment with you,' he added.

Her walls dropped a bit more.

'I'm not godsent,' Ezer said. 'If anything . . . Six is.'

The raphon's wings ruffled as she shook off a few flakes of snow. And for a while they stood there, just the three of them, staring up at the rare sun.

It was comfortable, this moment, and that surprised her.

'Arawn has journeyed across the Expanse countless times,' Kinlear said. Strange to hear him speak his brother's name after she'd learned the pain that was between them. A twinge of something that felt like *guilt* unfurled in her chest. Though she hadn't the faintest idea why. 'He has battled and taken out darksouls more than anyone could keep track of. The King Lordach needs, with my father's inevitable end. But me?' He sighed. 'I've spent my life inside the Citadel, staring through the glass at a world that isn't mine to know or explore. I can look . . . but I cannot touch. I thought I would die as forgotten as the ones who've abandoned us. I thought . . . my eternity would be *nothing* compared to Arawn's.'

She glanced sidelong at him.

She never would have guessed the darkness that threatened to steal him away. The sickness that would not quit. The pain of his loss, when it came to Soraya.

How utterly unfair that a Sacred like him would die young. The same fate as one who *could* wield . . . and yet he'd never been granted even that small gift.

She felt like he was paying penance without ever having done anything wrong.

He cleared his throat. 'When the War Table approved the Black Wing Battalion, I was overjoyed. It gave me a sense of purpose. A chance to do something in this war, other than be the broken prince. The one people look at, and think, *what a shame, he cannot be what his father wishes him to be. He'll never be like Arawn.*'

'That's not what they think,' Ezer said gently.

He raised a brow.

'They adore you, Kinlear,' she said. 'Because you are different. Because you are a sort of mystery no one can quite unravel. And I think people are drawn to that. We're fascinated by things we cannot understand. It's why you and I share a love for Six.'

He laughed, his breath soaring away in a puff of white. 'Mystery or not, now there is hope for the first time. Something tangible. A chance to win this war. A chance . . . for me to finally *mean* something to my people. And I am honored, Ezer. So honored by your yes. It was the greatest gift you ever could have given your kingdom. And by proxy . . . the greatest gift I have *ever* received.'

His words washed over her, sweet as honey.

She felt light as air.

'You are the first Raphonminder known to Lordach. The first in history!'

'Even if Lordach doesn't know?' Ezer asked, with a held-back smile. 'I suppose I am a mystery, too.'

He shrugged. 'We can be mysteries together, you and I.'

She smiled at him. 'I think I'd like that.'

Six was purring beside her, eyes still closed, beak tipped up to the sun.

'Do you want to try and ride her?' Kinlear asked. 'Before the storm returns. It always does.' His smile fell . . . and suddenly he was coughing again.

She didn't ask him if he was all right.

She knew he wasn't.

She just stood by, a silent companion as he uncorked the vial around his throat and pressed it to his lips. His coughing subsided, and when he looked at her . . . she felt the urge to reach out. To take his hand and let him know he was not alone.

They had a shared destiny now.

'Ready?' Kinlear asked. 'We'll walk at first, so you can learn the way she moves. Are you certain you won't use a saddle?'

'Absolutely not,' Ezer said, at the same time Six's tail twitched twice. 'The darksouls don't. Better to blend in, anyhow, and besides . . . I don't think she's meant for one.'

Ezer remembered the words of the librarian.

Gods help the person who dares tell a cat what to do.

So, she wouldn't tell her at all.

She'd let Six choose, the way no one ever had for her.

'She's your raphon,' Kinlear said. 'You have every bit of power now, to do as you please.'

Power.

Something she also had never had.

She turned to Six.

'Are you ready to ride? Is that what you want?'

The raphon looked to her.

And with her dark, trusting eyes, she stared at Ezer, and twitched her tail, *yes*.

CHAPTER 26

Another week had passed.

The sky was pink this morning.

Which meant another snowstorm was already well on its way.

Ezer adjusted her position on Six's back and pulled her hood lower over her eyes. She was grateful for the new runes Kinlear had ordered the Citadel's seamstress to stitch upon the fabric. They were meant to weigh the hood down, to keep snow from her eyes and prevent it from falling back in the biting wind.

'Come on, Six,' she said. 'A little faster now.'

Her mind flooded with a sudden vision.

A beautiful black raven, nestling down inside a pile of sticks . . . a nest, filled with lovely little trinkets.

'You can rest when Kinlear says we're done,' Ezer told her. 'I know you've got more in you.'

She could have sworn she felt Six sigh beneath her.

But the raphon broke into a lope, and Ezer buried her fingers into the soft black feathers at the base of her neck and leaned in close, so the wind rolled over her.

They'd worn a pathway into the ground, a perfect ring of paw prints in the snow. Six's movements were fluid, soundless as she loped. It was utterly fascinating how so large a beast could be so quiet.

But Ezer supposed that was the point of a predator.

To be able to sneak up on anyone at any time.

'Good!'

Ezer glanced to the left, where Kinlear stood in the center of the ring, wearing his fur-lined cloak that glowed with delicate gold runes.

'Now do the figure eight again, but don't hit me, *please*.' He pulled his cloak tighter around his middle. 'I still haven't recovered from the first time.'

Ezer rolled her eyes, because it wasn't *her* fault that just yesterday, Six had thrown her off and sent her careening against the prince, where they both came up trembling, covered in snow.

It was because Six saw a bird.

And she'd wanted to chase after it, marveling at the tiny little winter robin that had soared past, curious at Ezer's presence as they always were.

'You're being dramatic!' Ezer called, as she imagined Six performing the figure eight. Herself, seated perfectly on her back, not falling, thanks to the base of Six's wings also supporting her at the sides.

A vision of that tired raven flitted into her mind.

'I'll give you double lunch,' Ezer said. 'Come on.'

She received a vision of a large raphon paw, shoving a full bowl of food away.

'Fine,' Ezer said. 'I'll scrounge up another bauble from Kinlear's supply of lavish royal jewelry. Will that suffice? You'll need a new cage soon, if you're to fit all your little prizes.'

At that, she could have sworn Six pranced into the shape of the figure eight, keeping Kinlear safely at its middle. Where Ezer pointedly realized his hands were now bare of *all* rings.

'Now you're just showing off,' Kinlear said, when they had gone past him far too many times to count. When even Ezer was tired, her legs aching, her mind focused on the bathhouse – fleetingly excited at the prospect of running into a half-naked Arawn again – instead of the snow all around. 'Now try to get her to lift off just a few feet. Lean close. Don't fall. We don't want to heal another broken leg so soon.'

Not like two days ago, when Alaris had practically wrung Kinlear's neck as he'd helped Ezer limp in. And Arawn had nearly beheaded him right after, in the hall.

Even the torches had blazed with a flash of brighter fire. Like his magic was coming back, when it came to *her*.

Ezer blew out a breath.

Her stomach turned as she thought of herself in the sky.

'Now, flap your wings,' Ezer said to Six. 'Just a little bit.'

Six tossed her head twice, for it became easier for her to argue with Ezer that way, when she couldn't see the twitching of her tail.

No.

'Yes,' Ezer said.

The raphon flapped her wings.

But not to fly.

She flapped them to throw Ezer off balance, and before she realized it, she was face-down in the snow.

She came up cursing, sputtering through the wet and the cold.

'Anything broken?' Kinlear asked.

Ezer glared up at him as she swiped snow from her cloak.

'No?'

'No,' she growled, glaring at Six. 'Only my pride.'

'Pride,' he said with a smile, 'Is not something death cares about. Now start again.'

Another two days of riding lessons, and the raphon still wouldn't use her wings. Six just wanted to run.

'You're not a cat right now,' Ezer spat. 'You're a raphon. Meant for the sky!'

She sent Ezer a vision.

A cat, lazing in the sun, purring and perfectly content to be on the ground.

'She's done great work, but she's hit a plateau,' Kinlear said from the edge of the circle, where he rested on one of the boulders. He often sat more than he stood, these past few days.

'It's because she doesn't know who she is,' Ezer said. '*What* she is.'

How strange, that the sentiment hit close to home.

She was more like the raphon than she thought.

'We have only a few days until the War Table will request the Demonstration,' Kinlear said. 'A leader for every pillar of magic will attend. And if she isn't ready . . .'

'I know,' Ezer cut him off.

The wind whipped up the cliffside, sending a flurry of snowflakes into Ezer's vision. A fine morning to test out flying, for at least there was mild visibility. Ezer stared out at the Expanse as she slid down, patting Six on her sweaty neck, where feathers turned into fur.

And then Ezer felt the raphon's beak weigh heavy upon her shoulder as they stood and stared out at the world beneath them.

'You have to fly,' she told her. '*Please.*'

Six only sighed.

'The war is getting worse,' Kinlear said. 'We needed three carts yesterday to bring them all back.'

Ezer's stomach turned, thinking of that.

They came piled high, corpses shredded by battle the night before.

And as she turned, Ezer could see them now: the body collectors out there in the Expanse, far away beneath them. It was the only time, in daylight, that they could safely collect their dead. When the darksouls and wolves were hidden away inside the Sawteeth . . . biding their time to kill again.

A few armored war bears pulled heavy wooden carts meant to gather the fallen, while servants loaded them on to be burned.

The bodies were small as Ezer's thumbnail from here . . . but still large enough to fill someone's entire world, back home.

Death was strange. Because here, in the north, it became common.

It became a number instead of a name.

Ezer heard the whispers in the halls as she walked, following Arawn to the training room each night, where she failed to conjure any magic. But slowly, she began to block his advances with her sword. And once – only once – she'd landed a single hit to his side.

Though she suspected he'd allowed her to, if only to boost her confidence. Now that Kinlear wanted Ezer and Six to cross the Expanse, she was grateful Arawn had encouraged her physical training.

Grateful for every aching part of her body, because it meant he'd pushed her beyond the limits she'd initially thought for herself.

She was no longer weak.

No longer a shadow of what could be.

And though she'd come to love her days training with Six and Kinlear . . . it was her nights with Arawn that she craved.

His solid presence as he guided her, his impressive strength and swift movements.

And the look he had in his eyes each time he circled her in the training room, with nothing but a blade held between them.

You challenge me, Minder, he'd thought to her last night as he circled her, his voice like a caress against her mind. *In more ways than one.*

And why is that? she'd thought back. The moonlit swam across them, bathing them both in silver.

His breath tickled her ear as he'd leaned in and whispered aloud, 'Win this fight, and I'll tell you.'

She was so distracted he'd knocked the sword from her grasp, and his secrets had stayed safe with him.

'What will it take?' Kinlear asked Ezer now, and she was instantly colder as he pulled her back to the present. 'An entire castle full of gold to convince Six to fly?'

'I don't know,' Ezer said. 'But *she* has to be the one to decide.'

'It reminds me of someone,' Kinlear said, chuckling as he looked at her.

She scooped up a snowball and tossed it at his feet.

He looked like he would repay the favor, until Six growled behind Ezer.

'It's haunting,' Kinlear said, 'the two of you together. The nightmares I have each night, when I see you in my dreams.'

She blinked at that. 'You dream of me, Kinlear Laroux?'

He suddenly found the sky quite interesting.

'Tomorrow,' Kinlear said, ignoring her question with a grin. 'We'll try with her again.'

Six let out a soft growl, and a vision entered Ezer's mind.

Kinlear's white cane, left alone in the snow. Covered in blood.

She gasped and nudged the beast in the belly... and promptly felt Six's paw stomp down over her boot.

'*Be nice*,' Ezer whispered.

The raphon's tail twitched twice.

'Well,' Ezer said, glancing sidelong at the prince. 'Tomorrow should be . . . fun.'

'Speaking of *fun*,' Kinlear said, and gave her a wicked grin. 'Tonight is Absolution.'

CHAPTER 27

'I can't wear *this*!' Ezer squealed in protest at the gown Izill laid on her dormitory bed.

It was not black, for starters.

It was a pure, snowy white.

And far too little fabric to be considered *clothing*. At least, for someone who had spent their days in dark leather and hooded cloaks better suited for warmth than becoming a spectacle.

'You can and you *will*, or I'll be infinitely offended seeing as I'm the one who requested it from the Ehvermage seamstress,' Izill said. She *tsked* and swiped salve over the new bruises on Ezer's arms. All of them, courtesy of Six. 'This is our way, Ezer. A gift given by the Five so that we can appease the humanity within us, the release we all need when we've been so pious to keep the laws.' She smiled and picked up the dress, holding it out to Ezer. 'A shame I won't be able to dance tonight, as I'm needed for extra hands in the kitchens. Now, please. Just put it on. Then you can run back here and bury your beautiful figure beneath shadowy, raphon-scented fabrics once more.'

'But . . . I'm not feeling well,' Ezer lied.

'Gown,' Izill said, and pointed to the bathing chambers. '*Now.*'

She yelped as Ezer tossed a piece of chocolate at her – she'd been busy stuffing her face, while Izill expertly combed through the tangles in her dark hair – and with a huff that reminded her of Six, Ezer trudged to the bathing chambers.

Gods, she thought, as she slipped into the dress and turned to the enormous mirror that took up half the wall. *This most certainly will* not *do.*

The dress was a noblewoman's dream.

It was made of pristine, alabaster silk that shimmered in the torchlight. The sleeves were long, the neckline modest, for of course even on Absolution, the Sacred had limits. But the fabric that swam across her skin left little to the imagination, given how closely it hugged her every curve. White and silver sparkled glittered across the hem, gradually turning the entire bottom half of the dress aglow. It almost looked as if the wind were embracing her.

The same way Avane's dress looked, on the many-headed statue.

She sighed, thinking of such power.

Because some part of her knew . . .

The wind was a bit like Six. She would not tell it what to do.

'It's *devastating* on you, Ezer,' Izill squealed, as Ezer emerged, her arms wrapped around her middle. She sighed longingly. 'What I'd give for a dress like that.'

'Take it,' Ezer said.

'Quiet,' Izill shushed her, and sat her down in front of a dressing mirror near the fire, where several others were already putting the finishing touches to their looks. Each one was in the color of their pillared god, with small details to match their magic.

And Ezer had never felt more out of place.

'So what am I to do at this festive occasion?' Ezer asked. 'Without *you* by my side?'

'It's Absolution Day!' Izill said as she began to work at Ezer's curls. 'For one, enjoy the winterwine. Just . . . go slow. And don't bother asking how I know. We *all* know what it's like to wake up the next morning full of regret.' She laughed softly to herself. 'As for what you're to do? Well . . . it's the only time you'll not pay penance for crossing our sacred boundaries with an Unmatched. Kisses, of course, and nothing more.' When Ezer frowned, she said, 'What? You thought us *completely* pious?'

Another woman giggled and tied a red silk mask over her eyes. 'I'd need more hands to count the number of partners Prince Kinlear has taken into the shadows on Absolution.'

For some reason . . . that made her stomach sink.

'And what about Prince Arawn?' she dared ask.

'No,' Izill said. 'Never, for him. Not once, in all his days.'

Izill tied a beautiful white feather mask over her eyes.

And for a moment, as she let the conversation of the other Sacred women wash over her . . . she could almost pretend she had grown up here, a part of this world.

That maybe she *had* been able to invocate. And maybe . . . she would have been Matched with someone.

Perhaps a prince with eyes as cerulean as the sea.

But as she left the room behind, following the flock of other women in various shades of dresses to match their magic . . .

Ezer caught a glimpse of herself in full.

She looked like a true Sacred, the mask concealing nearly every dark, raised scar on her face. Her hair was lovely, cascading down her shoulders and back in perfect ringlets. Not a snarl in sight, thanks to Izill.

She belonged here. The wards had proved it, when they let her in. She had a job and a purpose, a mission to complete . . .

So why did she still feel like a Ravenminder locked away in a tower?

Because you are not like them, her mind hissed. *Because you are still a mystery to yourself, despite all you have discovered.*

She curled a fist around her mother's ring.

And as she left the dormitory behind, her gown glimmering in the torchlight . . .

A part of her still felt like she was dragging her old chains.

*

Absolution took place in the training room.

A comfort, at least, that she knew the space by now. But when she entered, expecting to see the enormous room bare . . .

She found it transformed.

Music flowed from the right, where a group of musicians plucked at stringed instruments. Tables and chairs had been brought in, piled with food and desserts in elegant displays that towered far over her head like sculptures themselves.

Masked Sacred drank from golden goblets: the famed blue winterwine that could only be harvested in the north.

Ezer had never seen true dancing, beyond snippets of what she'd witnessed in rundown taverns with Ervos.

But here . . . the Sacred danced.

The middle of the room was a whirlwind of every pillared shade, as Sacred Knights and Scribes spun about like they'd been practicing for centuries. Their movements were elegant, sweeping, perfectly in time to the strings.

And for a moment, with the late afternoon light spilling through the window wall, the dancers concealing the Expanse and the shadowstorm, far beyond the glass . . .

She could picture the war being over.

She could imagine the end of the Acolyte, and a world like this – the jewel of the north – being safe to go on as it pleased.

Forever . . . instead of just these few, fleeting hours. For when true night fell again . . . death would return like a promise. And some of the Sacred hiding behind these very masks, sweeping past her on the dance floor . . .

They would become nothing more than swords in the snow.

Nothing more than names on scrolls.

Ezer smoothed her gown and made her way to the winterwine table, needing a distraction from the emotions that washed over her. She'd tried ale and wine before, but she'd never loved the feeling it gave her. The loss of control.

She'd seen too much, what it could do to someone like Ervos.

A pang of sadness hit her anew.

Gods, she missed him.

She wanted to tell him everything. She wanted him to meet Six, stand at her side, help her with . . .

'I thought *I* was the only one capable of looking so fine in both black *and* white,' said a voice behind her. 'And yet . . . here you are.'

And Ezer spun to find herself face to face with Kinlear. He wore a white mask in the shape of a wolf's snout, his suit a lovely pale velvet with gold eagle wings stitched into the front pocket.

Simple, for him, despite his telltale golden chain and elegant white cane.

She smiled.

He was made for days such as this.

'You clean up well enough, Prince Laroux,' Ezer said. His familiar face was a relief. She smiled and leaned in as if to sniff the air around him. 'Though . . . there's a lingering scent of something strange upon you.' She wrinkled her nose. 'Is that . . . war bear?'

Kinlear's eyes sparkled as he caught on to her game.

'Oh, it's something far worse,' he said with a wink, and held out his arm for her to take. She obliged, and he led her about the space, his cane clacking almost in time with the music. His voice dropped as he leaned down towards her as if sharing a secret. 'I heard a rumor there's a strange and deadly beast hiding in this very castle.' His lips nearly grazed her ear as he whispered, 'A *raphon*.'

'*No*,' Ezer gasped, and feigned surprise. 'Surely there must be someone to Mind it?'

'Oh, there is, My Lady,' Kinlear said. 'A fine Raphonminder. The best there ever was—'

'The *only*,' Ezer corrected him, but he lifted a finger and continued.

'She is strong and brave and a little bit feisty, as Raphonminders should be. But rest assured. She's brought down to earth by the *brutally* handsome assassin she's rumored to train it with.'

'Brutally handsome?' Ezer asked and lifted a brow beneath her mask. 'Are you certain?'

'Certain as death,' Kinlear said. 'They say he's so handsome one can hardly look upon him without drooling into their winterwine.'

At that, she laughed. And found herself warm and comfortable, as she held on to his arm.

She no longer feared him.

She could not fathom a world in which this prince, charming as he was, would dare lift a blade to her chest.

He stiffened, suddenly, his eyes narrowing through his mask.

'And there is his nemesis,' Kinlear said with a sigh. 'We could run.'

'We will do no such thing,' Ezer said, and squeezed his arm.

She'd turned to find Arawn walking towards them through the crowd. His hair was braided back as usual, but instead of white, he wore red. It was the first time she'd ever seen him in color.

Warmth spread through her as he walked closer.

His mask was in the shape of flames and made with such a brilliant mixture of yellows and oranges, it truly *could* have been fire from Vivorr.

He came straight towards them. A solid presence to part the sea of Sacred.

Kinlear tensed beside her, where her hand still rested in the crook of his arm.

She had the sudden urge to pull it away, but then Arawn was before her.

And she was between *them*, the twin princes who stared at each other like they were on two different sides of a silent war.

'Kinlear,' Arawn said as he stopped an arm's length away. 'You look . . . well.'

Kinlear lifted his chin and placed his free hand atop Ezer's. She did not miss the way Arawn's eyes slid to their hands. How they narrowed beneath the mask for a breath of a second before he looked indifferent once more. 'I think it's all the time spent in the outside, with our dear Raphonminder,' Kinlear said. 'She has been quite healing for me, in more ways than one.'

Ezer swallowed the lump in her throat.

Her palms were sweating. She looked up at Arawn, begging him to meet her gaze.

But he stared at his twin like it was just the two of them.

'Not quite so healing for *her*,' Arawn said. 'What with the brutal injuries that Alaris must fix, time and again.'

'The Raphonminder is strong,' Kinlear replied. 'She can handle it.'

'May I remind you,' Arawn added as he stepped a bit closer, and Kinlear's grip on Ezer's hand tightened even more, 'that after she is done with you, she trains *here*, in the darkness, with me.'

'Learning how to protect herself better than the last you took beneath your wing, I hope,' Kinlear said.

And she could have sworn Arawn's fist curled.

'*She*,' Ezer said, removing her hand from Kinlear's arm, 'is standing right here. Between two brothers who refuse to forgive one another for a past that is *neither* of their faults. That lies with Soraya alone.'

At the sound of her name, the tension broke. The two brothers looked to her like she'd spoken a curse aloud.

'It's the truth,' Ezer said. 'And telling it is what Sacred do.'

'Forgive me,' Arawn said, clearing his throat. 'I . . . don't know what came over me.'

But Kinlear only sighed, and reached out as a servant skirted past them, golden goblets balanced on his tray.

'It's the winterwine,' Kinlear said, handing Ezer a goblet. The liquid inside was blue, and glowing as if by magic. 'It takes the limits off. Makes the walls we usually have . . . come crumbling down.' He looked to Ezer and noticed her gaze on Arawn. With a loud sigh, he said, 'I've suddenly discovered I have somewhere else to be. Anywhere, really.'

But then he leaned in and pressed a kiss to Ezer's cheek.

His lips were soft, and she sucked in a breath, surprised at his touch.

'Tomorrow, Raphonminder,' he said as he backed away, 'we'll take Six back outside and make certain we do not fail.'

Ezer nodded. And together, they watched him go, fading into the crowd like a ghost.

To hell with it, Ezer thought. And took a sip from her goblet, lingering on the feeling of instant lightness in her bones that could only come from magic.

'That was . . . interesting,' Ezer said. 'Were you two ever close?'

'Too close,' Arawn said with a shrug of his massive shoulders. 'I suppose . . . war takes more casualties than lives alone.' He watched Kinlear's back, then sighed deeply as he turned back to her.

And she could have sworn . . .

He looked *nervous*.

'I can't believe I'm asking this, but . . .' He glanced over his shoulder. 'I'm supposed to be seen doing court fineries. Pretending that the things I worry about, like my father's soon-to-be passing . . . do not exist. At least for tonight.' Another sigh, in which he took a long pull from his goblet. His lips shone as he asked, 'Would you dance with me, Minder?'

She thought her eyes might pop out of her skull.

But she took another few sips – half the goblet's worth – and answered him breathlessly, 'Yes.'

*

His hand engulfed hers as he led her to the middle of the training room. And as the music turned, and the sweeping melody overcame them . . .

His hand settled carefully over her hip.

She sucked in a breath, because though he'd trained with her, sparred with her . . . this was different.

This was a tender touch, the kind of thing shared between lovers.

Which they most certainly were *not*.

'I've never danced before,' Ezer said, her voice a bit breathless as he guided her through the sea of dancers. 'Certainly not in a gown like this.'

His gaze lowered, sweeping down her body before they shot back upwards to her face. And then stayed *only* on her face.

Like he was trying very hard not to drink in the details of her.

The way the fabric clung to her body like a second skin. He'd done the same in the bathing chambers, and suddenly she was thinking about *him* in such a state, and . . .

Gods, she suddenly felt like she needed air.

'Well,' Arawn chuckled. 'Lucky for you, Minder, I am a prince. And a very unfortunate side effect of that is an extensive knowledge of dancing.'

He took charge of their bodies together, spinning her round like she was made of air.

They spun past a couple in Dhysis' gold and then Aristra's green. The colors seemed to muddle together, the motions so fast that she suddenly found herself tripping over her own feet.

Damn the heels Izill had forced her into.

Damn how good it felt when Arawn caught her.

And lowered her, slowly, into a dip, his hand dangerously close to the small of her back.

'Careful,' he said, as he held her there, his face so close to hers she need only lift her head . . . just in the slightest . . . to press her lips to his.

If she dared.

She could discover all the things she had in her dreams.

She could taste him . . . *have* him the way she never had before . . . if only he felt the same.

Warmth shot all the way to her toes.

He lifted her slowly, his hand sliding across her back.

'Winterwine is potent,' Arawn whispered as he righted her. 'It is why we are only allotted one glass. The ones who fight tonight won't drink at all. Though some . . . find their ways around the system.'

'And you?' Ezer asked, breathless in his gaze. 'What will *you* do tonight, Firemage?'

His eyes slipped to her dress again.

'I . . . will stay up later than I should,' he said. The music changed around them, and he lifted her, spinning them again. 'Most likely, I'll send every lackluster thought I have towards you until I bore you to sleep, and the speaking stone goes cold.'

Behind his mask, his eyes were like twin crystals, so blue she could have drowned in them, could have—

'*Ezer.*' The wind sighed her name, as if in warning.

Like it was calling to her through the warm fuzziness of the winterwine, reminding her not to fall.

Not to sink into something she would not be able to climb out of, when morning came. When he would be untouchable, *forbidden*, yet again.

But she dared place her hand upon his chest, as they turned.

She dared feel the way his heart slammed against her palm, dared relish how the heat of him licked her skin like a promise.

He cleared his throat.

'How is Six treating you?' Arawn asked.

So painfully, he'd changed the subject.

His eyes roved across her again . . . but this time it was searching instead of hungry. Like he was checking her for more evidence of injury.

He would see nothing beneath the long sleeves of her dress.

She was fully clothed, and yet in his gaze . . . she couldn't help feeling like she did in the bathhouse.

Like she was utterly bare before him.

'The injuries are part of the job,' she said, trying to keep a rein on herself. 'And nothing Alaris can't fix.'

She'd grown stronger when it came to pain.

It was temporary. It was . . .

Strangely liberating. Because each time she trudged her way to Alaris's healing room, it reminded her that she'd done something worth the healing.

It reminded her that she was fully alive.

But nothing compared to this, right now.

With her hand in his . . . and his fingertips on her waist.

'She won't fly,' Ezer said, and almost yelped as Arawn spun her wildly, dipping her down before lifting her up again so that their gazes met. So that she practically collided against him, chest to chest.

'Perhaps she's just not ready to,' Arawn said. 'They're her wings, after all. She can decide what to do with them.'

'Your father will kill her if we fail,' Ezer said, softly enough that only he could hear. 'And probably me, too.'

His hand curled tighter over her waist.

His blue eyes hardened beneath his mask.

'Then don't let him,' Arawn said. She noticed he did not argue about the punishment. And by now, she'd taken note of how many other Sacred had penance marks. It seemed that the more they had, the more they carried themselves with a certain stiffness . . . as if they feared stepping an inch out of line. 'Find a way.'

He never dropped her gaze, even as he expertly skirted past the other Sacred.

As if he saw only her.

They went past Kinlear. He took a goblet and tilted his head back as if to down it in one sip, then grabbed the hand of a beautiful Watermage in royal blue.

'Do you know what bothers me most?' Ezer asked as she snapped her head away from Kinlear. 'I'm *supposedly* Sacred, but I am neither a Knight nor a Scribe nor a Null, so I'm not even qualified to be a servant. I cannot invocate. And yet here I am . . . dressed in white like I belong here.'

She hadn't meant to say it.

But the words had simply tumbled out.

'I'm Unconsecrated, unclaimed, which makes me broken, or . . .'

'Broken things are beautiful, too,' Arawn said.

So softly, she almost didn't hear it.

She had never been called beautiful.

That word . . .

The music ended before she could let it settle against her soul, before she could *believe* it. And then he released her. They were at the edge of the crowd, standing before the wall of glass.

He lifted his own hand, whispered an invocation . . . and brought a tiny golden flame upon his palm. It was larger than a candle's flame, but still not enough to destroy a darksoul.

'You're not alone in your struggle, Minder,' he said. 'A lifetime of invocations granted . . . and yet this is all I have left. Every time I try . . . I think of how I couldn't save her. How I wasn't good enough, strong enough, devoted enough to—'

'Arawn,' she said, loud enough that his eyes slid to hers. She dared step closer, until their chests were nearly touching again. She felt her fingertips graze his, a spark of desire surging through her. 'You are *more* than enough.'

He inhaled at her touch. The flame in his hand suddenly surged.

His eyes met hers.

'The gods failed you,' Ezer dared to say. 'Like they failed my mother and father. Like they failed Ervos. It's okay to admit that.'

Like they have failed me, countless times.
Like they failed Zey.

She had fallen asleep clutching the Eagleminder's book last night, replaying every interaction. Replaying how pained Zey was. It was obvious now, in hindsight. And no one had tried to help her, except by making her pay penance.

What if someone had dared to try something different? Something that wasn't within the confines of the Five?

What she was saying . . .

It was dangerous.

And yet she could not stop herself from speaking truth to this prince.

'The gods cannot fail, Minder,' he said. 'Sometimes things don't work out the way we wish.'

'Maybe not in your mind,' she answered. The dancers began to swim before her, the colors melding into one shade. Her dress was suddenly too warm. The room, too stuffy. She longed for the darkness of night, the cold kiss of the wind, instead of all this . . .

This singular brightness.

This one day that would still end in another death-filled night. Absolution was all the Sacred had, a little tease of what life could be. Like giving a dog a bone, but only *after* he obeyed first. She suddenly hated it. 'I've seen the way the laws hold you back,' Ezer said. 'Perhaps . . . there are ways around them.'

'There aren't,' Arawn said.

And he sounded so sure, so certain, that even with the winter-wine fueling her bravery . . .

She let it go.

'Perhaps . . .' His eyes glanced past her nervously. 'Perhaps the gods will be merciful.'

She raised a brow.

'My father's time is short. His end is near. Perhaps . . . you may not have to make the Descent at all. If the gods call him home. Soon. *If*,' he whispered, and his smile fell. 'I would pardon you from your duty . . . if I were already King in his place.'

A month ago she would have wept at the thought of such mercy.

But now?

Now she caught a glimpse of Kinlear as he danced past, and he was laughing, so full of life it pained her. It made her remember, in a flash, every moment they had ever shared together, training Six.

'No,' she said softly, and shook her head. 'I think . . . I would still make the Descent. I'm fated for Six. Fated for *this*. I'll get her to fly. I just have to figure out *what* is holding her back.'

To walk away now . . .

It would leave her feeling like she'd denied the greatest part of herself.

The only gift, perhaps, the gods had ever given, and it came hand in hand with Kinlear and Six.

'I figured you'd say that.' Arawn frowned, following her gaze to where Kinlear spun away. 'Which is why I'd like to show you something. Would you care to take a walk with me?'

He held out a large, calloused hand, his eyes eager as he waited for her to take it.

And she was surprised how good it felt, how normal, when she laced her fingers through his.

With the winterwine in her system, she would have followed him anywhere.

She would have followed him to a shadowed alcove, where she could truly press her lips to his. She would have followed him to *any* of the places he'd taken her in her dreams. The library, the bathing chambers, the flour-coated countertops in the kitchens . . .

But it seemed her dreams would remain only dreams.

Because Arawn took her back to the place she'd spent countless hours in – the Aviary. They went not to Six nor the Eagle's Nest. But up the stairwell that led to the Ravenminder's tower.

Where it all *should* have begun.

They'd since found someone else to fill the job, she'd been told. The Ravenminder was at Absolution with all the others, but would soon return like everyone else, ready to send messages that gave names and faces to death.

It felt like days ago that she was doing the same.

It also felt like a lifetime, for so much had changed.

The door to the tower was old and wooden, and when Arawn pushed it open . . . it was an effort not to gasp.

The smell was just like home.

Crushed seeds, millet and corn and parchment, and a candlestick on a small table in the center of the room, and birds sleeping on perches all around. A perfect Ravenminder's tower, and for a second, she imagined Ervos sitting at that table.

She could picture her uncle turning to face her. He'd probably say, '*Come on, Little Bird. It's time for me to show you something new today.*' And he would point out some interesting fact about a swallow or a finch or a tawny owl. He'd tell her how to tame that specific breed, how to determine whether or not it was trustworthy to make the routes they required from one tower to another. But in the end, it was always ravens for her.

'Ezer?'

Arawn was staring at her, where she still stood in the doorway, watching the shadows like they might hold a ghost.

But there was no one at the table.

Just ink stains and a stack of empty papers, some of them already pre-torn to the perfect size for a messenger bird's scroll.

'How did he die?' Ezer asked suddenly.

She no longer felt the warmth of the wine.

She felt only sorrow, deep as the sea.

'A scuffle in the barracks, if I had to guess,' Arawn said. 'The soldiers may fight for Lordach. But they are not always kind to one another. Especially when so many of them come from prison cells. From dark places.'

'Was it fast?' Ezer asked. 'Or . . .'

'I don't know,' Arawn said. 'I wish there was more to tell you.'

She felt like there was.

But it wasn't his job to keep track of deaths. He was Lordach's crown prince, and Ervos was just another Minder in a tower. One who probably got drunk each night in the barracks down below, playing cards . . . cheating, when the desperation to win became greater than the guiding light inside him.

She turned away and focused instead on the tower.

The birds.

'Hello, friends,' Ezer said.

There were a few ravens inside, and they instantly perked up at the sound of her voice. Like they knew her, though they'd never flown her routes. Not this far north.

She held out a hand, and one of them fluttered towards her, landing on her wrist with sharp, dark talons. But she remained still, so as not to scare it. Not that a raven would ever spook around her.

Perhaps it had been there in the woods a month ago.

Perhaps, in that strange burst of magic that had yet to return, this was one of the ravens that had saved her.

'I've never seen such an ability,' Arawn said, looking at her from the doorway. 'It's like they know you. Like they trust you, just as Six does.'

Ezer shrugged and ran her fingertip across the raven's chin. 'It's been this way for as long as I can remember. And yet, when I'm faced with a test of normal pillared magic . . .' She blew out a breath, lifted her hand and sent the raven soaring back to its perch. 'I get nothing. Only silence from the Five.'

'If I were a god, I'd answer,' Arawn said.

She raised a brow. 'So now you think yourself a god, Arawn of Augaurde?'

'No,' he said, shaking his head, his eyes wide. 'Not in the slightest. I know my place, I know my – you're joking again. Aren't you?'

'Always,' Ezer said.

He crossed his large arms. 'I simply mean, it would be a fine gift, to give you the clarity you seek. Not to know your lineage, your background . . . it would frustrate me to my core.'

He motioned for her to cross to the window at the other side of the tower. Already, she could tell it would overlook the Expanse. And the Eagle's Nest, from above, if she peered out of it.

'I will rule all of this someday,' Arawn said. He released a frustrated sigh. 'A leader who cannot properly wield. I wonder how the people will respect me then.'

'You will be respected,' she said firmly. 'You already are.' She'd seen the way the soldiers looked at him in the halls. How they inclined their heads, not because they *had* to, but because they probably all knew of his pain. His loss. And still . . . he was here. Still, he would take up his father's crown and lead. 'I'll find my magic, and you will recover yours. And if we don't . . . there is always Realmbreak.'

'Realmbreak,' Arawn said. 'It's why I brought you here.'

He turned his gaze towards the view out the window.

Despite the twist in her stomach, she leaned against the stones and peered out with him.

The Eagle's Nest was like a giant glass orb from up here. The tower itself, far up in the steeple, higher than the peak of the dome. She could see the golden runes swimming across the glass, alive with the gods' magic.

'Just in time,' Arawn said. 'Look.'

The domed roof beneath their tower suddenly opened wide.

And the first war eagle soared out.

The climb was instantaneous, a burst of gold wings and feathers and a rider in white, soaring up into the sky, twisting once upside down before nose-diving, beak-first, over the cliff's edge.

She watched that fall the way a child would, when tossing a coin into a fountain. Wide-eyed and waiting until it hit the bottom.

At the last moment, the rider tugged on the reins, and the war eagle lifted its wings. It rose just enough to cross through the Snow Gates: those two towering black pillars that marked the opposite edge of Augaurde, and the golden wards.

Where the eagle's wings took over, and they rose steadily back to the sky.

'This looks far more terrifying from above,' Ezer said as she watched the next one rise from the glass dome and make the nose-dive. 'Why did you bring me here again?'

Arawn grinned. 'Because this is the highest cliff face in all Augaurde. It's the greatest challenge Lordach's war eagles will ever face.' He smiled. 'But the raphons?'

He pointed at the Sawteeth, small from here, with that ever-furious shadowstorm.

'Those mountains are made of nothing *but* heights . . . the kind that would make this cliff face look like child's play.'

Her stomach twisted.

'That's supposed to make me feel better?'

He blinked, like she still wasn't getting it.

'It's in her blood,' Arawn said. 'To fly from harrowing heights. Her own mother came from there, in the Acolyte's domain. And the raphon before that, and the one *before* that, too. It's who she is, Ezer. And if you're going to survive this . . . believe in her. Trust that she'll know what to do when the moment comes.'

She could picture it, the Descent, the fall, in her mind.

The wind biting at her hair, the—

Arawn placed a hand atop hers. It was steadying. Grounding. Warm, as it always was in her dreams.

For a moment, she didn't want him to move it away.

And it seemed like he didn't either.

So they stood like that, his hand just barely resting over hers, shoulder to shoulder, watching the sky.

She could feel his heartbeat.

It was fast, like hers.

'Let her do what she does best,' Arawn said. 'Just like a bird leaving the nest, she'll know what to do. And if you give her that trust . . .' A steady breath, as his shoulder rose and fell against hers. And when he spoke next, she could have sworn there was sadness in his voice as he slid his hand away. 'You'll be flying away from here in no time.'

PART THREE

THE RAPHON RIDER

CHAPTER 28

She found herself in the labyrinth again. But when she turned the skeleton key in one of the locks . . .

It wasn't her own memory she found.

It was the Citadel. The library, of all places.

And seated there on the floor, her back up against the bookshelves as she scribbled something in a journal, was a small, mouse-haired young woman in a brown servant robe. There was a midnight-black cat in her lap, purring loudly.

'I thought I'd find you here,' said a voice.

Ezer turned to see a young man, perhaps only seventeen, with dark curls and bright blue eyes, and a smile that was as warm as the sun. He wore Sacred whites, the crest of a Realmist on his chest. 'I've missed you, Styerra.'

'And you,' said the young woman.

And as she stood . . .

Ezer gasped.

Because it was her own face staring back at her. Without scars, without the ugliness, with a few more freckles on her nose, and much lighter hair. But the likeness was unmistakable.

Ezer stepped closer, knowing the young woman wouldn't hear her. But she said the word on her heart anyway.

'Mother?'

*

This time, when Ezer woke to Izill's voice, she was desperate to keep her mother's face with her.

'Morning! The prince beckons again,' Izill said, frowning as she stopped at Ezer's bedside. 'Was Absolution that bad? You look like you've seen a ghost.'

Ezer blinked wearily as she sat up. Her nightclothes were drenched in sweat. She felt a bit queasy, unsure if it was from the winterwine or the face so like hers in her dream. 'I think . . . I think I *have*, Izill.'

'Coffee with a friend fixes all things,' Izill said and shoved a steaming mug into Ezer's hands. 'Drink up and then tell me *everything*.'

Speaking soothed her, as did the warmth of the coffee. And as she ate, Ezer told her friend about her dream. Not every detail of the labyrinth, but about Styerra. About the face that matched her own.

'Styerra is a common enough name in the north,' Izill said with a frown. 'But it's more detail than we've had thus far. You're *certain* it was your mother?'

'I've never seen her face before,' Ezer said. 'But . . . I felt it, Izill. And even if I'm wrong, the resemblance was uncanny. It's more than I've ever had to go off.'

At that, Izill nodded. 'Perhaps the gods granted you a gift. A small blessing, to ease your wonderings.'

'Can they do that?' Ezer asked.

Because she'd never considered the labyrinth to be from the gods.

But what happened in her mind . . . it could only be explained by something like magic.

'Of course they can.' Izill smiled and took Ezer's empty mug. 'They are limitless. And *you* are going to be late. I'll do some digging on the name. If she was a servant, she clearly had no magic. Styerra, you said?'

Ezer nodded.

'You'd be surprised, what I overhear on my days inside the kitchens. I'll do my best sleuthing.'

With a swift goodbye, Ezer left the dorms.

A snowstorm was fresh on the horizon.

It was unfortunate weather. Because today, Kinlear wanted Ezer to leave the cliffside. It was Six's first time out of the runed circle of stones, and already, the raphon seemed anxious, pacing a hole in the snow as they talked.

'We've several hours to sunset,' Kinlear said. 'By the gods, it's cold.'

He looked exhausted. Even his runed cloak couldn't seem to warm him, and his cheeks were too shallow. He'd been so vibrant last night, dancing his way through Absolution. How quickly things could change when someone's own body was working against them.

She'd been with him less than an hour, and he'd already had to sip from his vial twice.

'We'll walk her the long way around the Citadel, out to the Sacred Circle. It's the furthest we can go before we run into another Gate. She needs experience. A break from this pattern and place.'

'And the War Table is letting us take her there?' Ezer asked.

Six pranced past her, tail twitching as she kicked up the snow with her paws. Now that she knew it wasn't going to kill her . . . she loved it.

Kinlear shrugged. 'Training requires it. And besides, we're inside the wards. The most dangerous thing in Augaurde is Six.'

'And you trust me,' Ezer said, 'with her? With . . . *you*?'

He smiled at her. 'Do I have any reason not to?'

She felt guilty as she thought of her dreams. His dagger, and the blood on her chest.

If anything, *she* had reason not to trust *him*.

But nothing she'd seen had come to pass. Not the moments

with Arawn, not anything with Six. Certainly not her own death at Kinlear's hands.

It was *his* death she worried about now.

He was too vibrant a person. Too bright a light to simply fade away early, a horrible fate for a man who hadn't the excuse of using magic to bring about his early end.

Already, Ezer's heart had begun to squeeze with a *missing* sort of feeling when she looked at him.

Like he was already half gone.

'No,' Ezer said, meeting his silver gaze. 'Nothing to worry about with me, Prince.'

He smiled. 'All right then, Raphonminder. Let's go.'

Six was not easy to guide down the cliffside by foot. They went the long way down, a path that led through the Thornwell instead of the black stone steps. It was not used often, for it was overgrown with trees, and too steep for Ezer's liking, but she and Kinlear managed to stay on Six's back without falling.

A true feat they should have celebrated . . . because though Six was built for scrambling down harsh terrain . . .

She ran into tree branches, and got distracted easily, batting at things with her enormous paws. She leapt off boulders and scratched at the snow every few feet, like an overgrown chicken.

'It's good we did this,' Kinlear said, breathless as he held on to Ezer. 'She's become unhinged.'

'She's just *curious*,' Ezer corrected him. 'Ravens are like that. It's best she works it out now.'

The raphon sent a vision into her mind.

A small black kitten batting at a ball of yarn.

Ezer laughed. Six was playing.

And she was happy. Truly happy.

So Ezer was too.

The snow fell heavier by the time they finally made it down the upper cliffside. They stuck to the edge of the Thornwell, avoiding the barracks in the valley down below. Then they were moving upwards again as the land stretched gradually towards another jutting cliff.

A violent cough shook Ezer's back, where Kinlear held on.

'Should we turn around?' she asked, glancing over her shoulder at him.

He shook his head and uncorked the vial at his throat. 'Gods, no.' He took a sip, then worked to calm his breathing. 'My mother arrives tomorrow. I don't think she'll let me out into the cold again.'

They passed through a thick line of trees – both of their heads covered in snow, thanks to Six's wings knocking a heavy branch down – and when they came to the other side . . .

'Ah. Here we are,' said Kinlear.

Ezer's eyes widened.

The Sacred Circle.

She'd seen it through the library windows with Kinlear, what felt like forever ago now. But even though she knew just how big the standing stones were . . .

Seeing them in person stole her breath away. She had to crane her neck back to see their tops, and even then, they faded into the low-hanging clouds.

A ring of twelve, each stone protruded from the snow like they were only extensions of the earth. They would have blended perfectly with the snow, were it not for the runes carved into every square inch of them.

She dared push Six closer.

'Can I . . .'

'Go ahead,' Kinlear said, as the raphon stopped.

And Ezer placed a hand on the closest stone, marveling at the fact that she was touching something *older* than Lordach's first kings and queens.

As old as recorded time, and then some.

'Can you read them?' Ezer asked.

Kinlear shook his head. 'It would take me centuries to read every rune. But the overarching story of each realm is the same. The realm's creation, the gods, the inevitable attempt of mortals hoping to be just as great. And the Sacred.' He sighed. 'The names change, of course, depending on the realm, but there is always a placeholder. A set of souls meant to take the blame. To hold the punishment of imperfection so the rest can enter the Ehver when the Five call us home. Every stone was once the same . . . until the Thirteenth. And as ours darkens . . . we believe our fate is tied to whatever ended theirs.'

He pointed past Ezer to the stone in the circle that had tendrils of black stretching across its surface.

Cracks in the stone that could have been shadows.

A stone that was impenetrable by any sort of weapon. Even Sacred magic.

And just beside it was an empty space. A gap, where the thirteenth stone used to be.

Realmbreak was suddenly too soon.

The wind shifted, cold and biting. And Six's head turned, eyes narrowed as if she sensed something.

'What is it, Six?' Ezer asked.

The raphon huffed and scraped an impatient paw across the snow.

She turned so that now she was facing the exit, where the wardlight glowed a brilliant gold. One step beyond those tall obelisks, the Forest Gates that held them safely within a magical bubble of the gods' protection . . . and they'd be helpless. As good as dead, if the enemy found them.

Six began to walk slowly toward those gates. Daringly close to the exit.

'Six. *Stop*, before you get—'

Her words trailed off as a vision filtered into her mind.

A raphon, bleeding and dying as it lay on the snow. It looked like Six, but Ezer knew it wasn't, because her belly was swollen.

She was pregnant.

Sadness washed over Ezer as she saw the raphon trying to stand, screeching in agony. Her darksoul rider was dead, a creature with long, jagged claws that lay several yards away on the snow.

And her wings were broken, snapped in two.

Six's mother.

It had to be.

Voices broke through the memory, and the raphon collapsed again, just as the wardlight shimmered, and a group of Sacred passed through the Gates.

'Bind her up,' said a voice. 'She's too far gone. We may get some research out of her, at least . . .'

Something whizzed past, sinking deep into the raphon's back leg. A rune-marked arrow. The raphon yelped and went silent, pulled into deep sleep. Sacred converged upon her, with ropes and chains.

Just like that, the raphon became a prisoner.

. . . And inside of her belly, so did six others.

The vision ended.

Six kept walking towards the Gates.

'What is she doing?' Kinlear asked. 'Turn her around.'

'*Go*,' said the wind. The whisper had arrived out of nowhere. '*Go, Ezer.*'

'No,' Ezer said. 'She needs to see it.'

'See what?' Kinlear asked.

Ezer glanced over her shoulder, locking eyes with him. 'The place where her mother was captured.'

They passed through the wards. The magic was cold on her skin, tickling her cheeks and nose. It felt like a bubble *popping*. It felt like . . .

Like Ezer could breathe again, without the weight of magic.

The forest around them was calm, quiet, like there was no war at all.

Six walked a few paces into the small clearing and paused, sniffing the snow.

'You were here,' Ezer said gently. She glanced over her shoulder at Kinlear, who looked at her, puzzled.

'How do you know that?' he asked.

She shrugged. 'Six remembers. Sometimes . . . she shows me things.'

To his credit, he didn't prod any further. 'We captured her mother here,' he said. 'A perfectly executed trap, with runes and war eagles well placed. We didn't know she carried the pups until she'd already fallen. A happy accident, I suppose, because it brought us Six.'

The raphon's tail twitched twice.

Ezer pursed her lips, running her hands down the side of Six's neck, as if to say, *I'm here*.

In the distance, a raven cawed.

'She's seen the spot. Now we need to go back,' Kinlear said. 'This isn't safe, Ezer.'

But something in Ezer's belly told her to stay.

And Six seemed to sense it, too.

'*Ezer*.'

The wind blew, rushing past her.

She urged Six a few more paces forward, past a grouping of fat evergreens perched in the snow.

And there, just on the other side, was a graveyard.

'What . . . is this place?' Ezer breathed.

Kinlear looked down at the old stones. 'Many ancients were buried here. The tradition is lost to us. We burn the Sacred now, plunge their swords into the ground around the Sacred Tree.'

Ezer slid down from Six's back.

'What are you doing? We need to leave,' Kinlear said.

'Just a second,' Ezer mused.

The sky was darkening. It must have taken them hours to

get down the cliffside. It was getting too close to sunset, but she couldn't stop herself.

And neither, it seemed, could Six.

The raphon walked about, sniffing the ground. The stones were ancient, old enough to be dated several Realmbreaks past.

She read countless names, all of them half-buried by snow. For some reason, she kept going. The wind whispered '*yes*,' as if it were urging her on.

Six paused at the same time Ezer did.

Atop a grave that was old and broken. She knelt and swept the snow aside as best she could. The date in the stone had since worn away, but the name . . .

Ezer's eyes widened.

'Wrenwyn,' she whispered. 'Wrenwyn . . . Lavor.'

Six's paws stopped just at the edge of it. Her wings drooped upon her back, and she inclined her head. Like she knew this stone.

This place.

Ezer glanced up at Kinlear, who still sat on Six's back.

'Wrenwyn the Wrong,' Ezer said. 'She was buried here?'

Kinlear shrugged. 'I suppose she was.'

'She was killed on her wedding day,' Ezer said. 'A terrible end.'

The raven cawed again.

Kinlear shook his head. 'Perhaps in your version of the story. In others, she survived. She was brought back to the temple. That was the Aviary, at the time, where she spent years fading away slowly. She was confined to her rooms for protection from those who wished her ill. One of her siblings became King in her stead.'

'When did she die?' Ezer asked. 'In your version of the story.'

Kinlear shrugged. The wind lifted his curls from his eyes and he shivered and coughed. As if his warming runes weren't doing enough for him. He quickly reached for the vial on his throat, uncorking it.

There seemed to be only a drop left.

'We'll go,' Ezer said. She grabbed Six's halter and began leading her back.

'Some say Wrenwyn escaped,' Kinlear said. 'That she had help sneaking out of the castle. She made it far away from here, and when her brother sent his men after her . . . they made it to the Sawteeth. And were eaten alive by raphons. The first recorded instance of them hunting men.'

Ezer shivered at that.

She couldn't imagine Six eating anyone alive.

'Either way, the story is timeworn,' the prince said. 'It changes by the year. Wrenwyn is a figure for dark, strange stories, but the real one is probably far less thrilling.' He sighed and looked down at Wrenwyn's meager grave. A princess, buried alone and forgotten beyond the wards. A sad ending, for a tale Ezer had always loved. 'We need to go. It's almost sunset.'

The wind howled again, and Six lifted her beak, letting it roll over her.

Ezer smiled at another caw of a raven, because it was lovely, and it reminded her of her past, when things were simpler, when—

The raven's sound cut off with a strange, choking sort of screech.

'What was that?' Kinlear whispered.

Ezer's blood roared in her ears.

A low growl sounded in Six's throat.

Ezer looked to the treeline, but she saw nothing. Six stamped her paws, her tail twitching twice. 'Ezer,' Kinlear breathed. 'Let's go.'

The wind had gone still. It was utterly quiet, until another gust came. It kicked up the snow, and with it . . .

Something rotten.

The scent of death.

Ezer had just turned around, just climbed upon Six's back in front of Kinlear, when the wind whispered, '*Run.*'

And she saw the two dark figures that had landed behind them. Blocking the way to the ward Gates. Trapping them outside.

Shadow wolves.

Dark ichor dripped from their shadowy snouts. A low growl came from each of their throats as Ezer's body went cold.

'Ezer,' Kinlear breathed.

His hand went to the dagger on his hip. It was all they had to defend themselves. All they had . . .

Besides Six.

'*Fly,*' Ezer whispered. 'Six. You have to fly.'

She prayed the raphon would be faster than the wolves.

They closed in.

Six growled – Ezer felt it rumble through her body – and twitched her wings.

The wolves growled back and the scars on Ezer's face seemed to squirm with memory, as those long black claws carved up the snow with each step.

Help, she thought to the wind. *Send the ravens.*

But nothing came.

'Fly,' Ezer hissed. 'Six. Use your wings. You have to *fly*!'

The raphon shook her head, skittering and prancing backwards. A feeling of terror rose in Ezer's gut, and she knew it came from Six.

She was scared of the wolves, an enemy that was once an ally.

It was an effort to stay on her back. Ezer dug her hands into her fur and feathers, as if she could make the raphon feel her own terror. *Please. Fly!*

'Ezer,' Kinlear said. 'Get her airborne or we die.'

'I can't,' Ezer breathed.

The trees were at their back now, too thick for the raphon to make it through. To their left . . . the distant edge of the cliff.

'Six,' Ezer said. '*Fly.*'

The raphon nearly stumbled over the gravestones as she backed away.

Please, she begged the wind. *Help us, Avane.*

She tried, *desperately,* to invocate.

But the wind did not answer.

So Ezer held onto Six as desperation moved through her. As she felt something shift in her mind. An ember, come to life.

Six could send visions.

Perhaps she could too.

In her mind, she imagined herself dying. She imagined her body flayed open on crimson snow while the shadow wolves feasted upon her.

She imagined Kinlear, dead beside her, and Six . . .

Six standing alone in the snow.

Alone forever, without Ezer in this world.

She felt the moment that vision *whooshed* away from her. Like something had plucked it from her skull and sent it soaring.

Six inhaled beneath her.

Like she saw the vision.

The wolves stepped closer, and their wings snapped out.

They were going to lunge.

She was going to die.

'*Fly.*'

Six turned towards the cliffside, her paws rooted deep against the snowy ground.

'*Yes,*' whispered the wind. '*Fly.*'

Ezer had no choice but to hold tight as Six pushed off, taking three bounding steps . . .

Before she leapt into the open sky.

They fell.

Into the coming night, they fell.

At first, Ezer thought they would rise. But they began to spin slowly, as Six screeched beneath them, helpless. Lost, like a stone tossed out over the cliffside, falling too fast.

With each second, they picked up speed.

They weren't as high as the Aviary; they didn't have enough time to rise . . .

'Six!' Ezer screamed. '*Fly!*'

The terror in her veins made her arms and legs strong enough to hold on. She was falling, her hair ripped from its braid, the wind tearing at her skin, her cloak, the snow blurring everything in front of her eyes. Kinlear's grip was a vice around her middle, but she felt him sliding away.

Oh gods, oh gods.

'Pull up!' Ezer screamed.

They kept falling.

She could see the ground now. She could see the stones they would crash against, could imagine the way they would all be shredded.

'Six!' Ezer screamed. '*Your wings!*'

At the last second, the raphon snapped her wings out.

And caught the wind.

Ezer's stomach shot into her throat as they soared upwards. Kinlear was howling with laughter in her ear, and Ezer shouted, 'Yes, Six!'

They soared higher and higher, rising into the sky. The fear rose like bile in Ezer's throat. She was going to throw up, she was going to pass out—

No.

She forced herself to stay present for Six.

'You're doing it!' she shouted. 'That's it!'

The wolves chased after them, but Six snarled, and pressed faster into flight. The wind followed, whispering *yes,* as the wolves fell behind.

Ezer glanced back to see them banking, turning back towards the Expanse where easier prey awaited.

And for a moment, it all felt *right*.

Until the shadows erupted. Until the boom split the night, and in the distance, the war began.

A gust of wind crashed against them, and Six dipped in the wrong direction, like she hadn't a clue how to feel and understand the drafts. How to glide *with* them instead of against.

They soared over the treetops, too fast.

'Higher,' Kinlear said in Ezer's ear. 'She's got to go higher, or she'll clip the trees!'

Ezer tried.

But the panic had taken over her, just as it had taken over Six. The raphon dipped too far to the left, and she yelped a warning too late as Six's wing clipped a tall tree.

They spun sideways.

Everything blurred. The last thing Ezer heard was Six's screech before they crashed against the snow.

CHAPTER 29

She woke in her labyrinth, the skeleton key in her hand.

A safe space for the moment, because something in the waking world was wrong.

Ezer couldn't remember, couldn't place it.

She ran until she came to the hall that held her memories. She skidded on ice as she stopped before the door to where she'd last seen her mother – the face, so like her own.

She placed the key in the lock and practically shoved it down trying to get inside.

Ezer had stepped into the library again, but this time it was dark, as if hours or days had passed.

She spun around . . . and there she was.

Her mother.

Styerra was in the same spot Ezer had last seen her. She knew the young woman couldn't see her. But it was so real. As if they were truly together in a sea of books.

She stepped closer, peering down at the small woman as if she were looking at a better version of herself. Unscarred. Unruined by darkness and pain.

One delicate hand penned a note in a journal in her lap – the cover was worn, crimson leather – while the other hand stroked the black cat. It purred loudly, giving no mind to Ezer as she stood over them.

'Now, you keep prying eyes away from this, Saber,' said Styerra, as she finished up her note and closed the book.

Instead of taking the journal with her, she slid it onto the shelf.

The cat meowed in agreement, settling down on the floor as if to protect the secret. And Styerra scurried into the shadows, her brown robes flying behind her, a smile on her beautiful face.

The scene darkened, and before she knew it, Ezer was spat back out in the hallway.

The memory was over.

So she went to the next door, unlocked it, and crept inside.

She found Styerra in the library again. This time, Styerra's hair was braided back from her face, like a ribbon atop her head. The very same way Izill did her own hair. She had a plain face, like Ezer's, but without the scars it was easy to see her features. Her eyes were gray, her lips a pretty pink, and her smile was like a beam of sunlight. She grinned, ear to ear, as she rounded the corner between shelves, heading deeper into the library.

'Styerra.'

A hand reached out, and Ezer yelped until she realized it was the young man from before.

The young Realmist.

He was handsome with his dark curls, his blue eyes, his summertime smile.

Was this her father? She felt nothing when she looked at him, not like she did with Styerra.

'I missed you,' he said.

'Not as much as I missed you,' said Styerra. 'It's getting harder to find time, with your trainings.'

'And yet here we are again.' He smiled, lifted her hand and pressed his lips to it.

Ezer gasped.

Styerra wore a ring. The exact one that now sat on her own hand.

'Yes,' said Styerra. 'Here we are.'

Her stomach lurched when the two began to kiss.

She watched for only a moment, thinking it sweet, until the passion rose between them.

Gods.

It was like they were desperate for one another, as the Knight suddenly spun and pressed Styerra against the shelves. He leaned in hungrily. Like he could devour her whole.

Ezer turned away, stomach turning – gods, she'd never wanted to see her own mother doing that.

She left the library as quickly as she could.

The next door was much the same.

And the door after that.

Each time she entered, as the months seemed to go by, she saw nothing but the two lovers stealing kisses and secret moments in the darkness.

It was forbidden love, she knew.

A fate that would end in penance and heartbreak, for a Knight could never be matched with a servant. Their union would never be blessed.

Ezer watched it play out like a romance novel, door after door, memory after memory . . . her heart twisting each time she saw them together. They filled the journal with love notes, leaving it for the other to find later, to keep them connected while they were apart.

Beautiful, their love.

But doomed from the start.

She wondered when it would end. When they would be discovered.

She found out when she entered a door covered in thick cobwebs. The key struggled in the lock, as if the door did not want to be opened.

She forced her way inside.

She was back in the library again . . . but something had changed.

'You haven't come for me in days,' Styerra said. 'I wrote to you. You didn't answer.'

His face had changed, his expression pained.

'I tried to get here,' the Realmist said. 'I wanted to come, but it wasn't safe. I couldn't risk being seen with you.'

Styerra recoiled.

'You know what would happen,' he said gently. 'You know the penance would be worse for you than it would be for me.'

'I don't care,' Styerra whispered. 'I just want you, Erath.'

Ezer catalogued his name. Erath. She committed it to memory.

He reached for Styerra, but she backed away, still hurt.

'I heard the Masters came to your dorm. They turned it upside down, looking for Zeban. There's rumor from the other servants that he was ill. That he was caught speaking of something dark and dangerous.' Her voice shook. 'Something that defies the Five.'

'Zeban is gone,' Erath said. 'He made it out before they arrived. Someone warned him.'

'Who?' Styerra asked.

He released a sigh. 'I got him to safety. That's what matters.'

'Safety?' Styerra's eyes widened. She looked hurt that he hadn't told her. 'Where to?'

The Realmist chewed on his lip. He was tall and proud, as he stepped closer to her and whispered, 'Somewhere far away.' He took a breath, watching her carefully. 'Somewhere we could go. Together.'

'What?' Styerra shook her head. 'You mean to run? To bring him back?'

'Zeban isn't coming back,' he said. 'Not ever. And once we leave here . . . neither are we.'

'But . . .' Styerra's cheeks were flushed. Her lower lip trembled like she was holding back tears. 'There's nowhere for us to go.'

He took her hands in his, holding them up to his heart. 'Do you trust me, Styerra?'

'With my whole heart,' she said. She still had that ring on her finger.

And Ezer noticed he had a matching one.

'And I trust you with mine,' he said. He glanced over his shoulder and pulled her deeper into the shadows of the library. 'So, I'm going to tell you something, Styerra. Something that nobody can ever know. Only us.'

Styerra nodded.

'Zeban showed me something new and strange,' Erath whispered. 'Something he was given by Clarice.'

'She died months ago,' Styerra said.

He shook his head. 'She didn't die, Styerra. She ran. The Masters don't want us to know of it.'

'Why?' Styerra asked, wide-eyed. 'They'd never keep a secret. It defies the Laws.'

'They've kept it for ages. Because it offers freedom. A new way for the Sacred.' He reached into his cloak and revealed a small black book.

Ezer's heart began to pound.

Because the book . . .

It looked so achingly familiar, but in her dreams, she couldn't quite place it.

'It was uncovered decades ago, when some of the looters dug up an Ancient's grave, hoping for fine treasures. There were no bones in her grave,' he said. 'Instead, there was this.'

Styerra looked down at the book, her eyes widening.

'An Ancient . . . you have Wrenwyn's *book? She was cursed! You must put it back, get rid of it before it's too late.' She backed away. 'The gods will not be pleased.'*

'I've already read it,' Erath said.

Styerra gasped, shaking her head.

But he smiled, a disarming thing. 'Its pages, Styerra . . . they're unlike anything I've ever seen.'

And before she could stop him, he opened the book and showed it to her.

It was empty.

The pages, utterly lacking a single mark upon them.

Styerra's brow furrowed, a look that reminded Ezer so much of herself, she felt as if she were staring into a mirror. 'There's nothing here, my love.'

She reached out, as if to check his forehead for a fever.

But he shook his head and gently pulled her hand back down. 'Not at first. But Zeban told me if I would only read it, spend time with it . . . eventually, my eyes would be opened, and I would see.'

Footsteps sounded behind them, and he quickly hid the book. But it was only a Scribe passing through. The Realmist's blue eyes were bright, full of wonder as he looked back down at the empty pages.

Styerra's lip quirked. 'Something is wrong. You're tired from training, or perhaps you've spent too long out in the snow. You could go to the Masters, or the Healer, or even Draybor—'

The king.

'Draybor won't see reason,' he spat. 'I can't risk it.'

'Draybor is your friend,' Styerra pleaded with him. 'He loves you like a brother!'

'And he is also a crown prince, blinded by ritual and family ties. By a lifetime of Sacred lies.' He sighed and closed his eyes, breathing deep in frustration. 'No one can know until they are ready, Styerra. Zeban sensed that I was ready. Because of you. Because of us. So he shared it with me. And now I'm sharing it with you.'

He pulled the empty book out again.

'Sharing what, exactly?' Styerra asked.

He ran a thumb across the top of her hand, touching her ring.

'The book promises a different life. It is like the Sacred Text, but vastly different. It speaks of a different realm. A place without boundaries, where magic doesn't have to be earned by promises and deeds. It is given. And this realm, Styerra . . . it is a place where love isn't barred. Where a Knight and a Servant can be together. Forever.'

Her eyes widened.

She glanced at the empty book, then back at his eager expression.

'Where is this other place?'

'The Sawteeth,' he said. 'It's a pathway. An opening, and I think Wrenwyn was the one to discover it long ago. I think that's what made her different . . . able to wield without invocating. I think the others tried to kill her because they feared what she'd found.'

'Wrenwyn went to this place?'

'Yes,' he breathed. 'And . . . perhaps she is still there. Waiting for others to join her in freedom on the other side.'

'But that can't be true,' Styerra whispered.

'Perhaps the Masters,' he said slowly, 'have been controlling us, all along.'

'No,' she shook her head. 'They wouldn't do that.'

He closed his eyes, breathing deeply, like he was desperate for her to understand.

'Zeban went to find it. Others have gone before him, too, seeking the other place. And I think . . . if we run, Styerra, we can find it, too.'

He was speaking of the Acolyte.

He had to be.

'You're scaring me,' Styerra said. 'What you speak of, Erath . . . it's betrayal. It's madness.'

For a second, he looked angry.

'I love you,' Erath whispered. 'I would never lead you astray, Styerra. I would never lead you into darkness, unless I was *certain it was the only way for us to be together.' He looked at the ring on his finger. 'I've been matched.'*

Styerra gasped.

'I got the news last night. The Masters say the gods have matched me with another Realmist. I'll have to join with her, Styerra. To . . . lie with her.'

Ezer's stomach twisted.

'They say I must carry on the lineage. The magic. They say it is my duty to the gods to mate with her, and—' He closed his eyes, and a tear rolled down his cheek. 'And what we have will be over.'

Styerra began to cry.

Gently, she lowered herself to the ground, like the news of his matching stole all her strength away.

'I have three days before I make the Descent,' Erath said. 'They'll send me to complete the matching that night.' He set the book before her. 'Will you read it? For me? For us?'

'There's nothing to read,' she pleaded with him. 'There's nothing to—'

'Not yet,' he said. 'But there will be, if you believe.'

Ezer wished she could tell her mother not to read the book, that Erath was speaking of the Acolyte and he didn't even know it.

He was leading them somewhere dark.

He was leading them right towards Lordach's end.

But Styerra took the book.

'I will try,' she said.

Erath kissed her, relieved. 'I know you'll see. We're meant for each other, Styerra. I will not give my heart to another.' He kissed her on the forehead, even as another tear rolled down her cheek. 'We'll meet right after my Descent. I'll be in the Aviary, with Veren saddled and ready. Meet me there. We'll leave together to find freedom. And we'll never look back.'

He kissed her one last time before he turned and walked away.

Styerra wiped her tears. Then she stood, on trembling legs, and opened her cloak to hide the black book inside.

Ezer gasped.

Because there, just barely, was the beginning of a small bump.

A baby.

And Erath . . .

He didn't know.

Styerra ran her hands across it, cradling it gently, lovingly. Then she turned and walked away.

If she'd glanced back only once, she would have seen the figure that now peered out from behind a bookshelf. As if they'd been there the whole time, watching. Listening to Erath's every word.

He was tall, broad-shouldered, with a shock of red hair and a look of sorrow on his face.

Ezer's breath caught in her throat.

Because he wasn't supposed to be here. Because he had no part in this memory.

Because he'd told Ezer, for nineteen years, that he never knew who her mother was.

And yet there he stood, wearing brown servant robes like he was part of the Citadel.

Uncle Ervos.

She woke to pounding pain in the middle of her forehead.

Ezer groaned, wanting to sleep longer.

But the pain came again, followed by a *caw*.

Ezer opened her eyes, surprised to find a raven filling her vision. It was perched on her chest, illuminated by a spear of moonlight. And it was rearing back, as if to peck her awake again.

'Stop it,' she hissed.

The raven hopped away, giving her a glimpse of the trees overhead.

She was on her back, sprawled in the snow. Wet and shivering, and—

Oh, gods.

They'd crashed.

The last thing she remembered, she was on Six's back. Six was *flying,* and it was glorious, and Kinlear was laughing behind her and—

Ezer tried to sit up. Stars flickered in her vision as her head wobbled, and she thought she might be sick.

'H-h-help,' she whispered.

No footsteps came, but a groan sounded to her right. She rolled to hands and knees, gasping for breath. It was cold.

So, so cold.

Something caught her vision. A delicate golden glow, a few steps into the trees. The snow was carved up, a tree broken in half, as if they'd crashed and slid.

Where was Six?

The groan came again, and her mind registered the shape of runes, covered up by a fresh dusting of snow.

Kinlear's cloak.

Panic raced through her, shaking her awake.

There was little moonlight, but in the white snow it looked brighter. She could see the prince was on his side, darkness blooming beneath his head.

Blood.

'*Go to him,*' the wind whispered. '*Hurry.*'

Gods, her head.

It was going to explode.

With all her strength, she clawed at the snow until she reached Kinlear. He was still warm, thanks to his runed cloak, and his heartbeat was steady against her fingertips. She collapsed against him, wrapping her arms around his body. Holding him close. The warmth of his cloak seemed to rush through her, thawing her enough to calm the chattering of her teeth.

But her head . . .

Her eyelids began to shut.

'*Get up,*' said the wind again. '*Ezer!*'

She looked into the woods, trying to keep her eyes open. They were too heavy, and Kinlear was too warm, and . . .

The speaking stone.

She dug her hand into her pocket, a relieved sob leaving her throat as she curled her fingers around it.

You're late for training. Arawn's voice filled her mind. *Skipping out on me, Minder?*

She was so tired it took everything in her to think back to him.

Arawn. Darkness slid across her vision. *Help.*

The last thing she saw before her eyes slid shut again, was Six's enormous paw prints.

They led off, alone, into the woods.

CHAPTER 30

When she opened her eyes, she was back in the labyrinth, standing outside the doors that held Styerra's memories.

She unlocked another door, unsurprised to find herself in the library again.

It was just after sunset, by the look of the light just barely filtering in through the windows.

She found Styerra in the same spot she'd last seen her.

But this time . . .

Uncle Ervos was there.

Ezer almost couldn't believe it was him, for she'd trusted his word all her life. When she begged for answers about her mother, he swore he didn't know who she was.

A stranger, murdered by shadow wolves.

A woman without a name or a face.

But seeing him now, it was impossible to deny that Ervos not only knew her mother . . .

They had a deep bond.

She could see it in his eyes, as Ervos looked down at Styerra. He was younger and leaner but a giant for his age, nonetheless. That shock of red hair, the emerald eyes and soft smile. There was no mistaking her uncle's face.

Gods, she missed him terribly.

A fissure began in her heart, even as fury writhed inside her.

He lied.

All her life, Ervos had lied.

And yet here he was, before the shadow wolves had even arrived. Standing with Ezer's mother. His hand rested on Styerra's back, consoling her as she cried.

'When did he give this to you?' Styerra asked.

Her eyes were bloodshot and wet with tears. Her hands shook as he held out the small red notebook. The one she and Erath had passed love letters back and forth in.

There was a new entry, scribbled in black ink.

S,

The Masters know.
Leave this place, before it's too late.
Forget about me.
Live your life.

E

'He passed it to me just moments before the Masters came to our dorm,' Ervos said. 'They took him.'

'Where?' Styerra whispered.

Ervos frowned. 'A cell. He's committed treason against the Five, Styerra. You know what his fate will be.'

She gasped at his words.

'And there's little time before they come for you, too. The penance you'll pay for this . . . it's not the kind you can come back from.'

His voice was younger, but the sound of it was still so gentle, so purely Ervos that it made Ezer's own heart twist.

He'd spoken to her that way so many times. It was a steady, consoling voice, the kind that took all her fears away.

Styerra wept in his arms.

'I'm so sorry,' Ervos said. 'I wish there was another way. I won't let them do this to you.'

'He promised me,' Styerra cried. *'He said he'd found a place, a power ... a space we could be safe to be together, without the gods' laws to keep us apart.'*

'There is *no place the gods' laws cannot reach,'* Ervos said. *'Erath lied to you.'*

But Ervos was a liar, too.

And now ...

Now Ezer wondered what else he'd lied about.

'He wouldn't see reason,' Ervos added. *'I tried, but ... he's not well, Styerra. His mind is lusting for things that cannot be. And thank the gods I discovered it, because he almost took you down with him. Just like Zeban and the others. It's* all *a lie. The blank book, the strange god. A test, a trap, meant to show the gods who the unbelievers are. You must believe the truth and set Erath's lies aside. You must erase the poison he's tried to place in your mind. And you must run, before it's too late.'*

Styerra began to cry again.

She looked weak, not at all like the woman Ezer imagined her mother to be. A warrior, who'd fought bravely to fend away the shadow wolves so her newborn baby could survive.

But this woman, in this memory ...

She was just a child.

A brokenhearted child.

'I can't,' Styerra said. *'I have to see him, speak to him—'*

'You have to run,*'* Ervos said. *'The Masters know everything now. Someone turned him in. They know about the book.' He looked at Styerra's stomach. 'And the baby.'*

Styerra gasped.

Ervos held up his hands. 'I just want you safe.'

'But if I could just explain it to them, make them see reason,' Styerra started, her hands over her stomach.

'You can't,' Ervos said. His voice was almost panicked now as he glanced over his shoulder. Like someone would be rounding the corner at any moment. 'It's happened before, an unholy

union. You've placed a stain in the line of the Sacred, you've messed with the purity of pillared magic by carrying Erath's child. A child not meant for your womb. You know what the penance will be. For both of you.'

Ezer didn't have to hear him say it.

Death.

Death for Styerra . . . and her unborn child.

'Where would I go?' she asked.

'South. As far as you can get, with a new name, a new story. I have a horse secured,' Ervos said. 'We'll go together. Right now. There's a storm on its way. It will cover our tracks.'

'I can't let you risk that.'

Ervos smiled sadly. 'I'd risk anything for you, Styerra. You know that. I'll get you settled somewhere safe. I'll come back, throw them off your trail. No one will harm you or the child. I swore it to Erath. And I swear it to you.'

Styerra stooped to pick up her small bag of belongings, but Ervos lifted it for her, and placed a hand on her back, and guided her from the shelves.

'I'll protect you,' Ervos said. 'No matter what it takes.'

Ezer opened her eyes for a second time to find herself in a small cave, lit by a flickering orange fire.

She was on her side, a dark wing tucked over her like a blanket, with her head upon the pillow she'd come to know and love. Six's paw.

Safe and sound, and with her once more.

Kinlear was fast asleep a few feet away, another cloak draped over his shoulders like a blanket. No blood pooled beneath him, but he coughed and it was a ragged thing, wet and deep from within his lungs. He fell back to sleep, folding in on himself.

Ezer groaned and sat up, this time her head wobbling a bit less. There was a rune on her hand, glowing softly. She frowned at it, trying to make sense of the shape.

It looked like . . . a healing rune, Ezer realized. The same crossed shape she'd seen Alaris use on her countless times.

'Where are we?' Ezer whispered as Six shifted and settled one large dark eye on her.

Another vision filled her mind.

Arawn, rushing through the snow on horseback. Hooves thundered as he followed Six through the dark woods beyond the wards. How she'd found him, Ezer didn't know.

He fell before a pile of dark robes.

Ezer and Kinlear, asleep together in the snow.

With a circle of ravens around them, protecting them like tiny little sentries.

The vision shifted.

And there was Arawn again, tugging at Six's halter in vain.

The raphon had refused to go back to the Citadel, back to the safety of the wards.

'Please,' Arawn begged, and his voice broke. 'Please, or they'll freeze to death.'

Six just huffed in his face and walked deeper into the woods . . . where the mouth of a cave awaited.

It shifted again, another little snapshot of the past.

They were in the cave now.

'Come on,' Arawn growled, kneeling in the darkness while Six lay with her wings draped over both Ezer and Kinlear, her breath forming before her in too-large clouds. Frost coated the walls. 'Vivorr, please. I need you!'

He lifted his hands before him, whispering an invocation.

There were tears on his face, and he looked terrified, desperate . . .

'Not again,' he whispered. 'Please, not again.'

He looked back at Ezer.

And his eyes were so full of concern, so full of . . . of what they'd held when he looked at her in her dreams.

And then a flame, bright and burning, surged to life in his hands.

The vision ended.

Ezer sat up, her head spinning.

'You . . . went after Arawn for me?' she asked Six. 'For us?'

She'd reached out to him through the speaking stone. But there was no way he would have found them without Six.

The raphon twitched her tail once in confirmation. Her hot breath washed over Ezer's face, and she lowered her head, nuzzling Ezer's cheek with the tip of her beak. So gentle for an animal so large. 'Thank you,' Ezer whispered, and pressed a kiss to the raphon's feathered head. 'You saved us.'

Six began to purr and laid her beak back down against the cave floor. Almost as if she'd been waiting for Ezer to wake before she herself slept.

'Kissing a raphon. That's . . . certainly got to be a side effect of a concussion,' said Arawn. 'Not something you see every day.'

Ezer turned to find him standing at the edge of the firelight, a bundle of sticks in his arms. His eyes locked upon her, full of concern.

'I couldn't find you. The stone's tracking ability doesn't stretch beyond the wards. If it wasn't for Six thundering into camp . . .' Arawn said. 'She's lucky most of the garrison was out tonight. I managed to get to her before anyone else did.' He looked at the raphon. 'She saved you. A bond like that . . . it does not come often, Minder. Not even with the war eagles.'

He set down the sticks and walked slowly to the fire, careful to avoid Kinlear.

'Tell me what happened.'

He dropped another stick on the fire and sat down beside her.

'Shadow wolves,' Ezer said. 'It was my fault we went beyond the wards,' Ezer said, when Arawn practically growled towards Kinlear. 'Not his.'

He went quiet, listening.

'Six *flew*. She carried us away; she outflew the wolves, and for a moment, it was wonderful. Until we crashed.'

And now they were here. In a dark cave somewhere outside the wards.

'Six refused to go back to the wards, and now it's far too dangerous to journey by night. We can't go back until daylight,' Arawn said. 'I've runed the front as best I can to shield our scent, but I'm no scribe.' He looked down at her hand. 'I runed you, too. I hope it's okay, I didn't know what else to do . . .'

'It's fine,' she said. 'Thank you.'

Behind them, Kinlear began to cough again. They both turned, watching him.

'His vial is empty,' Arawn said.

Ezer remembered, from before the crash.

'It helps with the cough, the cold . . . a concoction Alaris made. I cannot replicate it.'

Ezer glanced at Six, who had lifted her head. And with a look . . .

She sent a vision towards the raphon.

It was simple, sending it outwards. Not a touch required, as if whatever was inside Ezer had unlocked itself. *Six, nestling near Kinlear the way she did with Ezer. Keeping his body warm and safe.*

The raphon lifted her head and twitched her tail twice.

'Six,' Ezer whispered. 'Please. He is our friend.'

And with a sigh, the raphon stood, padded across the cave floor, and settled back down beside the prince, tucking him away in the shadow of her wing.

'You speak to her,' Arawn said. 'How?'

Ezer noticed their arms were touching. Like he'd drawn closer to her of his own accord.

'Visions,' Ezer said. 'I don't know what sort of magic it is. But she's been giving them to me since the moment we met. Visions of strange things, beautiful things, silly things, even. And last night when the wolves came, when death was close . . . I was able to send one back to her.'

'Without invocating?' Arawn asked.

Ezer looked at him, brows raised. 'Of course not.'

He looked puzzled. Like she was something new and strange.

Ezer shivered. The fire was warm, but—

'Are you cold?' Arawn asked.

She shook her head.

'Minder.'

'Fine,' she said. 'A little.'

'I gave my cloak to Kinlear,' Arawn said. 'But . . . I've always heard Firemages are warmer than most.' And he surprised her when he lifted an arm, as if to welcome her to his side.

She stared up at him.

He gazed down at her.

And she sidled close to him, a sigh leaving her lips.

He *was* warm. A furnace, practically, and gods, it felt good as he draped his arm over her shoulders, holding her close.

'You still smell like a raphon,' he said.

She dug her elbow into his side.

'And you smell like ashes.'

They fell silent again, as they watched the fire together.

'Your magic came back,' Ezer said. 'Six showed me. You started the fire. A *real* flame, not just a candle this time.'

She felt him take a deep breath.

'You . . . have done something to me, Minder,' Arawn said suddenly. She could hear him swallow. 'Something I have not felt before. Something . . . that scares me.'

Her head was on his shoulder now.

She could hear his heart beating against her ear, and suddenly she got a flash of a vision from her dreams. His lips against hers, then brushing her scars.

'Why?'

He took an unsteady breath. 'When I found you in the woods, I thought you were dead. And it broke something loose inside of me.'

Ezer released a shaky breath and glanced up at him.

His eyes, the sharp angle of his jaw.

His lips.

'What sort of something?' Ezer asked. Because she was lacking words, and he was warm, and every fiber of her body was taut. Like she was a bolt of lightning, ready to explode.

This time, she knew it wasn't from the winterwine.

She knew it was all *her*.

'Something I'm not supposed to feel,' Arawn said. 'Something forbidden.'

His hand reached for her chin. He tilted it up gently, slowly, until she met his eyes again.

'And for the first time, Minder . . . I am doubting the laws for my matching. I am . . .' He sighed. 'I am not sleeping, because when I do, I think of you.'

Her heart felt like it stopped.

'When I see you, I feel like I can't breathe.'

She released a shaky breath.

'When I am near you . . . it is an effort to look away.'

'Why?' she whispered.

'Because you are different,' he said. 'You are . . . like nothing I've ever encountered before.'

'And that's a good thing?' she whispered.

'I'm still trying to figure that out,' he said.

He was shaking beside her, or perhaps that was her too, because suddenly she wanted him. It was like their dance from last night had never ended. Like she was still spinning in his arms.

'Are you afraid of me, Firemage?'

His breath hitched, and he was looking at her lips now, instead of her eyes. 'Terrified,' he whispered.

She wanted him the way her dreams did. She knew it was dangerous, and reckless, and she knew their time was fleeting. He was a rigid, pious, law-abiding Knight, *her future king*, and she was . . .

She didn't know what she was.

A Raphonminder.

One who might die the moment she passed into the Sawteeth.

But in this moment, she didn't care.

Because she might die right now, if she didn't have him.

'You can kiss me now,' she said, because she was feeling reckless and brave. Because she'd tasted the wind, touched the sky, and none of that compared to the feeling of *him* so near to her.

'I don't know that I should, Minder,' Arawn said.

She guided his hand to her face. He sucked in a breath as his thumb stroked her cheek, and she swore her heart almost stopped. 'I don't know that I care,' she said.

And they leaned in at the same time.

When their lips touched, her body melted into flames.

He kissed her slowly at first, gently, like he'd truly never done it before, but neither had she. They learned about it together, until her lips parted naturally, and his tongue slid across hers.

'Ezer,' he groaned.

Her name on his lips was her undoing.

He pulled her against him until she was on his lap, her legs around his waist, his hands at the small of her back, and suddenly he wasn't close enough.

She dug her fingers into his back, and he groaned against her, and she knew this was wrong, knew this was forbidden for them to be together, so *why* did it all feel so right?

A soft warning growl sounded out from Six.

'Well. This is certainly an interesting sight.'

They broke away, Ezer practically falling into the fire as they spun to find Kinlear frowning down at them.

His eyes, positively filled with rage.

*

'Kinlear,' Ezer gasped. 'You're awake.'

Six stood behind him, tail twitching in frustration.

Her dark eyes slid to Ezer, head cocked as if to say, *really? That couldn't have waited for another time?*

'And forgive me for interrupting . . . whatever this interesting little union is,' Kinlear said. 'You're lucky it was me that found you, or the penance you'd both pay . . . Father is *dying,* Arawn. You're soon to be King, and here you are, playing with her heart when you know you're soon to be Matched.'

'*Enough,*' Arawn growled up at him.

'It's the truth and you know it,' Kinlear snarled. 'This can *never* happen again.'

He was bent over at his middle now, forehead slick with sweat though he was shivering. A healing rune marked his own hand, and the blood on his head had dried, crusting his curls.

'That's our decision to make, not yours.' Arawn stood up. 'You need rest. You need to lie back down.'

'Because you want to be rid of me?' Kinlear asked. 'Or because you genuinely care for the state of me?'

Gods.

Ezer backed away from Arawn, suddenly feeling cold.

A bit broken.

Her lips were swollen, and she still tasted him on her tongue.

'Kinlear,' Ezer said, smoothing out her cloak. She was mortified. She stood and went to him, reaching out to place her hand on his arm. He was too cold. The runes on his cloak were already fading. 'You need to lie down again. You took a hard hit when we crashed, and—'

He pulled his arm away.

'I'm *tired,*' the prince spat. 'Tired of people telling me what I need. *Lie down, Kinlear. Rest, Kinlear.* I am the prince of Lordach. And I will *not* be commanded by you.'

'Brother,' Arawn started. 'Don't speak to her like—'

His words fell away as Kinlear began to cough again, until he was gasping. Until he bent over, the sound of something wet and terrible in his lungs.

He spat blood on the stones.

And when he came up to standing, his eyes were bloodshot.

'Calm down,' Arawn started. He walked towards him, reaching out as if to help.

'Enough!' Kinlear yelled. 'That's *enough*.'

His teeth were red. He coughed again, and reached for the vial around his neck, but Ezer already knew it was empty. So he cursed, recorking the vial with shaking hands, and let the chain fall against his chest again.

He wasn't himself.

'Kinlear,' Ezer tried, approaching him slowly, like he was a wounded animal. Her heart broke at the sight of him. 'Please. Sit down . . . with me.'

'I will sit when I'm dead,' he growled. He wobbled and placed a hand against the stones. 'I'm tired of resting. Tired of withering away in the shadows, while life goes on . . . and right beside me.' He glared at Arawn next, and something seemed to *shift* in his eyes. He smiled. But it was cold and thankless. 'But what perfect timing, since I'm awake. Since we're all three together now! Are you going to tell her the news, Brother . . .' Kinlear raised a dark brow. 'Or should I?'

Ezer glanced back and forth between the two men.

'I don't know what you're talking about,' Arawn said slowly.

The two were stuck in a glaring contest, the flames of the fire sending strange shadows across the cave wall behind them. Where Six had now begun to pace, her tail twitching back and forth as if she sensed the tension about to overflow.

'I only learned about it yesterday,' Kinlear said, looking back at Ezer. 'And imagine my surprise when I approached my dear brother to discuss how we should break the news to you . . .

only to discover he'd already known. He knew months ago, before either of us ever met you.' He looked back at Arawn, the other side to his coin. 'Since you've clearly grown so close, it only seems fitting that *you* should be the one to tell her.'

'Tell me . . . what?' Ezer asked.

'The truth,' Kinlear said.

She looked to Arawn now.

Whose eyes had suddenly fallen, downcast. 'Kinlear,' he said. 'Please.'

'She deserves to know,' Kinlear said, and coughed into his sleeve. 'Or were you going to carry on using her, hiding the secret until someday, she discovers it on her own? And it utterly *shatters* her.' He shook his head. 'You may be okay to play with her heart. But I will do no such thing.'

Ezer whirled on Arawn. 'What is he talking about?' She wrapped her arms around herself, suddenly cold. 'Arawn?'

His face was pained.

He wasn't looking at her anymore.

Why wasn't he looking at her?

'Tell her now,' Kinlear said. 'Or I will.'

Arawn glanced up. His eyes were haunted, utterly broken, as he looked at her and said, 'Your uncle isn't dead, Ezer. He's alive.'

A breath left her lips.

'What?' she whispered.

She could hear nothing but the roaring of her blood in her ears.

Could feel nothing, beyond Six, who suddenly paced to her side and pressed her warm body against Ezer's, like she knew she needed her strength.

'He's . . . inside the Citadel,' Arawn whispered. 'In the dungeons.'

She felt like she was going to crawl out of her own skin.

'Why?'

It was Kinlear who answered. 'Because he's a traitor, Ezer. Shortly after he arrived here . . . he discovered what we were doing with the raphons. He was the one who broke into the catacombs, where the raphon pups were kept.'

She shook her head, because what he was about to say . . .

She didn't think she would survive hearing it.

But Kinlear spoke anyway. 'He's the one who killed Six's siblings. He killed them *all*. And he almost killed Six, too. He's the one who left that scar on her beak.'

CHAPTER 31

The sun rose.

And Ezer led Six from the cave, out into a forest of fresh-fallen white. It was bitter cold, the sky heavy with the threat of more snow.

'Ezer.'

Arawn had no cloak, but he didn't seem to notice as he rushed after her, the snow blurring his features. 'Ezer, *please*. Let me talk to you, let me explain why I didn't—'

She turned Six around, so fast that her beak nearly collided with Arawn's face.

He stumbled back, eyes wide.

'You knew,' Ezer said, as she tapped on Six's shoulder. The raphon bowed, dipping a wing for her to climb on. 'From the moment you plucked me out of my tower. And you let me think he was dead.' She looked past his shoulder. 'Get on, Kinlear.'

The prince climbed on behind her, wrapping his arms around her middle.

All the while, Arawn stared up at them, his arms slack at his sides.

'You let me *mourn*, Arawn, for a loss that wasn't even real to begin with,' Ezer hissed.

'It is real,' Arawn said.

'He's *alive*!' Ezer screamed. 'He's *alive* and you knew the whole godsdamned time.'

Somewhere in the distance, birds rose from the treetops. She could hear their cries growing closer, as they came towards her call.

She felt like she was burning inside.

Like she was going to keep burning until it took everything down with her.

A raven landed in the trees overhead, cawing down at them.

Then another.

Gods, she had missed their mournful song.

'Please, Ezer,' Arawn's voice broke.

'Raphonminder,' she corrected him. 'You have no right to call me by name.'

Another raven cawed from above.

She could almost feel the sky filling with them.

She could almost feel the wind, whispering between their wings.

Six shifted beneath her, reminding her to breathe.

'His body may be alive,' Arawn explained. 'But his mind died to us all, long ago. What you will find in that dungeon . . . he's not the man you once knew.'

'Funny,' she said. 'I could say the same about you.'

And before he could say another word, she clicked her teeth and let Six carry her and Kinlear away. The ravens followed, a blade of darkness that sliced apart the sky.

'*There* you are,' Izill said, as Ezer and Kinlear burst through the black door into the warm halls of the Aviary, after returning Six safely to her cage.

Nearly all of the prince's weight was on Ezer's shoulders, her arms around his waist as she tried to support him before his legs gave out.

'You must have left early this—' Izill's face went ashen. '*What happened?*'

'Training mishap.' Ezer grimaced beneath Kinlear's weight.

Izill shouted out an order, taking charge, and suddenly a flurry of servants and Scribes lifted Kinlear away from her, just as his legs buckled.

'I'm fine,' he said. 'Really.'

But his words were weak, and he wouldn't stop trembling.

'Take him to Alaris.' Izill barked orders to the others. '*Now.*'

'Wait!' Ezer called out. She rushed after him, as he asked his helpers to pause.

Before she thought better of it, she leaned in and gently pressed her lips to his cheek.

'Thank you,' she whispered against him.

He was cold. He smelled like blood, and when she pulled away . . .

The sight of him held between two others, too frail to stand on his own two feet, made her chest ache.

'For what?' Kinlear asked.

'For being someone who is not afraid to break me,' she said.

He grinned, even through his pain. 'You are not easily broken, Raphonminder. And as luck should have it . . . neither am I. I'll send orders to let you pass into the prison. But what you will find there . . .'

'I can handle it,' she said.

He smiled weakly. 'I know.'

She watched as he was led away.

Before she could visit Ervos, Izill had forced Ezer to bathe and accept a hot meal.

It's not like he's going anywhere, Izill said after Ezer told her the truth. She brought Ezer a bowl of soup from the kitchens, along with a small bundle of chocolates.

It was the first time Ezer had *ever* had a true friend.

Her presence settled the nerves in Ezer's belly as she sat by the fire and awaited news of Kinlear.

And when news came by way of Kinlear's servant that he was

all right, along with a sealed letter meant to give her passage into the dungeons, Izill escorted Ezer all the way there.

'What do I even say to him?' Ezer asked. 'Where do I start?'

'At the beginning,' Izill said. 'You tell him *everything* in your heart – even the ugliest parts – because if you don't, it might haunt you for the rest of your days.'

She promised to be there at the exit when Ezer was done.

Ezer's steps echoed as she followed a rounded stairwell down, past guards and flickering magefire torches that cast an eerie blue glow on the stones. She walked until her legs felt leaden. With every step, her heart raced faster, until she came to the bottom of the stairwell.

'Cell 59,' a stone-faced guard said, after reading Kinlear's letter. And Ezer was on her way, counting the numbers as she went.

The smell was just like Rendegard.

She must have been far beneath the Citadel, deep in the belly of the rock on which the fortress stood, because the air felt stale. Cold, and lifeless.

She walked into the narrow hallway, past countless cells.

The men and women were mere scraps of things, covered in ragged blankets, curled up amidst their own feces.

A horrific place to be.

And not where she had ever, in a million lifetimes, expected to find her Uncle Ervos.

She approached cell 59 slowly, carefully, her heart in her throat. And when she came to the front and peered inside, she wasn't even certain Ervos was there until the lump of blankets on the cot shifted.

And a ghost sat upright.

At first, she thought the guards had directed her wrongly. Because the man inside could not be Ervos, kind and larger than life Ervos, a man whose laughter held such joy it could have shaken the stars from the sky.

The man before her was skin and bones. His tattered cloak hung from his shoulders like a sloughed skin. Tears blurred her vision. He was covered in cuts and bruises, gashes large enough they had to have been made by the tail end of a whip.

His cheeks were too shallow, the bones protruding from beneath his skin. His head was shaved, his shock of red hair gone.

She felt like she'd collapsed into another of her dreams.

He had lied to her, all her life.

As long as she'd been searching for the truth of her past. But now that it was right here before her . . .

She was suddenly afraid.

She backed up a step, but something pushed at her back. The wind.

'*Go*,' it whispered.

So, before she could stop herself, she stepped up to the bars.

'Hello, Uncle,' Ezer said.

He stiffened at the sound of her voice. Slowly, he looked at her, blinking into the torchlight as if she, too, were a ghost.

'Ah, my Little Bird,' he said. 'I was wondering when you would arrive.'

'What have you done?' Ezer breathed. 'Is it true?'

'All this time apart, and this is how you greet me?' he asked.

She crossed her arms. 'I know *everything*, Uncle. I know about the blood on your hands.'

'The . . . ah. The monster pups,' he said. 'I did what had to be done for the Five.'

'Not just the pups,' Ezer said, and rage ran through her as she curled her fingers around the cold bars, thinking of how lost and lonely Six had been all this time. Because of *him*. She took a deep breath. 'I know about *Styerra*.'

At that, he sucked in a breath.

And that was all the confirmation she needed, that what she'd seen in her labyrinth was true.

'All this time, you knew who my mother was,' Ezer said. When she was a crying child, awake at night, scared of the wolves and wanting a mother she'd never truly known . . . 'You fed me a lifetime of lies.'

His eyes had been downcast, but now they slid to hers.

And he *smiled*. The bastard smiled.

'*Styerra*. You look just like her. A gift to see her face in yours every day of my life.'

He said the name like a prayer. And something about it made her skin crawl. 'You lied to me. *Why?*'

'Of course I did,' Ervos spat. His hands shook as he reached up to scratch at his head, where cuts and bruises littered his skin like confetti. Some of them broke open, and blood smeared down the sides of his bald head. How long had he been down here, rotting in the dark? 'She made me promise.'

'Promise what?'

'To protect you.'

'*Protect me?*' Ezer asked. She curled her fingers tighter around the bars, wishing she could wrap them around his throat. She'd never felt such unbridled rage, and it made her shake worse than the cold. 'You hid the truth from me! My entire life, Ervos, I wanted to know who I was, who I came from, why I had these strangeties you begged me to hide. And you knew. That's not protecting me. That's *breaking* me!'

'I was afraid,' he whispered.

There were tears running down his cheeks now, making tracks on his skin through the dirt and blood.

'Afraid of what?'

'Of *you*,' he whispered.

She released a breath.

She shook her head slowly, like that had been the final dagger. She did not think she would *ever* be able to forgive him.

'I tried to stop it all before it began,' Ervos said. 'They sent for several of us, years ago, Ravenminders all across the south. I knew . . . oh, Gods, I knew they would come for you, too, after so many of us failed in their mission.' He sucked in a shaky breath. 'He's a monster, the second prince. The whole War Table, too, for allowing this. They claim faith in the Five but allow an abomination to live. I did what I could, before they stopped me.' He shook his head. 'Six months in this hell, and I thought the matter was settled. Imagine my horror, Little Bird, when I heard the guards' whispers that a beast had survived. And then, months later . . . I knew that the one to tame the last beast was *you*.'

She stared at him in disbelief.

He'd truly killed the raphon pups, in cold blood. Ervos, a man who had always *loved* the birds, had nearly murdered Six.

It didn't make sense.

It felt like a betrayal against her own soul.

'The raphons aren't what you think they are,' Ezer said.

He frowned. 'And neither are *you*.'

'What?'

He locked eyes with her. 'Do you remember the stories I used to share with you at night? When the wind was cold, and the nightmares drew near?'

'I don't want to talk about stories,' Ezer spat. 'I want the truth, Ervos. All of it. *Now*.'

'I'm trying to tell you the truth!' he hissed. 'The stories. Which was your favorite, Ezer?'

She knew the answer at once. 'Wrenwyn.'

He nodded, eyes wide. 'Yes, Little Bird. Wrenwyn the Wrong. She was Erath's – your father's – blood. Far back in his line. So . . . that makes her half *your blood*.'

But that was impossible. Because Wrenwyn was royalty, a princess from long ago. And . . .

'Erath wasn't a prince. He was just another Sacred,' Ezer said. He stepped closer to the bars. 'Because Wrenwyn Lavor was stripped of her title, long ago. Her brothers never bore a living heir, and the family line died out. The Laroux rose to power then . . . so says the written history. But the stories – the ones passed on in private – say Wrenwyn *did* survive. She'd become a martyr of sorts, a beacon . . . and Erath was just another fool who fell prey to her lies.'

'The lies of what?' Ezer asked.

'The darkness,' Ervos said. 'The Acolyte's call. She *lived*, Ezer, an entire life beyond the Citadel, and when she grew old, she returned and brought with her a book. It was one of secret symbols, full of *lies* that have stained the truth of the gods. She claimed there was something better out there. Something more powerful.' His hands were shaking as he curled them over the bars. His fingernails had been pried away. 'Your father had her blood, Ezer. And he died trying to find what Wrenwyn wrote about. Your mother died for it, too.'

She'd seen it play out, in her memories.

'She was *safe* where I took her. She should have been *happy*. But there she went anyways, packing to go north to the Sawteeth when the wolves came. She was going to take you, too. To run *towards* a danger far worse than the Masters.' He swallowed. 'So, I stopped her. I protected you from her . . . I kept you safe. Like I promised I would.'

She didn't know what he was saying.

But she felt like she was going to be sick.

'What did you do to my mother?' she breathed.

'She did it to herself,' he snarled.

He shook his head and slammed his hands against his skull.

'I tried to erase it,' he said. 'I tried to forget that night. But it's haunted me every day since.' He started to cry. 'I protected you.' A whimper. 'I kept my promise to my Styerra.'

Her whole body was cold.

This was *wrong,* something in his eyes was utterly wrong.

'The past is done. Styerra is finally *free* of the lies. The false love. What I had for her was true.'

No.

It wasn't love.

He looked wild, mad.

He looked . . . like a man plagued by obsession.

'All the days we went to the census, I removed your name. I kept you safe. And when I left . . . I made a deal that the prison master would keep you away from the north. He broke it, took his coin for putting your name in the draft. You aren't supposed to be here.'

She gasped.

'You . . .' She shook her head. 'You told him to keep me there? A prisoner? Working for *years* in your place?'

'Of course I did,' he said. 'You loved the birds. You were happy, Ezer.'

'I was alone!' she yelled at him. 'You abandoned me!'

'I did what I had to do,' he said. There was no regret in his voice, in his eyes. 'And now it is your turn. I've heard the stories. I know about the mysterious Minder from the south, who plans to travel north . . . to kill the Acolyte.' He shook his head. 'You cannot go, Ezer.'

'Why not?' she asked.

'Because you are blood of Wrenwyn!' he shouted. 'A child of two traitors who laid down their vows to the gods. They killed Erath as penance. They nearly killed Styerra, too. But I kept her safe . . . and her fledgling who was never meant to be.'

It took everything in her not to wish him dead right now.

He took a wheezing breath.

'I broke the laws for *you*. For her. The gods have been punishing me for it ever since. You are not strong enough, Little Bird, to resist the call that your mother and father died trying to answer.'

'You think me weak?' Ezer asked.

'No,' he said. 'I think you share blood with the ones who believed the lies in the Shadow Tome. And blood, it seems, is often stronger than common sense.'

She'd not heard that name before.

'I think Wrenwyn was telling one truth,' Ervos said. 'I think . . . it was the Acolyte, that dark power, that called to her. But it was not a safe space to find freedom. It was a trick, and whatever Wrenwyn did in her time away . . . I think she's the one that unlocked it. I think *she* set the Acolyte free, and now thousands are dead because of it. Thousands more will die, if we do not win this war.'

'Which is exactly why I *must* go north!' Ezer growled.

'No,' he said. 'This is my fault. All my fault. I shouldn't have interfered; I should have let the Masters do what they must . . .'

Her whole body had gone cold.

'If you hadn't, I would be dead,' Ezer whispered. 'Do you truly believe I did not deserve to exist?'

'No,' he said. 'I don't know, Little Bird, oh *gods*, forgive me.' He shook his head and banged his fists against his skull. 'I was blinded by love for Styerra. I was blinded by a different love when I got to know you. I saved you, and that makes me a sinner, too.' He was weeping now. 'This is my penance.'

She didn't know what he was talking about.

She felt like she was watching a man with half a mind.

'You cannot go north,' Ervos said. 'Because the Acolyte will take you. He will see what you are, the blood of Wrenwyn, the first to believe. And he'll turn you, too. You need to run south, get as far as you can from his call. Before it's too late.'

She backed a step away, shaking her head. 'You stole *everything* from me. My life. My family.'

'I am your family,' Ervos hissed. 'I protected you. I—'

'I hope you rot in here,' Ezer breathed. 'I hope you die knowing that Styerra's child *hates* you for what you did.'

He started to cry again, shaking his head.

'Please, Little Bird,' he said.

She curled a tight fist over her mother's ring. 'I'm not a little bird anymore, Ervos. I found my wings. And I'm going to ride my raphon across the Expanse. And prove you wrong when I destroy the Acolyte.' She took a deep, settling breath. 'Goodbye.'

He was already dead to her, already gone.

Perhaps . . . he'd never been real at all.

'*No*,' Ervos shouted after her. '*Ezer!*'

She kept walking.

He beat his fists against the bars. He rattled the door, screaming her name.

'*Don't let him take you, too! EZER!*'

She left him in the darkness, a wailing ghost.

And not a single tear slid down her face.

CHAPTER 32

She returned to the labyrinth with a gasp, already feeling for the skeleton key in her cloak pocket.
Her heart raced as she unlocked the next door.
Ezer found herself standing right on the edge of a northern wood. The air was crisp with the feeling of fall, her favorite time, even in Rendegard.
The aspens danced in the wind, leaves the color of burnished gold.
Tucked inside them, just at the edge of the wood, was a small cottage with a thatched roof and a white picket fence. And just beyond it, standing in a lovely little garden, was Styerra. Ezer unlatched the gate and approached, her steps soundless.
Styerra held a letter in her hands.
A letter from Ervos.
Ezer would know his handwriting anywhere.

My dearest friend,

I'm not able to visit to tell you in person. But you deserve to know.
Erath has indeed paid his eternal penance.
I know this news will pain you, as it pains me.
Perhaps, in some way, this will give you the freedom to move on.

I will visit soon.

Yours,

E

A single tear rolled down Styerra's cheek as she turned away and placed her trembling hands over her belly.
The ring from Erath was still on her finger.
It winked in the sunlight as she headed inside.

Ezer entered another door.

This time she was back at the cottage, while Styerra and Ervos tended to the flowers in the garden. A baby Ezer slept soundly in a basket beside them. She was perfect, with round cheeks and not a mark of claws upon them.

Butterflies danced through the spring foliage. A chicken scratched at the ground, searching for bugs.

And a raven sat perched in a tree overhead, watching Ezer's basket like a guardian.

Styerra was laughing, her smile bright as Ervos tucked a flower behind her ear. She smiled and stood on tiptoe to press a kiss to his cheek.

She paused.

And then, slowly, questioningly . . . she kissed him on the lips.

Ervos gasped against her.

'I . . . I'm sorry,' Styerra said and pulled away. Ezer noticed, then, how she still wore Erath's ring. Styerra reached down to it almost instinctively, twisting it with worried fingertips. 'I don't know what came over me.'

Ervos looked up, his mouth frozen open like he was lost for words.

'Please don't make it weird,' Styerra said.

'Why would I make it weird?' Ervos asked, raising his red

brows. 'I think . . . that I might live the rest of my life in wanting, Styerra, if you don't kiss me again.'

So she leaned in for another, just before a whip cracked in the distance.

The moment broke.

'More soldiers,' Styerra said as she peered across the woods. A whole troupe of them, nomages marching north. 'In the village, they say people are disappearing. They tell terrible stories of monsters in the night.'

He spun to face her. 'You promised not to go to town.'

'I only needed flour for bread,' Styerra said. 'I was careful. No one spoke to me.'

He sighed and pulled her to him. 'The only monsters out there are men, Styerra. The ones who would give good coin to bring you in. I just want you safe here. With me. Promise me you won't leave this place again.'

'Okay,' Styerra whispered.

This time when Ervos held her, the happiness had left her eyes.

Another memory unfolded behind the next door.

There were muffled voices as Ervos and Styerra argued.

They didn't want to wake Ezer, who slept soundly in her small basket at the foot of the bed.

'Where did you get it?' Ervos was saying. 'Is this why you keep going into town?'

He pointed to the table, where a worn black book sat.

Small. Insignificant.

But powerful enough to reshape someone's entire mind.

Styerra shook her head. 'I wasn't even searching for the Tome, Ervos . . . but there it was in the village, almost calling my name. The merchant gave it to me, free of charge. And this time, the pages weren't empty.'

'What do you mean?' Ervos asked, carefully reined fury in his voice.

'I mean Erath was right,' she breathed. 'This whole time, he was right about the Shadow Tome. I'm such a fool for not seeing it before, but . . . I'm taking Ezer with me. We're going north, to find freedom beyond the Sawteeth.'

Ervos looked horrified. 'What?'

'Come with us,' Styerra said. 'We'll go together, discover a new way of living, a new god to—'

Ervos stood so fast his chair tipped over. The baby Ezer flinched but settled, still fast asleep. 'You'll get her killed, Styerra. The wolves are out, hungry for blood.'

'I have faith now,' Styerra said. 'We'll make it there alive.'

'Faith?' He let out a bitter chuckle. 'I've done all I could to keep you safe. To keep her safe. I've given you all of me. And still . . . I am not enough. Your heart always goes back to him. Even in the grave.'

A tear slid down his cheek as he looked at the ring she still wore on her finger.

And he turned and walked towards the cottage door.

'Where are you going?' Styerra asked. 'Don't walk away from us again.'

He left the cottage without looking back.

The memory shifted. Now it was dark.

She was outside in the wind, in the snow.

And something was not right.

She stood outside the cottage. The moon was high in the sky, illuminating the shapes of wings and snouts that stalked about.

Shadow wolves, hungry for blood.

Ezer sucked in a breath.

This was the night her mother died.

Fires raged in the background, showing distant trees and cottages ablaze. Ezer looked around frantically, as if she could find her. Save her.

She found Styerra on the doorstep of the cottage, her chest torn open. Her body drenched in red.

'Mother,' Ezer breathed, and ran to her.

Styerra lifted a trembling hand, and for a second Ezer thought she saw her. But then a voice shouted, 'No!'

And Ezer gasped as something rushed through her, like she was truly a ghost. Ervos fell at Styerra's side, his hands hovering over her like he didn't know what to do, how to fix her, how to make the bleeding stop.

'Gods, oh gods,' he breathed. 'Stay with me Styerra. Please!'

'Erv . . . Ervos,' Styerra gasped.

Somewhere behind them, a person screamed. A howl broke the night, then a snarl that sounded like teeth ripping through flesh. The scream cut off.

'I'm sorry,' Ervos sobbed as he pulled Styerra into his arms. 'Oh, gods, Styerra. I'm so sorry. I never should have left you here alone.' Then his face went cold. 'Ezer.'

'Inside,' Styerra gasped. 'I . . . led them away.'

He tried to lift her, but she cried out in agony. Blood soaked the snow in rivers beneath her, and he slumped back down, sobbing.

Styerra's hand touched his cheek. Her ring was soaked in blood. 'Keep her safe, Stefon Ervos.' It was the first time she had used his full name. 'You must . . . promise me.'

'I promise,' he said, as his tears fell. 'I love you, Styerra. I have always loved you.'

She smiled. 'I can . . . see his face,' Styerra breathed. 'My heart.'

'Who?' Ervos asked.

She struggled to find her final breath. And then she said the last word like a promise. 'Erath.'

She died in his arms.

The wolves howled again. Somewhere behind him, another scream rang out.

But as Ervos looked down at Styerra . . . he no longer held a look of mourning. Nor did he look like a man in love. His face had changed at Styerra's final word, at the mention of Erath's name. He looked down at her now with hatred in his eyes.

'You chose him over the gods,' he whispered to her. 'Over me. And it killed you in the end. Like I always knew it would.'

With bloody fingertips, he slid the Ring of Finding from Styerra's cold finger. A final tear slid down his cheek as he looked at her.

'That's the last thing I can do, to protect you from him. You will not find him in death.'

He turned and stumbled into the cottage, where the door hung from its hinges. Awful claw marks marred the wood floors as if the shadow wolves had come inside to get to Styerra. To get to Ezer.

He paused on the threshold.

Because the cottage was utterly filled *with black feathers. Some still tumbled down from the rafters, blowing in the breeze where the windows had been shattered.*

'Where are you?' Ervos breathed. 'Ezer!'

He scrambled to the bed, breathless as he threw back the covers. Feathers danced through the air like living shadows.

But no Ezer.

'Please,' he begged. 'Gods, please.'

And then he saw the blood smears on the trunk at the foot of the bed. A handprint, like Styerra had held on to it when the shadow wolves attacked. Like they'd dragged her away from the place she'd made her final stand.

Ervos gasped and pried open the lid.

. . . And there she was.

Ezer, bundled in a blood-soaked blanket, with three horrible gashes across her tiny face. She was silent, unmoving. As if she were already gone.

'No,' Ervos breathed.

But then the baby Ezer opened her eyes at the sound of his voice. She let out a squeak, painful and broken and so, so weak.
But she was alive.
And clutched in her tiny little fists were more black feathers.
'It's okay,' Ervos whispered, as he lifted her into his arms, tear tracks staining his face. 'I'm here, Little Bird. I'm here.'

Ezer woke with tears on her own face, safe and sound inside Six's cage.

She was warm from Six's wing, draped over her side.

But the rest of her wasn't quite right.

It was a weariness. A burden to know what Ervos had done. To know that her mother had died so terribly . . . to finally remember what had happened that night in the dark.

With her last act, Styerra had placed her baby, bleeding and broken, inside that trunk . . . and led the wolves away.

Ervos had found her there, just as he always said. That part of the story was true.

But the rest . . .

The cottage filled with black feathers. She knew it was from her birds. That they had come for her, just as they had two months ago in the woods.

But . . . how?

And *why*?

Everything before that night, and everything after.

Everything she thought Ervos was.

It was *all* a lie.

She allowed herself a moment to mourn for her mother and her father.

For the life they could have shared, the three of them, if they'd run away *together* from the Citadel. But Erath had never known about the secret Styerra carried.

And he never would, because Ervos had stolen their connection away. He'd slid the Ring of Finding from Styerra's finger in hatred, not in love. So Erath would *never* find her on the other side.

Ezer felt sick as she looked down at the ring and curled her hand into a fist.

'I'm sorry,' she whispered to the ghost of her parents. 'I'm so sorry for what he did to you.'

And when she released her fist . . .

She released Stefon Ervos from her heart, too.

Kinlear came for her that morning.

'You look haunted,' he said. 'But lovely all the same.'

'I'm going to take that as a compliment, Prince,' she said, as she stepped out of Six's cage.

His tunic and cloak were a soft white with warming runes swimming across the surface. The buttons were open, revealing his pale chest and the vial that hung on his skin, the liquid a bold red. With his dark curls and his eagle cane . . .

He looked like a mystery, once more.

'And you look very much *alive*,' Ezer said and smiled through her scars. 'Don't ever do that to me again.'

'I'll warn you; princes aren't very good at keeping promises.' He winked. 'But for you, I shall do my very best.'

To her surprise, he pulled her into a hug.

She sucked in a breath, surprised at his touch. She was stiff at first. A flash of her dreams, his blade, her end . . . it all came to her in a rush.

But a killer would not hold her like this. A killer would not stake his mission upon hers, his future, his *life*. So, she settled into his warmth. The smell of him . . . it had become familiar and safe.

'What's done is done. I've closed the door on Ervos. He confessed everything. My father died a traitor. My mother died a victim. And I suppose in some ways, that makes me one, too.'

She did not tell him about the feathers, nor the suspected

birds. Something about that part felt personal. A secret to be kept safe until she could discover what it meant.

'You don't have to be a victim anymore,' Kinlear said. 'You can change that part of your story. *We* can change it. Together.'

She met his eyes. 'Together.'

For three days, they did nothing but train with Six. Ezer did not see Arawn.

Countless times, the stone in her pocket warmed.

But she ignored him until it went cold.

For days, she and Kinlear practiced mounting and dismounting, until they had it down to seconds. Six snapped her wings out, and soared in small, swooping circles around the clifftop, responding to every motion of Ezer's body. Kinlear's grip stayed strong around her middle, and when Ezer leaned, he leaned. When she shifted her weight back to slow, he shifted with her, until they rode as one.

When the sun set, they spent an hour in the darkness together, making Six stay on the cliffside to watch the shadows. Learning not to fear the storm, not to panic as she had before.

When the cold became too much, they took dinner inside the catacombs. Izill brought heaps of food to the outer door . . . along with letters from Arawn.

'Send them back,' Ezer begged her friend each night. 'Tell him I never even opened them.'

'It will hurt him,' Izill said knowingly and pressed a kiss to Ezer's cheek as she took the letters back. 'And *you*, if you don't face him soon enough.'

But Ezer couldn't bear to see him.

Not yet.

While they dined on the floors just outside Six's cage, they pored over maps of the Sawteeth, planning their entrance and exit. The Masters' plan was as good as it could be, all from the intel they'd gathered from tortured darksouls. From Ehvermages who could sense when a person was lying or telling the truth.

They need only execute these simple steps.

Leave the moment Realmbreak hits – the Long Day – three days of sunlight – their best hope in terms of time.

Find the black doors, the entrance to the Acolyte's domain.

Make it to his ritual, right before the sun sets.

'Kill him on his throne,' Kinlear said, twirling his dagger in his fingertips. The dagger she knew all too well from her dreams. 'And if we're right . . . the shadowstorm will break. The wolves will disappear. He'll have nothing to protect his army any longer. They'll either die with him or be scattered without if they somehow survive. We can go in by daylight after that. And end this once and for all.'

'And if we're wrong?' Ezer asked as she tossed Six a bleeding steak.

Spoiled creature, she thought and smiled as the raphon devoured the snack.

Kinlear's eyes met hers. 'It's a little late for that. I have prayed, day and night, that my blade will be steady. That my hand will be swift.'

'And I'll be waiting,' Ezer said. 'Hiding in the Sawteeth for your signal, to carry you away, victorious. The prince who saved Lordach.'

'And the Raphonminder who was crazy enough to help him do it,' Kinlear said, and smiled at her through his fear.

'And what about the godsblessing?' Ezer asked. She knew it was the one thing he couldn't tell her. The one truth he'd held back. A shield, was all he'd said. A shield instead of a sword. 'Will we be able to make it back?'

She'd thought it would be something like a fresh set of wards. Perhaps a true *wall* that none could pass.

'We will,' Kinlear said, holding her gaze, 'so long as we don't miss the deadline. End of Realmbreak. Just before the sun finally sets on the third day.' He swallowed and looked up from the map. 'Ezer. . . if I should fail . . .'

She shook her head. 'You won't.'

'But if I should . . . you must leave me. Fly back here and get behind the wards before Realmbreak ends. Promise me you'll leave me behind if it goes wrong.'

'No,' she said.

She took his hand and laced her fingers through his.

He sucked in a breath at her touch, and some part of her wondered, with how he looked at her . . .

Strange, to desire him sometimes.

To see how they would work together, if her heart had opened to him first.

'I won't leave you, Kinlear Laroux.' She gripped his hand so hard her fingertips went white. 'And you will *not* fail.'

CHAPTER 33

She got the news when she woke. The Queen had arrived. So today was the day of their Demonstration with the Descent.

Six stood still as Ezer brushed her and oiled her feathers.

'Are you ready?' Ezer asked.

The raphon's tail twitched once.

Yes.

And in her mind, Ezer received a vision:

That same dark feather, floating alone in an endless sea. But the wind came and lifted it. And the feather soared away, no longer alone. No longer lost.

'Good girl,' Ezer said. 'Just try not to crash this time.'

The raphon lifted her head, her dark eyes unblinking as she stared at Ezer.

A huff, as she considered and cocked her head to the side.

And then her tail twitched twice.

'That's hardly comforting,' Ezer said.

But then Six set her heavy beak down on Ezer's shoulder, the weight so much more than it had been just months ago. And another vision came.

The dark feather soared towards the Sawteeth. And even in the wind, even in the snow, it did not falter.

It fought like hell to reach the other side.

*

When she stepped into the Aviary halls, Izill was waiting for her, an enormous box in her hands.

It was wrapped with a delicate golden bow.

'From the prince,' Izill said. '*Kinlear*,' she added, when Ezer's eyes widened as she unwrapped the box.

A weapon. A short sword with raven's wings for a hilt.

The very same one from her labyrinth.

'Where is this from?' Ezer asked.

Izill pursed her lips in thought. 'They gather many weapons on the battlefield. It could have been forged by anyone in Lordach for all I know.'

Ezer gasped as she lifted the blade and found it nearly weightless, a far cry from the training sword she'd begrudgingly used. This one . . . this was a work of art. It felt like it was made for her.

Black diamonds shimmered on the pommel, embedded into whatever substance the sword was made of. She held it to the light, and it sparkled like it was spun with stars.

Some part of her wanted to place it back in the box, because it was yet another part of her dreams coming true.

And she knew – oh gods, she *knew* how it would end for her.

I'll change that part, she promised herself. *I will not fall to Kinlear's blade.*

Izill led her to one of the many countless rooms inside the Aviary and braided her hair while Ezer ate breakfast.

The food tasted stale today.

Even the water felt dry on her tongue.

'A warrior's braid,' Izill said as she worked with careful hands. 'So everyone can see how strong you are.'

Ezer had never spent much time looking at herself, not wanting to see the ugliness of her scars. But when Izill was done, and she'd guided her towards a mirror . . .

'Look at you,' Izill said. 'You are *radiant*.'

She'd braided her hair back away from her face . . . the better for others to see her shadow wolf marks.

They stood out, stark raised black lines against her pale face. In the past, she would have winced at the sight of them. But today, she did not see her smallness, nor her scars.

She saw strength staring back at her.

She saw who she really was for the very first time.

'Thank you,' Ezer whispered as she took Izill's hand and squeezed it tight.

'Don't thank me,' Izill said, and led Ezer from the room. 'It's you who is about to give everything for us. Just . . . kick the Descent's ass.'

Then Izill gasped like she was surprised she'd uttered the word.

'I won't tell anyone,' Ezer whispered with a wink.

They left the room together, hand in hand.

Kinlear was waiting for her in the catacombs when she arrived.

'Ezer,' he said as he turned to her, leaning on his cane. He had on a matching dark cloak. 'You look . . .'

'The hair was Izill's doing,' Ezer said, her cheeks reddening.

Kinlear smiled and reached out to tug the end of her long braid. 'I was going to say *lovely*. But I don't think that's it.'

'No?' she asked.

Kinlear said, 'You look fierce. Formidable. Strong.' He smiled and tucked a strand of hair behind her ear, his touch lingering on her cheek. 'You look like Ezer, the very first Raphon Rider of Lordach, worthy of her name.'

And then he leaned in and ever so gently pressed a kiss to her cheek.

It was soft.

Delicate, like he was taking his time.

Testing the moment.

When he pulled away, he stayed there, his lips just beside her ear.

'Are you ready, Ezer?' he asked.

He smelled like red wine and woodsmoke, and she was surprised at how good it felt to be close to him. To feel his words sighing into her ear.

'Yes,' she breathed.

When he pulled away, he was smiling again, his arm held out to her.

She took it.

And together, they turned towards Six.

A small crowd had gathered at the cliffside, just at the top of the black stone steps. The Masters, dressed in white with their golden armbands, all of whom made up the War Table. And with them, crowns upon their heads, were the King and Queen of Lordach.

The King was sitting in a wheeled chair.

As if he no longer had the strength to walk. And right there beside him . . . Ezer averted her gaze from Arawn.

'You're a quick study,' Kinlear said as she led Six across the snow. 'So be aware, my father looks like hell froze over. Bow to him. Don't speak unless spoken to. My mother?' He chuckled. 'Gods help you. *And* me.'

'What?' Ezer yelped. 'Why?'

'She detests me,' Kinlear shrugged as they crested the hill. 'Because she thinks me the weak link of our family line. An embarrassment that never should have been. Today, we prove her wrong.'

Her heart sank, but she had no time to question him further as they closed in on the crowd.

'Mother. Father,' Kinlear said as he stopped before his parents and bowed respectfully. 'Brother,' he added, glaring at Arawn.

Don't look at him, Ezer thought. *Don't you dare do it.*

It was an effort not to raise her eyes, not to let her heart ache for his.

The King hardly looked like himself. He'd wasted away . . .

stringy white hair, shallow cheekbones, his body so frail beneath a mountain of runed blankets it was a wonder the chair had made it across the snow at all. His eyes were milky white, and he squinted, as if he struggled to see.

Her heart stuttered.

This was what the power of the gods did to a mortal body.

This was perhaps the worst, most undeserving penance of all.

His sole purpose was to serve the Five, to strive for perfection under the weight of their laws. He'd protected the weak, led his army with glorious invocations granted . . .

He'd fought against the Acolyte with everything he had.

And now he would die early.

A victim of what the gods created him to do.

It was no wonder he seemed to hate people like her.

Queen Dhyana sighed as she looked down at him. Like she had no love for the King, no sorrow that she would lose him soon . . . only a duty to stand at his side as his Matched.

She was the picture of Arawn. Pale, white hair, soft blue eyes. Wrinkles formed at their edges, despite her being only in her forties, for she was a powerful Realmist who helped sustain the extra food source in Touvre, Lordach's capital.

She'd invocated plenty, to ensure her people survived.

Her eyes slid to Six and narrowed. 'So this is the beast that nearly killed my son. An ugly thing, isn't it?'

Fire churned in Ezer's gut. And then Dhyana's cold eyes fell upon *her*. 'And *you*. A bit small for a Rider, wouldn't you say? And quite the pairing you two make, scarred as you are.'

'*Mother*,' Arawn warned.

But Ezer *wanted* her to look.

Wanted her to see what good Lordach had done for those like her. The ones raised in forgotten shadows . . . called to war anyway.

Kinlear sighed. 'Your presence in the north is uplifting as usual, Mother. I think you'll soon see that my Rider is more than capable of ensuring the Black Wing Battalion remains a successful mission. She's proven herself to me time and again.'

'You are not the one to decide.' His mother turned her icy gaze on him. 'Look at you, Kinlear. Standing in the cold ready to catch your death, trying to play savior. You're dressed like a sloppy tavern bard when you should be inside, resting—'

'A prince does not *rest*,' Kinlear said. His voice was so firm, it almost felt like he'd yelled the words. 'This is my last chance to do something of worth for this kingdom. I've worked, tirelessly, to ensure the raphon flies. I will not back down now. Not when future peace is so close.'

'The future,' the Queen said carefully, 'that lies in your brother's hands when he is king soon. Not yours, Kinlear. I hardly doubt that *this* –' she waved a hand at Ezer and Six, who had broken character by now and was sniffing playfully at the snow. Ezer jabbed her in the side – 'can survive what is required to save Lordach.'

Gods, the Queen *was* awful. Truly awful.

Perhaps it was better not to have family.

Perhaps Ezer had been spared.

'Yes, we're all aware Arawn has a future,' Kinlear said. 'And if you want him to keep it . . . you'll spend your time praying for my success, instead of wishing I would go back inside and hide. I am done hiding, Mother.' He took a breath, like he was forcing his cough not to appear. And then, in a way that made Ezer's lip twitch with the effort not to smile, he added, 'I'll have you know that this cloak is *designer*, straight from Touvre. And certainly not anything a tavern bard could afford.'

'Enough,' the King spat. His voice was pained. 'We are here for the Descent.'

'I'm glad you see reason, Father,' Kinlear said. 'Shall we begin?'

'Yes,' the King said. 'Make the Descent.' His milky gaze slid towards Ezer. '*Alone*.'

Kinlear gasped. 'But—'

'The Rider goes *alone*, Kinlear. Until she has proven her worth. Should she survive the Descent . . . we'll take our vote then.'

The cliffside was clear before her.

The open sky, empty and waiting.

Too soon, the test of her bond had arrived. Too soon, she asked Six to bow, so she could climb on.

There were only the two of them, alone with the wind.

Kinlear stood beside her, looking up. His grasp utterly white on the eagle's handle of his cane as he watched her settling herself, her hands in Six's feathers.

'Do me a favor, when you're in the midst of it?' Kinlear asked.

Ezer released a heavy breath, a cloud of white. 'A little late for favors, isn't it?'

But he cocked his head and smiled. 'When you make the Descent . . . enjoy it.' He placed a hand on Six's neck, and to her surprise, the raphon did not stiffen, or twitch her tail twice. She leaned into his touch, purring softly. Like she finally trusted him. 'Just . . . don't die.'

Ezer's stomach turned. 'Thanks for that, Prince.'

And then his hand fell away and he was gone, back to join the others who stood watching.

She glanced back and found Arawn with them.

She saw his hand reach for his cloak pocket, and her speaking stone warmed.

She reached for it on instinct, perhaps because in moments . . . she could die.

Six can do this, he thought to her as their eyes locked, and she felt like they were worlds apart. *She must do this . . . so that I can make it right. So that I can earn your forgiveness, one step at a time.*

Her dark heart shifted.

A tiny, insignificant crack, and it allowed a tendril of his light to shine through.

He'd lied to her.

But his lies didn't feel the same as the ones from Ervos. They felt more like stones instead of boulders, more like broken pieces they could still form back together, if she wanted.

She'll do just fine, Ezer thought to him, fingertips around the speaking stone. *As for earning my forgiveness . . . you already have it.*

She would not linger on hatred.

But even as he smiled, relief flooding across his face, she thought back, *it is my trust, Arawn Laroux, that you must earn once more.*

She released the stone and turned away from him.

She closed her eyes and felt the snow on her face, heard the whisper of the wind in her ears that said, '*Fly, Ezer.*' She focused on the warmth of Six beneath her, and the steady beating of her heart.

She blocked out everyone, everything, but the two of them.

She dug her hands into Six's feathers, leaned forward and whispered, 'Okay, Six. Let's fly.'

The raphon broke into a jog, and Ezer settled into it. The rhythm of her body, the beat of her heavy paws against the snow.

Six's wings snapped out when they were twenty paces from the edge.

They were lovely, casting a dark shadow across the cliffside, where morning light had begun to spill through the snow, a beam of beauty in the chaos.

Six's wings were a drum.

Ezer's heart matched them, until they were almost at the cliffside.

Beat.

Beat.

Beat.

She could feel the moment they lifted off the edge. It felt like pressure upon her shoulders, and the wind became colder, stronger.

Her stomach dipped as they careened down, down, past the window wall in the Citadel, the rock face mere inches from Six's paws.

Ezer held on, as the wind pulled at her cloak.

Her hair.

Her breath left her lungs as they picked up speed, as they fell, headlong, towards death.

She was going to splatter on the rocks.

She was going to end up broken for good, and Six would break with her, and—

Trust her, Arawn's voice appeared in her mind. *Trust Six.*

And the second she thought it, a vision filtered into her mind.

A beautiful sunset.

A feather, drifting gently in the wind as it headed for a cluster of mountain peaks. Not the Sawteeth's fierce dark crown, but someplace different. Someplace where the mountains were smoother, softer, wholly covered in white.

Ezer practically gasped at the shift in vision.

Because while her body tumbled down from the cliffside, her mind was rooted to the spot, somewhere else.

If she imagined away the wind, the cold, the rocks at the bottom of the cliff and the seconds between herself and death . . .

She let herself sink into that beautifully painted vision from Six.

There was no battlefield, no cloud of living shadows. Instead, there were distant rolling mountains, thousands of them as far as the eye could see, and in their center, a glittering blue lake. Its shoreline was crusted with ice, and when she looked out across the water . . . she saw the reflection of a black-winged raphon.

And with it, a rider – herself – perched atop the raphon's back.

They flew like they were one body, one soul.

The wind was a breeze instead of a torrent. The sky was a place to dance instead of fight, and as they flew . . .

Others joined in with them.

Ravens.

An entire flock, guiding them as they sang a mournful song. They headed into the wilderness, where no one could stop them.

Not even the wind.

'Thank you,' Ezer whispered, and she stayed there, safe and sound and warm in her mind, while Six led the way. While Six faced the fear for her.

And Ezer was not afraid.

When it was over, when Six carried her safely back up towards the cliffside, and landed . . . the King nodded his approval. The Queen's cold blue eyes held her . . . and so subtly, she approved with a lift of her chin. The Masters, too, and the vote was decided then and there.

'You were magnificent,' Kinlear said as he came to greet Ezer.

He held out a hand to help her down, but she did not need it.

She was capable on her own.

'Tomorrow,' he said, as Ezer stopped before him.

'Tomorrow?' Ezer asked.

He nodded, his eyes bright, as he turned and looked across the Expanse. 'The vote was four to one.' Ezer wondered who that one denier was. The Queen? Or . . . she hated to think it . . . Arawn? 'Tomorrow . . . at the dawn of Realmbreak . . . we fly.'

CHAPTER 34

When she entered the labyrinth, she found herself back in the cottage.

Her first home, where she'd lived with Styerra and Ervos in the woods.

The last time she saw it, the floorboards were covered in black feathers. Today it was as if years had passed once more.

'Strange,' Ezer said, because she'd never begun here.

She was just about to turn and head back to the hall of memories . . . when she heard footsteps.

And suddenly a hooded figure emerged from the frozen tunnel.

Ezer gasped and reached for her blade, but a gust of sudden wind knocked it from her fist.

It clattered to the floor, useless.

'There's no need for weapons,' said the figure. 'Not with me.'

Ezer sucked in a breath, because she knew that voice. And when the figure lowered her hood . . . it was her own face staring back at her. Without the scars but lacking none of the sorrow.

'Mother?'

Styerra smiled. 'Hello, Ezer. I've been working towards this moment for a very, very long time.'

*

Styerra looked about the cottage with a sigh. Like she couldn't believe the state of the place. She crossed to the table and pulled out a chair. Ezer winced as it scraped against the dusty floors with a screech.

'Sit,' Styerra said. 'There's not much time.'

'You can see me?' Ezer asked. 'This is . . . real?'

Styerra smiled. 'It's taken all my energy, all my time, to find a way to meet with you.'

'But . . . how?' Ezer sat across from her.

'Death holds many secrets, my dear. I fear I can't spill a droplet of them without repercussion. But this is real. And important. There's little time to waste, so . . . let us begin . . .'

Ezer nodded, too shocked to argue.

She could see the mark upon Styerra's finger where her skin was a bit paler, the place where she'd worn her beloved ring. Her eyes slid to Ezer's hand.

Where that very ring now sat.

'All my life, I tried invocating. I failed, of course, and was cast aside. Useless, to the Sacred, except to serve them.' Styerra pursed her lips, like she was still annoyed. 'I feared you'd end up like me, too. But the night I died . . . when the wolves came for you. Something happened, Ezer. Something I cannot explain.'

She spoke like she knew Ezer had seen her memories behind the doors. Like they were old friends, catching up. 'It wasn't from an invocation, for I was not so lucky as to wield magic, even near death. But you . . .' Her eyes widened, like she still didn't believe it. 'You were just a baby. How could you invocate? But the moment the wolves attacked, just after they managed to swipe your beautiful face . . .' She frowned, shaking her head as her eyes fell to Ezer's scars. 'It was not me who led them away. It was your ravens.'

Ezer sucked in a breath.

'A thousand of them strong,' Styerra said. 'They protected you, fought for you as if you'd called them, or maybe they'd

been sent, but . . . it was you, Ezer. You saved yourself. With your beautiful magic.'

Ezer shook her head.

It couldn't be.

But . . . she had seen the feathers inside the cottage.

She had seen the way the baby Ezer had them clutched in her furious little fists. And she could imagine it, the very same thing that had happened two months ago, in the woods.

An army of ravens.

For her.

'But . . . how?' Ezer asked.

'Your ancestor, Wrenwyn . . . she could do what you do. Magic, raw and real, that does not require invocating. That does not have to pay a price.'

But if that were true . . .

It would change everything for the Sacred, if they could only learn. If only they could stop relying upon the granted invocations to the gods.

'There are a rare few that possess your ability,' Styerra explained. 'Very rare, for only those in Wrenwyn's line can wield without invocations.'

It didn't make sense.

And yet . . . it explained her entire life. Her connection to the birds. To Six. Her ability to call upon the ravens, when death was near . . .

Her dreams.

'What am I?' Ezer dared ask.

Because . . . she couldn't be Sacred.

Styerra frowned. 'That is a question I cannot answer. But there is another who can. Another who your father believed in. Wrenwyn, too.'

'The Acolyte?' Ezer asked.

Styerra nodded.

She flickered for a moment and winced.

Her hands curled like she was in pain.

'I doubted Erath when he first told me of this other power. How could I, born and raised in the Citadel, taught the laws of the Five, witnessing the glorious magic from them . . . how could I ever think there was anything different?' *Her eyes glittered.* 'But he was right. The gods are not alone, Ezer. The Acolyte is far more powerful than they think.'

A tendril of fear shivered through Ezer.

She needed to know more, had to know more, but first . . .

'What happened to my father?' *Ezer asked.*

Styerra sat forward, her expression darkening. 'I suppose I'll never fully know. I was meant to find him in death. That ring you wear on your thumb was meant to bond us. A way to seek one another, a map for our souls after we left this realm behind. But when Stefon—'

'Ervos,' *Ezer said.*

'You knew him as only his surname, yes.' *Styerra nodded.* 'When he removed it from my dead finger . . .' *she lifted her hands, frowning at the space where she once wore the ring,* 'it wasn't so he could hold on to some fond memory of me. It was because he knew that he would never have my heart. He took the ring to ensure that I would never find your father again. Not in life. And not in death.'

A horrible fate, to wander aimlessly in the afterlife, searching for a love that might never be found. Ezer's blood went cold.

'Why would he do such a thing?'

Styerra placed her hands in her lap. 'Wouldn't you, to save the one you loved? We would have been killed together, Erath and I, and you along with us, Ezer . . . if Stefon had not lied.'

Ezer had read thousands of stories in her life.

But none were quite so bitter. Quite so broken and sad.

'Stefon loved me. But he loved the idea of me more. A perfect, pious Sacred woman, who was content to do the Five's bidding and never think twice about what else might lie beyond. Because *like I once did . . . Stefon believed that the Five, and their thousand impossible laws, were the only way. And to deviate from that way would mean a fate worse than death. He forged the letter from Erath. I do not believe your father would ever have left without me.'* She closed her eyes, and when she opened them, the sadness was replaced with anger, burning like an ember. *'I tried to show Stefon, that final night. But his eyes were not ready to see. His loyalty to the Five, too strong. It's why I lied to him, told him that I was the one to draw the wolves away. He would have treated you like the book. Like something to be feared, instead of cherished.'* She looked at Ezer's pocket. *'I know you carry the Shadow Tome with you.'*

The book.

The symbols.

The blood drained from Ezer's face as she reached into her cloak pocket . . . and found Zey's empty journal there. The one that she'd been thumbing through, night after night. It hadn't ever made the journey to her dreams before.

When she set it on the table between them, the pages fluttered open.

It was still empty.

Styerra smiled at the pages. Like she could see what Ezer could not. '*When the Acolyte was set free, only the ones who could see through the cracks in the Five were able to decipher the message. Stefon saw nothing on the pages, like so many others. But I was awakened. I didn't find the journal in town, like I told Stefon. I had kept Erath's book with me, the last thing I had of him. In secret, I began to read it. And after you were born . . . I began to see the symbols.'*

This was wrong. Ezer knew it was wrong, and yet . . .

'What did they say?' Ezer asked, glancing down at Zey's empty pages. *'The symbols.'*

'Your eyes aren't opened yet,' Styerra said. *'Not fully. And there is nothing I can say, nothing I can do, to sway you to open*

them all the way. That must happen in your own time. For most, it never will.'

'But that book, that raw power you speak of . . . it comes from the Acolyte,' Ezer said, horrified. 'The same power that caused a stone in the Sacred Circle to turn black. An entire realm. Gone. It's coming for us, next. All of Lordach will be gone if he wins the war. It's the same power that killed *you*. And did this to me.'

She tucked her dark curls behind her ears. She lifted her chin, so that Styerra would be forced to look at her three hideous scars. 'How can you worship a power like that?'

Styerra looked as sad as she had the day she left the Citadel. *'I wish I could tell you what it all means. I wish I had been given the chance to teach you and be the mother you deserved. I was going to leave with you, the night the wolves came. I was going to go north to the Acolyte.'*

'To a monster,' Ezer said. 'You were going to take your newborn baby to a monster.' She stood up, chair scraping, desperate to put space between them. 'He started a war after you died. He's murdered thousands, women and children and men who never even stood a chance against him. He's—'

'And yet . . .' Styerra leaned back, holding her gaze. *'You have bound yourself to one of* his *monsters. And by all counts, dear daughter . . . I would say that Six is good. There is always another side to the story.'*

Ezer's heart stuttered. 'How do you know about Six? About the book I carry? About—'

Styerra's image suddenly flickered.

She let out a painful gasp.

'What's happening?' Ezer asked.

'Time is running thin. I cannot give you everything . . . but I can at least give you this answer. When I died, a young woman met me on the fringes of life and death. The doorsteps to the Ehver. She gave me a choice. To end my journey . . . or to go

back and watch over you until you were ready. A spirit guide. The cost, of course, would be to delay my eternity. My peace.'

A cold sense of dread washed over Ezer.

'You . . .' she whispered. 'You chose . . .'

Styerra nodded. 'I chose you, Ezer. As I would over and over again in every lifetime, no matter the cost.'

A choice like that . . .

It was love.

True, selfless love that left Ezer breathless.

'I didn't fly away to the Ehver,' Styerra explained. She winced again, and spoke faster, like she was racing the wind. 'I found myself here, in this labyrinth. A place full of my own memories. For a decade, I walked them alone. A purgatory, if you will. But as the years passed, more doors began to appear. They were full of your *memories.' She smiled. 'This labyrinth . . . it is your mind, your soul – and mine – tangled into one.'*

A breath left Ezer's lips.

'I called out to you for years,' Styerra said. 'But you didn't hear me. I thought my job as spirit guide fruitless. Until Stefon gave you the ring.'

Realization dawned on Ezer.

'It's you,' she said. 'You're the whisper on the wind.'

'Not the wind.' Styerra laughed softly. 'It doesn't have a voice, dear girl, but I most certainly do. I protected you. Truly protected you, the way only a mother *could.'*

And then she flickered again and gasped.

Ezer watched her body begin to fade, like she was truly a ghost.

'I've held on for years. As long as I could. But I grow weary, and my strength . . .' Another flicker. 'Each day, it wanes. The stronger you become, the less you will have need of me, until eventually . . . this labyrinth will be gone. There will be no voice on the wind. You will have only the birds. Only the magic that lies dormant within you, waiting to be unleashed.'

'But what is it?' Ezer asked. 'Please. You to have to help me understand. I can't do this on my own. I can't . . .'

'You have never been alone, my love,' Styerra said, and a tear ran down her cheek, glistening as if made of starlight. 'When you are ready . . . you will step into that power. And you will soar.'

'And what if I never do?' Ezer asked. 'What if, my entire life, I am nothing but a stranger to myself?'

'You know exactly who you are, Ezer. You need only accept it.' She flickered again. 'I must go.'

'Not yet,' Ezer begged her. 'I'll die tomorrow, without your help.'

'No,' Styerra said. 'For I believe you are fated to go north. To see the Acolyte face to face, the way neither I, nor your father ever could.' She reached out, with a wavering hand, and tried to touch Ezer's fingertips. But they went right through her. Instead, she placed them on the book that still lay between them. The empty pages. 'I believe you were always meant to be the one to bring our family to the truth. To see it with your own eyes and decide whether you end him or join him. Whether you side with the Acolyte. Or fight for the Five.'

'But—'

'The symbols,' Styerra said. 'Keep your mind open to them, and they will show you the way.' Her body was fading too fast, the cottage walls now visible through her. 'I never had the chance to say it, not with words. But I will now, as my final parting gift. I love you, Ezer. My daughter. My heart.'

And just like that . . .

She was gone.

Ezer woke to the sound of rumbling.

It was still the middle of the night, the war raging beyond the wards.

Six was curled up beside her, fast asleep. One of her paws was warm and soft beneath Ezer's head, a fine pillow she was now certain she couldn't sleep without. The other was wrapped over Ezer's stomach . . .

Like she was one of Six's beloved treasures, a thing to be held and kept close.

'It was my mother, all along,' Ezer whispered. 'The voice on the wind.'

Ezer had sought answers all her life. And now that she had them . . . she somehow felt even more lost. Like she'd been floating, and now she was falling.

'Who am I, Six?' Ezer whispered into the dark. '*What* am I?'

Because despite what Styerra had said – *you know exactly who you are* – she didn't. And she feared she didn't have time to discover it. Not with the journey tomorrow.

'I'm afraid,' she said. 'I don't even know if you chose me because of *me*. Or if you had to, because of my magic. Perhaps you never even had a choice.'

Six winked open an eye.

And then a vision fluttered into Ezer's mind.

It was the night Six escaped. She leapt through the Eagle's Nest, hopping from tree to tree.

Six came across a youngling. A boy who looked up in terror and screamed like he was staring at a monster. Six leapt away, closing in on the barn and the stalls where the war eagles slept.

She found herself on the ground, facing two Sacred Knights.

And when they beheld the raphon – a raphon that was scared and lonely and desperate to be free – their faces shifted.

That was fear in their eyes, too, like they were staring at something that did not deserve to exist. And there were others behind them rushing out of the barn, a flurry of cloaked Sacred with invocations on their lips and hatred on their faces.

Six leapt for the nearest tree, her claws scraping away at the bark as she faded into the canopy.

The vision jumped forward.

She saw herself, standing paces away from Arawn on the path, so small beside him, as he dove and pulled her to safety.

The vision jumped again.

And there she was, standing in front of Six.

Ezer, with blood staining the palm of her hand. It was not terror in her eyes . . .

It was strength.

It was a bravery that did not falter as she faced the raphon and whispered a challenge.

'Go ahead. Make it count.'

The vision broke.

'You chose me,' Ezer said, sorting through what she'd just seen, why Six had chosen *that* memory to share with her. 'Because I saw you for what you are. Not a monster. I saw you . . . as a bit like me.'

Six's tail thumped once.

She settled her scarred beak in Ezer's lap as she cried. As she let out the anger, the fear, the frustration. She purged everything she'd been holding in.

She waited until Six was happily snoring away, her enormous paws twitching in sleep, before she left the catacombs.

There was one thing she still needed to do, a matter she needed to settle, before tomorrow.

But when she came to the black door and reached for the handle . . . it swung open from the other side.

'What in the—' Ezer's words fell away.

It was Arawn.

CHAPTER 35

'Ezer,' he breathed.

'What are you doing here?' she asked.

She hadn't seen him since yesterday.

His normally perfect warrior's braid was loose. His cloak was rumpled, not pressed, and his eyes were wide, like he hadn't expected to find her standing there either, her hand on the door.

'I was . . .' He looked over his shoulder, like he was searching for some sort of excuse. Then he sighed and said, 'I came to apologize.'

'Why?' Ezer asked.

'Because I lied to you. Because you deserved to know the truth, even if it would break you.'

'Do I look broken to you?' Ezer asked, and stepped out of the doorway, closing it shut behind her. 'Do I look like some fragile, feeble thing?'

'No,' he whispered.

And though he was three times her size, right now as he stood before her, he seemed small.

He looked like the broken one.

'You look brave,' Arawn said. 'You look bold, and . . .' He paused. 'And *angry*, Ezer, which you have every right to be. I shouldn't have lied. They teach us that as one of the first laws. We promise to uphold it when we take our vows, and despite myself, when it came to you . . . I still broke it.'

'Why?' she said again.

'Because . . .'

'One chance, Arawn.' She held up a finger, her eyes locked on his. 'You have one chance right now, and if you do not tell me the truth . . . I will walk away from you. I will leave this place tomorrow, come sunrise, and you will *never* see me again. Even if I survive.'

He let out a breath.

'If?'

'I'd be lying if I said *when*,' Ezer told him.

His eyes shone silver at their edges. He was holding back tears.

Please don't say it was to protect me, Ezer thought. *Please don't say it was to keep me safe.*

Because she wanted, just once, for someone to let life happen to her in *her* way.

To let her fall if she was to fall, because at least that was freedom. At least that was living.

'I did it . . . to protect myself,' Arawn said. 'Because . . .'

He glanced away.

'Look at me, Arawn,' Ezer said.

His eyes opened. And he looked like he could hardly stand as he said, 'Because I didn't know you that day in the tower. All I knew were my orders, and they were to deliver you here, to have you become any other soldier.' He sighed. 'But you aren't any other soldier. You are . . .'

'What am I?' Ezer asked.

Her heart was beating against her rib cage. *Move closer to him*, her body said, but her mind . . .

Gods, her mind was sick of being manipulated.

And she couldn't stand the thought of being hurt again by someone else's actions, like she was a rock tossed about in the sea.

'You are stubborn,' Arawn said. At that, she recoiled.

'What?'

He nodded and stepped a little bit closer. 'You are crass, and you are curious to your own detriment, but I adore how much it keeps me on my toes. And you are perhaps the messiest eater I have ever met. Worse than Six.'

She glared at him then. 'If this is supposed to be a slew of compliments, Arawn . . .'

'You are brilliant with her, and you are bold to spend your days with Kinlear, and *gods*, the way you speak to people, the way you challenge them . . . the way you do not falter, not even when it comes to a shadow wolf . . . it's like you aren't even afraid, Ezer.'

He stepped a little bit closer.

This time, she did not back away.

'You are everything I am not. Everything I wish I could be, because you do not bend to the will of anyone but yourself.'

'That's not true,' she said.

Her entire life had been about bending to the will of others.

She was sick of it. Sick of being told who she was by people who had their own opinions of her. But every word Arawn had just said . . . he was right.

Because he saw her.

He saw her when she didn't even see herself yet.

'I didn't tell you at first,' he said, 'because it's my duty to hold the secrets of the Citadel. Why would I offer that up, risk penance and punishment, for a stranger? For a woman in a tower with a mountain of debt upon her head?'

He sighed.

'And when I *did* get to know you . . . why would I wish to break someone who seemed already broken? Because I was broken, too, Ezer. I couldn't even conjure a flame to save you, but you didn't need me to. You saved me, and then you saved yourself in those woods, and however you did it, I don't know. And I don't care. Because . . . everything about you, that's what I love.'

Her heart started to *thump* at that word.

Love.

He stepped closer still. 'And once I knew who you were . . . I couldn't speak the truth aloud.'

'It wasn't your choice to make,' Ezer said.

'I know that. And I was going to tell you, but the more I got to know you, the more time we spent together, the more you challenged me and frustrated me . . . the more you began to step into who you are here . . . the more I realized, Ezer of Rendegard, that *you* could not be broken. But I could.' He swallowed, and his hands shook at his sides. 'I could be broken if I lost you. So, I hid the truth. And it was wrong of me, and I am a coward for it, and I will spend months, years – gods, whatever it takes – trying to make it up to you.'

His words were beautiful.

They were lovely, wonderful, heartfelt things, and they slid over her and through her, making it hard to remember to breathe.

She'd been so angry with him, so betrayed by his lies, for he'd pretended for months that Ervos was dead. But somehow his wrongdoing paled in comparison to all she'd faced inside her labyrinth. The awful memories of Styerra and Erath.

And Ervos in the cell far beneath her, rotting away for murdering five innocent raphon pups. But she liked to imagine he was there because of what he'd done to Styerra, and to her.

'I have been lied to my entire life,' Ezer said. She hadn't the chance to tell him about her mother, but when it came to Ervos, he knew. He understood. 'And you expect me to forgive you? To fall into your arms and . . . and what then, Arawn? You'll be king soon. And . . . we are *not* to be Matched.'

He took a deep breath, and his hands went slack at his sides, like he was surrendering.

'I do not expect anything from you,' he said. 'Never, Ezer. Your choices are your own to make. I am asking – I'll beg if I have to – if you will forgive me. If you will trust me again.

Because I've lived my entire life in the Citadel afraid of making mistakes. When we make them here . . . we pay. When we make them against the gods, our eternity is on the line. Our magic.'

He looked at his hands. He frowned. And when he looked back up at her, his eyes were shining again.

'I'm asking for grace.' His voice cracked. 'Something I have never known. From anyone.'

And the way he said it was so utterly broken, so raw and real, that she felt her walls go down.

They'd both been wronged.

They'd both faced darkness, in their own ways. She might die tomorrow. She might die and never feel love, but . . .

But tonight.

Just for tonight . . . perhaps she could.

'We shouldn't do this,' she whispered. 'It's forbidden.'

'I know,' he said. And suddenly she was terrified of this ending. But then he reached out and ran a hand down her cheek. Towards her neck. Her collarbone. His gaze was molten as he looked back up to her. 'I cannot live my life, Ezer, not knowing what it was like to have you. I'll pay the penance. I'll pay it a thousand times, if it means one night together. One night . . . where we are *free* to love who we please.'

Her own eyes widened.

Because there it was again.

Love.

She reached behind her and opened the door to the catacombs. The cold and the darkness poured out. But she laced her fingers through the front of Arawn's cloak, met his eyes, and pulled him with her over the threshold.

'What are you doing?' he asked.

'I'm taking you some place private,' she said as she shut the door behind them, bathing them both in darkness.

He was raising a pale brow, the way he always did when he

looked at her. Like she was a question he'd happily spend his life trying to answer.

'So you can kill me?' he asked, and she could practically hear him smile.

'No,' Ezer said. 'So I can kiss you.'

She pulled him down to her. And when their lips met, the cold was gone, and there was only fire in its place.

They reached the edge of themselves in the darkness, and when the hunger rose, and the space between them was still too much to bear . . .

'I don't know how—' Ezer whispered against his lips.

'Neither do I,' Arawn whispered back.

So, they learned together.

And it was beautiful.

And fleeting.

And the choice was theirs to make.

She had no dreams in Arawn's arms.

There was no labyrinth, no whispering wind.

She found only warmth and silence.

They stayed together in the darkness, until the rumbling of the battle subsided. The floor was their bed. His body, her blanket, and when sleep was hard to come by . . .

She told him everything. The book, the labyrinth, the secret of her mother. Ervos's manipulation.

'What if we've been wrong the whole time?' Ezer asked him.

She couldn't see him, but she could feel him all around her. The way his fingers ran up and down her spine, tracing the shape of her. Testing the feel of her skin on his. 'In what way?'

'What if the gods are not alone?' Ezer said. 'What if the Acolyte is some other sort of god? Some deeper power, intent on punishing the Five for locking the Sacred in a lifetime of laws they cannot measure up to? What if . . . this entire time, we've been fighting for the wrong side?'

His fingers paused at the small of her back.

'What you speak of . . .' he whispered. 'It's dangerous, Ezer.'

'I know it is,' Ezer said. 'But so is *this*.'

Her head was against his chest, her ear pressed just over his heart so she could hear the way it beat steadily . . . and how it quickened when she ran her own hands across his skin. 'I'm just wondering. *What if?*'

'I wish I knew,' he said. 'But that is the point of faith. To question. To struggle to understand what is right and what is wrong, and in the end, all we have to trust is our soul.'

'And what does yours say, Firemage?'

He let out a deep breath. 'My soul has not known, for a very long time, which way it leans.' She could hear him swallow. 'I know that Soraya believed in what Zey and many others believed. I know they all died for it.'

'My mother and father, too,' Ezer said.

'But countless others I have known and loved . . . they fight for the Five. And I believe in them, too. That their souls are good, and their hearts and minds are in the right place.'

'What if I don't know if I've ever believed,' Ezer said, 'in anything?'

She swallowed a lump in her throat. To be so honest, so raw with someone . . . she'd never had anything like it in her life.

And later, if she failed, it could all be whisked away.

'Later,' Arawn whispered, as if he sensed her thoughts. 'You'll see with your own eyes. And . . . you'll make it across. You'll find the Acolyte.'

'And what if what I find isn't what we thought?' Ezer asked. 'What if the darkness is really the light? What if Lordach was wrong about the Five, all along?'

'Then you'll have to make it back to me,' Arawn whispered. 'So, we can face the truth together.'

She nodded.

And then she kissed his neck, and he leaned into it, and before she knew it, they were intertwined again, and the sun was rising beyond the darkness, and her fate was barreling towards her.

And she didn't want time to press on.

But it did.

It was the first day of Realmbreak.

When the door to the catacombs opened, Kinlear found Ezer there alone, standing by the door to Six's cage while the raphon finished a meal of bleeding meat. Like nothing had ever gone on, in the wee hours of morning, between a Minder and a Firemage.

'Ezer.'

She spun as more footsteps sounded, and Izill stepped into the torchlight.

'She insisted,' Kinlear said with a small smile. 'She is quite terrifying, despite her size. I swear, the two of you could have been sisters.'

Ezer rushed forward and pulled Izill into a hug.

'You'll do this,' Izill said against her. 'And then you will come *home*. We'll spend far too long in the library together, eating chocolate and drinking coffee and sharing stories and—' Her voice broke, and when Ezer pulled away, Izill was crying.

'Don't do that,' Ezer said. 'It will make me cry, too.'

Izill nodded. And then she surprised Ezer by walking right up to the bars of Six's cage. Anyone else would have balked, screamed at the sight of the Acolyte's beast. But Izill wrapped her fingers around the bars and said, 'Keep her safe, Six. Or you will have *me* to deal with upon your return.'

The raphon lowered her head in acceptance and began to purr.

It was not a grand exit, with people gathering on the cliffside to watch them go.

There was only the King and Queen, the Masters and Arawn.

The snow fell gently from the sky. The wind whistled past her ears and for the first time . . . it was *only* the wind.

No whisper.

No voice upon it, guiding her in what was to come.

'Today marks the first of Realmbreak,' the King said, as they stopped before him. 'You have until the third day before night returns. The godsblessing, Kinlear . . . you'll want to make it back before that final hour.'

'I know,' Kinlear said.

'And I . . .' His father's milky eyes shone. 'I may no longer be here.'

Ezer's stomach sank to her toes.

But Kinlear showed not a hint of emotion.

'Kinlear.' The Queen suddenly stepped up.

She placed a tentative hand on his cheek. She frowned, disappointed in the son that would never wear the Lordachian crown. Kinlear was doomed for death no matter what the outcome was. It was the only reason they'd sent *him* . . . instead of Arawn. Instead of any other warrior.

'I will never know why the gods willed you for this,' the Queen said. 'But if it must be so . . . do not fail. Do not squander your only chance at greatness.'

A spike of rage went through Ezer.

But Kinlear only chuckled, like the insult rolled off his shoulders. 'I suppose that's as heartwarming a goodbye as you're capable of giving, Mother. I'll carry it with me to the other side.'

Ezer hated them all suddenly.

She hated the Masters for how they punished with penance, showing no mercy for a single slip-up . . . but especially the King and the Queen. Because Kinlear was their *son*. And in their eyes . . . he was expendable.

He was a lamb already headed for slaughter, so they were okay with sacrificing him early.

Six shielded her as she shifted, so that she and Ezer stood alone while the others said their goodbyes. And in that fleeting moment of solitude . . . Arawn stepped up beside her to say goodbye.

No one noticed them as he placed his hand on her cheek. His fingertips ran gently across her scars as he kissed her and whispered, 'Ezer. Come back to me.'

'I will,' she said.

'Promise me.'

And as she pulled away, suddenly she understood why some people lied to the ones they loved. It was wrong and it made her blood run cold and her insides twist, but she was certain it would be better for him. Better for the moments they'd shared and the hope she wanted to leave him with, so she looked into his eyes, and told him, 'I promise.'

His smile made the lie hurt less.

She turned away and climbed onto Six's back, where Kinlear already sat waiting. He frowned down at them, like he'd seen the kiss. Like he *knew* what had transpired between them in the wee hours of morning. He wrapped his arms around her middle, holding her closer than normal.

'Goodbye, Brother,' Kinlear said down to Arawn. 'Don't worry. I'll take care of her. The way no one did for Soraya.'

The look of pain on Arawn's face nearly had her climbing back down to him. Instead, Ezer turned Six away. Before she could stop herself, she clicked her teeth and urged Six into a run.

The fear chased her like a hungry wolf, and it sounded like her uncle's voice.

You will fail.

You will die the moment you cross over that border, Little Bird.

The sky is a dangerous place for a girl without wings.

But she'd found her wings.

They were dark and wondrous and safe, and as Six reached the cliff's edge and leapt into the waiting sky . . .

Ezer did not close her eyes.

She wanted to see it, wanted to taste it and dive headfirst into the fear that had followed her all the days of her life.

She should hate her uncle for the choices he made, the sins he'd committed in the name of protection. But for all the things Ervos had said and done that were wrong . . . there was one thing he was right about, and Ezer still believed it in her bones.

As she stared at the snow-covered ground as it closed in beyond the point of Six's scarred beak, Ezer thought . . .

Do it afraid.

And she did.

For herself, she did.

PART FOUR

THE ASSASSIN

CHAPTER 36

The Expanse was harrowing from above.

Fitting, Ezer supposed, for a killing field.

She directed Six to the bottom of the cliff face. The towering black Snow Gates rippled with gold, the last remnants of the wards that surrounded Augaurde.

Six's wings shot out from her sides at Ezer's touch, and the drop became a bank, Six's paws kicking up the snow as she just barely clipped the surface.

Climb, Six, Ezer thought, and the raphon's wings fell into a glorious, steady rhythm as she caught the wind like it was an old, trusted friend. The wardlight rippled as they passed through.

And they were out.

Away from the Citadel, so fast she wondered why she'd feared this flight at all.

The sky was a glorious place for a woman with wings.

'Gods,' Kinlear breathed as they rose steadily, away from the snow and the frozen chasms, away from the tracks of countless soldiers marching north. 'That was . . .'

'*Incredible*,' Ezer breathed.

And then she did something she thought she'd never do.

She threw her arms into the sky.

And screamed in delight.

Kinlear laughed behind her, the sound so joyful she knew he felt it, too.

Freedom.

The greatest gift they'd ever been given. Because of Six.

Hours ago, this very same sky was full of magic and shadows, darksouls and Sacred riders clashing. But in daylight, it was calm.

It felt like a reset, to know the daylight would not wane for three days.

It was as if the gods had chased night away.

It was almost quiet, were it not for the wind ruffling through Six's feathers, a lovely sound she'd always appreciated from the incoming birds each time they landed in her tower.

Six dipped to the right as a gust of wind came through, offering them a glimpse of the view beneath her wings.

Ezer's stomach flipped, but she held fast to Six's feathers, trusting the raphon to hold steady. To never let her fall . . . or at least catch her if she did.

The frozen fog that covered the Expanse was lighter today, so Ezer could see the body collectors were already out as they soared over. Through the snow muddling her vision, she could see splashes of crimson and black, and large outlines that marked the fallen beasts.

'It was somewhere out here that we lost Soraya,' Kinlear said suddenly.

Ezer glanced over her shoulder to find him staring down at the Expanse.

'What was she like?' Ezer asked.

He chuckled against her back. 'Bold. Daring. Beautiful. She was a lot like you, always content to challenge what is known.' He sighed. 'But challenging people does not bode well in the Citadel. Soraya paid penance quite often. And when the penance became too much to bear . . . she left.'

Like Zey, Ezer thought.

She hadn't told a soul when she'd eventually packed Zey's

book in her cloak pocket. Some part of her couldn't let it go, even though the pages were still utterly empty. Even though she did not believe the story of the symbols to be true.

She'd leave it somewhere in the wilderness on the other side. A tribute to the Eagleminder . . . because there would be no sword plunged into the snow around the Citadel's ancient tree for her.

The wind shifted, and the snow began to fall a bit harder. Six held steady, heading towards true north, that ever-present ring of black mountains just visible before her beak. And the shadowstorm above it, with dark shapes swimming through the sky. It truly never stopped, no matter the time of day.

What sort of man, Ezer wondered, could handle such raw, endless power?

Perhaps Wrenwyn was right. Perhaps it truly *was* a god on the other side.

Or – she shivered – a devil.

'The night she left,' Kinlear said, and coughed as his sickness was spurred on by the frigid wind, 'she claimed that the Acolyte could save me, could heal my ailments in ways that the magic of the Five never could.'

'But . . . you said that's impossible,' Ezer said.

He shrugged against her back. 'People deal with grief differently. Some run from it. Others try to fix it. Soraya was a fixer, even when we were children. My sickness was only another battle for her to fight.'

The shadowstorm rumbled, silencing his sigh.

'I asked her for hard proof. She showed me a small black book. She called it the Shadow Tome and claimed it was full of promises and hope for healing. She said it was *alive*. That it called out to people. To those who were ready to see and believe.' Ezer's heart sank. Soraya . . . another one lost to the darkness, just like her mother and father and Zey. He paused, and she felt his eyes on her back. 'Have you ever heard of a book like that, Ezer? A book that *lives*?'

She was about to tell him yes, of course she had, because she carried such a book in her cloak pocket now.

But something within her knew it was better to lie.

'No,' Ezer said, as easy as breathing. 'What did her book say? Was it true?'

The distant shadowstorm rumbled again, and Kinlear tensed.

But Six stayed the course, unbothered, as if she finally understood the sound and feel of the Acolyte's magic. Like it was calling her north, instead of warning her away.

'Kinlear?'

For a second, she wondered if she was wrong to doubt the driving in of that knife, night after night.

He nodded against her back, and said, 'I looked at it. Every page.'

Ezer's breath hitched.

What if he was leading her north, all along, not to kill the Acolyte. But to try and discover him for himself? He was a prince without a ruling crown. He was doomed to die. What if he believed what Soraya said?

What if Ezer was wrong about him?

But then he said, 'It was empty. Completely blank.'

It was an effort for her not to sigh in relief.

'I knew then that her mind had been poisoned. She was going the same dark route others had before, defecting.' His grip tightened as Six shifted, catching an updraft. 'I wanted to turn her in. I wanted to keep her there in the Citadel, until someone could make her mind right again. But then I remembered the others that had defected. The ones who paid penance . . . until they couldn't pay any more.'

Dread began to stir in her gut. Because she knew what he meant. Six glanced back, sensing her unease.

'They burn the bodies,' Kinlear said, so softly it was nearly carried by the wind. 'It is a traitor's death, to us, the fire so hot that not even a finger bone is left behind. Nothing for the gods to seek . . . so that they can't even make the journey to the Ehver when they die.'

It was sick.

She was going to be sick.

For all the things the Citadel stood upon. For all the talk of the gods' grace . . .

She wanted to scream.

'I confronted her about it. I think she sensed that our hearts were already on opposite sides. Because she left that night. Arawn was on watch. It was *his* fault she got out, *his* fault she got past him.'

His heart hammered against her back.

'The thing I can't figure out is *where* she got the Shadow Tome from. We searched her belongings after she left. It wasn't there. But I have a feeling it's because she'd already passed it on to someone else.'

Ezer's blood went cold. What if Soraya had given the book to Zey, and now that very book, the one that had ruined Kinlear's betrothal . . . was in *her* cloak pocket?

'I'm so sorry,' she said and shifted her weight nervously.

He could never know. It was too risky.

He nodded against her shoulder. 'So am I.'

And then the sky erupted.

The boom was enough to feel in her bones. The shadowstorm was *above* them instead of before them.

'We're nearly there,' Ezer breathed.

She pressed her hands to Six's neck as the fear threatened to overtake her again.

'Ezer,' Kinlear said and suddenly reached for her hands as he held on to her waist. Inches from the black book. 'I've known it from the moment I saw you with your hand on Six's beak. Because of you, I won't be forgotten when I die.'

She hated his inevitable end.

'Because of you . . . I'll slay the Acolyte,' he said. 'I'll bring glory to Lordach. We'll be remembered forever, the prince and the raphon rider.'

'The *warrior*,' Ezer corrected him. 'Today, you are a warrior. Now let's find the Black Door and the Acolyte.'

He nodded. 'And drive in the blade.'

Three days before darkness returned. It had to be enough time.

His lips were inches from her ear. 'Will you promise me one thing, Raphon Rider?'

She nodded.

'When we make it back . . . save a dance for *me* at the next Absolution? I want every eye in the Citadel to see how victorious we are . . . together.'

Her heart did a nervous little leap.

But not in the way he would have wanted it to.

Because in the back of her mind, she still saw Arawn, how he'd looked as she flew away from him.

Broken.

She nodded. 'My hand is yours. Though . . . I can't promise I won't step on your toes.'

'Step on them all you want.' Kinlear's voice was nervous. 'Break them if you wish it. I'll bear the pain, so long as you dance with me.'

He suddenly coughed and released his grip on her as he went for his vial.

So Ezer took a deep breath and faced the shadows. Dark tendrils spilled from the clouds like reaching claws, but the shadows were also thick between them – a true veil of living darkness.

They were ten wingbeats away.

She could tell Six to turn back, and she knew the raphon would listen. She could fly them somewhere far away, leave this war behind and start life anew.

But Styerra's words came back to her. There could be answers about her magic on the other side.

'Ezer,' Kinlear said suddenly, just before they reached the shadowstorm. She turned to look at him one last time, with his hood now covering his face. 'Will you go with me into the dark?'

But before she could answer him, before she could fully register what that might mean, she felt her hair stand on end.

The tip of Six's beak reached the shadows.

The light collapsed.

It was so dark, she could barely see her own hands held before her, even with her scarred eye.

Six soared right into the Acolyte's magic.

And then *through it*.

It moved away – that dark veil of power. The shadows folded outwards around the shape of the raphon like the tendrils itself were told not to touch a feather upon her wings, nor a single tuft of fur upon her body. And as the shadowstorm cleared for Six, it cleared for Ezer and Kinlear.

Just as Kinlear's intel had promised.

'It worked,' he breathed.

They were inside the Sawteeth, inside the Acolyte's domain.

And Six . . .

She let out a victorious caw, and Ezer smiled as the darkness was whisked away. As light found them once more. She felt it in her own bones, her blood.

Six was finally home.

CHAPTER 37

The wind died down the moment they passed through the veil of darkness.

She turned to look past Kinlear's narrow shoulders, just in time to see the shadows fold back in on themselves, closing the gap where Six had just flown through.

She was surprised that she could still see the other side, a muted gray instead of snow white.

The Citadel was so far away, it was barely a speck on the horizon.

Incredible, Ezer thought to Six. *You are incredible.*

Hundreds of warriors had died trying to do what they'd just done. They had tried magic and might, all manner of onslaughts against the shadows . . .

But all they needed was a raphon.

So simple, the trick. Because the Acolyte had never needed to fear someone taking one of his own beasts, taming it, and flying it right back home.

Ezer smiled.

This was the perfect place for winged monsters to thrive.

The Sawteeth could have been weapons themselves, each one intent on stabbing the sky, and they stretched so high she couldn't see their peaks for where the shadowstorm swallowed them up.

It churned above them, and rumbled the way the seaside

storms always did: like a furious beast waiting for the moment to unleash itself. But the shadows did not strike inside the Sawteeth. They remained only on the perimeter, creating a barrier.

A safety net of magic that was untouchable for anyone who served the Five.

How did it know, she wondered, when someone defected? Did it count the darkness in their heart? Did it unfold for them, the way it had unfolded for Six?

Had Zey ever made it to this side?

She couldn't picture anyone surviving past this point without a raphon.

The landscape beneath them was far more deadly.

Endless facets of black rock stretched on and on, so sharp even at the lowest points that it would have been impossible to pass on foot. One wrong step, and you'd spear yourself. One slip on the sharp, upward climb, and you'd be impaled to death.

There were no trees, no color at all beyond shadow black and snow white.

Flakes swirled in Ezer's vision making her shiver, despite the runes on her cloak.

Kinlear coughed against her, sudden and violent.

'Are you all right?' Ezer asked him.

He kept coughing. Each tremor of his chest was a reminder of the time he was losing. How he would soon fade away.

'I'm fine,' he said as he uncorked his vial and took a sip of the medicine.

She didn't know how long he had until that small vial ran out. He had only one extra, and now that seemed not nearly enough.

And then it was quiet again, as Six soared further north. The Sawteeth stretched on for miles and miles, an endless landscape.

'There's nothing down there,' Kinlear said. 'Not a single creature.'

But something had caught Six's attention, for she suddenly banked to the left, then dropped into a fresh current of wind.

They were joyful, her movements, like she was exploring. Perhaps Ezer should let her lead.

Each wingbeat carried them deeper into the mountains, until they were surrounded by them in full, with two monstrous peaks on either side. For the first time, a bit of her hope waned.

They could search this harsh terrain forever and never find a trace of the Acolyte.

And the further they flew, the darker it seemed to become.

The plan felt silly now. A far cry from possible, until—

Six let out a soft caw.

Ezer felt a jolt of *recognition* swim through her from their bond.

'What do you see, Six?'

The raphon picked up speed as they came around the first two peaks.

The world stretched on as far as the eye could see, every part of it split by black mountains capped in white. And right there in the very middle stood a peak no one could have seen from the Expanse, for it was smaller than the others, hidden right in the center.

And out of that small peak funneled a line of dark winged creatures.

'Ravens?' Kinlear said.

'Not ravens.' Ezer's scars stretched as she smiled. '*Raphons.*'

Wild raphons.

They had burst from the darkness below, where the black rock was thick, and the shadows were deep. It was an entire line of raphons, soaring skyward, some full-grown and others barely fledglings. There were so many Ezer couldn't count their number.

Six seemed to pause in the sky, her own breath held as she watched them and listened to their cries.

Your kind, Ezer thought as she buried her hands in Six's fur. *Your family, Six.*

But as soon as she thought it, she realized that *she* was Six's family too.

The kind that was found instead of given.

Six slowed to give the flock space as they climbed higher into the sky. As the wind howled past them, the raphons turned. Some flipped backwards, their wings tossed by the wind, their tails curling, their bodies belly up, as if they were in free fall.

As if they'd done this a thousand times.

Then they dropped from the sky.

Their wings flattened against their dark backs, and their beaks were like spears as they dove.

It was glorious.

The most beautiful sight Ezer had ever seen, and she could *feel* the adoration in Six.

The need to join them in flight.

'Go ahead,' Ezer whispered.

And she smiled as she let all control go.

Six kicked into another gear. Her paws tore at the sky as if she were running across solid ground, and Ezer dug her hands deep into her fur as she went faster, faster, until they reached the edge of the flock.

'Ezer,' Kinlear warned. 'I don't think we should—'

'We *must*,' Ezer breathed.

Six let out a screech.

The sound rumbled through Ezer, and her eyes were wet from tears as Six joined the others.

Another raphon was suddenly beside them. Another came up behind, and another below. They were *inside* the flock now, surrounded by wings of blackest night. Ezer's heart could have burst from her chest. All her life, she'd watched winged creatures fly.

And now she was one with them.

She'd never felt more alive.

Six let out another caw.

The sound was beautiful and urgent. A question, she sensed.

And the raphon beside them answered.

The beast had an enormous feathered black mane, its beak double the size of Six's. A male, and beside it soared a smaller female and her pup. A family unit.

The male croaked, as if answering Six's question.

Six cawed back.

Ezer couldn't understand them, but she sensed excitement brewing.

A vision entered her mind.

A rock, being tossed into a deep sea.

'Hold on,' Ezer yelped to Kinlear.

Just before Six snapped her wings shut.

And *dove*.

Snow blurred in her vision. She couldn't hold back the cry that left her lips as Kinlear gripped her like a vice and they tumbled down, down, higher than the Descent had *ever* been. Arawn was right. Raphons were made for this.

For a second, the fear tried to rear its ugly head again.

But then she remembered who she was.

No longer without wings.

She was the Raphon Rider.

She was *Six*'s Rider.

And she didn't care anymore how far the drop ahead of her was, how dangerous the flight.

She did it afraid.

And she loved every damn second of it.

'Ezer,' Kinlear yelled. 'She's not stopping!'

'She will,' Ezer said.

She didn't dare pull up.

She didn't dare stop this flight.

'Ezer!' Kinlear cried.

'Not yet!'

She could see every detail of the snow. She could see the rocks they might be impaled upon, and she *relished* the danger. This was living, this was how it felt to be inches from death and still scream for the joy building in her heart—

Too soon, Six's wings snapped out.

They caught the wind so fast, Kinlear slammed against Ezer's back with a rush of breath.

'Are you *insane*?' he breathed.

Because she was still laughing, and tears of joy ran down her cheeks.

'Relax, Prince!' she yelled, as Six leveled out. 'She had us the whole time.'

'Gods,' he said as he gasped for breath. 'I've created a monster in you, Ezer.'

And then he was laughing, too, as Six circled lazily around the mountain.

It was then that Ezer saw it: the opening right on the side.

Like a dark, yawning mouth.

'Kinlear,' she gasped, and pointed. '*There*.'

An outcropping of black rock, almost like a landing pad, appeared before them. *And more raphons*. Several lounged with their tails or paws hanging right over the edge, like they had no fear of tumbling overboard. A few pups bounded back and forth, leaping onto their mothers.

And Six was suddenly diving again, right towards that flock.

Growls sounded out, and dark eyes turned skyward as Six landed and jogged to a sudden stop.

Ezer and Kinlear sat frozen on her back.

But not a single beast moved towards them as if to attack. Mostly, they sniffed the air and clicked their clever beaks.

Six clicked back at them, like she was only saying hello. There were paw prints leading into the darkness: a massive, yawning cave, so black that it seemed like a blanket had been draped over it, so no one could see what lay beyond.

It wasn't a black door. But . . . it was as good a start as any.

Like she was drawn forward, Six padded into the mouth of the cave.

Torches on the rock walls suddenly flared to life. They blazed with purple fire. Not magefire, but almost like liquid darkness, the flames black in their center. The sconces they sat on were in the shape of hands with long black talons, the blazing fire held in their palms.

'Darksoul hands,' Kinlear whispered.

His voice was so quiet, like he was afraid to speak.

There were several boulders inside, raphons of all sizes lazing atop them.

'Where is she leading us?' Kinlear whispered.

The torches led downwards, deeper into the cave, where the walls shone with hoarfrost, and strange, jagged symbols were carved into the rock.

Ezer's heart gave a little tremor.

Were these the same symbols her mother claimed she saw in the Shadow Tome?

The same ones from her own labyrinth?

They were confusing at first, angular and sharp as the Sawteeth. But the deeper Six walked, the more the shapes began to make sense.

Ezer swore she saw words mixed among them, but when she blinked they became only the symbols again.

Her head was swimming, her heart was racing too fast, and—

A vision from Six slid into her mind.

The raphon rider soaring over the icy lake, a castle with dark, twisting spires in the distance.

The wind was gentle, and Ezer was at peace.

And when the vision flickered away . . .

Ezer relaxed and stared at the symbols.

Perhaps it was because she'd seen them so many times in her sleep. Perhaps it was because they had always felt so familiar. But this time as Six took her deeper into the darkness . . .

She understood them *all*.

It was a story carved into the walls.

Ezer slid her gaze across the symbols, drinking in the strange language. It was the story of a time long ago, when men walked with gods, and magic had freshly entered the realm.

There were six of them. *Six* gods, instead of five.

They depicted a great split between the six. When a terrifying power – a cloud of darkness – overtook the light.

It sounded just like what they were facing now.

But in this depiction . . . the roles were reversed.

The *darkness* was made up of five.

And the light . . . the light was only *one*.

'What do they mean?' Kinlear breathed against her. She'd nearly forgotten his presence, so lost in her new understanding of the symbols. Like some part of her mind had been off-center. And now it had just shifted back into place.

'I . . . I don't know,' Ezer lied.

The symbols faded the further they went into the cave. But more signs of life soon appeared. Small, natural pools of water gathered. Raphon pups lingered by the edge, playing in the shallows. Some yowled, and others cawed, like they were caught in an adolescent phase between cat and bird.

Six's head was on a swivel. She began to purr.

All about the space, there were piles of sticks and golden, shimmering things. Pommels of Lordachian blades. Bones. Helmets and shields with various house symbols.

And some were far older, with sigils Ezer did not recognize, like they'd been here for centuries. Like they were special treasures, set aside to admire.

'Nests,' Ezer breathed.

Little treasure troves, just like Six had inside her cage. She looked about, wide-eyed, drinking it all in. Somehow, it felt more holy than visiting the stalls of war eagles.

The raphons lived raw and free.

More torches flickered on as they went. She kept waiting for darksouls to come pouring out of the darkness. For a wave of enemies to overwhelm them. She reached for the blade on her hip, but suddenly it felt so insignificant.

What could one blade do against thousands of darksouls?

What could one woman, and one man, do to fight back against the Acolyte's might?

This plan seemed so futile now. They were walking right towards their doom.

And still . . . neither she nor Kinlear turned around.

So she let Six go on, as if some part of her were magnetic. As if whatever was in that darkness ahead . . .

It called to her very soul.

More symbols drew Ezer's gaze as they entered another great rounded cave. This one, far larger than the last and still lit by the strange sconces.

The symbols spoke of thousands falling to that great wave of darkness.

Thousands upon thousands, whose eyes were sealed shut by it. But after quite some time, only *one* was able to crack them open. To remove the scales from them and finally see.

Wrenwyn.

Ezer's own ancestor.

And then there were other names, ones she'd never heard of before, shaped down the cave wall like an ancient family tree.

A lineage.

Where would she be among them? And how many others, she wondered, were like her? Sharing Wrenwyn's blood? Sharing the ability her mother spoke of . . . to wield without invocations?

To have *raw* magic.

Untethered by the gods.

'Ezer,' Kinlear whispered, because she was too busy looking at the symbols, reading the story, to notice what lay beyond. '*Look*.'

Six came to a stop, and Ezer gasped as she glanced forwards.

Because there, at the back of the cave, was an enormous black door.

CHAPTER 38

The door looked carved by magic.

It was entirely black, embedded in the cave like a portal to another world. It towered above their heads, as tall as the Citadel. Ezer had to crane her neck back to see its rounded top, where more symbols arched over it, but they were so high up she couldn't read them.

'This is it,' Kinlear breathed. 'The entrance to his domain.'

'Six found it,' Ezer said.

The raphon's tail twitched, *yes*. She lifted her head as if she were quite proud of herself.

Kinlear slid down from Six's back, his hands trembling. Ezer didn't want to leave Six's warmth, her comfort.

But Kinlear was already limping towards the door, and her heart squeezed at the sight of him.

So she pressed her hand to Six's neck. *Stay*.

'Wait,' Ezer whispered after Kinlear. She caught up and laced her arm through his, because suddenly she couldn't bear the thought of him being alone.

He needed this. He wanted to do this, to be the one to make his mark on Lordach. He wasn't a warrior like his father or Arawn. But now, if he made it inside and his dagger found the Acolyte . . . he would become a hero.

The savior of so many lives, and he'd go down in history for doing it.

'Careful,' Ezer whispered, as they stopped just before the door. 'We don't know if there are traps guarding it.'

'Why would there be?' Kinlear asked. He smelled like the liquid in his vial, sickly sweet as crushed flowers. 'This is all as the intel promised it would be. A black door, an entrance, and . . . how else would the defectors make it inside, if not by this door?' He glanced back over his shoulder, at the fading light of the outside world.

'That door is *ancient*,' Ezer said, because anyone would be able to sense the strangeness of this place. The sort of *holy* feeling that came with it, as if even the air they breathed was filled with the sighs of spirits long lost to time. The closer they got, the more her head spun, almost as if she'd drunk winterwine. 'What if it's cursed or—'

Kinlear lifted a dark brow. 'That's why it isn't *you* who's going to risk it, Ezer.'

'Don't touch it,' Ezer hissed, but before she could stop him . . .

The prince placed his hand on the door.

She held her breath, waiting for something terrible to happen.

The Citadel's wards could sense who was pure of heart and who was not. The shadowstorm too.

Surely this would be the same.

She waited for the ground to shake, or shadow wolves to come pouring out of the darkness behind them, or for the raphons to turn on them and attack, an ambush well played. But nothing happened.

There were no traps, no monsters.

And when Ezer glanced back, Six just sat there preening, her beak nipping at her paws, like she hadn't a care in the world.

'See?' Kinlear whispered. 'Nothing to worry about, Raphonminder.'

But the door did not move. And Ezer felt it again, that pull towards it.

Like the door itself was intoxicating.

'Do you feel it, too?' Kinlear frowned. 'The . . . strange power?'

And then he frowned, as if in pain. Another cough left his lungs. The sound was wet, far worse than it had been before. He tried to grab his vial, but his hands were shaking too much.

'Here.' Ezer uncorked it and held it to his lips.

He drank the foul liquid like it was water in a desert.

And as Ezer recorked the vial, she realized . . .

It was empty.

'How much do you have left?' Ezer asked, her eyes meeting his.

He shrugged. 'Enough.'

And then he let out a small chuckle.

She echoed it, like they were both drunk, indeed.

The door . . . what was it *doing* to them?

She felt like the shadows had grown eyes now. Like the darkness was swimming around them. She placed a hand on Kinlear's chest to steady herself.

'We have to find a way inside,' she said. 'Before we pass out, or—'

'Or *what?*' he said and grinned haphazardly. 'It feels lovely. Like the sun on my face.'

The door was definitely making her head swim. Because he was warm, and she could stay here forever in the darkness, comfortable in this strange, shadowed haze.

She suddenly couldn't remember *why* they were here.

Or where *here* even was.

She focused on the closest thing to her.

A prince, she thought. *I am here with a prince.*

She giggled.

'I love the sound of it,' Kinlear breathed, and he wobbled where he stood. 'Your laugh. Your joy.'

His face was so handsome. It was so much like . . .

She couldn't remember, suddenly.

She saw only Kinlear Laroux.

Something was whispering in her mind. A voice she knew, as wind tousled her curls, but it was muffled. She could barely hear it as she stared at her hand on his chest.

The world around her began to swim.

But *he* was solid. He was . . . intoxicating.

She leaned forward, and breathed him in.

Six huffed in the background and turned her back to them.

'You gave her to me, Kinlear,' Ezer whispered. Her words . . . were they slurring? '*You* are the reason she is free.'

No one else had ever believed in her like he had.

No one else had ever given her as sweet a gift.

'Ezer . . .' He grinned down at her as his hand slid atop hers. She could feel his beating heart, and in the back of her mind, she knew that soon . . . it would go still. She pressed closer to him. 'A lifetime in the Citadel . . . and *you* are the greatest thing that's ever happened to me. Do you know that?'

She shook her head as he coughed again.

As his outline blurred, and she had to blink to resettle herself again.

'All the waiting, all the hoping, the prayers for true healing that did not come.' He nodded. 'It was all worth it. Because of you.'

She could have sworn his skin was glowing, that his eyes had become stars, that his dark curls would be so *soft* if she just reached up and ran her fingers through them.

That strange voice called to her again, but she shut it out.

Because she was melting into a puddle of warmth, and . . . and through the veil, she knew, by the way he was looking at her . . .

He *loved* her.

'Ezer,' he whispered.

A strange little shiver ran up and down her spine.

She did not back away.

'There's something I want you to know, before I . . .'

She was floating. Perhaps she was dead.

But her heart wouldn't be pounding this hard if she were dead. And that feeling in her bones . . .

She licked her lips, and noticed his gaze dropped to them.

Something powerful, unexpected, shot through her.

Desire.

'Ezer,' Kinlear breathed.

'Yes, Kinlear?' Ezer whispered.

And he stepped even closer, and lifted a hand to her cheek, and tucked a strand of hair behind her ear.

He was her mystery.

And suddenly she wanted to solve him.

'I think . . . I have known for a while now,' he whispered. He smiled, his eyes glassy as the dark power pulsed from the door. 'When I look at you . . . when I am near you . . . it becomes so much clearer.' His hand drew lazy circles around hers, and it set her on fire. 'I need you to know, Ezer. I think . . . I think I am falling—'

She couldn't bear it any longer.

Gods, she was *ravenous* for a taste of his lips.

So she stood on tiptoe and kissed him. A gentle thing, just a peck, but . . .

It only made the wave of desire surge.

'I'm sorry,' she said, because he wasn't kissing her back. And—

'Don't,' he whispered against her lips, and she'd never seen *that* look in his eyes before, with a hunger that made her toes curl. 'Don't you dare apologize. I want to experience you.' Her heart roared in her ears. Or maybe that was the pulsing power of the door. 'I want . . . I want to *live*, Ezer. Before I die.'

He kissed *her* this time.

He was passion incarnate, and suddenly she wanted to drown in him.

He washed away everything else, and even as he broke the kiss, gasping for breath as he fought away a cough . . . she found herself reaching for him.

And pulling him back towards her.

'Ezer,' he breathed, and then their lips were meeting again, and he tasted sweet, and he felt warm and safe and for just one moment, she could imagine the way his body would feel against hers when—

A growl sounded.

And something nudged her, so hard she fell backwards, and landed on the stones.

She looked up, gasping, to find . . .

Six.

The raphon clicked her beak and breathed into Ezer's face, warm and stinking . . . and suddenly enough to push the desire away.

A vision entered her mind.

Ezer, standing on a snowy cliffside . . . with a different man.

Arawn.

Gods.

Shame washed over her. How had she forgotten him?

And then she remembered where she was. The mission. The timeline.

The Acolyte.

She'd lost herself to the pull of dark power, what had to be some sort of strange protection set in place, like a test for weak minds, those not capable of carrying on. And . . . Ezer stood and wiped dust from her cloak.

She had almost failed it.

'That . . . shouldn't have happened,' Ezer said, and wrapped her arms around herself. 'It was the door. It was the *power*.'

'Not for me,' he said. 'Not all of it, at least.'

She paused, her lips parted in question.

He took her hands gently and held them against his beating heart.

'You chose *him*,' he said gently. 'Didn't you?'

'I . . .' She didn't know what to say. So, the truth was what came out. 'In another life . . . I might have chosen *you*.'

He squeezed her hands and leaned in close, so that his lips were a sigh away from hers. 'And would you choose me still if he was standing right beside us?'

Her silence was answer enough.

'In another life,' he said, his hands cradling her face, 'I would have proved to you just how well you and I could fit together, Ezer. How deeply I could love you, day and night . . . until the only Laroux brother on your mind was *me*.'

'Don't say that,' she whispered.

And suddenly she was cold without him, as he backed a step away.

'It is the truth. And I am man enough to admit that I cannot have you. Not . . . forever. Not the way he could.'

Her heart squeezed, full of guilt, but she did not regret it in full.

Because if the door hadn't pushed her to kiss him . . . a part of her would always wonder what it would have been like. Even after he was gone.

So she took his hand and squeezed it. 'You deserve to live, Kinlear,' she said. 'And you've plenty of life left. You have an Acolyte to kill. And you promised me a dance when this is all said and done.'

'I could give you more than a dance,' he said. 'I'd give you anything you wanted, Raphon Rider. I'd give you my soul if you asked.'

His smile was playful. Devilish, as his thumb caressed her cheek, and it was almost her undoing. She didn't know if it was from the intoxicating, dark power pulsing off the door . . .

Or her own feelings.

Her heart was a traitorous, wretched thing.

She could have stayed in this cave forever with him, if not to explore what they could have had together . . . then certainly to freeze time and keep him from facing his inevitable end.

But that tiny whisper in the back of her mind – her own conscience – told her that her choice was already made.

And it wasn't him.

'Would you help me open the door?' Kinlear asked.

She nodded. 'Of course.'

And together, they turned to it. But they could find no way to open it, no matter how they ran their hands across it, no matter how many places they tried to find a fold in the stones, a gap, a hidden handle.

'*Ezer.*'

It surprised her, the whisper. She hadn't known if her mother's spirit was still with her.

'*Blood.*'

Something seemed to shift inside of her, and she knew what her mother meant. She reached for the small blade on her hip. It glittered beautifully as she unsheathed it and held it to the purple torchlight.

'What are you doing?' Kinlear asked.

The power of the door threatened to pull her under again as he stepped closer, his hand on the small of her back.

'I think we should try blood,' she said, and stepped ever so slightly away. She could still feel heat where his fingers had just been. 'It's what called Six to me at first. If it worked with one of his raphons, perhaps it will work with this door too.'

She looked at Six, who stood paces away.

The raphon twitched her tail once.

Her breathing went from steady to slightly hitched as she held out her right hand and poised the tip of her blade above it.

'No,' Kinlear said. 'Use my blood.'

She didn't listen. The pain was quick, and red soon ran from her skin like a river, dripping down the stones. Before it slowed, she turned and pressed her hand to the enormous door. She could feel its power, like the heartbeat of a great, slumbering beast.

She gasped as the door drank her blood hungrily. That overpowering feeling swam through her, begging her not to release her hand. To stay her and bleed herself dry, if only so the door could taste her for eternity.

But then Six let out a croak, and Ezer ripped her hand away.

The symbols suddenly flared to life, filling with dark tendrils of shadow that curled from the cave walls, as if they had indeed been hiding before. As if called by magic, they filled every symbol upon the door, undulating like snakes, until suddenly . . .

A great rumble, as enormous locks on the other side slid open. Dust rained down from the cave ceiling and, with a great groan . . . the door clicked open.

There was only darkness beyond.

A *whoosh* of frigid air swam outwards, kicking up eddies of dust around their ankles.

Kinlear looked at her the way she imagined she always looked at him.

Like she was *his* mystery, too.

'What is it,' he said aloud, 'about *you*?'

He turned and pried one of the torches away from its clawed sconce. The purple flames flickered even as he held it out to the waiting dark.

It was thick, like it was swirling with real living shadows, the kind that would not be chased away by firelight.

But then Ezer noticed something on the side of the wall.

A groove, shining with dark liquid.

Something strange crawled up and down her spine, a feeling that was not quite right. She'd seen those grooves before.

She pried another torch off the wall, and leaned just over the threshold, dipping the purple flames into the groove.

It burst to life, with a tendril of fire that snaked away, down into the darkness until the entire rounded tunnel was lit.

Ezer's heart felt like it stopped, and she sucked in a breath.

It was her labyrinth.

CHAPTER 39

It couldn't be right.

But there was the frost forming in strange whorls upon the rounded walls. There was the groove and the fire and the ice-coated cobwebs that hung in the furthest edges. The feel of the wind was the same. The cold was ancient and alive.

It was her labyrinth, indeed.

But this one was five times the size. Enormous tunnels stretched high over her head, large enough for any size army to pass through.

Large enough for a raphon.

Ezer backed away, shaking her head. 'It can't be.'

'Can't be what?' Kinlear asked.

'I've dreamt of this,' she whispered, as her breath formed before her in a white cloud. There was no use hiding it now.

Kinlear gave her a strange look, and for a moment she thought he might say something. But then he coughed again, and he had to reach for his second vial.

'Are you sure you want to do this?' Ezer asked. 'We can still go back. We can find another way.'

'No,' he growled and wiped his mouth. 'This is my fate. I have to see it through.'

More blood marked his sleeve. His lungs were giving out on him. He needed to go back home, where Alaris could heal him as best she could, strengthen him with runes and give him more time. The Long Day would give them plenty of time, now that they knew where to find the Door.

But what if it changed places? What if you could only find it *once*, or . . .

'Ezer,' Kinlear said, as if he sensed her hesitation. 'We can't turn back now.'

She was to wait here, to be his exit plan . . . *should* he succeed. But . . . now there was no way in *hell* she'd let Kinlear go inside without her. He needed her help and this was *her* fate too.

'I'm going with you,' Ezer said.

Kinlear whirled to face her. '*What?*'

'You're not going alone.'

He opened his mouth, like he was going to protest. 'Ezer, it's too—'

'Dangerous?' she finished for him.

His lips snapped together, and he nodded.

'Good,' she said. 'I think we've established I belong in dangerous places, Prince. Or have you forgotten all I've done to make it here? I'm not the shivering thing you met months ago. Or would you tell me to stay behind, safe and hidden, the way others have done to you?'

'I would never hold you back,' Kinlear said. His eyes were on fire. 'I would *never* stop you from doing anything you wanted to do, Ezer.'

He released a breath.

For a moment, they stared at each other, chests rising and falling.

She wanted to kiss him again.

She wanted to . . .

He held out a hand. 'After you.'

At that, she lifted a dark brow. 'We've a raphon for a *reason*, Kinlear Laroux.'

*

It was like walking inside her own dreams, but this time she wasn't alone.

This time, she had a prince and a raphon, and they were both hers, in their own way. They walked silently down the tunnel, Six's paws so quiet it was like she was born for this. For stalking her way into shadowed places, seeking prey.

The tunnel spat them out into a main corridor.

It was exactly as it was in her dreams. A wide entrance, the mouth that connected countless other tunnels. Her waiting room, where she found herself most nights when she opened her eyes.

She turned Six in a circle and looked at every arched entry, every shadowed tunnel waiting to swallow them whole.

To go straight, in her dreams, would have been to enter the place of her mother's memories.

To take a left would lead deeper into the labyrinth, until she came to the door of the old cottage where she'd last seen Styerra. Where she'd first called upon the ravens as a baby, desperate to be saved.

Mother, Ezer thought. *Help me. Where do we go?*

The icy wind sighed past them, ruffling Six's feathers, but Ezer heard no whisper. Perhaps Styerra had well and truly let go.

'Which way?' Kinlear breathed into Ezer's ear.

It was too quiet, too calm, too utterly empty inside.

But then Six lifted her beak, sniffing the air. And before Ezer could stop her, she took them into one of many tunnels to their right. Kinlear dipped his torch into the groove, and it burst into life, the purple tongue of fire stretching down into the depths.

Ezer took a step back.

It was lined with doors.

The very same as in her mind. But as they crept closer, she noticed that every door was ajar. And like the rest of this space, there was not a darksoul in sight.

It was like everyone had picked up and left at a moment's notice.

'It's true then,' Ezer whispered. 'They must be at the ritual.'

She swallowed the knot in her throat. It was all falling into place, this plan. And soon . . .

They would discover the Acolyte.

They would see his face.

They passed door after door, peering inside with breaths held, as if they'd find darksouls waiting there to attack. Signs of life were everywhere, and it was so utterly strange to discover that it looked like a soldier's barracks, instead of a lair for monsters.

There were cots and worn blankets, a room with a large table for dining. Some of the beds were rumpled, while others were made perfectly, the blankets smoothed, the pillows fluffed.

Like the darksouls were still *human* inside, capable of setting things up the way they pleased.

But that wasn't possible.

Every story told about the darksouls was that once they bowed to the Acolyte . . . they traded their spot in the Ehver. They lost their humanity and became as good as shadow wolves, hungry for blood and death.

And beyond that . . . where *were* the shadow wolves?

She hadn't seen a mark of them, hadn't heard a single howl.

'This feels wrong,' Ezer whispered. 'It feels . . .'

'Like the Citadel,' Kinlear breathed. 'But they all deserted.'

They passed into another tunnel and found a small library of sorts. One that was lined with symbols and books, an old stone table in the center with parchment and pen and ink. Ezer itched to open the pages and discover what lay inside, but there was no time.

Another room was stacked to the brim with worn black cloaks woven in a fabric she'd never seen before. 'We should change,' Kinlear whispered. 'Blend in.'

They weren't runed, but they were warm to the touch, and they shimmered with a sort of living shadow. Ezer and Kinlear quickly removed their own robes and dressed in darksoul ones, with hoods deep enough to hide their faces.

This is all wrong, Ezer thought.

For it was utterly silent. As still as death.

An army of thousands was supposed to be here, and they'd walked right in. And not a single soul had come to stop them.

Six carried on into the twisting tunnels. Every so often, Kinlear coughed as silently as he could, the sound echoing just enough to alert any guards.

But no one came for them.

'Where are they?' Kinlear growled. She could sense the frustration rising in him. He'd made it here, and yet . . . it felt like they were too late. 'I have to do it, Ezer. I have to find the Acolyte. I *have* to be the one to kill him.'

'I know,' she whispered. 'You will be.'

The tunnel forked three ways, frost curling up the walls, some places so thick with ice she didn't think Six would be able to pass. Their breath became clouds before them, morphing the way the walls looked, but Six kept going like she was certain of the path.

Like some part of her knew the way.

They saw what looked like cages for shadow wolves, filthy and reeking of death. There were bones piled up in corners, and whips leaning against walls. They passed a training room for magic, enormous and domed and full of blackened burn marks on the walls and floors.

And at some point, Ezer was beginning to wonder if perhaps the Acolyte and his followers had gone elsewhere to another mountain inside the Sawteeth. Maybe they moved constantly to keep themselves hidden in the event that someone made it through the shadows and the strange, intoxicating mind trap the door gave off.

Maybe Realmbreak would end . . . and they'd fail simply by running out of time.

But just as soon as she was about to tell Six to turn back, fearing that they'd get lost, and end up stuck in here forever . . . light came from up ahead.

And the reek of dead things, and the sound of voices.

They came into another massive entryway, and Six stopped. And slowly, so slowly, crept forward just enough that they could peer around the corner, Ezer's scarred eye seeing despite the shadows.

A spike of fear stabbed Ezer's heart.

Darksouls.

There were hundreds of them. Enough to fill the cavern as they filed through an enormous set of black doors.

They looked human at first glance, all of them standing in a line. Each one wore the same cloak as Ezer and Kinlear, with hoods pulled low.

But it was their hands that struck fear in Ezer's heart. Their terrible, clawed hands, capable of rending flesh and bone in one swipe.

They watched for a few moments, utterly silent. The wind seemed to sigh towards them, instead of away. Like it had changed course to hide their scent.

She couldn't look away from those claws, long as daggers, utterly black.

What would cause a person to want to give up their humanity in such a way? To become a monster?

Kinlear hid another cough, and the wind blew a bit harder. Taking the sound elsewhere, and Ezer knew her mother was with her still.

But she doubted Styerra's spirit would be here much longer. She couldn't rely on her to save them should things go south. If only she knew how to call upon that *raw magic*, as Styerra claimed. If only she knew how to wield. But there would be no birds, here. Not this far beneath the earth.

And as Ezer watched how many darksouls there were . . .

She knew there would be no hope of leaving this place alive.

Not if Kinlear didn't strike true.

And what about after? Would the entire army fall? What if they were wrong about that part too?

Her stomach turned. She could run, take Kinlear and Six and retreat to the other side.

But this was her calling. Her fate, impossible to ignore. She'd never convince Kinlear to leave now. And to abandon him . . .

It would break her heart.

So she stayed, because of fear, because of morbid curiosity . . . because some part of her still needed to see the Acolyte's face. To realize her mother and father's dream for them and discover the truth.

One by one, the darksouls entered through the doors. Like a war meeting or a worship session, for each one bowed their heads as they entered, and made their way down a set of crude stone steps just inside.

'We'll slip in with them,' Kinlear said. 'It's our best chance.'

A boom rumbled the mountain around them.

The doors stayed open, enough that she could suddenly see something moving within. A pillar of darkness in the middle of the enormous room.

A pillar made of living shadows.

They snaked upwards, spiraling high into the ceiling.

And she could see . . . before more darksouls obstructed her vision . . . a figure on a raised dais in the center, clad in black.

Arms raised to the sky, as shadows shot upwards and away from their body. Like they were feeding the dark cloud that hung over the Sawteeth, far, *far* above.

It was pure power, horrifying. Beautiful and deadlier than she ever could have guessed.

'The Acolyte,' Ezer whispered.

The darksouls began chanting and roaring, loud enough to make Ezer's blood go cold, loud enough to rumble the cave around them.

Dust rained down from the walls as another burst of shadows erupted into the sky.

'It's time,' Kinlear whispered. The line of darksouls was shortening. The doors began to creak as they started to close.

She nodded, but fear was filling her veins with ice now.

They slid down from Six's back.

'*Stay*,' Ezer thought and pressed a kiss to the raphon's beak. She sent a vision to her. *Six, settling into her life with the raphons here.*

Six, wild and free.

She could have sworn Six whimpered as the vision reached her.

'I love you,' Ezer whispered, as she wrapped her arms around the raphon's neck.

'Ezer,' Kinlear whispered. 'The door's going to shut. We have to go *now*.'

A dark wing wrapped over her back.

And Six's tail thumped once in goodbye.

Ezer felt like she left a part of herself behind as she turned and took Kinlear's hand.

Together, they stepped out of the safety of the tunnel.

And joined the darksouls inside, just before the doors slammed shut.

CHAPTER 40

It was an enormous amphitheater inside, lined with carved stone seats. And darksouls so numerous, she couldn't count their number. Ezer and Kinlear were simply swept up in the current as the line descended the stairs. Every few seconds, they paused, as someone at the very bottom reached the dais.

It sat in the middle of an enormous pool of pure dark water, connected by a single runway of stone. It was lined with darksoul guards in shimmering black armor, helmets concealing their faces.

And at the very end, guarding the enormous black throne . . .

Ezer's stomach lurched.

Two shadow wolves. The largest she'd ever seen, chained by manacles large enough to hold Six. As if, even beside their creator, their wild nature could not be trusted or tamed.

Turn back, Ezer's mind whispered, but that was her own fear speaking, not the wind. *Turn back now or you die.*

Kinlear's hand squeezed hers as the crowd shifted.

And they caught a glimpse of the Acolyte for the very first time.

He sat upon the onyx throne and was clad in all black robes. Shadows – living shadows – swam around him, concealing his face from view, but she could see his body was that of a man. And his hands . . . they were not claws, as the stories had said. No, they were fully human, covered in fat rings as he rested them on the arms of his throne. Each arm ended in a carving of a raphon's head.

Four figures sat with him. Two to his right, two to his left.

His Darksoul Sentinels.

They had the claws shared in stories, so long and dark they curled at their tips. They made the shadow wolves' claws look small.

And as Ezer and Kinlear drew closer . . . the world came down to only that dais.

Ezer could feel every beat of her heart, could hear the roar in her ears as she clung to Kinlear's hand. She couldn't stop this.

But every part of her wanted to now.

The line paused as the Acolyte lifted his hands, as if gathering his energy. And then shadows shot from his fingertips. Two colossal beams of darkness, cast out from his bare hands. They spiraled up into the ceiling, where the cave stretched so high she could see that it was open at its top. She could see the belly of the shadowstorm far above it.

The Acolyte was the source of its power.

Suddenly their plan felt foolish.

Would a blade even kill him? Did he even *have* a heart any longer, or blood in his veins, a life source to drain?

Closer, closer, they marched down the steps. They were over halfway there now, each step filling her with more terror than the last.

She watched as another darksoul – a woman – made the march across that runway of stone. The wolves snarled but did not move to attack as she bowed before the throne. The Acolyte's Sentinel held out a black blade.

The darksoul ran it across her palm.

She stood, squeezed her fist . . . and let droplets of dark blood spill into the shimmering black waters.

Blood, Ezer realized. It was darksoul blood that filled the lake.

A sob of terror rose in the back of her throat.

'Kinlear,' she breathed, gripping his hand like a vice. 'We can't do this.'

She could have sworn he shook his head, *no*.

Ten steps.

'Kinlear.' She dug her fingernails into his skin. '*Please*.'

But it was too late.

They were on the runway now, passing the first set of helmeted guards.

She could feel the heat coming from the lake. The blood.

They were three darksouls away now. She caught sight of one of their faces as a darksoul man shouldered past her, his hand freshly cut.

His eyes.

His eyes were no longer human. They were pure darkness incarnate. Even the veins around them swam with darkness, like shadows swimming beneath his skin.

She could feel the ground rumbling beneath her and hear the *snick* of the blade running across the next darksoul's hand.

She couldn't tear her eyes from the wolves guarding the Acolyte's feet.

Kinlear was two away now.

Oh gods, Ezer thought. *If you were ever real at all, stop this madness now.*

Once Kinlear cut his hand . . . he would be revealed.

Because he would bleed red instead of black.

'Ezer,' he whispered, turning sideways to lock eyes with her from the shadows of his hood. His words were so hushed and so fast, she could hardly decipher them. 'I tried to tell you before in the cave, but . . . you kissed me before I could say the rest.'

The wolves snarled again.

'When I said I'm falling,' Kinlear whispered and smiled . . . but it wasn't quite *his* smile. 'I meant, I'm falling out of love with the gods.'

And then his hand slid from hers, and something strange raced through her. A cold, unsteady sort of feeling, like the world had just turned sideways.

She watched in horror as he knelt. And instead of driving the blade into the Acolyte's chest . . . instead of doing what he'd promised . . .

Kinlear Laroux bowed.

'My Lord,' he said.

'Ah, the young princeling,' said the Acolyte, 'Child of Draybor Laroux. Your eyes have been opened at long last.'

His voice was human. It was young and accented like Arawn's, heavily northern, and . . .

And she recognized it.

'I wish to join you, my Lord,' Kinlear said. 'I wish to lay down my allegiance to the Five.' He was crying as he added, 'I wish to live forever . . . belonging to you.'

The Acolyte inclined his shadowed head.

'A final test,' he said, 'and you will be welcomed here, my child. You will be *free*.'

There was nothing Ezer could do, nothing she could say, as Kinlear took the Sentinel's blade and split his skin wide open.

For a second, Ezer felt like she was floating. Like she was outside her own body as she watched him bleed.

And it was not red.

It was a deep, soulless black.

He was gone.

Kinlear Laroux, child of the king, a loyal servant of the Five . . .

He had defected right there before her and joined the other side.

Suddenly, she couldn't breathe.

She couldn't even gasp his name as the Acolyte lifted a hand and sent a bolt of shadow into Kinlear's chest.

It melted into him, and before her very eyes, he shifted.

He *changed*.

His hands, long and beautiful, morphed into darksoul claws. He screamed through the pain of it, and she watched in horror as his eyes, his beautiful, moonlit silver eyes, shifted to a darksoul black.

He did not look at her as he walked away. He followed after the other darksouls, a part of them now. She noticed, with a pang in her chest, that he had no limp. No cough. And he stood so tall, so proud . . . that she knew, somehow, he'd been healed of his ailment. Just as Soraya said.

But at what cost?

He was gone.

His very soul might have just died before her.

And now it was up to her to finish the job.

She didn't have time to think about how utterly wrong she'd been about him.

He'd lied.

Oh gods, he'd lied to her, and she'd taken it all for truth. And she'd carried him here, brought him right to the Acolyte's feet. She'd *kissed* him. She'd betrayed Arawn for him.

She was horrified, furious, her body so frozen in shock that she thought she might not be able to take a step. But then she was next, and she stumbled forwards, her hood low over her eyes.

The wolves snarled. She could feel their hot breath on her face as she knelt, trembling.

'You wish to join us, child,' said the Acolyte. 'You made the journey to the Door, called to the dark as others have been called before. You made it past the defenses and proved yourself deserving.'

That voice.

She *knew* that voice, and perhaps it was why the wind suddenly whipped around her, as if it recognized it too.

The Sentinel handed her the blade.

With trembling hands, she took it. And held out her palm as if she were about to slide it across her skin.

Do it, she told herself. *Do it afraid.*

She thought of thousands of names on bloodstained scrolls. The countless deaths and disappearances. The way her mother had looked, flayed open on the snow while she died.

She thought of Arawn, still waiting for her on the cliffside.

She thought of Izill.

She thought of Six.

You're going to die someday, Ezer told herself. *You might as well die for this.*

And at the last second, she lunged forward, thrusting that blade up into the Acolyte's chest.

Right into his cold, black heart.

CHAPTER 41

She'd done it.

She'd killed the Acolyte.

Ezer gasped and stumbled away. The blade was still stuck in his chest, handle deep.

It was the first time she'd taken a life. The first time she felt the crunch of skin and bone, the squelch of a heart beneath a blade.

Her entire body trembled, overcome with emotion as she stared at him.

She waited for him to fall. To slump over, a sign that she'd completed the kill.

But the Acolyte . . . *laughed*.

He chuckled as he looked down at the pommel of the fine black blade, and said, 'You didn't think it would be *that* easy, did you?'

He reached up with hands covered in dark jewels. And slowly, delicately, he slid the blade from his chest.

There was no blood upon it. Not even a drop as he examined it, twisting it left and right before he handed it back to his Sentinel with a flourish.

'Pathetic,' the Acolyte hissed.

Ezer made a choking sort of sound, halfway between a scream and a sob, as his shadow wolves rose, hackles raised.

'You could have bowed to me and found life,' the Acolyte growled. 'Instead . . . you will die.'

A second later, her blade was in her hands. But before she could even hold it out, something cold clamped over her wrist.

She gasped as she looked down to see a tendril of pure shadow slithering across her skin like a snake.

'A clever attempt,' the Acolyte said with a frown. 'But not effective against those who cannot die.'

The shadow squeezed, and her sword clattered to the floor.

Then guards were at her back, blocking her exit.

'No,' she gasped, as one of the Sentinels rose.

The shadow held her in place, impossibly strong.

She screamed as the Sentinel reached her. The sound tore from her, ragged with terror. It changed to a cry of pain – white hot, surging through her so fiercely she saw spots – as the Sentinel dug its claws into her skin.

They cut through her like a knife in warmed butter.

Red warmth spilled down her arms, and she didn't dare move to pull herself away.

She'd failed.

A sob tore itself from her.

Kinlear had lied to her. He'd left her for dead.

And it was all for *nothing*.

'Take her away,' the Acolyte said. He held out a hand, and the tendril of shadow slithered away from Ezer, back into his palm like a snake. It coiled up his arm, until finally it disappeared into his chest . . . filling the hole she'd just carved into him. 'Question her, torture her if you must, and if she relents . . . throw her to the wolves.'

'*No!*'

She was going to die.

She hardly recognized her own scream as the Sentinel dragged her away. Her heels scraped on the dais but it was no use. The pain in her arms – it was blinding.

'Kinlear!' she screamed his name, hating that she dared call out to him, but she had no one left. '*Kinlear, you bastard!*'

He was nowhere to be found as the crowd parted.

Please, she begged, hoping her mother would hear her. *Please, don't let this be how it ends. Send someone, send something.*

But there were no ravens, here.

She wanted to *live*, she wanted to—

The wind suddenly howled past her, a furious gale. It circled her body and swept away, carrying with it the scent of her blood.

Right towards the dark throne.

'Wait.'

The Acolyte's voice called out from behind her. Sudden and commanding.

The Sentinel paused. Fresh pain struck Ezer like a bolt of lightning.

'Who are you?'

She was going to pass out.

'I asked you a question, *Sacred*.'

She tried to speak, but she had no voice.

'*Who are you?*' the Acolyte demanded.

He stood from his throne, moving towards her with predatory grace. Shadows swirled outwards from his feet, as if he were walking on a dark cloud.

He stopped before her . . . and a cold tendril of his power stretched down and lifted her chin.

She hissed at its touch.

'Take note, child,' the Acolyte said, 'of how I, enemy to the Five, give even an assassin such grace.' The shadow pressed deeper, cutting into her chin as he forced her to look up at him. 'What is your name?'

'I'm no one,' she sputtered.

'*The truth*,' hissed the wind. '*Tell him the truth!*'

'It's no use lying,' the Acolyte practically purred down at her. 'I can sense that you are—'

He paused.

As if he'd just noticed something . . . and suddenly the shadow at her chin recoiled.

She sucked in a breath.

'Where did you get that ring?'

His voice was a rough whisper. And though she could not see his face, she knew he was looking at her hand. At Styerra's ring.

The wind caressed her, a reminder that she was not alone.

'It was my mother's,' Ezer growled, as hatred rose in her. 'A woman who died believing in *you*.'

'Your name,' he said again. 'Speak now, before I send you to your death. She flinched as one of his shadows slithered across her face. Across the dark scars on her cheek. 'This time, my wolves will not miss.'

'*Tell him*,' the wind hissed.

So she looked into that dark, depthless hood. She thought of the life she'd lived, the things she'd done. The mysteries she'd uncovered that parts of her wished she never had. She took a breath and said, 'My name is Ezer. The Raphon Rider of Augaurde. Descendant of Wrenwyn.'

He knelt before her . . . and the shadows that concealed his face suddenly melted away.

Ezer thought, for a moment, that perhaps she was already dead. Perhaps she was just lost in her own dreams again, a nightmare that had twisted itself up all wrong.

But the pain in her body reminded her that it was real, it was true.

And the man standing in front of her . . . the Acolyte . . .

It was Erath.

Her father.

'*Erath*,' she breathed.

He had aged elegantly, his jaw broader, his face leaner. But it was impossible to deny . . . it was him. He had the same dark curls, the same half-smile. It was only his eyes, wholly black, that were different.

The wind danced through his curls now, almost joyfully.

Like Styerra was saying *hello*.

He closed his eyes and leaned into it. Like he sensed Styerra's presence too.

'Styerra was always good at hiding things . . . but this? This . . . is a surprise, even to me.' He looked at her truly now. Every detail of her face, and it took everything in her not to shy away. Not to avert her gaze. 'You . . . are all the best parts of her.'

'You left her behind!' Ezer screamed. 'And it was *your* wolves that killed her.'

The wind whistled, tossing Erath's curls about . . . not quite so joyfully this time.

'Restless beasts, my wolves,' he said, and waved his hand. 'They are not always as loyal to my commands.' Shadows reappeared, soaring towards him from the darkness like little birds to flit about his head. 'And from what my shadows tell me . . . you also brought a wayward raphon.'

Ezer gasped.

He laughed, the sound cold and biting. 'You thought you could just walk into my fortress, unannounced? I knew the moment the Door opened. My shadows see *all* things. Even the Shadow Tome you carry in your pocket.'

Cold dread filled her, because this was true power before her and around her, power that could put a Sacred Master to shame.

Enough to shatter worlds.

'Take her to a cell,' Erath said to the Sentinel still holding her in place. 'And capture the raphon. I'd like to dig into its mind. See what secrets lie in waiting for me.'

'*No!*' Ezer screamed. '*Please! Please, don't touch Six!*'

But her time was up. She was already being dragged away again into the darkness.

Away from the Acolyte.

Away from her father.

CHAPTER 42

The Sentinel took her somewhere deep in the labyrinth.

She tried to remember the path, tried to hold on to the twists and turns she'd spent so long traversing in her own mind – but terror had blinded her now.

'P-please,' she begged. She'd lost too much blood from the claws still gripping her body. It was so cold she could see frost forming on the torchlit walls. 'Please, just *let me go.*'

A sob scraped the back of her throat as they stopped before a cell. 'No. Gods, no—'

She screamed again as those claws were suddenly ripped out of her arms.

'We do not speak of the enemy inside these walls,' the Sentinel hissed and leaned close enough that she could see into the shadows beneath his hood.

She could have sworn she saw fangs as the beast shoved her inside.

She didn't know how much time had passed. It could have been hours or days that she lay there, curled up on the black rock.

Alone, bleeding, cold.

Three days.

That was all they had before the Long Day ended, before Realmbreak was over . . .

And she would not make it back in time.

She had failed.

She'd failed Arawn. Izill. Alaris.

She'd failed Six.

Her father . . . Erath . . .

She was the Acolyte's *daughter*.

She laughed at the sheer madness of it.

But was he even Erath? Or was he someone else wearing Erath's skin? He was supposed to have been killed by the Masters; another lie she'd believed. At this point, she wondered if she'd ever learn the real truth.

She'd told Six to leave her, should anything go wrong. But some part of her knew . . .

The Acolyte would not let her raphon go.

It was the image of Six imprisoned *again* that drew Ezer to her feet.

She tried to pry open the barred door, but found it had no handle. She tried pounding her fists on it, screaming Erath's name.

Please, she prayed. *Please, don't let them hurt Six*.

Because she wouldn't be able to survive that. She wouldn't be able to get past knowing the raphon's death was *her* fault.

'Why?' she whispered into the dark. And she wasn't sure if she was speaking to the gods or to herself, to her mother's spirit on the wind, but somehow hearing her own voice kept her panic from spiraling out of control. 'Why did it come to this?'

She paused, cocking her head.

Because that was the sound of footsteps in the dark.

She had no time to gather herself before the door was pried open.

And a darksoul . . . a darksoul she knew, stood on the other side.

'Zey,' Ezer breathed.

'Wolf Bait,' said Zey.

She was once achingly beautiful.

Now she looked like the queen of nightmares.

Her pale, buttery hair was wild and free from its Sacred braid, with rings of black tied to the strands. Her eyes, once the color of the sea, had darkened to a pure, depthless black. The telltale dark veins spread outwards across her face. She wore darksoul robes.

And when she crossed her arms in a very Zey-like way . . . Ezer saw claws, where her fingertips once were.

She had completely changed.

'You're still alive,' Ezer whispered.

Zey smiled, and those were fangs in her mouth. Fear rushed through Ezer, even as Zey stood twenty paces away.

She knew the darksoul could kill her in a breath if she wished it.

'I'll admit, I'm surprised. I didn't think you had it in you.'

'To make it here?' Ezer asked.

Zey chuckled. 'All this time you pretended to be lost, to be a fledgling . . . and it turns out you weren't Unconsecrated, after all. You are *his*. The Princess of Shadows.'

'I didn't know,' Ezer spat. 'Have you come to kill me?'

'Quite the opposite. I've come to offer you a final chance at life.' Zey looked pointedly at her cloak. 'No sense hiding it anymore, Wolf Bait. Let's see it.'

With trembling hands, Ezer reached for the small black book in her inner pocket. She held it out, wincing as she imagined Zey's claws reaching for it.

But the darksoul didn't move. 'It's not for me. The Shadow Tome became yours the day you picked it up.' She smiled with her fangs. 'Open it.'

'Why?' Ezer asked.

Zey rolled her dark eyes. 'Because every part of me wants to rip out your throat. But as you are still on the precipice of being redeemed –' she clacked her dark claws against one another – 'I cannot kill you yet. Open the Tome. Read it. Before it's too late.'

She turned to go.

'Wait,' Ezer said.

Zey paused and glanced over a shoulder.

'Six,' Ezer whispered. She could barely ask the question. 'Is she . . .'

'Safe,' Zey said. Relief flooded Ezer's chest, until Zey said, 'But I cannot promise you for how long.'

She sat in the darkness for hours after Zey left. She knew that outside, the Long Day was still here, if only for the fact that the war had not resumed. She would have felt the rumble in the stones.

Beyond that, it was impossible to tell *when* it was. As if the darkness had stolen all semblance of time away.

Had the gods turned their eyes to this realm?

Had they granted their godsblessing?

Whatever it was . . .

The king himself had warned Kinlear that he needed to be home before the blessing was granted.

Read the Tome, Zey had said. *Before it's too late.*

She didn't want to. Everything she'd been told was to turn *away* from the darkness, to deny the Acolyte, to walk with the Five. And on the other side, she'd seen that darkness in full. She'd seen Kinlear, a man she'd thought loved her . . . completely abandon her.

She was a fool to believe in him.

He'd left her for dead. Just as Erath had done to Styerra.

But *why*?

Why would anyone . . .

The wind suddenly gusted through the cell, and she knew it was her mother's doing. It fluttered past her, flicking open the pages of the Shadow Tome.

And when Ezer looked down . . . she saw the symbols.

The ones she'd seen in the entrance to this domain.

She slammed the book shut.

'Stop it,' she hissed to Styerra. 'I thought you were gone.'

The wind rustled past her again, flicking open the pages.

'I said *stop.*'

But her eyes went to the symbols . . . and she paused.

What sort of book could be powerful enough to get someone to lay down their own religion, to step aside from everything they'd ever known and believed in . . . and choose to follow the Acolyte instead?

Even if it led to death.

Even if it led to a journey across the Expanse, cold and alone and uncertain of what they'd even find on the other side.

'One page,' Ezer whispered.

The wind circled her in a cold embrace as she looked at the symbols.

And began to read.

At first, there was only One.

The One created time and space and a string of realms twelve in number, upon which were breathed the very first signs of life.

The pillars of magic: wind, fire, air, realm, and the Ehver.

The One reigned over all in peace.

But as time wore on, peace became lonely. So, with a great burst of power, the One called upon each pillar of its creation to breathe new life.

And soon were born the Five.

They were given control over the twelve realms, so long as they kept a single vow:

They would bow to the One for eternity.

For a time, all was as it should be. The One ruled, and the Five obeyed.

But soon, the Five began to grow wary of the One. All creation sang the One's praises, even their own pillars of magic.

The Five longed for adoration, too.

A root of bitterness sprang up in them . . . and with it, they devised a plan to turn the One into the None.

Together, they gathered their power and created a new realm.

A thirteenth: a place of chaos instead of pillared balance, which they fashioned into a mighty cage.

They fooled the One into going inside . . . and sealed shut the door.

Without the One, the Five realized that they, too, needed worshipers, and so they gave of themselves to create something new entirely:

Humanity.

Lesser beings, weak and insignificant and meant only to serve the Five for all their days.

But the Five soon learned that humanity was restless, and even when the Five walked among them, Humanity complained. Humanity groaned.

Humanity was never satisfied with what the Five gave them, always hungering for more.

Over time, Humanity began to worship itself instead. They bowed to the strongest, the prettiest, the boldest.

And when they did, their belief in the Five waned.

And so did the power that the Five claimed, their hold on the Thirteenth realm beginning to waver, until a crack formed in the cage they had created.

A hairline fracture, just enough for the Five to fear the One's ultimate return.

'We need to make Humanity worship us again,' the Five said. 'We need to make them believe in us, fear us, so they will never forget about what power we hold over them.'

So the Five gave a kernel of magic to Humanity. They chose the ones most pliable. The ones they were most capable of controlling, so that their hearts and their minds would never turn away from the Five.

And they called them the Sacred.

Each one was given a pillar of magic to wield, and a vow to keep.

It came as a book of laws, a thousand strong. A single day of Absolution, to show the Five's grace. And should the Sacred obey . . .

Then someday they could join the Five in the Ehver and live in glory for the rest of their days.

'A prayer for a bit of power,' the Five promised the Sacred. 'So long as your heart remains pure and true.'

And the Sacred, loyal to their bones, obeyed.

Each time they wielded, their strength waned – a failsafe, created by the Five, to ensure that Humanity still knew who was in charge.

Each time they wielded, the Sacred proved to Humanity just how powerful the Five were. Each time someone saw and believed, the Five kept their strength.

And the Thirteenth Realm remained a cage.

It existed like that for eons.

The Sacred had more Sacred, and they obeyed the book of laws, and all was good and well.

Until one day, when a Sacred child heard a whisper on the wind.

Her name was Wrenwyn, and she awoke by night, swearing she heard someone cry out for help.

For revenge.

For freedom.

Night after night, the One whispered on the wind, and Wrenwyn listened.

'I hear the call,' Wrenwyn told that whisper. She turned her eyes north and made a promise: 'I'm coming.'

CHAPTER 43

She awoke to the sound of her cell door opening.

Ezer sat up, blinking wearily, the Shadow Tome inches from her fingertips. She'd fallen asleep before she could read any further.

Kinlear stood in the doorway, a torch in his hands.

Her breath hitched, and her eyes welled with tears, because he looked nothing at all like the Kinlear she'd pressed her lips to, just hours before.

'Ezer,' he said, almost reverently. 'My heart.'

'I am *not* your heart,' she hissed. 'What have you *done*, Kinlear?'

He was no longer weak and waning. He stood tall and strong in his dark cloak, and though it was still his face, his freckles, his curly dark hair . . . he was already changing before her.

His silver eyes were black as the night. His teeth elongated when he smiled, and she took a step back, her heart racing.

'Come with me,' he said. 'Into the dark.'

And then he held out a hand, like he wanted her to take it.

But it was *not* his hand.

It was not his long, ring-covered fingers that he had so willingly turned bare, bit by bit, to help her train Six. His palms stretched out, and where his fingertips once were . . . he had darksoul claws.

'Why?' Ezer asked him. She was crying again – traitorous

tears, because how dare she cry over him, after all he'd done?

'Why did you do it?'

He turned his head sideways, as if he were confused by the question.

'Isn't it obvious?' His voice was more like a purr, a sound that sent shivers up and down her spine. 'I was tired of dying. Tired of fighting for a Five that would never save me.'

'Was it worth it?' Ezer asked, shivering as he held her in his cold, dark gaze. 'To trade your soul?'

He huffed out a laugh, and she realized with an ache that the vial on his neck was gone.

He no longer needed it, nor his cane.

'My soul is free,' he said. 'And soon enough, yours will be, too.' He stepped closer, reaching out with those long, dark talons. She inhaled, frozen before him, as he slid them across her scars. 'We can be together, Ezer. *Forever*.'

'I will *never* be with you,' she whispered.

He sighed. And then he smiled, his claws pausing on her neck. 'You won't be with him, either.'

She didn't dare move until his hand fell away.

'Come,' he said. 'Your father awaits.'

He turned away, leaving the cell door ajar.

And she had no choice but to follow.

They passed countless other rooms, the doors open to reveal that everyone was back inside. Some were sleeping, some were training. Others knelt and prayed or pored over copies of the Shadow Tome, and it was all so normal. So calm.

So utterly different to what she'd ever expected it to be.

He led her back to the throne room that had been filled with thousands of darksouls before.

Now it was empty. Save for the shrouded figure that sat upon the black throne.

And – Ezer's breath hitched – the raphon that lay at his feet.

Six.

She looked up at the sound of Ezer's footsteps and twitched her tail once.

Yes.

No, Ezer wanted to tell her. *No, Six, it isn't good.*

Because though Six did not look harmed, though her fur and feathers were clean and every part of her wings and paws intact . . . she was not safe.

Kinlear dropped to a knee before the throne, bowing his head. 'My lord.'

Her heart twinged.

A prince did not bow.

A prince did not bend to the ruler of another kingdom. And that struck Ezer the most about how much he had changed. How utterly gone he was.

This was another creature entirely.

'The One has been fed well,' the Acolyte said. 'Another night of feasting and praise has brought its freedom closer,' he added, looking at Kinlear. 'You are dismissed. But do not go far. I may have need of you.'

He held out a hand to where the pool of darksoul blood had been.

But now it was fully dry, like the banks of a river that had been washed away. All the blood that had been fed into it, from thousands of darksouls was gone. And in its place . . .

A crevasse, so deep, she knew if she fell into it, she would fall forever. It seemed to sigh as she peered into it. To breathe of power, like it harbored a sleeping giant within.

'Ezer,' the Acolyte said. 'Blood of my blood. The daughter I never knew, and yet it seems the One did.'

His voice was a smooth, poisonous thing. It rolled over her and sent shivers down her spine.

'Are you going to kill me?' she asked.

He chuckled. 'Have you so little trust in your own family, Ezer?'

'*You* are not my family,' she growled.

Six's tail twitched twice, agreeing.

The Acolyte shifted. Shadows swam between his fingertips in warning. 'Look at the darkness, daughter. What do you see?'

There was a path of rock that circled the enormous crevasse. Darkness moved inside, swirling as if alive.

'Shadows,' Ezer said. 'Your little pets.'

He laughed at that. 'Your ire. Your rage. I can taste it. It comes from *me*.' He sat back in his throne. And though time had aged him elegantly, hardened the lines of his face . . . when he smiled, it was exactly as he had in Styerra's memories. 'And they aren't just shadows. They are an extension of the *One*. And this—' he glanced at the crevasse, 'is our connection to him. Our pathway that will someday become a door. We need only win this war.'

She watched the deep shadows sigh and roll. Like . . . the crevasse was breathing.

'You read the Tome,' he said. 'I can see it in your eyes. I can sense it in the questions you aren't asking.'

'I have questions,' Ezer said. 'But I'm not certain you'd tell me the truth if I asked.'

He sat back, crossing one leg over another, and the movement was so human, so casual, it gave her pause.

'Try me,' he said. And then he sighed. 'You look just like Styerra. I never knew about you, and that is the truth. If I had . . . perhaps this all would have gone differently. I wouldn't have left the Citadel. I wouldn't have left *her* behind.' He frowned, and his shadows crawled up an arm, settling around his shoulders in a comforting embrace. 'But if I hadn't . . . I wouldn't be here now. And the One would still be starved, locked deeper in its cage, and *you* . . . you would be alone in this realm, Ezer.'

'That isn't true,' she said.

Her eyes slid to Six.

He caught her glance and smiled knowingly. 'Raphons bond

deeply to their riders. We have Wrenwyn to thank for that. It was one of her first acts as Acolyte.'

Wrenwyn.

Her ancestor.

Wrenwyn, the story Ezer had always loved . . . was once the Acolyte on this very throne.

Erath looked down at Six, who sat still as a statue, looking only at Ezer. 'You can keep her for yourself, if you come to our side. Stay with her here, forever. Ride her into battle if you please.'

'I won't battle for you,' Ezer said. 'Set her free. Isn't that what you speak of so much? Freedom for all?'

He chuckled, and Six's tail twitched twice, like she hated the idea of it.

Run, Ezer thought towards her. *Fly away from here.*

But she knew Six would never leave her.

Even if it led to the raphon's death.

'I would have torn apart the entire realm to bring you home to me. When someone becomes the Acolyte . . . they are given great power. Beauty. Riches that run soul deep. I was granted the gift of shadows. A glorious display of unpillared power, for light cannot survive in true darkness.'

A pillar of shadow erupted from his hands, spiraling up into the sky, where the hole in the mountaintop lead to the shadowstorm.

Their protection from Lordach's advances.

'Now that you are here . . .' He smiled at her, and she fought the urge to flinch. 'All is right again. You are *home*, Ezer. Where you were always meant to be.'

There was something behind his words that she couldn't quite place. A danger. A promise.

'You told Styerra you'd come for her that night in the Citadel. And instead, like a coward, you sent a godsdamned letter to break her heart. You were a coward, Erath. And you left her behind to die, with a baby in her womb.'

His shadows lunged towards her.

But a lifting of his hand, and they recoiled, settling upon his lap like a cat. He ran his fingertips across them as he spoke, ever the soothing master. 'The truth tells so much more than speculation can. Stefon, an old friend of ours, was truly clever. I'll give him that. But he took advantage of our trust. Mine and Styerra's combined.'

'What does that mean?' Ezer asked.

He shrugged and looked into the crevasse. She could sense the power inside it.

She could sense, if she dared listen . . . a voice upon the wind.

Not her mother's, for this voice was far away.

So far, she almost imagined she was hearing it sigh her name. And with it, a request.

A promise.

'The past is unimportant. It is but a blink, a flash in the grand scheme of time now,' the Acolyte said. 'But to you, weak and human, I can sense the true story is still important. So, I'll tell you this: Stefon visited me first in our dorms, before he visited Styerra that night. I can see so much more now, than I did back then. But you . . . for some reason, Ezer, I never sensed *you*.' He sighed. 'He came in a frenzy, a man shattered by grief. I held him while he wept at my feet, while he gathered the strength to tell me Styerra was *gone*. He told me the Masters had captured her, ripped her from his grasp in the kitchens. He told me they killed her – the ultimate penance for her wrongs – and they were coming for me, too. So I fled. I went to the Aviary and took my eagle . . . and soared away from the Citadel, never to look back.'

A disgusting lie, her uncle had crafted. He'd ripped a family apart. He'd taken everything from them. Ezer, Styerra, even Erath, long ago.

Before he was *this* . . . this dark monster on a throne, caressed by shadows.

'After that, I assume he fled with Styerra. He used her fear, her love for *you*, to take her away from me.'

The shadows began to swirl at his feet, angry as the storm far overhead.

'I made it here. I discovered the Acolyte before me. And now . . .'

'What *are* you?' Ezer asked.

'I am the Acolyte, dear child. A voice for the voiceless. I am a host. A vessel, with Wrenwyn's blood in my veins, and I am sworn to carry out the commands of the One until my time is done.'

'You're a murderer,' Ezer said.

His shadows seemed to *hiss*, like snakes. But he held them back from her. 'Your mind is still weak. Still young and mortal, and though you read the Tome . . . you still aren't ready to *see*. That final choice is yours, Ezer.'

'What the hell is that supposed to mean?'

Before her, that dark crevasse was still whispering.

She heard it clearer now as hatred swam through her. As his shadows circled at his feet like hungry hounds, just waiting to be unleashed.

She wished she could control her own magic. She wished she could send an army of ravens to shred him, bit by bit.

But when she reached for her power – an ember, a spark – there was *nothing* to grasp hold of.

'When I made it here, when I came to the same door as you, I found a child of Wrenwyn's . . . the Acolyte. She was my ancestor. My blood. I'd never had true family before, not like that.'

Her heart was beating all wrong.

Her breathing was too shallow.

'She was not ready to pass on. So I killed her,' Erath said. The shadows slithered across his body and up the sides of his face. 'I swung the knife and took her place.'

She backed up a step. The shadows turned and slithered back towards her as they sensed her fear. They were hungry for it.

He was still lost in his story, like he'd been waiting his whole life to share it with someone.

'I loved Prince Draybor like a brother,' Erath said. 'Once I became the Acolyte, once I mastered my newfound magic, I flew back across the Expanse to reason with him. I found his father dead, and Draybor finally king in his place. I tried to show him what *living* looked like. I asked only for a chance to share the truth with his people.' His voice darkened. 'Instead, he called me an abomination. He declared war upon me and vowed to slaughter each person who turned to my side.'

'The darksouls,' Ezer said. 'The monsters.'

'They are not monsters,' Erath growled. 'They are creatures, once weak, made strong. I created the shadowstorm to keep them safe. And while the war rages . . . it is only because we need *time*.'

'For what?' Ezer asked.

'Time to borrow more souls,' Erath said. 'Time to uncover the key. The Five hid one in each realm, fragments of a master key meant to unlock the Door to their infernal cage. We believe . . . that a key is being held *inside* the Citadel. Somewhere behind the safety of their Wards.' He smiled. 'And as we gather more souls, more who will deny the lies of the Five, we grow stronger. Our onslaughts increase.' He looked at the crevasse in the cave floor. 'We will keep giving the One the souls it requires, and in turn, the One will strengthen us, sending through the reinforcements we need, until we find the next key.'

The *next* key.

Which meant . . .

'We must unlock the realms, one by one,' Erath said. 'And when the Long Day ends, and Realmbreak comes to pass, the Five will indeed give a blessing – a curse – to Lordach.' He leaned forward, dark eyes on hers. 'Their King has fallen. A new one has risen in his place.'

Her heart gave a terrible tremor.

That meant that Arawn . . .

Arawn was *King*.

'And what he will ask of the gods, what blessing *he* will request . . . one of my own tells me it will be far worse than what his father would have chosen. It would have been a set of wards for *all* of Lordach. But this king? He will ask for a weapon instead. A way to counteract my power. A way to destroy my shadowstorm. And then this stronghold . . . it will no longer be safe.'

Arawn's own words came back to her.

What my father will ask for – and what I would ask for if I were already King – they would not be remotely close to the same.

She couldn't imagine a weapon being able to break through the power the Acolyte held.

She could see only Arawn, Izill, Alaris, all the people she'd come to know and trust . . .

Dead.

Dead at the hands of this monster before her.

'What will you do if you win the war?' Ezer asked. 'What will you do if you manage to break through, and find this key?'

'I will first give everyone a choice. Join us . . . lay down your belief in the Five . . . or die.'

Her stomach turned as his shadows circled his throne.

'And then I will unlock the Veil that holds this realm back from the next. And we'll be able to go through.'

'Through to *where*?' Ezer asked.

The Acolyte smiled. 'Into the next realm, just as my ancestors did to gain entrance to this one. They found its key and came here to conquer. My job is to carry that on, until we enter the next realm. And the next. Until *all* realms see and believe the truth. We will crush the Five, realm by realm. And when all of humankind stops believing their lies . . . the Five will *finally* fall. They will lose their hold on the Thirteenth Realm. We will hold all the keys to unlock the cage. And the One will finally be *free*.'

It was an eternal darkness he had planned.

Like dominoes falling, taking out realms one at a time.

Piece by piece.

She looked at that crevasse.

She could hear the hissing whisper now, stronger than before.

'Why are you telling me this?' she asked. 'I tried to kill you.' And then, because she guessed he could already sense it, she added, 'I still would if I could.'

His shadows stretched towards her, but he pulled them back, reined them in with a simple squeeze of his fist. 'Blood of my blood,' he said. 'You are more like me than I realize.'

'I'm nothing like you,' she said.

She hated this man, this monster.

He'd killed her mother with his own wolves, his own creation . . . and he hardly seemed to care. He was blind to all he'd done, every wrong, because he believed it was *right* so long as it was in the name of the One.

He was the villain in her story. And she was the hero that would secure his end.

Erath looked down at his hands, at the shadows swimming between them. 'The sheer *power* available to me is endless. But imagine, Ezer . . . what it would be like if we were to join *together*. If you could take that furious magic churning inside your veins . . . and unleash it in the name of the One.'

She backed up a step.

Suddenly, she felt sick as the pieces began to click into place.

She shook her head. 'I won't join you.'

'You will,' he said. 'Because you are my blood. My bones. My breath.' His shadows slithered away from him, reaching for her across the dais. She sucked in a breath as they began to circle her.

Like sea wyverns surrounding their prey.

'You have been lost in this realm,' he said, 'a fledgling with no one to show you our ways. I will teach you. I will show you just how glorious is the gift of our blood.'

Something shifted in her chest.

She looked at Six and nodded subtly.

The raphon's tail twitched once.

'You're *home*,' Erath said. 'Falling into the footsteps of fate. And someday, when my time is done . . . I will have trained you so well, that you will be able to lead better than I ever could. You, Ezer, Child of Erath and Descendant of Wrenwyn . . . *you* are going to take my place. Someday . . . you are going to become the next Acolyte.'

Horror washed over her.

'But like me . . . you may need a little convincing. Let us pray that you will be strong enough to survive it.'

CHAPTER 44

She turned and ran.

She'd made it three steps to Six, ready to leap on her back and soar away, when Erath drawled, 'Stop her.'

A *whoosh* of power, and suddenly his shadows had locked around her ankles, her wrists, faster than she could gasp at their icy touch.

'Let me *go*!' Ezer screamed, as panic tightened in her chest.

She tried to stumble backwards, but the shadows were too strong.

And then suddenly Kinlear was at her back, his body cold instead of warm, strong instead of sickly. 'Don't fight it, Ezer,' he hissed into her ear. 'Don't fight what the One has fated for you.'

'You will *never* have me,' Ezer spat. 'I will fight you until the day you—'

'Silence,' the Acolyte hissed.

Her words died on her tongue. Fear took anger's place, because a tendril of shadow now swirled at his fingertip.

Shadow . . . that was slowly forming into the shape of a blade.

And it was pointed right at Six.

A sob rose in the back of her throat. 'Don't,' she begged. 'Don't touch her.'

'Bring her here,' Erath sighed, and then Kinlear was pushing her towards the throne. Then *past* the throne, to the enormous crevasse in the floor where the pool of blood once sat. 'To the Veil.'

Her toes were right on the edge. It was only the shadows holding her back now. Her breath froze as she looked into the endless dark abyss . . . as it seemed to sigh and breathe her in.

It was hungry for her.

She could sense it.

A desperate sob rose in her chest.

'You *are* fated to join us, Ezer,' the Acolyte said. 'But you must make the choice yourself. You must see to believe. Listen to the voice! Let the whisper prove to you what glory and freedom awaits.'

'Let me go,' Ezer begged. 'Please, Erath. For Styerra, let me *go*!'

'I was afraid you would say that,' he said with a *tsk*. 'Which is why I will offer you the same mercy I give every survivor we find on the battlefield, inches from death. We bring them here, to the Veil. And the One offers them a choice. What will it be, Daughter? Will you die . . . or will you *live*?'

Horror raced through her as his shadows *squeezed*, like constricting snakes. So tight, she cried out. And then they were turning her around. Spinning her so that her back was to the void, and only the shadows held her from tumbling in.

Kinlear stood a breath away.

'Ezer,' he sighed. 'Don't fight it anymore. Join us. We could do great things together.'

'No,' she gasped as his hand lifted the blade from his hip.

Six screeched, fighting like hell to get to her, but the shadows had bound her, too. 'Kinlear, *please*,' she begged him through tears. 'Come back to me. Think of *before*, think of everything we've been through. You love me. You *love* me, Kinlear. You would never hurt me.'

'I do love you,' he whispered, and smiled through his fangs. She flinched as he leaned forward and kissed her. 'But I love the One more,' he sighed against her lips.

She gasped as he pulled away.

Six screeched and thrashed like she felt the blinding pain for herself.

Because when Ezer looked down . . . she found Kinlear's blade buried deep in her chest.

'There's only one way out of this,' Kinlear hissed.

Ezer cried out as she ripped the blade from her chest. She stumbled, her body numb and cold, as the blade clattered to the stones.

'Die, my love,' Kinlear said. 'Or choose to join us and live.'

His face was the last thing she saw before she fell into the abyss.

Into the darkness, she fell.

She could hear Six screeching, fighting against the shadows to get to her, and as the light from above faded, and the surface shrank . . .

Something dove in after her.

Two dark wings.

Six.

She felt the raphon swoop beneath her, and the feeling of falling disappeared as Six's body caught hers.

There was no pain.

There was only warmth as her eyelids fluttered closed.

'*Ezer*.'

She gasped at the voice.

Because it wasn't Styerra.

She knew at once . . . it was the One.

It was ancient, and powerful, a voice that she felt rumble through her.

'*Please*,' she thought to it, while she clung to Six. She thought Six was flying up, but there was no surface in sight. They were lost in the darkness, so thick that not even Ezer's scarred eye revealed a thing to her. '*I'm not ready to die*.'

She felt now that they were in some place *other*.

A place not quite living and not quite dead.

'*Then you must listen to the last truths of the Shadow Tome . . . and believe.*'

And as they tumbled through darkness . . . the One told her the rest of the story.

'*It was in the black mountains, a land of darkness and omens, that Wrenwyn discovered the whisper. It came from a crack in the stones, a fracture in which the One was able to peer through, for the belief in the Five had waned just enough that it was able to free its voice.*

A single tendril of its soul.

A mere shadow.

'*I am the One,*' *it told Wrenwyn, and the princess knelt there on the edge of the world as it promised her many things.*

Power and freedom, a life without holds on her magic. A life without laws to keep, where no one could tell her what to do, or who she was, or what to believe.

She wept as she listened, for she'd never had a choice of her own.

It was always the will of the Five, and the Masters, who forced it upon her.

'*What must I do,*' *Wrenwyn asked,* '*to hold on to this promise?*'

The One had only a single request:

'*Become my Acolyte.*'

A mortal representative, someone to go before and sow distrust in the Five.

Someone to build an army and find this realm's key.

'*Join me,*' *the One promised.* '*And you, and all your ancestors, will rule upon earthly thrones.*'

And so Wrenwyn became Lordach's first Acolyte.

She shed her own blood into the mountain and allowed the One to feed upon it. Her humanity changed, but her soul was filled with power.

And it was wild, and wondrous, and strange.

It gave her wings of blackest night . . . for with her newfound power, she tamed the first raphon.

The One shared with her all the knowledge of the darkness.

She learned of new creatures, of new magic, from the realm conquered before. She learned a language that was beyond the comprehension of the Five.

And with it, Wrenwyn penned the truths in the Shadow Tome.

Only those who had doubt in the Five would be able to decipher it, to learn of its secrets and truths, for it needed to happen slowly.

Without mistake.

Too fast, and the Five would turn their eyes upon Lordach.

Too fast, and they would notice the tendril of the One's soul that had gone missing from his cage.

They would silence him. They would cut off the root of power he'd taken centuries to sow . . . and stop it all before it started.

The Shadow Tome spread slowly across the land, and Wrenwyn turned many with eyes to see towards the north. When they arrived, they need only shed their blood into the mountain to feed the One proof of their belief. And their soul would be opened, and a tendril of the One would enter them and set them free.

They danced with the One, instead of marching to the Five's false light.

Wrenwyn bore a child, and raised her in the ways of the One. And when she grew old, her soul finally ready to pass on . . . Wrenwyn's child was given the same choice:

Live free in the dark. Or die loyal to the light.

The child chose freedom, and so as the One promised, it was through Wrenwyn's own blood that arose the next Acolyte.

*

The One's voice faded away.

Six continued to fly through the darkness, and past the tips of her wings, Ezer saw visions soaring by. Glimpses of memories in the dark.

She saw Styerra, sobbing in the Citadel's library as Ervos lied, and used the fear of the Five to make her flee.

She saw Zey, her eyes filled with hatred as the Masters carved her hand with penance and told her she'd failed them again.

She saw Izill weeping before a statue of the gods. 'Whatever I've done to cause you to turn a blind eye to me . . . please. I beg of you, forgive me. Grant me the gift of magic.'

She saw a beautiful, dark-haired Sacred – Soraya – with penance marks all over her back as Kinlear held her and she sobbed through the pain. 'I didn't mean to disobey,' she cried. 'Why do I still resist?'

She saw countless Sacred forced to wed before the Masters for the sake of strengthening the Five, not a hint of love in either partner's eyes. She saw Styerra's joy wither and die when Erath told her he'd been Matched with someone else.

The vision shifted . . . and suddenly Ezer saw *herself, standing alone in the rain as Ervos boarded the prison wagon and left her behind.*

She saw herself in the woods, a shadow wolf inches from her face.

She saw the ravens saving her.

She saw Six with a bleeding handprint on her scarred beak.

She watched her kiss with Arawn. It was forbidden by the Masters, and yet it had felt so right.

She saw her own Descent, as the wind tore at her braid and together, she and Six soared down to the depths.

How many others, Ezer wondered, had spent their lives trying and failing to live up to the Five?

How many others would *never* know what it was like to be free?

'*Ezer*,' the One whispered, as the visions faded away, and suddenly she could see the light again. '*Choose now, before it's too late.*'

She could see the golden doors of the Ehver up ahead. She could see a line of bobbing lights – souls – waiting to meet the Five, face to face. The world beyond the doors was warm, and the light was lovely, like the sun on a summer's day, and she turned Six towards it, ready to go *home*.

But then she saw the scroll at the entrance.

It unraveled before her, eternities long, glowing with every rule that had ever been written.

To fail is to fall, it said at its top, and she realized what it meant . . . as a soul tumbled *out* of those golden doors. She could see its light already dimming, hear its ragged scream as it was cast out. Even after death . . . perfection was the Five's way.

Ezer reached out. She caught the soul before it could fade. It was cold, a tendril of light that died in her fingertips and turned to ashes.

She gasped as it crumbled away, caught by the wind.

'Choose,' the One whispered, and its voice was distant now.

So Ezer clung to Six.

And made her choice.

CHAPTER 45

The moment she chose, the world shifted. The darkness lightened until she could see the surface again, and Ezer directed Six towards it.

They landed on the dais with a *whoosh* of air from Six's wings.

There was no pain as Ezer dismounted.

There was only cold, coming from the hole in her cloak where Kinlear's knife had once been.

She looked down and frowned.

'Ezer,' said a voice.

She glanced up to lock eyes with the man on the throne.

She couldn't remember why she'd been so afraid of him before. Because he was just a man. And she . . .

She knew now, how to kill the Acolyte.

Her footsteps were silent as she walked to him, feeling weightless.

Feeling . . . *powerful*. She cocked her head to the side and closed her eyes as she breathed deep, her body whole once more. Whole and *different*.

She could have done without the dark claws that now tipped her once-human hands.

'My child,' Erath said. 'Look at you. Magnificent.'

'I wish to do as the rest of the darksouls did,' Ezer said. 'I wish . . . to give of my blood to the One who remade me. As my first act on this side.'

'You will learn fast,' he said, and smiled as he reached for the ceremonial knife. The one that had cut through countless darksoul hands earlier.

The one that was impeccably, perfectly sharp.

'Would you join me?' Ezer asked. 'It feels as if all of this was set in stone, long ago. The Acolyte . . . and the daughter spared just for him.'

Erath obliged, his depthless eyes soft as he got down on his knees beside her. As he bowed, his hand outstretched for the blade to cut across. He bled shadows, tendrils that pooled beneath his hand and then regathered again. Just like the wolves when Arawn cut them in the woods.

And as Erath handed her the blade, and she held out her own hand, as if she would slice it . . .

Erath's words from earlier came back to her.

I swung the blade.

He did not stab his predecessor. Which meant . . . he hadn't gone for the heart.

It was just as Arawn said, when he'd tossed her a dagger in the woods. A lifeline against the shadow wolves.

Go for the throat.

So she did exactly that.

She was faster, stronger, than she'd ever been before. And perhaps it was because she'd been touched by the One, given a tendril of new power when she made her choice. Perhaps it was because, deep down, her soul knew this was her last chance.

But when she sliced that blade clean across her father's throat . . .

Her magic unfurled within her.

She had only a second before his shadows recoiled enough to heal him.

She lashed out with a fury she'd never known. A *power* she'd never felt before now . . . but it had always been there, writhing within her.

Magic to match his own.

His shadows tried to heal him, but her own stood in their way.

He was older, wiser . . . but she had been reborn.

She put all of her fury, all of her past, into her power. They had grown wings like birds, and they soared against his as she screamed, her body filling with newfound magic.

His life faded just like the wolves in the woods.

'*Styerra*,' Erath said, as he lay there on the dais floor. A sad, struggling thing. 'Let me . . . be with her now.'

She knew what he meant.

And it was with a smile on her face that she knelt as his side and whispered, 'You will *never* see Styerra again. Not in life, and not in death.'

She reached out to the ring he kept on his hand, the one that matched her own. And she did what Ervos had done. And pried the ring of finding from her father's hand.

He was too weak to fight her now.

And with a sigh, a rattling breath . . .

Erath died.

The shadows slithered away from his body.

And curled up at *her* feet, instead. She swore she could feel them purr against her as she looked at what was left of her father.

A pile of dark clothing, and an empty throne.

Ezer sat down upon it, surprised that it fit her shape perfectly. Like it was made for only her. And at her side, Six sat proudly.

A soft growl revealed her distaste as Kinlear approached the throne. Six was not pleased, after what he'd done.

'Ezer,' he said. 'My hand is yours. My heart, too, if you will have it.'

She glanced up at him. His eyes were dark as night. His lips had curved in a fine, fanged smile, and a part of her relished it.

She remembered how he'd kissed her, and she shivered as he bowed before her, took her clawed hand in his own, and pressed it to his lips.

He was stronger than he'd ever been. He was *alive*, without fear of the future.

It would be so easy to accept him.

So easy to forget the fear he'd placed in her heart, when he drove his blade in.

So easy to forget who she once was.

But as Kinlear backed away . . .

She remembered it all.

Every godsdamned moment.

'You killed me,' Ezer said. 'And now . . . you will spend *forever* serving me until you prove your allegiance.'

A breath, and the shadows left her. She could feel them like an extension of her own body as they locked around his wrists.

And she relished it as she forced those shadows to haul him away. She ignored him as he cried her name, trying to fight his way out of her power.

But she was stronger than him.

Stronger than anyone now.

Her Sentinels arrived with a breath, a thought, and bowed before her, acknowledging that she was the Next.

'The storm, Acolyte,' one of them said, dark eyes wide in wonder. 'You no longer need to control it?'

'A gift,' Ezer said, 'A blessing this Realmbreak.' She looked down at the second ring she wore, a new one, to match her mother's. 'I traded Erath's soul to sustain it.'

It meant that he would have no future in the Ehver.

He would cease to exist.

It was the darkest act she'd ever done, to steal a man's eternity.

But it was a small price to pay for freedom.

She would not be anchored to Erath's shadowstorm, forced to live her life in this darkness.

No, she would ride into battle *with* her army.

She would feel the moonlight on her face, let the wind dance against her, as she led them all to victory. She would break through the wards into the Citadel.

She would find the hidden key.

'Bring Zey to me,' Ezer said aloud. The Sentinel – the one who'd thrown her in a prison cell – came back with Zey and with a breath, a single thought . . . her shadows choked the life from him.

And then Ezer elevated Zey in the man's place.

'Acolyte,' Zey said with a grin, as she bowed at Ezer's throne. 'The darkness looks good on you.'

Ezer smiled at her.

'The Long Day ends within the hour,' said another of her Sentinels. 'Should I prepare your raphon?'

'No,' Ezer said. 'Prepare the army instead. Come, Six.'

She climbed on and smiled in relief.

The shadows had not stolen their connection away. If anything, the connection had brightened, had become a blazing fire that no one could put out.

Six lifted them into the sky.

They soared upwards, climbing with the wind, out of the mountaintop and into the storm of shadows . . .

Ezer turned her eyes south, to the land that had oppressed her all her days.

She squeezed a fist over her mother's ring.

I will avenge you, Ezer thought.

She thought of Izill, still trapped behind the wards . . . unable to see the truth, for how bright the Five's false light.

She thought of Arawn, now a *King*, who she prayed would be ready to embrace her. To take one look at her and be willing to See.

I will avenge them all.

She burst through the mountaintop just as Realmbreak

ended. As the full moon rose in the sky, she soared through the shadowstorm, and into the Expanse.

Fly, Six.

On two dark wings, the Acolyte soared.

And the battle began.

Acknowledgments

It's wild to be here again, writing a *thank you* to those who helped shepherd me in my journey to completing another book. I never thought I would, because several years ago I told my agent, 'I quit. I can't write the next book because there isn't one.'

The business of publishing had stolen my joy. And I walked away.

I came back only because of Ezer . . . a woman locked in a tower, who is a direct reflection of my own creativity trying to claw its way back out into the light. And because I've never read a book about a raven gryphon before, and if they don't exist in real life . . . well, now they do in these pages.

This book took over 350,000 words, five totally different drafts, and what I thought at the time was failure. Instead, it was growth, because *Ravenminder* is the embodiment of *not* quitting. Even when I wanted to.

Thank you, first and foremost, to God, my savior. You have guided me and given me the spirit of stubborn grit that's carried me through so much in life. Anything I've tried to quit I've eventually gone back to and conquered, no matter what it took.

To you, reader, that's my challenge: *Don't quit. Conquer.*

To my incredible agent, Peter Knapp, along with Stuti Telidevara, Danielle Barthel, and everyone else at the wonderful Park, Fine & Brower Agency: thank you for being the reason I could step away from writing, find my creative heart again, and come back stronger. To say I'm grateful is an understatement. But I'll say it again in case you've forgotten: thank you for giving me the gift of time and thank you for being the champions for this story. Thank you to Philippa Milnes-Smith, Eleanor Lawlor and the team at the Soho Agency for helping this story find a home across the pond. It's the perfect place.

To my editor, Kate Byrne at HQ, thank you for answering the countless emails with all my wild ideas, and never once balking at them. Instead, giving me the freedom to fly. Thank you for challenging me.

To everyone else at HQ, thank you for believing in me and this book and giving me what is absolutely the most BEAUTIFUL cover I could ever have imagined. I. Can't. Handle. It. (You gave a *Hunger Games* fangirl a purple book just like the Haymitch story, and that gift is not lost on me.)

To my husband, Josh: *I love you.* You are my steady rock. You are calm pretty much *always,* gracious when I need more time to create, and the inspiration for every romance thread I will ever write.

To my mom (and sister) who spent countless hours entertaining the kids so I could sneak away to a coffee shop and work . . . it's only been possible because of you. Thank you forever and then some, for giving me the space to think and create.

To my mother and father-in-law (bonus parents) who have whisked me away to the mountains many times: my favorite scene with Six and Ezer exists because I wrote it while shivering on a balcony in Breckenridge, watching the snow fall. Thank you for the adventures.

To my sweet kids, thank you for allowing Mommy the grace of time to create – and being sure to pull me out of 'work mode' to play. Homeschooling you was the best decision I've ever made. But wait until you're older to read any of mommy's books, please.

To Cheeto, the feral barn cat we rescued: sometimes you're a jerk with daggers for claws but you inspired so much of Six and I actually really like you now.

To my close friends and church family, thank you for liking every post and leaving fire emojis to boost my confidence.

To Anthony and Brittany Gonzales, y'all helped me solve the biggest plot hole of my life. Thank you for the dinner convo and whiskey cake that saved this story.

To the readers who have stuck with me through every world and word: thank you for being my champions.

To the writers who inspired me: I never would have done this, never would have had the courage to *try*, without your stories first paving the way.

I'll keep trying, even when it feels impossible. Even when I'm scared to fall.

I'll do it afraid <3

H|Q

ONE PLACE. MANY STORIES

Bold, innovative and
empowering publishing.

FOLLOW US ON:

@HQStories